To

Joe Moody

from

the Ex Berliner

Reinhold Esher

Sarasota, FL
2/23/2017

The Bridge of Love to Freedom

Reinhold J. Kerstan

First Edition: November 2015

Printed in the United States of America

ISBN: 978-1-939237-40-8

Published by Suncoast Digital Press, Inc.

Sarasota, Florida, USA

Dedication

This book is dedicated to my wife, Inger,
the love of my life.

We met and were married in Sweden fifty-seven years ago.

Inger continues to be my inspiration and the
supporter of our international family of five, each
of us born and raised in a different country.

Acknowledgments

My life has been an outstanding adventure by the grace of God, who deserves my greatest thanks.

This novel is historical fiction, except for the parts that aren't.

I owe a depth of gratitude to those who told me their life stories, which somehow found their way into this book—even though with careful changes. Many friends and colleagues granted me extensive interviews and helped me widen my horizon of the whole world.

When writing this book, it was Barbara Dee from Suncoast Digital Press, who became my trusted and appreciated editor. Her professional skill and talented insight into my story often surprised me, pleasantly. I thought of myself as a published writer and an accomplished communicator. But it was Barbara Dee who ironed out flaws in my idiomatic peculiarities and Germanisms. Thanks, Barbara, for your energetic and kind support!

And a very special thank-you to my wife, Inger, for her patience and understanding, when my writing sometimes took me to a different time frame and forgotten world. I could always count on her support.

Reinhold Kerstan

Preface

Dealing with one of the darkest periods in Germany's history had a cleansing effect on me. I am unable to explain why and exactly how, but it did. The lives of millions of people worldwide were effected by Hitler's rush to World War II. I was one of them. However, my conscious decision not to think of myself as a victim but rather as a victorious survivor, made writing this fictional story of the German Anleger family meaningful and possible.

"A book writes itself" is a common saying among authors. In reality that is wrong. A lot of time, patience, research, writing, and rewriting go into a book. Without these, perseverance, and a team to help with editing and proofing, no book would ever be ready for publishing.

Still, there is an inexplicable, driving power in writing a book. When I wrote my autobiography, *Blood and Honor* (David C. Cook Publishing, ©1980), it felt like as if I had opened up a dam after many years and let the held-back water of remembrances flow. No research was needed, because I had lived every word and minute of what I was writing about. My only handicap seemed to be that my pen could not write as fast as the thoughts were coming. Constantly I had to sort out and often discard what I thought were interesting details, in order to keep my narrative from being cumbersome and too lengthy.

It was totally different when writing the book you are holding in your hand. I had made a short list of people who were to be the main characters of my story. As a person who was born in Germany and had lived for sixteen years in Berlin, I had sufficient knowledge about the political events during the six decades I wanted to write about. Determined to write a fiction book based on true historical happenings, I threw myself into diligent writing, to experience what many others writers had gone through before me: the characters took on their own life, made their own decisions and plans, and started leading me, instead of I guiding them.

People I had never known in reality were thrown into situations I was familiar with.

They mastered challenges and solved problems in ways I had not thought of before. Then I willingly let them set the course and take on the life I had given them. Yes, fictional characters do that!

On many nights, when I was writing late after midnight, I was full of anticipation—where would my characters take me, who would they meet, and what would they say? At times I was tempted to stop them from what they were doing in their world, realizing that following them might mean more work for me. But they just turned a deaf ear on me and kept going—to my delight!

Enjoy reading about world-changing events in the 1900s, being mindful that most of the characters are the product of my imagination except for those real people you will easily be able to identify, taking their rightful place in Europe's and America's chronicles.

Chapter 1

A knock at the apartment door made 16-year old Norbert jump to his feet. As he tiptoed to the window, louder knocking chilled his pounding heart. "Police!" Had they managed to get to him before he could …? There was no time now for reflection. He moved the heavy curtain just far enough to see a black limo parked across the street. Right underneath his window, he could make out the contours of another vehicle, a police car. Two uniformed men were standing in the dim cold light of a street lantern, the only faint illumination on this starless night of March 18, 1948.

They have come in full force as if to get one of the big boys, he thought. He moved away from the window and looked around. Besides the worn mattress on a steel bed frame, there was no other furniture in the room; no pictures on the walls; nothing on the floor, not even a rucksack that a man on the run would have been expected to have.

Thinking of his well-prepared escape plan, Norbert slipped into the kitchen and squeezed himself into the apartment next door through a narrow hole in the pantry. Just when he had pulled himself through, he heard another pounding at his apartment door and then the crashing sound of splitting wood. The police had cut short their wait by kicking in the door with rough boots. Once in the neighboring apartment, he moved swiftly to the balcony door of the living room. He didn't need any light, even though it was pitch black around him. For many weeks, he had practiced his escape over and over; in his mind he saw every step, even in the dark. He pulled at the door release, but it did not move! For a second he panicked. Then he remembered that he first had to flip a latch in order to pull the release. With his heart pounding, he continued, just the way he had rehearsed it. He climbed the narrow iron staircase leading from the balcony to a flat roof, which former tenants had used as a garden. With hurried steps, he felt his way to a compost pile of branches, weed cuttings, and rotting leaves. The hole he had dug at the bottom of the large pile was like a narrow tunnel that fit his slim body tightly. Once he was inside, he carefully disguised the entrance. All there was left now was to lie perfectly still and wait.

He didn't have to wait long, because minutes after he had tucked himself into his hiding place, a man with a flashlight and a policeman groped their way across the roof. Ravaging through the empty apartment, they had soon discovered the hole in the pantry that led to the neighboring apartment. Since it was too small for them, they just had broken down the door to the adjoining apartment. Yet, they had found nothing suspicious but for the wide-open balcony door.

"Nothing! There's nothing here! I told you so!" the man with the flashlight shouted, while the light beam scanned the rooftop.

"Perhaps he is hiding in this garbage pile here," said the policeman, kicking at the branches.

"Man, are you crazy? Who would crawl into this stinking hell? Let's go!" There was an air of superiority in his voice that clearly marked him as the man in command. Without a word, the policeman turned and the men made their way back to the staircase.

"I tell you, he must have jumped to the balcony below. Let's search there!"

"That's just a vacant apartment," the policeman said, still convinced that the fugitive might be in the refuse pile, which by now was swallowed up by darkness. But his secret service colleague had already made his way down the staircase.

"Stinking hell" they had called Norbert's hiding place. They were right! Norbert put his hand over his nose and mouth. It didn't help. He suppressed a gagging cough. The compost stench was stronger than he had expected. Still, he had come too far to give up now. Tomorrow he would be in the West—if there was a tomorrow.

The "West" referred to the Western Allies Sectors of Berlin, the former capital of Germany. The occupying Allied forces had divided the city into four sectors: American, British, Russian and French. The Russian Sector, by far the largest slice, was in the east, thus called "The East," in contrast to the other sectors, called "The West." That is where Norbert belonged, that is where he had come from, and that's where he wanted to fight his way back to.

When he had roamed the streets of Berlin as a little boy, there had been no East and West. His parents had spoken of the *Reichshauptstadt*, the capital of the German *Reich*. To him it was just Berlin, his city. It took a lost war to split up his once beautiful city into four sectors, but mainly into East and West.

His date of birth was April 20, 1932—yes, on the twentieth of April, the very same day all of Germany celebrated Adolf Hitler's birthday each year. As far as he could think back, it had always been a national holiday, which for him meant no school.

Norbert, or "Norbi" as his peers called him, was a short, slim boy whose curly dark brown hair gave him an almost feminine appearance. Perhaps he was not even that short, but since he regularly had to wear the worn-out clothes of his three older and taller brothers, he always looked as if he had not managed to grow into them fast enough. At times, when he would protest his fate of having to wear his brothers' hand-me-downs, Hans, the eldest brother, would laughingly comfort him, "Be glad you don't have to wear Heidi's old dresses."

Four years older, his sister Heidi was the ever-smiling sunshine of the family. With her curly blond hair and blue eyes, she attracted like a magnet all the neighborhood boys of her age and even older ones. That pleased her mother Gertrud, who seemed to relive her own youth in her daughter whom everybody called her "spitting image." The sons all looked more or less like Karl, their father: brown, full hair, thick eyebrows, thin lips, prominent chins, broad shoulders, and well-proportioned bodies.

"There is something eerie about the Anleger boys," Mrs. Mueller, a long-time neighbor, would say to her coffee-*klatsch* friends when they gossiped about their neighbors.

"Isn't it incredible how they all look alike?"

4

"Yes, and what's even more amazing, they all resemble their old man to the 'T'."

"You think Heidi is their real daughter?"

"Why not? Look at Gertrud...Heidi looks just like her mother."

"Ya, but isn't it strange that Heidi is stark blond, while her brothers—well, forget it!" With a broad sweep of her arm, Mrs. Mueller seemed to wipe this topic aside in order to pick on some other neighbors.

Karl Anleger was an engineer at *Siemens-Halske*, a large company in Berlin, a branch of the giant German Siemens Concern. Almost from the beginning of the war, his company had switched its production from large electrical clocks and other electronic instruments to products needed by the war machine. Exactly what his company was producing, Karl never told his family. Whenever one of his boys asked him what he was doing at work, he would laugh it off with "Waiting for *Feierabend*," which was a reference to the factory whistle at five o'clock, signaling the end of another workday.

At first, it looked as if Karl would not be drafted. While almost all of the men in his neighborhood had to report to military recruiting centers (either right at the outset of the war in September, 1939, or later in 1940) Karl had been declared *unabkoemmlich* (indispensable). It became increasingly embarrassing to have to explain to his family, neighbors, and friends that the government considered him of greater use to *Deutschland* at home rather than at the front line. On the one hand, he was glad to be near his family; on the other hand, he

5

envied the men who could serve the fatherland in the military and were admired both by their peers and loved ones at home.

His pride was really hurt when, in summer of 1943, his son Hans, on his sixteenth birthday, was drafted as a *FLAK Helfer* (eight-point-eight anti-aircraft gunner). It had been a special honor for Kurt and Waldemar, both members of the *Hitler Jugend* (Hitler Youth Movement), to accompany their brother to the garrison in Potsdam, a suburb of Berlin where Hans was to be stationed. On that day, all three wore their uniforms to demonstrate that they considered it a privilege to serve the fatherland in their own ways. Hans, a tenth-grade high school student, had recently helped evacuate the patients of a hospital which had taken a full hit in an allied air raid. For his bravery, he had received the Iron Cross 2nd Class medal, which now decorated his uniform.

Kurt was ten years old when the war broke out. That same year he had to join the *Deutsche Jugend,* the younger branch of the Hitler Youth Movement. In 1941, as a twelve-year-old *Pimpf* (a general nickname for a member of the *Hitler Jugend*), his school district selected him along with twenty other boys and girls to visit the Chancellery of the German Reich. They brought flowers and greetings of good cheer to the *Reichskanzler* Adolf Hitler, who had just recovered from a severe illness. Even though the encounter with Hitler had been a disappointment for the Hitler Youth delegation—the meeting was very brief and uneventful—the pride of having been part of the honor task force never left Kurt.

Waldemar's claim to fame for Germany was his nightly duty as an air raid night watch. While most of the people of Berlin during those alarms sought refuge in air raid shelters,

Waldemar would pedal his bicycle to the watch center where men of all ages had to report. In case of a bomb attack, they were sent to the rooftops of the four- and five-story apartment houses in search of incendiary bombs, which, when discovered, they had to render harmless by putting sand on top of them. Waldi was only twelve years old when he had to prove his manhood by performing this task, and he had managed to convince everybody—except himself—that fear was something he had never experienced.

Karl Anleger was not able to accompany his sons to Potsdam because his work at *Siemens-Halske* had become a never-ending burden. Often he had to work 14 or 15 hours a day. So when in October, 1943, he received a draft notice after all, he was genuinely relieved. And his relief turned into joy when he arrived on the northern German island of Usedom and discovered that his son Hans had also been stationed near Peenemünde on this small island in the Baltic Sea. While he was working on a top secret project which later was to be known as *Vergeltungswaffe V-1*, or "Doodlebug," as the citizens of London would one day call it, his son Hans manned the anti-aircraft guns against allied air attacks.

Like all of the other German girls her age, Heidi had joined the *Bund Deutscher Maedchen* (BDM) when she was ten years old. That was in 1938, one year before the war broke out against Poland. Now, five years later, she was a highly-trained and well-accepted leader among the BDM, even though she was the youngest among her leadership peers. As a "girl of Aryan descent," she was the prototype of what the Third Reich wanted a German girl to look like, and to be. She had never put any makeup on her fair-skinned face, and her blue eyes framed by blond curls had never seen the inside of a beauty salon. She knew that she was beautiful, but of greater importance to her was her wish to be of use to her fatherland. She was intent on being a model BDM girl who was always on time for classes and meetings and set an example as an excellent student. Her teachers admired her quick wit and charm—except when she pleaded with them to get a day off in order to serve meals to soldiers at the various railroad stations in Berlin.

"What do you mean, 'I must have another day off for railroad station duty'?" her homeroom teacher snapped at her. "During the last two months you and your BDM girls have had six days out of school. Don't you think that the Red Cross and the Sisters of the Inner Mission can take care of our *Landsers*?"

"I know they can. But there is so much more that needs to be done. Just the other day a Red Cross official asked me if I could come back every day."

"And what did you say?"

"I told him, I would think about it," Heidi answered with a disarming smile.

"And what do your parents think of all this short-changing of your education?" The moment the teacher asked the question, he knew that he had used the wrong approach. The smile on Heidi's face died as she stretched herself to full size in front of her teacher.

"You know yourself that my concern for Germany's victory is of greater importance than the concern for the feelings of my parents," she declared.

Just as taken out of their BDM leadership manual, the teacher thought. But he kept his thoughts to himself. Over the years, he had learned that even the party membership badge on his lapel was no protection against overzealous youngsters. Some months before, several of the older students had made it quite clear what they thought of his lack of enthusiasm for the Third Reich, and he had not missed the underlying threat in their remarks. So the next day, Heidi and her BDM platoon marched to the Anhalter *Bahnhof* where, for the next ten hours, they handed out refreshments, fruit, and warm soup to the thousands of soldiers coming from or traveling to the battle fields.

Norbert tried to move his stiff limbs without making the slightest noise. He knew that he would have to get out of his hiding place soon, or else he might suffocate. But just when he was about to push open the cover of his tunnel, he heard the sirens of two police cars. Were they still searching for him? He couldn't take any chances. So close to freedom, he could not afford to make any mistakes! Doomed to remain immobile in his self-made prison, his mind again reeled back to the past.

He had to admit that these had been years of many mistakes, both in his own life as well as in the life of his family. He realized that calling the harsh events in the past "mistakes" was probably incorrect. Rather, they were "unfortunate happenings." Besides, his family shared many of the same happenings with millions of other Germans.

The avalanche of mishaps had started with the arrival of a sad letter from Hans. His previous cards and letters always had been full of glowing reports of victorious defenses against British bombers. Shortly after having completed his brief

9

training as an anti-aircraft gunner, he had reported five "kills." Then, in one night, his 8.8 FLAK had shot down two planes within one hour. To celebrate the unusual victory, his gun crew had gotten a day off, which he spent with his father.

In a cozy bar, they tried to drink each other under the table. Hans had been drunk before, but never in front of his father. That day they sat man-to-man—talking, laughing, drinking, and fueling each other's longing for home. Then, in the stupor of too many drinks, the father put his arm around his son's neck and whispered into his ear, "Hans, I tell you, you haven't seen a thing yet!" When Hans just stared at him, Karl Anleger continued, "Have you heard of our *Vergeltungswaffe,* or *V-1*? Let me tell you, Hans, I am working on it. It's the greatest thing the Germans ever have developed."

"We are defending the V-1?" Hans blurted out.

"Shhh, son!" his father quieted Hans' alcohol-magnified voice. "Yes, this and a few other 'military gems' you are defending from the Tommies. They are trying everything to destroy it, because they know that they will be the first recipients of our new miracle weapon."

"When will it be ready for action?"

"In two or three months. We could deploy the *V-1* now, but there is still some adjusting of the steering mechanism to be done. You have no idea how many *V-1's* we had to destroy in midair, because they were heading for the wrong targets."

"To our victory over the British!" shouted Hans, as he raised his glass.

"Yes, to our victory with the help of the *Vergeltungswaffe*," beamed Karl, carried away by the thought of glory (and his state of drunkenness). They downed the drinks, and while they waited for another round, Karl pulled out one more trump. Looking sternly at Hans, he spoke in a hushed tone this time.

"Guess what, Hans…some of us are working on an even more effective and destructive *Vergeltungswaffe*, that doesn't even have a name yet. Just like the V-1, it is jet-propelled, but it looks more like a real plane. It will have a much farther range and—." Suddenly a waitress stood at the table with a security officer in plain clothes at her side.

"Here, this man is spilling it all out," she said, pointing at Karl. "He told this young *Flakhelfer* about a new weapon he is working on, and he also...."

"Alright, alright!" the officer cut in. Glaring at Karl, he gestured for him to stand up. "Get up, you drunken swine! You are under arrest. Pay your tab and follow me!" Karl Anleger, who had been a Captain in World War I, recognized instantly that the man in front of him was not a civilian. While he scrambled to his feet, he also realized that his former rank would not impress the arresting officer.

Before Karl could fully stand, Hans thundered at the intruder, "How dare you arrest this man? He has not said anything against Germany. As a matter of fact, we are here to celebrate last night's double victory of my *Flak* unit."

Before Hans could continue, the security officer signaled two of his men to attend to Karl. Then, looking at Hans again, he asked, "Is this man in your unit?"

"No, of course not! He is with the Army, while I am with the *Luftwaffe*."

"Well, young man, then you better stay out of this!" The officer turned to Karl and led his two men as they held each of Karl's shoulders and walked toward the exit. Hans stood paralyzed. He wanted to shout, scream, do something; but no words came out. He stared in disbelief as the four men moved quickly away. The security officer turned back to him and yelled, "Make sure you forget what you have heard and seen tonight—for your own good!"

As Hans saw the last glimpse of the back of his father's head, he began to feel the effect of adrenaline overpowering the alcohol and started toward the door. The bartender and the waitress blocked his way.

"Not so fast, tin soldier," said the bartender, making the gesture of counting money. "First you have to pay." Hans had enough money to pay for their drinks. His motions were mechanical, as if he had not fully understood the events of the last few moments.

Then he was outside in the cold December night. He had to find out where they had taken his father and what would happen to him. In the rush of the threatening events, he had not even had the chance to tell the security people that the man they were arresting was his father. Or had he held back this bit of information on purpose?

A quick glance at his watch told him that it was almost midnight. He had to report for duty at 24:00 hours. Duty came first. So he hurried back to the military base. Should he tell his buddies what had happened? Or perhaps just his commanding officer? Before he reached the guardhouse, he had made up his mind to tell nobody. Things would fall in place by themselves; they always did. The immediate challenge was to make sure that nobody noticed that he'd had too much to drink.

"Man alive, where did you come from?" Bert, his Flak buddy, asked as Hans almost bumped into him at the door to his room.

"What do you mean?"

"Well, with that spirited breath of yours, you better stay away from the stove. You'll burst into flames!" Bert hit him jokingly on the forehead, as if to test his safety upon impact. "Seriously, Hans, you look like hell. You better hurry up—in two minutes we have to report for duty."

Standing in the walled earth shelter next to the huge gun, Hans could not forget the scene at the bar. Why had his father spilled out weapon secrets? That wasn't like him at all. For years Hans had been mad at his father's silence; now he was angry with him for having talked too much.

Somehow, the hours ticked away. It was seven o'clock in the morning. The sun was about to come out. His head was pounding and he was consumed with the thought that soon he would hit the sack and sleep for three days.

"Alarm!" Instantly the crew was at full alert. They waited for the giant searchlights to cut open the dark night and detect the high flying bombers. Then they would blast their deadly load into them. But this morning, everything was different. Suddenly there was the roaring sound of dive-bombers, board guns, screams and crumbling buildings. The enemy attack had come as a total surprise.

Hans had to deal with a different kind of surprise. One of the explosives had hurled him through the air and smashed him against the earth wall of the neighboring Flak unit. He felt as if he had broken all of his bones in the fall. As he reached for his hurting chest, his hand touched the blood-warm stump of his left upper arm. Blood seemed to be everywhere. Where was the rest of his arm? Numbness crept through his body. Frantically searching for the severed arm piece, he made an even more devastating discovery—his left hip was totally smashed. His leg was still there, but he could not move it. Warm blood poured from several parts of his body. Darkness spun in dim glowing circles and finally made him black out.

Weeks later, when Hans was finally able to write from his hospital bed, he wondered how much he should tell his family back home. He decided to write nothing about the arrest of his father. However, he told his family of the decoration for bravery he had received, and about the loss of his arm, and of the left leg that doctors had to amputate a few days after the fateful attack.

I don't know what I will do or when I'll come home, Hans had written in that first letter. *I know there won't be much I can do, because, frankly, my other leg is almost paralyzed, too. Still, I am glad that I was able to fight for our fatherland.* Mother Anleger had cried for days. Neither her boys nor Heidi were able to comfort her. At night, they heard her cry out, "Karl, Karl! If only you were here! You would know what to do." Strangely, there was no news from Karl Anleger.

Months later, when a military ambulance brought Hans home, Heidi, Kurt, Waldemar and Norbert all tried to spend as much time with him as possible. However, Hans was different now. He seemed so much older, especially after he and his mother had a hushed talk all through an entire night. They had heard their mother cry, had heard her call out for her Karl; afterwards there had been nothing but loud sobbing. Only after the war, when they were informed that their father had died in a concentration camp, did they find out that during that night Hans had told their mother about the arrest at the bar in Usedom.

Norbert was disappointed that Hans had shown no excitement on June 13, 1944, when he had come home from school announcing that Germany had just successfully exploded the first *Vergeltungswaffe* (V-1) over London. Kurt, who had just started an apprenticeship as a tool- and die-maker, grabbed Heidi and, along with Waldemar, danced a victory dance through their apartment. Even Mother Anleger had managed to put a smile on her weathered face. Only Hans had grinned a rather queer smile and mumbled, "A week ago, Hitler didn't know what to say regarding the invasion by the Allied Forces in Normandy, and now he wants us to believe that a new, victorious day has come for Germany." Kurt was especially annoyed by Hans's remark. Since his visit to the *Reichskanzlei* and his personal (though brief) contact with Hitler, he had tirelessly defended the genius of the *Fuehrer*, in spite of the frequent radio announcements of German retreats and losses.

"You should be ashamed, Hans, for having so little faith in the strategy of our *Fuehrer*," Kurt admonished his brother. "Adolf Hitler has told us all along that the day will come when he will prove the German superiority. Well, the day is here!"

"Rubbish!" Hans said. "I heard last night that the offensive of the Americans has shocked the German troops at the western front. The enemy has come with 6,500 landing boats and with more than 10,000 planes, while we have only 350 planes over France."

Heidi looked at Hans in disbelief and disgust. "You mean, you—you have listened to BBC London again?"

"No, you needn't listen to London to see that Germany is..."

"Yes, yes, you have listened to the enemy!" Heidi screamed at her brother.

"Alright, so I did! So what?! If we are such a great nation, what harm will it do us when we listen to claims of the English?"

"Children! Will you keep peace, please!" Gertrud Anleger broke into the heated argument. "What is it with you? We don't know where your father is. Hans comes home crippled for life. Waldemar risks his life every night looking for incendiary bombs on the rooftops. And now you have to hurt each other over a man who doesn't seem to care one way or another about what will become of Germany!"

"Mother!" Heidi said. "That 'man' is our *Fuehrer* Adolf Hitler! I love him and serve our fatherland. You should be telling Hans to do the same." Then Heidi used the opportunity to reveal her plan to ask for leave from school in order to join the movie extras in the making of the propaganda film, *Kolberg*. "Even our school principal has encouraged us to enlist for it," she said.

"Why, of all the people, would they want you girls to appear in the movie? Don't they have a thousand other, more qualified extras for their filming?" Mother asked.

"Yes, they have thousands of other extras, and 6,000 horses, and thousands of soldiers in Prussian uniforms for this movie. It will depict the victory of the Germans over the Slavic barbarians in *Neu*-Stettin in 1807."

"Who cares about 1807?" Hans hissed through his teeth. "How about a victory in 1944 or 1945?" Kurt jumped into the conversation.

"Now you are getting close to the truth," he said to Hans. "With the V-1 in action, it will not take long for Germany to win the final victory."

Suddenly Hans sat up on the sofa, where he spent most of his time, raised his left arm stump as in a salute and sang in a mocking tone, "*Deutschland, Deutschland ueber alles—,*" the beginning of the German national anthem. Heidi was outraged. In two long steps she was at his side, grabbed his stump and jerked it down. She was about to slap Hans across the face, but Hans lost his balance and fell over onto his back.

"*Kinder, Kinder!*" Gertrud made another desperate attempt to make peace among her children. Tears were streaming down her face. Suddenly she looked old and worn. Also Hans was crying. t was not because of physical pain, which had become his daily companion. Rather he thought of the night with his father in Usedom, of his most likely miserable condition now, of his brothers' blind faith in the New Germany, of his sister's fanaticism. What had become of the once happy Anleger family?

Waldemar, who had stayed in the background during the violent family encounter, walked up to Hans, helped him back into a sitting position, and just stared at his brother. "Hans," he finally said, "Hans, don't you remember that you always told me that a German boy doesn't cry?"

"I didn't teach you that," Hans snapped. "Our Hitler Youth leaders beat that into our brains. Maybe it works for those bastards, but I surely need to shed a few tears now and then."

"It works for me," said Kurt, as he stood in the middle of the room. Then, without another word, he walked out the door, slamming it shut with full force.

The twentieth of July, 1944, was another upsetting day in the Anleger household. Gertrud was sitting next to Hans, mending the socks of her growing boys. Hans had just made a sarcastic remark about how much work he was saving his mother by just having one leg. Kurt had not heard because he was deeply engrossed in putting together an album, called *Gross Deutschland*. The printed pictures came from cigarette boxes of the brand "R6." Waldemar, at 14, now in his fourth year of *Oberschule*, was doing his homework even though it was vacation time. He liked to get over the "stupid assignment," as he called it, of writing about the most memorable event during summer vacation. Since recently he had managed (almost single-handedly) to prevent a house from bursting into flames by dumping sand on five incendiary bombs, he had decided to write the report on this exciting happening.

Both of the younger brothers played "Battleship," which irritated Heidi who was writing a letter to one of "her" soldier friends at the eastern front. The radio played softly. Suddenly, the light entertainment music changed to classical sounds.

Only Hans seemed to notice the changing mood of music. Then an announcer urged the listeners to stay tuned for a very important newsflash. Eventually all Anleger ears were tuned in. During those days, the broadcast of classical music usually preceded tragic news, such as the loss of a German ship, the giving up of a military stronghold, or the announcement of casualties with carefully manipulated statistics.

Nobody was prepared for what was to come over the radio next. With an emotion-filled pathos, the newscaster announced that at exactly twelve o'clock noon an attack had been made on the life of the Re*ichskanzler* Adolf Hitler. A certain *Oberst* Claus Graf Schenk von Stauffenberg had participated in a strategy-planning session the *Führer* had scheduled that day in the *Lagerbaracke* at his eastern headquarters, Wolfsschanze I, in East Prussia. Stauffenberg had placed his briefcase with a medium-sized bomb against the leg of the table next to the feet of Hitler. Then, making up an excuse, he had walked out of the bunker and gotten into his chauffeur-driven car. Before leaving the *Wolfsschanze* compound, he had heard and seen an explosion that convinced him that Hitler must have been killed in the blast. After all, he had placed the bomb less than six feet from the *Führer.* Thus, he put the machinery for a *coup d'état* (called *Walküre)* into gear by informing his military confidants in Berlin of the successful assassination.

Less than 15 minutes later, a special newscast shed a different light on the situation. Inexplicably, Hitler had suffered only minor injuries, while some of his generals were killed or severely wounded, even though they had been farther away from the explosion.

Then Hitler's voice came on the radio. He spoke only a few sentences, yet his words were filled with stinging hatred "against those damned assassins who would pay for their cowardly act," Family Anleger sat in stunned silence.

"Too bad he made it." Hans's slowly spoken words tore apart the silence like a blinding lightning. "I wish he would at least have lost an arm or a leg." Before he could continue, Heidi let out an unearthly scream. Then she dashed for the door.

"You will regret that remark!" she shouted over and over, while she struggled with the lock of the apartment door. The gall of her brother's remark against Hitler had put her into a frenzy. Finally she managed to rip the door open, storm down the hallway staircase and out of the building. Gertrud Anleger and her boys did not move. Life seemed to have come to a standstill. All they knew for sure was that Hitler was alive. But what about Heidi? Would she report Hans to the authorities? For many years Hitler Youth propaganda had drilled into Germany's youth to turn in anybody who made derogatory remarks about the Third Reich and its leaders.

Chapter 2

Airman Fred Harrington could not believe that he and his buddies had to cross the Atlantic by ship. It was 1948. Early spring storms whipped up the sea. He had never been at sea before—in fact, he had not even been in a boat. There was not much water where he came from. Iowa was blessed with endless fields of corn and sunshine, and his family owned a turkey farm near Sumner. The only body of water in his experience was the shallow pond behind the barn where his parents had threatened to dunk him whenever he was a "bad boy." From his older brother he knew that the bottom of this pond was full of soft, putty-like excrement that was more dangerous than quicksand. Fred's brother knew because one early spring he had broken through the thin ice and the soft bottom had almost swallowed him up, even though the water seemed to reach only up to his waist.

Fred thought it was a disgrace that hundreds of highly-trained aviators could not be taken to their destination in fitting style rather than on this lousy, shaky, stinking, troop transporter. At first, the weather had cooperated, but now the wind and chop added to his misery. He had sat on deck reading whatever he could get his hands on. Back in high school, he had discovered that there was more to the world than corn, turkeys, and the feather-dotted, murky pond. That's why one day he drove sixty miles to the next Air Force recruiting center to volunteer for military service—"but overseas, please!" There was no guarantee of such an assignment, but with German grandparents on his mother's side, he stood a good chance of eventually being shipped to the European theater. He decided to take his chances and hope for overseas deployment. Still, he never imagined this kind of degrading voyage for a member of the elite Air Force. His only comfort was the chance to read a lot.

Roaming through the ship's library, he had found a brand new book on the "Marshall Plan." He had once met General George C. Marshall, the father of this plan, while on a high school trip to Washington, D.C. Now he was intrigued to read how this former commander of the Western Allied Forces in Europe and Asia, who had inflicted deadly wounds to Germany and Japan, had come up with a plan to help the German population overcome the horrors of war. Even though the official name was the "European Recovery Program," all newspapers and even the book in Fred's hands referred to the program as the "Marshall Plan."

Another book which captured his interest was about Thor Heyerdahl sailing from Peru to Tahiti on the primitive raft, "Kon-Tiki." Being on a much, much larger and yet shaky ship himself, he just could not imagine how Heyerdahl and his five friends could have sailed the ocean nearly 5,000 miles without going crazy. From back issues of *Stars and Stripes*, the newspaper published for American GIs around the world, he picked up hundreds of useful (and useless) news items: the creation of the autonomous nation of Pakistan after breaking off from India; Christian Dior's "new look" of half-long dresses without shoulder straps, made possible by wire-supported brassieres; the first sightings of UFOs in USA and Europe in 1947; the mounting friction in Berlin between the Social Democrats and members of the newly-created communist SED (*Sozialistische Einheitspartei Deutschlands,* or, Socialist Unity Party of Germany); Mahatma Gandhi's assassination on January 30, 1948; etcetera... .

When one of his buddies surprised him with a paperback edition of Norman Mailer's *The Naked and the Dead*, which had just come off the press, he momentarily forgot his seasickness. Mailer, just a few years his elder, put into words what he had always felt: Wars are a senseless waste of energy and material.

As a youngster, Fred had cheered for the victorious Allies and had been happy over every German plane, tank, and soldier who had been "finished off." To him, every uniformed German was a Nazi—until one day when Grandpa Schweigert had taken him aside to show him that there was more to Germany and her people than those brown-shirted party bosses and the black-shirted SS storm troopers.

Fred vividly remembered the day in July of 1944 when the wireless reported the news of the failed assassination attempt on Adolf Hitler. His grandfather tried to explain to him why and how all this had come about. During the following days, he read of Hitler's fury, which was directed against all those who had been part of, or who knew about, the plot. It was incredible that eventually more than 5,000 German military and civilians were "liquidated" in retaliation, as Nazi newspapers put it. As much as he pitied the conspirators whom Hitler had executed, he just could not understand why the German masses did not rise up to do away with Hitler.

From his love for music and literature, he knew that the German people were an intelligent and creative nation. Yet they had not been strong enough to prevent the rise of this dictator, nor had they come up with a plan to dispose of him. That day helped him make up his mind to join the Air Force in order to overthrow Hitler and his cohorts.

Fred was an outspoken, handsome young man with full hair, a rather high forehead, pronounced cheekbones, and a slightly too-large nose. When he smiled, his mouth sported two rows of perfect teeth. In high school he had not been tall enough to be on the basketball team, nor muscular enough to play football. However, he was an excellent gymnast and sprinter and, in fact, won the district title in the 100-meter dash.

His real strength was the academic field. Although he was the youngest of his classmates, he outdid most of them in just about all subjects. Because of his love for learning, he finished school one year ahead of his peers, making him popular with the girls and the target of envy and scorn with the boys. Nothing distracted him, however, from the pursuit of his goal to become a pilot.

So, without allowing himself a decent break after graduation, he had enlisted, had done well in his training, and now was on his way to Germany for his first turn of duty. His parents hoped that he would stay in the US until his twentieth birthday, but he managed to persuade his superiors to ship him out at the first possible opportunity.

"Can't you hear?" Somebody shook him roughly by the shoulder. "Hey, are you deaf?" Fred had been so deeply engrossed in reading *The Naked and the Dead* that he had not noticed all the sudden commotion around him. Had there been an alarm?

"What—what's going on?" he finally managed to ask one of the mates.

"A mine has been sighted, which is really bad news in rough seas." *A mine? Hasn't the war been over for three years?* There was no time now for further reflection. While the crew took alert positions, all others had to go under deck, even those who were seasick.

Below the deck, hundreds of young, enthusiastic American soldiers were bunched together tightly like a herd of cattle. There was nothing they could do but let fate take its course. There was not much anybody could do now except hope and pray, and that's exactly what Fred Harrington did. He had grown up in a Christian home where prayer always had played an important role. Even though as a teenager he had often been unhappy over the insistence of his parents that he attend church every Sunday, he now was glad that his trust in God made this situation more tolerable. Most of the other GIs either swore at the damned Germans who had left behind a deadly souvenir for them, or they just sat quietly staring into nothing, pretending that they were not afraid.

Chapter 3

Sergey Iliavitch Svertlov was the pride of his family. Born in 1924 in Moscow, he was the third of five children of engineer Leonid Svertlov, and Natasha Iliavitch. The family lived in a four-room apartment on the ninth floor at *Perulok Stanislavski* 249, about one mile south of Red Square.

After their wedding in 1920, Leonid and Natasha had endured, along with many of their fellow citizens, much suffering, food shortages, and religious persecution. Still, Leonid considered himself a lucky man. As the chief supervisor of the main water station in Moscow, he was a respected man among his colleagues and in his neighborhood. His wife Natasha was a graduate of Odessa University, down by the Black Sea. Some whispered that her parents were Jews, but nobody was sure, and the Svertlovs never talked about their past. Besides, Natasha's father had been killed as a soldier in World War I. Her mother had always treasured the military medals as proof that her husband had been a loyal, brave soldier, to the point of laying down his life for his fatherland Russia.

Yet, even Leonid's father had a bout with ill fate. As a man of high principles, he had spoken out against corruption among his government coworkers. He knew well that he would not reap praise for his action, but he never anticipated banishment to Siberia. After all, he was a war veteran. He had served his country well. Still, to speak out against the Soviet government was a *transgression* the people in power would not forgive.

After ten years of deportation, Grandfather Svertlov returned from Siberia a broken man in body and spirit. Years of hard labor in the extreme climate, the total isolation from his family, and the constant harassment from his guards and some of his peers had made him into a man who had given up on speaking, perhaps even on thinking.

Sergey remembered his grandfather's homecoming. It was a day of excitement, hugs, kisses, and lots of tears. It seemed that all family members and neighbors were forever crying and embracing each other. Even though Sergey had been only a little boy on that day, he remembered that his grandfather had not spoken a single word nor had he shed a tear. Like a distant spectator he had let people hug him, touch him, and wash his face with their tearful lips. But he did not even squeeze the little hand of his grandchild, which Sergey had put into the weathered and wrinkled hand of the old man, back from Siberia.

The grandfather had come home to live with them in their Moscow apartment. That made for a crowded situation, especially after the fifth Svertlov child arrived. However, since he never complained or made any demands, he was like a piece of furniture which everybody had gotten used to, without any thought of whether it still was useful or not.

When the war broke out against Germany in 1941, Sergey was seventeen years old. His father and two older brothers were drafted into the military two weeks after the declaration of war. Before leaving, Leonid had explained to his mute father that he and his two sons had to go to war now. Suddenly there seemed to be life in the old man. Stiffened from lack of use, Grandfather Svertlov's cracked and shaking lips could hardly form words. Leonid had to strain to hear his father as he pleaded, "Don't go. Don't go. Don't go, my son." Standing next to his father, Sergey also heard those words, the first he had ever heard from his grandfather. Then Sergey saw how his grandfather's eyes filled with tears; the Siberian snowman's eyes finally were melting.

Now, seven years later, all this seemed like ancient history to Sergey. He was on the way to Major General Kotikov, the Chief Commanding Officer of Germany's Eastern Zone and the Eastern Sector of Berlin, both occupied by Soviet troops. As a university graduate, he had been drafted into the Intelligence Unit that reported directly to the *Kommandant*. Though many of the regular infantry soldiers would have envied him for his cushy job, Sergey hated his assignment. As a civil engineering student, it had been his hope to be put one day into the pioneer battalion that was in charge of building bridges and military accommodations. But the war had ended while he was still a student. By the time it was his turn to be enlisted, the government simply put recruits wherever there were vacancies, regardless of their educational backgrounds and skills.

Sergey's dark brown eyes matched his full hair. At the Moscow University, he had been the dream of many female students and the victim of many pranks caused by jealousy. One early morning, after a long night of boisterous drinking in the apartment of one of the assistant professors, he woke up to find himself officially engaged to the sister of Professor Gudanov. All he remembered was the roaring loud music of the band when he had entered the apartment of the professor, a man whom he very much respected and considered a friend.

He also remembered the endless toast after toast to peace, friendship, Mother Russia, and Final Victory. But who in the world was the gorgeous girl with almond-shaped eyes, now in his arms? Then, very slowly, it all came back to him. Yes, this was the woman he had been introduced to by Professor Gudanov a few months prior to the party. Somehow, meeting the stunningly beautiful sister of his professor had spurred him on to even greater zeal in his studies. After some weeks, when he had to admit that this lovely girl was not responding to his frequent "attention-getters," he gave up on her. Strangely enough, that was the moment when she started pursuing him. Confused, he did not know how to handle the situation. To meet her at the party, therefore, was more than he had ever hoped for.

Yet, the unexpected end result overwhelmed him. Amidst drinking, laughter, shouting and more drinking, their engagement was announced. As it turned out, the engagement was rather unsuccessful. Six months later, both partners were happy to get off the road that would have led to marriage. Soon Sergey found out that breaking the engagement had also broken the friendship of his assistant professor. He was glad that graduation was only a few months away, because somehow both studying and girls had lost their glamour for him.

All this was far away from his mind now as he was heading for the tall, gray *Kommandantura,* a building pock-marked by hundreds of grenades that had chewed away on Berlin's formerly stately Ministry of Commerce. The two guards in front of the arched entry saluted stiffly as he approached them. His responding salute came automatically. His mind had been working feverishly for more than an hour. How could he explain to Major General Kotikov that so far his mission to find that crazy German youngster had been unsuccessful?

"You mean that incorrigible rascal is still un-caged?" thundered Kotikov. The Major General was standing in front of Lieutenant Sergey Iliavitch Svertlov, his legs spread apart, arms planted into his hips, his round belly shaking in fierce tremors.

"*Da*, Comrade Kotikov, Norbert Anleger is still at large. As a matter of fact, we are not even sure that he is still in our sector." When Sergey saw his superior's thick eyebrows rise in angry questioning, he quickly added, "Anleger may have defected to the West some days ago."

He still stood at attention, and he feared that the bullish Kotikov's rage could explode right into his face, possibly wiping out his career with the Intelligence Service. The explosion never came. Instead, Kotikov suddenly turned around, shuffled through some of the papers on his desk, and with a big thump, threw himself into his armchair. Seeing his commander in emotional disarray, Sergey permitted himself the freedom to stand at ease. Since his major general did not say anything, he kept quiet, too. The silence seemed to last an eternity.

"Comrade General," Sergey said, finally trying to end the awkward silence. His superior, however, did not hear him. His mind was trying to put things together, which proved to be a difficult and painful task. Since he was one of the officers who had liberated Berlin, Moscow headquarters had made him the commander-in-chief of the Russian sector of the city. He remembered how elated he had been, how swollen with pride as his driver toured him around in an open Jeep to inspect "his" city, his empire.

Yes, the high brass in Moscow this time had given the command to a worthy fighter of the Red Army. After reaching the suburbs of Berlin, his unit then had fought district after district, street after street, to either drive out or destroy the German foxes in their holes.

Kotikov would never forget the almost insane fighting in the densely populated district of Berlin-Neukölln. The Soviet headquarters had told him that he could count on little resistance in this district, since it was the part of Berlin that once had harbored more German communists than any other Berlin district, or any other large German city. He soon had found out that the optimistic message from Moscow was based on wishful thinking.

Fighting his way slowly from Berlin's Köpenick District to the District Neukölln, he soon realized that he was in for a major battle á la Stalingrad. The test of his strength came when his troops approached the city hall of Neukölln. It was a huge sandstone edifice stretching over an entire city block. The tower was an imposing solid stone block structure. Even though the hundreds of windows of the city hall were barricaded either with sand bags or heavy boards, they were by no means unattended. Out of each window frame spit deadly bullets and heavy grenades. Several attempts to persuade the defenders to give up, via a bullhorn message, had failed badly. The last attempt ended with the death of the German prisoner who had been forced to shout into the bullhorn: "Give up, you damned Nazis! Stop shooting! Throw away your weapons! Leave the building with your hands up! Give up and live, or you will all die!"

Seconds later, a German rocket killed not only the negotiator, but also took twelve Russian soldiers to their death. That's when Kotikov requested heavy artillery to do its deadly pounding. The exploding grenades were a danger not only to the fanatic defenders but also to the conquering Russians close by. They watched with a mixture of fear and relief as the explosions tore piece after piece out of the sandstone building. The fighting Russians could not believe that the relentless shooting from inside never diminished. When their guns tore open the third floor of the city hall, the shooting from the second and fourth floors seemed to escalate.

On the third day, the Major General asked for several wild-firing *Stalin Orgel*, as the Germans called the gun that could fire twenty or more grenades out of twenty connected barrels in less than a second. Yet, in vain he had watched for a white flag, indicating surrender. By then his troops had solidly surrounded the entire city hall. The pounding of the guns continued all through the night. Finally, after four horror-filled days of relentless shooting, the former city hall was reduced to a large, silenced pile of smoking rubble. It was the 27th of April.

When searching the smoldering ruins, his soldiers had made a blood-chilling discovery. During all these days they had not fought against heavily-armed soldiers, but rather against 13- to 17-year-old Hitler Youth in brown shirts, many of them wearing their Hitler Youth shorts. In their blind fanaticism, they had defended the city hall to the last man, or rather, last boy. Thinking of his own son back in Russia, he momentarily felt deprived of military glory. *Who wanted to fight and kill children!?* Only the "hurrah" victory shouts of his soldiers brought him back to military reality—in war the rule is either to kill or be killed.

"Comrade General," Sergey said, attempting once more to get the *Kommandant's* attention.

"Yes, what is it, Comrade Svertlov," the major general replied in a disturbed mood.

"I have come to give you a report about the German spy Anleger, Comrade General, and now I am waiting for your further instructions."

"Further instructions!" Kotikov mockingly echoed. "Further instructions! Further instruction won't catch this blasted German kid." Then he continued, even though speaking more to himself: "We threw out the Nazi bastards, but the Berliners did not thank us. We liberated their city, but they ran after the American troops, as if it had been those cowards who had freed them. I made Professor Arthur Werner the first post-war mayor, yet the Berliners called him *Kommunist Emil* and kicked him out of office. We gave them the chance to hold free elections, but more than half voted for the Social Democrats, while our Communist Party did not even get twenty percent. We relocated their specialists from their bombed factories to the Soviet Union and gave them jobs, and they called it deportation."

"You are referring to the *Ossawakim Programme*?" Sergey interrupted the commander's flow of complaints.

"I know the name!" Kotikov cut him off. And after a little pause, which was to show the young lieutenant how annoying his interruption had been, the commander-in-chief continued his monologue.

"We fed their school children with daily meals, but they refused to study the Russian language and spent their last German marks on American chewing gum. Every time I make a suggestion in the Allied *Kommandantura,* I can count on the vetoes of the American, English and French imperialists. Tell me, Svertlov, how can anybody run a city under these circumstances?" Svertlov knew that it was better not to answer this, which was only a rhetorical question anyway, to which nobody seemed to have an answer.

Chapter 4

Norbert knew that he could not stay any longer in his foul-smelling hiding place. It was better to be shot fleeing than to slowly suffocate in a garbage pile on the rooftop. With cat-like stealth he crawled out of his tunnel. The chill of the March night cut through his thin clothing like razors. For a moment he could not control the shivering of his arms and legs. He vigorously rubbed his arms until he was ready for the descent. But where was he to go? He knew that they would be waiting for him—if not the *Volkspolizei,* then the Russians. Why were they hunting him as a spy, anyway? He had never worked as a spy, neither for the West nor for the East.

By now I know both sides and probably would make a good spy, he mused, as his feet haltingly sought safe passage across the roofs of several houses. Then suddenly his step met only air and he fell, halting as he seemed to be suspended in midair—cold and dark air which revealed no clue to Norbert what had happened. Somehow in the last second he had been able to grab a beam above his head, preventing him from falling into the pitch-black nothingness.

Norbert tried to focus. "How stupid of me!" he hissed. "Naturally, this is the ruin of house number 79." He was remembering that the roof he had tried to walk across disappeared in a bomb blast many months before. Still dangling and feeling the weight of his body pull hard, his eyes slowly adjusted to the darkness. He surveyed the rugged ruin. Yes, this was it! This neck-breaking ruin provided a safer escape route than the staircases of the other houses. All he had to do was let go of the beam and hope for a safe landing on the rubble of the third floor twelve feet below. His heart pounded. His breath seemed to stop. Was it stupid to jump into what could be a death trap?

Then one of his hands let go, quickly followed by the other. To his amazement, no broken steel beam or other sharp objects had pierced him. In a split second he was on his feet looking for a further escape possibility. He searched in vain for stumps or beams in the wall which would have permitted him to lower himself to the second floor. To his horror, he discovered that there was no second floor—it must have collapsed in the explosion. He could just make out piles of debris as he looked down two floors below him. To climb back up to the roof was impossible. He would never make it. Brittle ruins were less solid than rocks in the mountains. Suddenly he remembered a movie he had seen once. A mountain climber had worked himself to an impasse. In order to shake off his pursuers, the mountaineer had leaped down a steep gorge, much higher than this ruin here. Why not jump here and now?

Without much further thought, determined to get back to the street, Norbert protected his face with his arm, closed his eyes, and jumped. With a big thump he landed on top of the rubble on the first floor. It was a good, though rather violent, landing. *Bruises, not breaks*, Norbert thought. Just as he was getting up, he heard an eerie sound. With a screechy moan, the entire floor gave way, triggered by the sudden impact. The overloaded floor beams cracked and let tons of rubble go. Norbert tried to ride out the sudden avalanche of dirt and bricks. The crushing masses whirled him down all the way to what once had been the basement.

It's over! was all he could think. Everything was finished. Attracted by the crashing sound, now the police would certainly come and find him buried in the rubble. Yet, miraculously he survived the fall uninjured. Frantically, he dug himself out of the mass of dirt, splintered wood, broken glass, and dust. A few minutes later he reached the street, just in time to see that two men were running toward the house at number 79, or rather the burnt-out ruin, which now was engulfed in a thick cloud of dust. Using the dust cloud as cover, Norbert pressed himself into a niche in the wall. The moment the pursuers tried to climb down into the ruin's gaping hole, he dashed off, racing in the direction of the Western sector. He knew that he was only a few hundred yards away from the heavily-guarded border crossing. Oh yes, the guards would be another hurdle, but right now it didn't matter. He just wanted to get away from the two dark shadows who were determined to hunt him down at all cost.

As he ran, he tried to convince himself that crossing into the West would be a piece of cake. He knew his city well, especially the streets and houses along the border. Entering a vacant factory building whose roof had been blown away during the last days of the war, he rushed toward the door that led to the basement, which in turn had an underground passageway that would lead him to the West.

The door was hammered shut. More than ten thick nails had been driven into the solid planks, making the opening of the door totally impossible. Norbert clawed with his fingers at the boards. They did not give an inch. He felt trapped. Suddenly, he knew a better solution. Quick steps took him to the second floor where empty window frames filtered dim light from outside. He tiptoed to the window and peered cautiously into the quiet night. He climbed into the window frame and jumped, reaching out to grab a broken window frame that was dangling away from the building like a hinge. The frame took a violent jolt outward. For a second, Norbert hesitated; then he let go. When his feet hit the pavement of the street next to the factory wall, he realized that he was in Western territory.

He had made it! In wild ecstasy, he zigzagged the street, shouting unintelligible words, until a blinding flash of light brought him to an instant halt. Years of street survival had sharpened his instincts—he knew to be on guard at all times. Yet for a few moments he had dropped his cautiousness, and right away he would have to pay for it—again.

"Where do you think you are going?" At these English sounds his heart started beating again. *Good God*, he almost thought that he had run back into the Eastern sector, rather than racing toward freedom. Now he saw it. These soldiers were Americans. Actually, he could not clearly see them, but he could hear and almost feel them.

"I—I'm…" is all he could stammer before he collapsed on the cold pavement. When he opened his eyes, he noticed that he was alone. He was lying on an army cot, covered with a soldier's coat. Quickly he got up and peered through the window. Outside stood two GIs talking to an American officer. Where in the world was he? In the middle of the small room stood a desk cluttered with hundreds of papers, pencils, cardboard stubs, business cards, a pack of *Lucky Strike* cigarettes, and a small radio. There was yet another stack of papers piled on the desk chair. A bookshelf held a few books, but was used mainly to store empty cups, a coffee maker, framed photographs, and a baseball trophy. The wastebasket was overflowing with a hodgepodge of mangled newspaper, tossed documents, and paper cups. The only wall without a window displayed a life-sized pinup girl.

While Norbert's eyes were still fixed on the scantily-clad pinup girl, three Americans entered the guardhouse. "Ah, I see that you are up," one of the GIs said. Without waiting for a response, the soldier posted himself in front of Norbert, taking the role of an interrogator.

"What is your name?" he demanded. "And what made you jump from that factory window? Who else was with you?"

Norbert looked at him, then turned his head to the officer. During the months of several arrests and time in East German prisons, he had learned to play up to the highest-ranking person present, especially in the case of an interrogation. And, the best thing was to say nothing.

"Thank you, soldier," the officer said, motioning back the overzealous guard. "I'll take it from here." With this he reached for Norbert's arm and led him from the sentry booth to his Jeep.

"You'll come with me," he said. "First we'll have something to eat, then we'll get back to business. You look as if you could stand some food." Food sounded absolutely heavenly to Norbert. He couldn't remember when he had properly eaten the last time. However, once his hands wrapped around a thick double-decker hamburger, he surely remembered how to eat! A huge ice-cream soda also helped to quench his appetite.

He was back where he belonged! He felt he no longer cared what would happen next. He would tell the Amis anything they wanted to know, even though he had no idea what they would ask. One thing he knew—that he would never, ever be caught again in the East. *Never!*

Chapter 5

Hours after the German mine alert, Fred and his buddies tried to convince each other that they had never been afraid of a possible explosion. After all, this was 1948, almost three years after V-E Day. Again, Fred was totally engrossed in Norman Mailer's book. The further he got into it, the more he was confirmed in his conviction that wars are a terrible waste of manpower and energy. Even though he was proud that he had enlisted, he fervently hoped that his main job would be to secure peace rather than to fight a bloody war.

His father must have instilled that conviction in him. Fred remembered the days when he and his father would walk along the fence of their turkey farm. While thousands of turkeys were eagerly scratching and searching for food, there would always be a few who were looking for a fight. And they always found equally belligerent partners, with whom they would battle, often to their death.

"Look at those dumb cocks," George Harrington would say. "They are too stupid and lazy to find food, so they get into a fight, which leaves them in much worse shape." Father and son understood each other without much conversation. When Fred was on a date or a school-meet, he usually was the life of the party. But with his father he didn't have to put up a front. There was something about this man, this down-to-earth farmer, that made Fred want to listen rather than talk.

It was different with his older brother, Jim. Fifteen years older, Fred had always treated him more like an uncle rather than a brother. When Fred was only six years old, Jim had married and moved to Utah. When the kids in school teased him that Jim had become a Mormon, Fred did not know how to respond. Frankly, as a first-grader, he really didn't know what a Mormon was, and Cindy, his brother's wife, looked and seemed to him just like any other young woman.

One day, his father took him along to Oelwein, a town not far from Sumner. Fred thought the people there really looked strange. The men wore black trousers with wide suspenders, blue shirts, and giant-brimmed black hats. The women had their heads covered with polka-dotted scarves, wore gray blouses, and wrapped their wide bodies in huge aprons. He had laughed when he saw the horse-drawn black buggies with high, thin wheels steered by bearded men.

"You must not laugh at those people," his father admonished him. "They are the Amish folk, who live and worship in their own peculiar ways."

"Do they believe in God?"

"They surely do. As a matter of fact, if all of us Christians would show such strength of faith as they do, the world would be a better place."

"But would we all have to go around in strange clothes and ride in buggies?"

"Of course not," his father chuckled. "At least I hope not."

In later years, Fred met Amish and Old Mennonite people at various occasions. He admired them in a strange way, even though he did not know why. Some of their girls were really pretty, yet they were too shy for his taste. And they seemed totally disinterested in the things that meant the most to him: music, literature and dating—not necessarily in that order.

The Harringtons belonged to the small, old-fashioned Baptist church in Sumner. German immigrants who had come from East Prussia, Poland, and Russia before World War I had founded the congregation. Many members had kept up their German traditions and transplanted them into the Iowa culture. For years, all of their church activities were conducted in the German language. Eventually some of the church services and weddings were held in English, yet all of the choir songs were in German so only those who understood and spoke German could join the choir.

During World War II, many of the German settlers in the Sumner area had faced mockery, bullying and ethnic persecution from their pro-war American neighbors. Nobody knew whether it was true, but rumor had it that in 1941 the Governor himself had issued the order that all ethnic German congregations had to sing their hymns and choir anthems in the English language *only*. However, that was easier decreed than done. Some of the old immigrants truly did not speak any English. Thus, they had to give up on singing altogether, or they would just keep on singing in German.

Harrington, on the other hand, was of English descent. He would have felt much more at home in a modern American church. But when he had courted Anna Schweigert, a lovely German girl with a slight accent, he had not been much of a church-going man anyway, even though he considered himself a Christian. One day, Anna invited him to come along to her church. Even though he understood almost nothing of the sermon, prayers, and songs, it did not bother him as long as he could sit close to Anna. He loved her beautiful voice and he enjoyed the warm, open welcome he received from her family. George's first church visit in Sumner was the beginning of a life-long active affiliation with that Baptist church.

The test of his faith came when his oldest son, Jim, returned home from his university studies and introduced to them a young, attractive girl from Utah.

"Utah…is that where the Mormons live who practice polygamy?" Harrington had asked and embarrassed his son. Jim was taken aback that his father would use or even know that term. With a few well-chosen words he set his father straight—and all who wanted to listen to him.

"Yes, Cindy comes from a Mormon family," Jim said. "And no, her father is not a polygamist. Her family is just as normal and proper as any of the families in Sumner. Oh yes, the most important thing, last—we're planning on getting married."

The wedding was harder on George Harrington than taking care of his turkeys during a tornado. The ceremony, in many ways, was similar to ones he was accustomed to. But when the bride and groom were invited to step into the "Heaven Room" for a special "sealing ceremony" open to Mormons only, the Harringtons knew that their Jim was lost to them. Little Fred, on the other hand, did not mind any of the events of the day. He had discovered a beautiful little girl among the wedding guests whose attention he was trying his best to attract. They caught each other's eye several times, and Fred was set on keeping her in sight. At the end of the day, he had made up his mind that one day he would marry her. However, the next day he realized that he had forgotten to ask for her name, and nobody seemed to know which girl he was talking about.

Now he was almost twenty years old and still not married. As far as he was concerned, he would stay that way, at least for a few more years. He was glad to feel free to embark on this see-the-world adventure. He hoped they would anchor in an English port. His father's folks came from Brighton. Secretly he had made plans to visit his English aunts and uncles, or at least their graves. However, as soon as they seemed to approach land, the ship turned again, losing the land slowly out of sight again. The ship's new destination was Cherbourg in France. Even though Fred was somewhat disappointed, he was looking forward to applying his two years of high school French, and everybody knew that the French girls were gorgeous!

However, once they had landed in Cherbourg, the ship transformed into a madhouse. Fred almost got separated from his unit. MPs checked him out, once he stepped on land. They were loaded on trucks that, in a two-hour ride, took them to a military base further inland. Like all of his buddies, Fred fell asleep during the ride. The loud orders of a barking sergeant woke them up. Boy, that was some kind of welcome for U.S. Air Force troops!

Three days later, he still had not seen a single example of the famed French mademoiselles. Neither had he seen a single American airplane. It seemed all he had done was fill out questionnaires and a bunch of other papers. Slowly it dawned on him that his captain in training school might have been right when he once proclaimed, "Often the tour of duty turns out to be just that."

A few weeks later, it was official that he and twenty other pilots would be transferred to Berlin, the "Western Island" in communist East Germany. That same night, most pilots were bent over maps of Germany and also studying other European nations.

"Where the hell is Berlin?' asked one of the men as he squinted at a map.

"Come on, you know where Berlin is," Fred said, trying to sound knowledgeable.

"No, I don't. You show me!" insisted the curly-haired Puerto Rican from New York City, who never before had been outside of the Big Apple. Fred's fingers traveled across the map along the Russian-American occupation zone border. He couldn't locate Berlin.

"I'll be ..."

"Here, I found it!" said one of the men, who was known for speaking only in emergencies. All eyes followed his finger. There it was! Not at the border, as Fred had supposed, but rather smack in the middle of the Soviet occupation zone. Now all admitted that they had thought of Berlin as a border city rather than an island in the center of the Russian Zone, ruled by the four Allied powers. The men continued studying the maps.

"I wonder if we will get to see some honest-to-goodness Ruskies."

"Why not? We'll be right there where they are hanging around."

"Yeah, but if they step on my feet, they'll be hanging for real."

The waiting for the transfers was worse than the senseless pushing around of papers. Having been informed of their impending transfer, they had been relieved of any duties. Now some played cards, others solved crossword puzzles. Fred was devouring books again. There was so much to know in this world. When he found a small but rather sophisticated book on rockets and fuel-propelled missiles, all boredom was gone. He had a hard time accepting in his mind that the little country of Germany had managed to develop and deploy jet engines before any other nation. Even the U.S.A. had limped behind in that field. His only comfort was to read that Wernher von Braun and Hermann Oberth, the two outstanding German scientists and fathers of jet-propelled missiles and space flights who had headed the wartime Peenemünde Development Team on Germany's Usedom island, were now working on the American side, together with the American space specialists, J. Robert Oppenheimer and Robert J. Goddard. Only the future would tell how many German missile specialists the Soviets had managed to capture and press into their service.

The day finally arrived when Fred and his buddies boarded a plane for Berlin. When they flew across East Germany, his eyes searched the sky for Russian planes. But his flight was uneventful. There was a tense feeling among the young airmen as they flew across the Soviet occupation zone. None of them had been here before, but somehow they sensed that Berlin would be a special assignment with an unpredictable outcome.

All of a sudden, there was a Soviet plane right next to their plane. Fred could not believe what he saw. In flight school they had been taught that no commercial airliner ever approaches another plane with less than two miles distance. This plane, however, was right outside his window. He even saw the pilot turn his head with a face made out of stone. His buddies cursed in anger; other screamed at the Russian intruder, as if he could hear them.

"What is that devil trying to prove?"

"That bastard must be drunk!"

"I bet you, that commie is going to ram us." A mix of shouts, screams and loud monologues filled the American plane. They had read about the dangerous behavior of the Soviet air force which had buzzed American planes, had caused radio interference, and had flown too close. Now they got their very own taste of Russian craziness in the air. Just as suddenly as the plane had popped into close range, it tipped its wings and disappeared into thick clouds.

Before Fred could analyze this strange event, his plane was readying itself for landing in Berlin-Tempelhof. His eyes searched the approaching ground again. There was nothing but four- and five-story houses, then a four-lane street, a steel fence, a few trees that had survived the war, and—suddenly— the runway. The plane hit the runway awfully hard because the pilot knew that he had to bring down the plane's momentum to a speed that allowed making a turn after only a few hundred yards. The sudden turn to the right made everybody lean over. Then the pilot killed the two propellers on the right wing. Goodness, what kind of flight manual had the pilot read! This was not the prescribed procedure of how to land a plane. When

Fred turned around to the other airmen, he saw that they had arrived at the same conclusion. When he was deplaning, he could not hold back commenting to the pilot. "That was a hell of a maneuver you put on, sir…nothing from our books."

"That's right, son," the senior officer came back. "Our flight instructions also say nothing about how to handle strafing, close-flying Ruskies."

When Fred's feet touched German soil, he took a moment to reflect on his thoughts and feelings. He wanted to be able to describe to his grandparents back in Iowa the landing in the country which they had left over forty years before. When he looked at his calendar watch, he saw that it was May 1. Grandfather Schweigert had mentioned that he left Germany in the month of May in 1908. Alex and Hedwig Schweigert, such hard-working, dear people in Sumner, had managed to carve out for themselves a totally new existence in the United States of America. A full forty years had passed; strange and crazy years in a way, at least in Europe. Fred was eager to track Germany's history as far back as he could, to understand what made this nation of his ancestors such an unpredictable, strange partner in the world community of nations.

Chapter 6

All Lieutenant Sergey Svertlov could think of was how pathetically incompetent these East German secret service agents were. Instead of following Soviet orders, they tried to outsmart their communist allies, usually with devastating results. The case of Norbert Anleger, for example, was more proof of their incompetence. Svertlov knew the case almost by heart, and he also knew that this Norbert Anleger was really just a very small spoke in the wheel of the New Germany that had been created with Soviet help. Compared to some of the enemies of the Soviet occupation army and the East German administration, Norbert hardly deserved another look. It was this man's defiant spirit, however, and his seemingly miraculous escapes that kept the wheels turning and the hunt on. Frankly, Svertlov doubted seriously that Anleger was a spy. He knew of better ones. Yet, Svertlov was sure that this case would be the making or breaking of his career as an intelligence officer.

Just as he was reaching for the stack of German newspapers on his desk, there was a rap at his door. Who in the world dared to disturb him at this hour? He had instructed his assistant, who age-wise could have been his father, never to admit anybody directly to his office. Before he could respond to the knocking, the door flung open.

"Cousin Sergey!" shouted a tall, husky man who filled the entire door frame. Lieutenant Svertlov's face was blank. Who was this impertinent intruder? Realizing that his cousin Svertlov would not make the first move toward a family reunion, Private Anatoly Chukov, with a few large steps, went behind Sergey's desk and engulfed the surprised officer in a bone-crushing embrace. This totally non-military greeting shocked the lieutenant, yet he did not sense any threat, only a familiar warmth.

"Cousin Sergey! Cousin Sergey, don't you remember your cousin Anatoly Chukov?"

Svertov's brain was working in overdrive. Then he remembered. Yes, his father had a sister in Tashkent, who was married to a *kolkhoz* farmer by the name of Chukov. This bear around his neck must be the offspring of his father's sister. He had the man identified, but he could not adjust his mind to the intrusion into his office and onto his chest.

"Soldier, come to attention!" Svertlov shouted. But Anatoly would not hear of it. He kept his supposed relative in an iron-like embrace, while he tried to place a kiss on the officer's cheek. Svertlov finally managed to tear himself loose.

"I'll have you disciplined, you stupid ox!" he gasped, straightening his disheveled uniform. "Sit down, soldier!" he thundered, not trying to hide his displeasure over the private's unbecoming behavior. Suddenly Anatoly's enthusiasm died. Instead of sitting down, he came to full salute, his eyes fixed on the wall. He did not dare to look at Svertlov, who had flopped down in his chair. While Anatoly stood at attention, the lieutenant's mind was flooded with memories of a time when his father's sister and her family had visited Moscow. He recalled that he had felt ashamed at their peasant appearance and ignorance. Yes, there had been a boy, Anatoly, and a younger brother Sasha, and one or two small sisters. They had followed him around like little puppy dogs. So, this was his cousin Anatoly Svertlov Chukov. What now?

A few minutes later though, both had forgotten the ill-mannered reintroduction and the difference in rank. They were deeply engrossed, comparing notes as they recalled their past common experiences and exchanged family news. To his amazement, Svertlov discovered that Anatoly had traveled via Moscow, where he had managed to visit Svertlov's parents.

"You mean, my father is still pumping water for the ever-thirsty Muscovites?" Svertlov asked jokingly.

"You should say the 'ever-dirty Muscovites,'" countered Anatoly, who was totally relaxed now. "Some Muscovites use water for washing, as you know. But when it comes to drinking, all good Russians prefer vodka." That was the cue to bring out the drinks. After a few toasts to their families, to Mother Russia, to Uzbekistan (the home republic of Anatoly), to Joseph Stalin, and to the unexpected reunion in Berlin, their hearts were warmed up and their tongues loosened.

"Tell me, Anatoly, wasn't your mother one of those believers our State has tried to do away with?" All of a sudden, the hulky man from Tashkent seemed to shrivel in his chair. The potato vodka had made his speech slurry. His eyes were glassy, yet his mind was still clear. So clear, that he now felt stabbed with the painful recollection that this moment, this indulgence in nostalgia with his cousin, was a world apart from his usual life.

"It is true, Mother is a believer. Even my father used to go to church every Sunday, if not more often. The day before a German grenade killed him, he wrote a letter in which he admonished us to be strong in our faith and not to 'neglect the gatherings of the Christian believers,' as he called it." Svertlov stared at his peasant cousin, contemplating his ignorance.

"What about you? Do you believe that stuff, too?"

"What stuff?" asked Anatoly, trying to avoid a direct question regarding his religious convictions.

"Well, the Jesus fables, the Messiah stories, the Bible, and all the other pious nonsense."

"I don't know," said Anatoly, "I guess I do. At least as long as I was at home, all the Christian teachings seemed to make sense. I never thought of them as nonsense then." In spite of numerous drinks, Svertlov felt sober and keen to pursue his cousin's ridiculous and irrational ideas. And so, even when Anatoly tried to change the topic of their conversation, asking about the situation in Berlin, Svertlov hammered away with his anti-Christian arguments. Then he asked, "By the way, Anatoly, how come you are drinking vodka? I thought believers do not touch the devil's brew?"

That was too much for Anatoly. His eyes filled with tears, and he started sobbing. His quivering lips formed unintelligible words. Finally Svertlov could hear his cousin say over and over again, "Forgive me, forgive me, God!" He held his eyes closed, while the tears were running down his cheeks, leaving wet spots on his new uniform.

Svertlov was at a loss. He had meant to provoke his cousin, but had not expected the man to completely break down. His drinking buddy had turned into a weeping, sobbing heap of misery, not unlike the weeping *babushka* he had watched one day in Moscow as her husband was dragged out of a church and loaded into a police van.

Just then the telephone rang. It was his *Kommandant* who wanted to know whether he had any new information on the German escapee. When Lieutenant Svertlov had to tell him that nothing new had come up, Major General Kotikov went into such a rage that Svertlov had to hold the telephone receiver far from his ear. There was no point trying to respond. Kotikov's tirade was like a torrential river that could not be stopped.

Anatoly forgot about his own misery, looked up, and listened in disbelief to the flood of curses. "I think that man is very, very angry," he finally whispered, more in sign language than in words.

"That man is my *Kommandant*," Svertlov whispered back. After a long while he shouted into the receiver, "Yes, my *Kommandant*! Yes, sir! Yes, my *Kommandant*! *Da, da!*" tried to change the topic by asking about the situation, readying himself to salute whenever his invisible boss was through. Anatoly's face lit up when he watched his cousin end the almost one-way conversation by coming to attention and giving a stiff salute.

For a moment neither one of them said anything. Then the lieutenant's hand swiped the empty vodka bottle off the table. It bounced off the wall, smashed to the floor and shattered into small pieces.

"Damn it! Damn it! I hate that Kotikov," Svertlov said. "He may be a great warrior, but he has the head of a stubborn mule." Anatoly could hardly believe that his officer-cousin would speak so disrespectfully of his superior. Back home in Tashkent, nobody would ever have dared to speak like that about a commanding officer. Even though he didn't know what the phone call was all about, he could tell that it was important enough to forget about further socializing with his upset cousin.

"Comrade Svertlov, thank you for your time and your wonderful welcome," Anatoly said, bringing his huge body to attention. Sergey looked up in surprise. So much courtesy he had not expected from his Uzbek relative.

"Good night, Comrade Chukov," he replied, remaining seated. When his cousin left, he reached for the two empty bottles under his desk and sent them flying against the wall, where the first shattered bottle had left its mark.

Chapter 7

"Wait, wait, young man!" Major Blythe held up his hand, as if to shield himself from the gushing flow of words of his young prisoner.

"I am impressed that your English is so good. But now let's do everything in proper order!" After a sumptuous meal at the PX, the American officer had driven Norbert to his office located in the western part of *Friedrichstrasse*, where he wanted to find out more about the house-jumping escape artist. As long as Norbert had food in front of him, no real conversation had been possible. Norbert's main interest was to gulp down as much as possible. After all, he did not know when or if there would be another visit to the "land of milk and honey," as he called the American PX store.

Now Norbert felt full and relieved beyond measure as he sat across from his liberator, and he was more than ready to make up for the forced long silence of the last two days in his hiding places.

"So, as I said before," Blythe said, "let's do things right." The major reached for a note pad, adjusted himself into a comfortable position, and began his interrogation.

"Before I ask you anything, let me first of all tell you who I am. My name is Major Robert Blythe. My home is Chicago in the state of Illinois. But now my real home is the Army. I have been a soldier since 1941, right after the Japanese attack on Pearl Harbor."

He paused to study Norbert for a moment, and then continued, "I have been in Germany for three years—three long years. Do you know what that means? I came with the first American troops after fighting my way up from Italy across the Brenner Alps, then through Austria where I got fleas and lice in the God-forsaken military barracks of Wagrain. Then I made it to Germany to take a look at your *Führer's* Eagles Nest in *Berchtesgarten*—or what's left of it—and then I was deployed to Munich, and finally to Berlin."

Norbert did not know what to say. For a moment there was an awkward silence. Then, instead of getting lost in more memories of his European tour, the Major looked at Norbert and started his interview.

"Now to you, young man," he said. "How come you speak such good English?"

"I started learning English in school when I turned ten. For some years I studied English along with Latin and French, until the war's end brought a stop to my education. From then on there was no more Latin, no French, just lots of American—if you know what I mean." Major Blythe was not sure what he meant, but he was thinking that this escapee had mostly studied fraternizing with American occupation troops.

"What about Russian? Do you speak Russian?"

"*Njet, Tovarish!*" Norbert joked and laughed. "No, but I speak and understand enough not to be caught in a Russian black market roundup."

"Well then, first, tell me your full name."

"Norbert Anleger."

"Where do you live?"

"*Hermann Strasse* 245 in Berlin-Neukölln."

"Do you live with your parents?"

"No. My parents are dead. I live with my uncle and aunt—whenever I happen to be at home."

"Or when you are not running from the Russians, right? By the way, what were you doing on the Russian side of Berlin, since you actually live in West Berlin?"

"That's a long story, Major."

"I have time."

Instead of throwing himself into a long narration of his life, Norbert hesitated while a cloud of sadness slowly passed across his face.

"I was born in Berlin," Norbert began. "I have—I mean I *had*—three brothers and a sister. My parents were wonderful people. My father worked as an engineer for *Siemens-Halske* until he was drafted into the army in 1943. The government sent him to *Peenemünde* on the *Usedom* Island in the Baltic Sea. He was involved in the development of the V-I and V-II—you know—the war toys of Wernher von Braun. My father consulted with Dr. von Braun at least once a week." Major Blythe saw a flash of pride on Norbert's face before the young man continued.

"One fateful night, when Father and my brother Hans, who also was stationed near *Peenemünde* as an anti-aircraft gunner, had too much to drink, my father let out a few military secrets. He was arrested. We never heard from him again. But just a few weeks ago, an ex-POW visited us and told us that shortly after the war my father had died from never-ending torture and starvation in a former Nazi prison camp, which had become a Russian prison, and was occupied by almost the same prisoners as under the Nazis. There is no grave for him, and I doubt that we will ever receive an official document of his death." Norbert took a deep breath and let it out slowly, trying to remain in his role as the storyteller, not the heartbroken son.

"Hans, my oldest brother, did come home two years before the war ended. Actually, he was brought home in an ambulance—minus one arm and with a shattered hip. Because of a lack of much-needed medication, a few months after his return, his left leg had to be amputated. He was a broken man, in spirit as well as body.

"Not so for my brothers Kurt and Waldemar," Norbert continued. "They loved everything about Hitler and his war, about uniforms and the Hitler Youth, about the idea of serving the *Reich* and dying for the fatherland. Actually, for us Anleger kids —yes, me included —Adolf Hitler was an *Übermensch*. Kurt and Waldi both died for their folly, while I am still alive."

"Both? How?"

"Both my brothers gave their lives for the fatherland, on the same day and at the same place. Since my father was a concentration camp prisoner, a fact only the authorities knew at that time, and since my brother Hans was severely wounded, my brothers had been exempted from military service. One night, two military police showed up at our apartment. They asked Kurt and Waldemar to put on their Hitler Youth uniforms and join the hundreds of HJ-Kids defending City Hall in *Neukölln*. By then, Russian troops had already occupied most of Berlin."

All of a sudden Norbert was overcome with emotion. His eyes filled with tears which he quickly dried with his sleeve, being ashamed of his seeming weakness. Blythe remained silent. The horrors of war which he had experienced firsthand were far different from Norbert's horrendous experiences and personal losses. Slowly, Norbert continued:

"You've probably heard or read about the fate of the 600 Hitler Youth who defended the city hall to the last drop of blood. By the time they had all been slaughtered by the Russians, there were literally rivers of blood flowing in and out of the ruins of the *Rathaus.* When the news of the death of Kurt and Waldemar reached my mother, I thought she would go crazy."

"When was that?" Blythe asked.

"When was what?"

"When were they killed?"

"It was on April 27. I'll never forget that date. One week before, I had turned 13.

"You could say that I was lucky that I wasn't 14 yet. Otherwise my blood would have mixed with the blood of 600 stupid HJ heroes. At that time, though, I wished...I wished I had been among those fanatic defenders."

The major could see that Norbert's body was shaking. He had not interrupted the lengthy flow of his words and was surprised when Norbert seemed ready to talk some more. Yet from then on, Norbert's words came very haltingly.

"Major, you must be wondering why I remember the date of the death of my brothers. After all, what were two more deaths among the millions of lives Germany and other nations had sacrificed since the beginning of the war? Still, I will never forget April 27 and 28, 1945, the days when our already-hurting family totally fell apart.

"After the terrible news on the 27th, nobody felt like eating breakfast on the following morning. There was no decent food left in our house, anyway. Hunger is awful, but on that day we were all hurting much more from the loss of my brothers." Norbert blinked back tears as he recalled that painful scene.

"'I'll go outside to look for something edible,' my 17-year old sister, Heidi, announced to our silently sobbing family. We looked at her in disbelief. Did she think she was 'Wonder Woman'? How could she find food in a city reeking from death and charred by hundreds of flames?" Norbert stared at the wall behind Blythe, not seeing his current surroundings, only the apartment and pain-stricken faces of his family, years before.

"'No, my child,' protested my mother. 'Don't go out! We must stay together—you, Hans and Norbi are all I have left now.' But Heidi would not hear of it. Touching Mamma's hair and planting a quick kiss on her cheek, she was out the door." Tears rolled down Norbert's cheeks as he continued:

"Mother became hysterical. 'Why did she go? Why did she go?' Mother wailed. 'Even if she should find some weeds or potatoes, we have no fuel to boil water anyway!' Neither Hans nor I said anything. Then it happened! Without any warning, a sudden earth-shaking explosion engulfed us. The walls of our apartment shook and collapsed in all directions. The smell of explosive powder mixed with thick dust and black smoke made breathing impossible. A Russian grenade or bomb must have hit our apartment house and pushed the tall building into the ground, taking us for a deadly ride. There was no feeling of gliding or sinking—just crashing into utter darkness, into hell." Norbert fell silent. He did not seem aware that he had stopped speaking, but finally, he went on.

"*It's over,* was all I could think in the midst of this inferno. A bit later I analyzed my situation. *I cannot move my limbs. I have no arms, no legs, no body. Where is my head?*

Why can't I speak? Where am I? Where is my mother? Who else was with her? I need to shout for help, or I will die. No, I am already dead." Norbert paused and wiped his face with his sleeve.

Major Blythe exhaled, realizing he had been holding his breath. In a quiet voice, he asked, "How in the world did you get out of there?"

"Nobody ever told me how long it took the rescue team to dig me out of the rubble.

"I only remember that suddenly I saw a beam of daylight… and then I was free. Rough but careful hands checked my bones for breaks. 'Speak, boy, speak!' I heard somebody say over and over. *Why should I speak,* I thought. *I'm dead anyway. Or am I?* Suddenly I was back to life. The rescue team watched in amazement as I stretched my legs and arms, carefully twisted my bruised body, and wiped lots of dirt off my face. 'Hey, I am alive!' I finally shouted, hardly believing it myself. But there was no time for celebrating because suddenly the tragedy of the situation hit me."

"'Where is my mother? Where is Hans? What about Heidi? Where are they?' I cried out. 'They didn't make it,' I heard a man say. Then I drowned in darkness. I must have fainted because when I came around, I was lying on a military stretcher surrounded by uniformed personnel. My vision was blurry—my eyes were bleeding! All I could see was Heidi, bending over me, touching my face with her blond hair. But I remembered the rescue crew had told me, 'They did not make it.' I thought that meant Heidi was dead—perhaps this blond creature looking like Heidi was an angel."

"'Are you an angel from God?' I finally squeezed the words through my swollen lips.

"The mysterious blonde laughed, saying, 'I wish I were! No, I'm not an angel. I am your sister, you dummy.' Then she kissed my forehead and cheeks over and over. You know, when a teenage sister kisses her teenage brother, that's more than a miracle." Major Blythe shared Norbert's brief laughter, as Norbert continued:

"I wanted to know how long I was buried, so I asked Heidi, 'What day is it?' 'Today is the 28th of April,' she whispered. You see now, Major, why I remember the date of my brothers' death? Only one day later, I lost my mother and Hans, too."

Both men stared at the floor. What else was there to do? He had asked the young German to unpack his life story; now they were stuck somewhere between here and eternity.

With an even more strained voice Norbert continued, "But I still had Heidi—at least for a few days." Silence.

"A few days?" asked Blythe.

"Heidi and I buried mother—nobody could find enough of Hans worth burying—in a make-shift grave, actually just a hole in the ground of the debris-covered area, where once we had played as little children. That was on April 29." Norbert looked straight into the major's eyes.

"On the next afternoon," he continued, "two Russian officers of the Third Army victoriously hoisted the Soviet flag over the *Reichstag* building. About one hour later, Adolf Hitler committed suicide in his bunker in the *Reichskanzlei*—the chancellery. Both places were only a few hundred meters apart. That day was April 30."

There was a long silence, a painful silence.

"You will never know how I felt, Major. Never! Father missing. Three brothers dead. Mother dead. My Führer dead. Incidentally, the German media reported the distorted news that Hitler had died a hero's death—'shoulder to shoulder with his brave soldiers.'"

"The Soviet Army was swarming all over Berlin now. The end had come. The end for Germany. The end of my future. But I still had Heidi. She may have been four years older than I, but suddenly I knew that it was *my* role to protect *her*. I had to shield her. We had survived until now. Perhaps together we could survive a bit longer. Unfortunately, I had Heidi for only one more day." Norbert stared off into space again, saying nothing; Blythe waited patiently.

"May first had all the makings of a beautiful spring day," Norbert recounted. "The sun was shining, which almost made up for having no food. Heidi and I decided to leave all the rubble and anguish behind and go for a refreshing walk. We didn't get far, though. After only a few minutes, we ran into a marching column of Russian soldiers. We stopped and wanted to let them pass. Most of the soldiers were tired, disheveled, and 'victory-drunk.' We almost had pity on these exhausted marchers in dirty, torn uniforms.

"Suddenly their commander shouted '*Stoy!*' A quick stream of other Russian words followed—and then these soldiers fell on us. Brutal fists knocked me to the ground and held me there, while others ripped off my watch, jacket, and shirt. Then I saw ten or fifteen soldiers surround Heidi—jeering, pulling her hair, grabbing her breasts, and at last throwing her into the air. She fell into the arms of two soldiers, who tore off her clothes. She screamed, terrified…but the soldiers did not even hesitate. While fists were smashing into my face, my sister was gang-raped first by three, seven, or even more Russians who joined their frenzied comrades. After a few minutes, I could no longer look at this diabolic pack of wolves. When I refused to watch, a soldier's boot kicked me in the head, sending me, mercifully, into a coma." Again, Norbert's cheek became wet with bitter tears.

"When I woke up, I was lying in the street all by myself. Everybody was gone. I saw only a few torn pieces of cloth and some blood, where Heidi had been raped. My calls for her echoed in the burnt-out ruins around me. Heidi, the last living member of my family, was gone."

"Hold it, young man," the major said with a deep frown. "As much as I am sorry for you being beaten unconscious, you don't mean to say that your sister was brutally raped by ten or more soldiers of the Soviet Army."

"Yes, she was!" shouted Norbert, making the major blink and briefly shut his eyes as if he had been struck by the outburst.

"Sorry, Norbert, but I think that's just Nazi propaganda crap."

Suddenly Norbert was on his feet. He shook his fist close to the American major's face.

"Propaganda?! Propaganda crap, you said? I was there!" he yelled, his rage exploding now—at all that he had endured, at the despicable Russians, at the unbearable frustration of not being able to come to his sister's rescue. His face was red; his voice became a little less shrill but even firmer as he went on.

"God is my witness that every word is true. I am sure you know that for several weeks before and after the war, the victorious Russian troops officially had free reign to do with the Germans as they pleased—killing, burning down, raping, plundering, and more raping. Revenge was the accepted rule for the fighting, victorious Soviets."

When Norbert noticed that Blythe's face was marked by an incredulous expression, he let his fist land on a copy of *Stars and Stripes* on the desk in front of him.

"Your own papers here reported that in 1945, in Berlin alone, 87,000 women and girls were raped by the 'victorious' Russian soldiers and officers between April 24 and May 1— that's in ten days! Is that Nazi propaganda crap?"

66

Norbert was glad that three years ago he had learned to read and understand American newspapers. They confirmed his tragic story. Still very angry, he turned on his heels and walked toward the door. He had nowhere to go, yet he just had to leave this place. The memories of those days of death, pain, and shame were choking him.

Chapter 8

POLITICO-GEOGRAPHIC INTERLUDE

Long before the Russians Sergey Svertlov and Anatoly Chukov, and the Americans Robert Blythe and Fred Harrington set foot on German soil, Germany's so-called enemy nations had made plans how to handle a defeated Germany. In mid-1943, the Allies, having witnessed Germany's failure to conquer the Soviet Union and to block the Anglo-American landings in North Africa, seriously began discussing and outlining procedures for the days when the *Third Reich* would fall. As far back as October 1943, American, British and Soviet government representatives met in Moscow, where they agreed to form an "Allied European Advisory Commission," or "EAC," whose task would be to define how the "Big Three" would occupy and rule Germany after the war had ended.

Some months later, the plan was modified to establish an "Allied Control Commission," or "ACC," based in Berlin, which would run Germany as a single nation. Still, to avoid supply and communication problems, Germany was to be divided into three occupation zones. The Soviet Union would control 40 percent of Germany's pre-war territory and 36 percent of its population. The British would control northwestern Germany, and the Americans southwestern

Germany. Frankly, the USA would have preferred the control of northwest Germany with its large seaports, Hamburg and Bremen, and also the coal-rich, industrial *Ruhr* District.

Berlin, Germany's capital, would now be situated 110 miles inside the Soviet Zone. The three Allies agreed that Berlin would be controlled by the Big Three, each of their garrisons occupying one of three "Sectors." Unfortunately, this proposal looked less complicated and more peaceful on paper than in reality.

At the Yalta Conference in February of 1945—less than three months before the war's end in Europe—Roosevelt, Churchill, and Stalin approved the original plan, except for one change: The war-defeated nation of France would also become an occupier of Germany. Their Zone would be carved out of the American and British zones of Germany and the western Sectors of Berlin. The "Big Three" had become the "Big Four."

In the heat of all the wrangling over future dominance in Germany, the western access to Berlin did not appear to be a problem. Thus, the Western Allies neither arranged for, nor insisted upon, specific transit rights to and from Berlin—an oversight that was to cost them dearly in 1948 and 1949. However, being so close to the defeat of Nazi Germany, and with credit going to each of the Big Three, it was necessary and convenient to overlook differences among the war partners. Besides, all this was to be a temporary arrangement, with the understanding that after the war's end all occupying troops would leave Germany after two years—at the most.

There was still the "little" problem regarding which of the fighting nations was to be given the chance of conquering

Berlin. All Allied troops, down to the last soldier, wanted to be involved in the total destruction of Nazi Germany's crown jewel—Berlin, the capital of the *Third Reich*. The American troops were within 53 miles of Berlin when General Eisenhower, the Supreme Allied Commander, informed Stalin that his troops would move southward toward Leipzig rather than toward Berlin. Churchill, a well-grounded and experienced politician, was furious over Eisenhower's decision. His deep-seated distrust of the communist superpower prompted him to send a cable to President Roosevelt, expressing his fear that a possible victory over Berlin might give the Russians the impression that *they* were the real victors over Germany. Churchill foresaw "grave and formidable difficulties in the future" as the result of such a move. He pleaded with the American President, "…from a political standpoint, we [USA and Great Britain] should march as far east into Germany as possible; and should Berlin be in our grasp, we should certainly take it."

Nevertheless, on April 11, with President Roosevelt's support, General Eisenhower ordered his Berlin-bound troops to stop at the Elbe River, only 53 miles west of the Capital. The following day, Roosevelt died of a cerebral hemorrhage while in his home in Georgia, and was succeeded by Harry S. Truman.

On April 18, 2.5 million Russian soldiers launched their final offensive against Berlin, which was defended by only 1 million German soldiers, some as young as twelve years and some older than 80 years. The Russians outnumbered the Germans 4:1 in artillery and tanks and 3:1 in aircrafts. General Georgi K. Zhukov's forces approached directly from the east.

Berlin formally surrendered to the Soviets on May 2, 1945. General Karl Weidling represented the German *Wehrmacht* and signed the surrender against the will of the new German leader, Admiral Doenitz, Hitler's successor.

The capitulation of Germany to the Western powers, one day earlier in Reims, France, was not acceptable to Stalin, who feared that a secret peace had been struck between the Western Allies and Germany. Thus, Stalin arranged for another unconditional surrender ceremony of all Germany on May 8, this time in the city his troops had just conquered, Berlin.

Finally, after five years and eight months, the infernal war was over. The Soviet Union had lost 304,000 officers and soldiers during the final battle for Berlin. German military losses were close to one million, which includes the soldiers taken prisoners by the Soviets. About 100,000 civilians lost their lives in just a few days of total horror. More than 6,000 suicides of Berliners were registered in the weeks after the war. The pre-war population of 4.5 million was down to barely 2 million, two-thirds of whom were wounded or old men, women, and children. One million unidentified corpses were either buried under mountains of rubble or were decaying in the streets and in burnt-out buildings.

The city looked like a demolished mausoleum without electricity, gas, drinking water, or sufficient food. Most of the streets and roads were unfit for traffic. Only tanks, Jeeps, and bicycles could make their way through the maze of ruins, bomb craters and now nameless streets. No streetcars operated. One third of the subway lines were flooded. Only the "Black Market" flourished, since the survivors were forced to barter their furniture, furs, carpets and jewelry in exchange for flour, sugar, salt, potatoes, oil and smokes.

When the newly elected American President Harry S. Truman visited Berlin in July 1945, he wrote:

"A more depressing sight than that of ruined buildings was the long, never-ending procession of old men, women, and children wandering aimlessly along the autobahn ... carrying, pushing, or pulling what was left of their belongings."

Facing the cadaver-city Berlin and the other mostly-destroyed metropolitan centers of Germany, the Western Allies had no plans and no ideas where and how to begin the reconstruction. The ACC, which was to rule Germany, was overwhelmed by the task to the point of paralysis. Hastily-called meetings discussed (endlessly) such questions as "How should new city governments be established?", "Should new political parties be permitted?", "How and when should free elections be held?", and "When would Germany be ready for a free press?"

In contrast, the Soviets for some time had made concrete plans how to rule Germany, should they succeed in conquering the entire country. Now that they had only one third of the territory, they concentrated on applying their ideas and enforcing their laws in their Russian Zone.

Even before Germany's official capitulation, Stalin had sent to Berlin a group of German exile communists, who during the war years had taken shelter in the Soviet Union. Once back in Germany, they formed the "Committee for a Free Germany." They also founded anti-fascist cell groups in all of Berlin's districts (boroughs), which were to take over the civic administration leadership. All this was done in great haste because of fear that with the arrival of the Western troops in Berlin, the chance for a Soviet-directed rule over the entire city would be over.

With the Western Allies still absent from Berlin, the Soviet Military Administration appointed a City Council to run the day-to-day affairs. They also set up a communist-run police force, a "red" radio station, newspapers, banks, and a 5-tier rationing system, with the highest-calorie rations going to communist public officials. Prisons which the fighting troops had emptied ("liberated") were quickly filled with citizens who dared to speak out against the Russian dictatorship, not unlike the prisons in the Soviet Union. While the deportation of specialists, scientists, and highly qualified workers to the USSR (known as *Ossawakim*) was to start in 1946, the Soviets did not lose a day in dismantling machinery from factories, steel mills, and technical centers, which they shipped to the Soviet Union. Thousands of still usable furniture pieces were trucked away. Even all surviving livestock was "dispatched" to Mother Russia.

By the time British and American forces finally entered Berlin on July 4, 1945, they faced a plundered city with a communist-dominated administration. Colonel Frank Howley, who in June of 1945 had commanded a Berlin-bound U.S. Advance Party and had been forcibly stopped by the Soviets 50 miles outside of Berlin, years later told reporters:

"We went to Berlin in 1945, thinking of the Russians only as big, jolly, balalaika-playing fellows who drank prodigious quantities of vodka and liked to wrestle in the drawing room. Suddenly we discovered that Russian officers had been briefed

73

that WE were their enemy, merely enjoying an armistice, and they regarded us as such."

Over the next few months, the Western Allies discovered that the Soviets were merely doing in Berlin and Germany what they had been doing across the eastern European continent—installing communist regimes. Poland, Bulgaria, Romania, Hungary and Czechoslovakia had already tasted the power of Soviet-implanted "People's Governments."

However, the attempt to make Germany (or at least East Germany) a Soviet satellite turned out to be more difficult than with the other "liberated" Eastern nations. When the Soviets tried to merge the Communist and Social Democratic parties into one major "Socialist Unity Party" (*Sozialistische Einheitspartei Deutschland, or SED*), most Social Democrats protested vehemently. The first post-war election in Berlin in October, 1946, gave the Social Democrats (SPD) and Christian Democrats (CDU) a 71% victory, while the Communistic SED Party did not even register 20 percent.

The disappointing if not disastrous outcome of the election infuriated the Soviet occupiers and set off a string of harassments and bullying against the West. Most of the Berliners in all Sectors, however, stood on the side of the SPD and CDU. They voted the anti-communist Ernst Reuter to be their Lord Mayor of Great Berlin. However, the Russian veto blocked the Social Democrat Reuter from taking up his duties as mayor until as late as December, 1948.

With the support of the Soviets, the Communist SED suggested the formation of a "United Germany" and a centrally-administered City of Berlin. None of the Western Allies went for these suggestions. The Western Allies finally realized that it was impossible to collaborate with the Soviets and their eastern German puppet administration.

One year before (March 5, 1946), Winston Churchill, traveling with President Truman in the USA, had spoken of the danger of unchecked Soviet behavior. He said:

*"A shadow has fallen upon the scenes so lately lighted by the Allied victory... From Stettin in the Baltic to Trieste in the Adriatic, an **Iron Curtain** has descended across the Continent. Behind that line lie all the capitals of the ancient states of Central and Eastern Europe. Warsaw, Berlin, Prague, Vienna, Budapest, Belgrade, Bucharest and Sofia, all these famous cities and the populations around them lie in what I must call the Soviet sphere ... this is certainly not the Liberated Europe we fought to build up."*

For Germany, this "Iron Curtain" became a deadly reality in 1948. In February of 1948, the USA, Great Britain, France, Belgium, and the Netherlands met in London to discuss the fate of Germany. The Soviet Union did not attend out of fear that they would be outwitted by the Western Allies. At that London meeting, the Western Powers agreed to go ahead with their plans to merge the three Western Zones of Germany into a "Federal Republic of Germany" and to introduce a new currency.

Upon the return of the three major Western delegates to Berlin, they held a meeting with the ACC. The Soviet delegate, Vassily Sokolovsky, was anxious to find out what had transpired at the London conference.

"Had you been there, you would know," was the not-so-polite answer by one of the Western conference members.

Without a further word, Sokolovsky and his entourage stalked out of the ACC, never to return. The dice had fallen.

The Western Allies reacted swiftly. Without seeking the agreement of the Soviets, they introduced the "*Deutsche Mark*" on June 20, to be valid in the three Western occupation zones. The new currency was also to apply to the Western Sectors of Berlin. Every citizen of West Germany was permitted to exchange a per capita sum of 60 *Reichsmark* at a 1:1 ratio.

On the day of the new currency distribution, the Soviet commandant declared the *Deutsche Mark* invalid in the Russian Zone and in East Berlin. Furthermore, he declared that anybody possessing the DM "…committed a criminal offence and would be arrested."

Sokolovsky had no idea where the new currency suddenly had come from, anyway.

The Americans, on the other hand, knew that already in the spring of 1948, twenty-three thousand boxes containing the new *Deutsche Marks* had secretly been shipped from the USA to Germany and deposited at the *Reichsbank* in Frankfurt.

The Soviets responded by hastily imposing their own currency reform for the Soviet Zone of Berlin, to be effective on June 24. Their new currency, however, was not "new." They used the old *Reichsmark* with a paste-on coupon, calling it the "*Ost Mark.*"

The Western military commanders immediately proclaimed a currency reform in their three Sectors of Berlin, effective the next day, June 25. The currency for Berlin looked just like the one in the Western Zones, except for a large circled "B" stamped on.

The frustrated citizens in the divided city of Berlin could hardly find their way through the monetary maze. Which currency was valid where? Many East Berliners worked in the Western Sectors, but received their wages in Eastern currency to avoid possible confiscation of their money had the wages been in *Deutsche Marks,* or worse—they might have been arrested for having "committed a criminal offense."

The West Berliners who worked in the Soviet Sector, on the other hand, received their salary in *Ost Marks,* which they could exchange into western currency at the rate of 1:1. On June 24, 1948, the Soviet Military Administration ordered the stop of all passenger and freight traffic to and from Berlin. The Soviets also cut off all supply of coal, food, electrical power and other vital supplies from the surrounding Eastern Zone to West Berlin. The total **blockade** of Berlin was on. The Iron Curtain had divided Eastern from Western Europe and had used a bit extra curtain material to wrap West Berlin in its isolating, iron grip. It was to last almost one year.

Chapter 9

The shrill scream of the alarm clock tore Fred Harrington out of his deep sleep. He tried to open his glued-shut eyes. Where was he? Back in Iowa? On the Atlantic? On an airfield in France? Then it came back to him: He was in Berlin. He had arrived yesterday.

Five o'clock! No wonder he was still dead-tired. Sleep had escaped him most of the night. It could not have been more than two or three hours ago that he finally had relaxed enough to give sleep a chance.

Five o'clock. This must be May second, he thought. *The briefing session will be at seven. Don't these people have more sense than to start the day so damn early? This is just like back home on the farm!* A few minutes later he was wide awake. A cold shower did that every time. Fred quickly dressed and headed outside, cautioning himself not to expect a good ham and egg farm-style breakfast, but at least something to quiet his growling stomach.

"Hi, I'm Floyd from Detroit."

"Hi, I'm Fred from Sumner, Iowa," Fred replied. "I know, 'Fred' doesn't rhyme with 'Sumner' but it's home for me." Both soldiers laughed and even shook hands as they were standing in line to get breakfast. After they had received their portion plus hot coffee, they sat down across from each other. Floyd's smile seemed to be a permanent fixture of his face.

"Say, Smiley, what's up here?" Fred started a friendly conversation between bites of his hard roll and potatoes.

"Not too much now, Sour-face," Floyd came back. Fred looked around in feigned surprise.

"Are you calling me a sour face?"

"Yeh, I did. You should see your face. Are you scared, or what?"

"Scared? Scared of what? No, I'm just very tired." Fred gulped the last of his black coffee and looked over to the coffee refill station. "Didn't get much sleep during the last three nights."

"Sorry, I forgot that you just got here," said Floyd. "Were you stationed in France?"

"Yes, I was—and *stationed* is the right description, or should I say *stationary*? There was almost no action except for a few drill flights—on and off."

"Well, you won't have that complaint here. Once you have the three briefing days behind you, there'll be plenty of action."

"I sure hope so," was Fred's answer as he got up and hurried to the barrack where the briefings for the newcomers were to be held. As little as he had seen of Berlin, and as scarce as his knowledge was about the situation here, he could not help but feel that *here* the war really was not over yet. Sure, there was a truce with Germany, but what about the Ruskies? Were these troublemakers the new foes?

The briefing sessions had hardly begun when Fred's question about the Russians got a powerful answer. Instructor Harry Strong, though young in years, was an "old hand" in his position. The last two of his five military service years he had spent in Berlin, mainly as a traffic control technician for the US Air Force at the Berlin Air Route Traffic Control Center (BARTCC). Along with nine other American airmen, Harry would sit in front of huge consoles in a dimly lit room high up in the Tempelhof Central Airport Building. With these men, he would continuously watch the scanning lines of light which indicated an either inbound or outbound plane progressing cautiously towards the declared destination.

Since the end of the war, the Soviet Union had confined all Berlin air traffic to three designated routes crossing the Soviet Zone. The "southern corridor" Berlin, Fulda/Frankfurt, was the longest, at 187 nautical miles. The "center corridor" Berlin, *Braunschweig*, at 80 nautical miles long, and the "northern corridor" Berlin, *Dannenberg/Hamburg*, at 96 nautical miles long, were equally important for the traffic flow. Each corridor was exactly 20 miles wide.

The controllers in the towers, both in West Germany and West Berlin, had to make sure that all planes flew below 10,000 feet while they were in one of the corridors across Soviet-occupied territory. In addition, each flight bound for Berlin had to register with the Soviets and get a stamp of approval. Harry's control technician crew at Tempelhof Airport averaged 200 "directs" every day. Harry had to admit (even if only to himself) that the round-the-clock vigil over the "life-lines" to Berlin was a monotonous routine job. However, none of the controllers ever took their jobs for granted, especially not in politically critical times.

"You have no idea," Harry addressed the greenhorns, "what we went through during the ten days of the Little Lift, which the press is calling 'Operation Little Wittles.'"

Fred had never heard of a "Little Lift."

"When was that?" he asked. Seeing that his military audience was wide awake, the instructor continued:

"I'm glad you asked, Airman. It started on the last days of March this year. *Stars and Stripes* reported that for almost two years the Soviets had tried to push us out of Berlin. The agreement that Berlin would be administered by the Four Powers was a sore spot for the Russians. They were determined to do away with the three Western Berlin Sectors smack in the heart of the communist Russian Zone, before the Western Allies and the Germans got accustomed to this division.

"At first, the Soviets purposely slowed down the clearing procedures at the British/ US – Soviet Zones land borders. When the Western Powers complained, the Russians blamed it on technical difficulties. Eastern attacks by the German communist press worked hand in hand with the daily physical harassment and badgering by the Soviets. Western literature and newspapers were confiscated from passengers traveling in cars and trains bound for West Berlin. As part of the psychological warfare, rumors were spread that the Western Allies were about to abandon West Berlin. Slowly, confidence in the Western Allies' commitment to the Berliners was undermined.

"Then, on March 20, when, after the walkout of the Soviet Delegation, the Allied Control Council was dissolved, it became clear that the Soviets had an even more sinister plan. On the last day of March, a Soviet order was issued that all passengers and all baggage and cargo, to and from Berlin, would be inspected—even on military trains.

General Lucius D. Clay, the Military Governor of the US Zone and Commander-in-Chief of all US troops in Europe, was outraged by the Soviet order. General Clay feared that this was the beginning of an eventual *total* blockade of West Berlin. He sent three US military passenger trains through the Soviet check points with the order to prevent controlling Soviet military personnel from boarding the trains—this was a test. Were the Soviets just flexing their muscles, or was this inspection order an intimidation tactic with possibly more severe consequences?

"When the three military trains reached the Soviet Zone border, one US train commander permitted the Russian inspectors to search his train anyway. A few hours later, his train was free to continue its trip to Berlin. The other two trains, which did not yield to the Soviet inspection order, were detained until the next day, at which time they were turned back to the US Zone. Two British military trains likewise were turned around at the northern checkpoint.

"To avoid continuous dangerous confrontations, General Clay stopped any further military train and road transportation and arranged for an airlift, later known as the 'Little Lift.' In ten days our Air Force boys transported about 300 tons of supplies for our troops. The Soviets were shocked over the failure of their blockade, which had targeted the Western military. With egg on their face, they lifted their blockade on

April 10, even though their continued minor interruptions of road and rail traffic still give us a headache to this day."

Strong proceeded to tell the attentive airmen how hard the fairly short blockade had been on the entire Air Force stationed in Germany.

"I wish you had been here, boys. We needed every bit of help."

"Did the military suffer any shortages, say like tobacco, drinks, chewing gum?" asked a soldier in the last row. Laughter spread through the room.

"No it didn't. At least none of us felt deprived of any necessary items. But listen, men, worse things happened. Five days into the blockade, a Soviet fighter plane first buzzed and then collided with a British transport plane which was approaching the Gatow Airport in the British Sector. Both planes crashed. The Soviets lost their pilot. All fourteen passengers plus the crew of the British plane were killed."

"Any American casualties?"

"Yes, two of the passengers were American airmen."

There was a hush in the room. Fred's unspoken question, whether the Russians were now the foes of the Western Allies, had just been answered.

"What happened then? Weren't there any official protests?" another newcomer wanted to know.

"You'll soon find out how the Soviets react to formally-registered protests. The Soviet military commander of Berlin claimed that the British plane had violated Soviet air space and thus was to be blamed for the accident. Period!"

Fred and the airmen new to the Berlin situation could not know that much greater hostility from the Russians was waiting for them; this time, however, mainly directed toward the civilian West Berliners, but indirectly also toward the US, British and French occupation forces.

The three briefing days went by faster than the "new boys" had feared. After an intense introduction to the Berlin situation, the remaining lectures were more job-related, providing the airmen with detailed starting and landing procedures to use in the limited airspace, a thorough survey of Germany's topography, and thousands of other facts a pilot had to know.

Fred and the other airmen exchanged glances as they were being dismissed from the last briefing. Each and every airman had the look of determination; they were chock full of critical information, pride in their sense of duty, and resolve—no matter what lay ahead.

Chapter 10

All of a sudden, it felt like living on an island. Norbert had always been proud of Berlin, even after the war when not much of the past glory had survived. For him, Berlin was still the best place in the world. Not that Norbert knew much of the rest of the world. As a matter of fact, he had never crossed Germany's border into any of its many neighboring nations. Once a GI had asked why he liked Berlin so much.

"I think it is the *Berliner Luft,* the air of Berlin," Norbert answered, which had left the American inquirer more perplexed than satisfied. This Yankee surely had never heard of Germany's popular hit song, *"Das ist die Berliner Luft."*

"The Berliner *Luft*? What is that?"

"Forget it!" Norbert said with a dismissive wave of his hand. "You wouldn't understand."

But now, even Norbert did not understand what had happened to his city. Overnight, all traffic to and from Berlin had been blocked. Even though he rarely read a newspaper, he had picked up enough news to know that for many months the Soviets had tried to push the Western Allies out of Berlin. Living in the heart of the city, he had seen hundreds of communist banners "decorating" the war ruins, proclaiming the most outrageous and often silliest slogans. Many displayed the sayings of Karl Marx: "The highest being for man is the human being" or "A New Germany in Partnership with the Soviet Union is True Democracy." Others proclaimed "Striking is Cowardice and Sabotage" and "Yankee, Go Home!" The banners, though hastily made, were clear in their propaganda messages: "Activists produce more, because they work with a plan" and "You want electricity at night, vote for SED" and, of course, "Communism – the only Hope for Germany."

Norbert always had to chuckle when he saw the slogan, "What happens to Berlin, happens to Germany: What happens to Germany, happens to Europe." It was attributed to the Soviet foreign minister, Molotov, but it reminded him of Lenin's infamous statement, "Whoever has Germany, has Europe."

The confusing and irritating events on June 24, 1948, started early for Norbert.

Just when he wanted to use his electric shaver (which he had obtained in trade for a worn German military jacket on the black market), the electric power quit. At first he thought he had gotten a "lemon." (Checking later showed him that there was nothing wrong with the shaver "Made in USA" because then the electric power in West Berlin had been restored—at least for a few hours.) He needed a shave for the long day ahead and used his regular blade and shaving cream; however, when he tried to wash the foam off his face, the water pressure suddenly dropped and soon was down to a trickle.

"What next?" Norbert shouted at the mirror in exasperation. "Now I know why the Russians think of me as a spy. I look like one of their peasant Bolsheviks, our *noble liberators*. And had we stayed with their Moscow time, it would be pitch-black now, and my beard growth would not show."

Norbert's thoughts raced back to 1945, when the Soviets had introduced Moscow time for both East Berlin and East Germany. The two-hour time difference between Moscow and Berlin had caused chaos. People had to rise when it was still dark, and when they went to bed, the sun was still shining. Traveling from West to East Berlin and back to West Berlin meant changing the time on your watch twice—sometimes within one hour.

He returned his attention to wiping his face as he heard his uncle call out, "What's going on?" His uncle shuffled into the dismal kitchen where the bombed-out window had been replaced by a few wooden boards creating an "eternal darkness," as Norbi's aunt called it. After his apartment in the *Weise Strasse* had been destroyed, killing his mother and brother, the apartment of his relatives in the *Hermann Strasse*, also in Neukölln, had appeared to him like a paradise, or (to be more honest) like a severely trimmed-down version of a haven of respite. Still, it was far better than the damp, ice-cold basement in his destroyed apartment house where at first he had tried to survive for a few weeks. Then he discovered that the apartment building at *Hermann Strasse* 245, where his mother's sister and her husband lived, had survived the war almost undamaged. How glad he was, when they took him in as one of their own!

"I'm sick of these blackouts," Norbert said while he was eating at the kitchen table in half darkness.

"Don't eat it all!" said his uncle, pointing at three slices of bread lying on the table. "Those have to last the three of us for the rest of the day."

"I know, I know," Norbert replied. Just when his uncle started to join him at the table, Norbert got up, put on his shoes, and opened the front door.

"Where are you working today?" his uncle asked, as if he wanted to stay in touch with him throughout the day.

"Who knows?" called Norbert back, and closed the door behind him. Then he remembered something, opened the door again, and said in a half-whisper, "Say 'hi' to Aunt Hanni when she gets up." The closed door prevented him from hearing his uncle's reply: "Not *when* but *if* she wakes up."

Then Uncle Theo put his head in his hands and started to weep. He was afraid of the future. At one time, Hanna had been his attractive, strong-willed partner working in an ammunition factory. He was immensely proud of her. One day toward the end of the war, she lost half of her right thumb in a machine accident. He wanted her to quit the job and take time for healing and recovery. She would not hear of it.

"My job is too important," she had said. "What would the soldiers do without ammunition?!" Two days after the accident—the thumb stump heavily bandaged—she reported back to work. That's why he called her strong-willed, even though in his mind he spelled strong-willed "s-t-u-b-b-o-r-n." That was his Hanni, until the day her factory received a full artillery hit. For more than ten hours, rescue teams worked to pull the buried workers out of the rubble. Miraculously, Hanni was found and had received only a few scratches and bruises.

"Doesn't surprise me," Theo had bragged to his colleagues. "Hanni has seven lives.

It takes more than a heavy grenade to get her under." But then something else happened, something more tragic than being buried under a collapsed building.

One day Theo's wife was raped by two Soviet soldiers. Along with other factory employees, Hanni had been busy clearing the debris of the destroyed factory. All workers were constantly afraid that their shovels or picks might touch one of the hidden, unexploded grenades and set off a deadly explosion. Nobody imagined that a less dangerous looking group of Soviet soldiers would have a more devastating effect on them.

"*Frau, komm!*" The working crew suddenly found itself surrounded by thirteen of those war-battered "liberators." They were not drunk. Instead, their eyes were filled with hatred, and their mouths breathed pent-up anger and lust. The men of the crew quickly stepped in front of the women, pointing their shovels and picks to hold off the Russian attackers.

"*Davai, davai!*" they heard the Russians shout and saw them reaching for their holsters. But the German men did not move. One hateful eye met the other. Then when one of the Russians threw himself at one of the German women, two shots rang out; then five more shots. His Russian comrades had mercilessly cleared the road for rape by doing away with the shovel-carrying German men. What did it matter! The Russian soldiers had the mindset to do as they pleased, the more brutal the better. Ehrenfried, one of their famous Soviet poets, had stated in 1944 at a large gathering in Moscow:

"It should be an honor for every Soviet soldier to kill Germans. They do not deserve to be alive. So, Comrades, kill them—the more the better!"

The Soviet troops had not forgotten the encouragement to kill Germans; after all, the prompting came from the higher-ups in Moscow. Kicking aside the dead or wounded bodies, they seized the women, pulled them further into the ruins and then viciously raped them. Two more shots were fired, and nobody could tell whether women or more men were the victims.

Hours later, when Theo had just arrived home from work, Hanna suddenly appeared in the door frame. She had not rung the bell. She just stood there, clawing the wooden frame. Theo saw her tattered and blood-soiled work clothes, and he instantly knew what must have happened.

"Hanni!" he screamed like a wounded animal. At the sound of his voice, she let go of the door frame and collapsed into his arms. For three days she was in a feverish coma, at first gesticulating wildly and screaming in pain, then just lying there motionless.

Hanna was not dying, as Theo feared, when she no longer seemed to be part of this world. She recovered her strength after a few weeks, cooked meals, dusted the apartment furniture, and seemed to wait daily for Theo's return from work. Otherwise she really had turned her back on the world. She spent hours and hours in her bed, the blanket pulled up to her chin. At first Theo feared she might be feverish or cold. Then he realized that she now was suffering from something that neither he nor any medicine could cure. He resigned himself to the fact that this was his Hanni now, that she would never recover to her former self. That is why he had wept countless tears since that fateful day three years ago. However, he never indulged in his grief when she was around. He had learned to save his tears for the hours when he was alone. That is when he discovered that darkness was his best companion.

Norbert, on the other hand, had an insatiable appetite for light. June and July, with their long hours of daylight, were his favorite months. Would the looming blockade of Berlin by the Soviets take away all the joys and necessities of life such as water, electricity, fruit, milk, potatoes, movies? Somebody had told him that West Berlin alone had 30,000 babies one year and younger. Where would young mothers find fresh milk? How many of the infants were orphans? With all roads and railroads closed to transportation, how would these innocent little creatures get their nourishment?

Half-way to the subway station entrance, Norbert turned around and briskly walked back to his apartment house. In no time he got his bicycle out of the basement and headed for the border between West and East Berlin. Work could wait. Today he felt compelled to explore the situation first-hand. Besides, his work, if he wanted to call it that, was of little consequence anyway. For almost a year now, he had taken the short *U-Bahn* trip from Station *Leinestrasse* to Station *Hermann Platz*. At this square, in front of the former giant department store *Karstadt* (now a huge mountain of rubble), he waited morning after morning to be picked up by tradesmen, moving companies, or construction contractors to do hourly work for them. He felt lucky when they would hire him not just for a day but for several weeks. He was lucky frequently—the slim but muscular body of this 16-year old appealed to most of the labor scouts looking for workers.

But today he did not care about any of this. His bike carried him quickly past the *Goerlitzer Bahnhof* to Berlin's famous river, the *Spree*. Here was the *Oberbaumbrücke*, one of the official crossing points from West to East Berlin. This morning, cars, trucks, horse-drawn carriages loaded with *Berliner Kindl* beer kegs and bottles, cyclists, pedestrians—all formed a chaotic mix of honking, shouting, swearing, and even weeping West Berliners whose crossing into East Berlin had been refused. A detachment of heavily-armed Soviet soldiers yelled unintelligible orders to the crowd. Norbert assessed the situation and knew that here was the end of the line for him.

Pedaling along the well-marked East-West border, he soon reached the *Prinzen Strasse* checkpoint, where he came across a similar chaotic scene. Here, however, Soviet tanks and soldiers were lined up, powerfully demonstrating that would-be trespassers would be punished or perhaps even shot. Since he had seen more than enough of the destructive force of tanks in his young life, Norbert had not the slightest urge to challenge the Eastern authorities now.

As he continued his strange ride along the border, he saw sign after sign alerting or warning Western traffic participants in three languages: YOU ARE LEAVING THE AMERICAN SECTOR. Then moving further northwest: YOU ARE LEAVING THE BRITISH SECTOR. Finally in the northern part of Berlin he came across the sign: YOU ARE LEAVING THE FRENCH SECTOR. Today, however, it seemed that there was no chance of leaving from any of the Western sectors to cross the border into the East. During the night, each of the crossing check points had been sealed off. His anger level rose. How could the Western Allies permit the Soviets such an outrageous act of strangling his city? He had the sinking feeling that the Ruskies this time would succeed in choking West Berlin either to the point of surrender or death.

Suddenly he had an idea. He needed to see for himself what the situation was like at the border between West Berlin and the Eastern Zone—not just the Eastern Sector. Traveling for a few kilometers, he turned his back on the Eastern Sector and made his way to the *Grosser Stern* with its *Siegessäule* (Column of Victory). A strong wind helped him reach good speed. On a normal day, this could have been an interesting tour, stopping at the *Brandenburg* Gate, the Opera House, and the Olympic Stadium. But this was not a normal day. Only briefly he stopped on the high bridge across the *Havel,* the other famous river of Berlin. Looking at the blue peaceful water below and the clear sky above, he could not imagine why another war seemed to be looming on an unseen horizon. Was this newest Russian attempt to strangle West Berlin "only" another move to occupy *all* of Berlin, driven by their obsession to take over *all* of Germany? What had Molotov predicted? *What happens to Berlin, happens to Germany; what happens to Germany, happens to Europe.* Norbert also recalled a song (sounding completely idiotic to him now) which he had learned as a Hitler Youth member:

> "*Es zittern die morschen Knochen*
> *der Welt vor dem grossen Krieg.*"

> *The morbid bones of the world*
> *are shaking in fear of the great war.*
> *We have conquered the fear;*
> *for us it has been a great victory.*
> *We will march on*
> *until everything tumbles to pieces.*
> *Today only Germany belongs to us,*
> *tomorrow we'll own the whole world.*

He mused about how fitting this song was for the Soviet expansion tactics. After gobbling up Estonia, Latvia, Lithuania, Poland, Ukraine, Czechoslovakia, Romania, Hungary, and Bulgaria, now Austria and Germany were next on their acquisition list. Norbert shivered at the thought.

"No, never!" he puffed out aloud over and over, as he tackled the slowly ascending street toward the checkpoint *Heerstrasse/Staaken*. Still about two kilometers away from the checkpoint, he came across hundreds of cars, motorcycles, and trucks of all sizes. All had been blocked from crossing into the Russian Zone. His bicycle was the only bike here. The lines at the inner-Berlin checkpoints had been long, but they were nothing compared to what he found here. Many truckers had gotten out of their vehicles. They were standing in groups, smoking, gesticulating, and discussing what would become of them and Berlin should the Russians cut off Berlin for a long time—or even permanently.

Norbert used the anger-filled situation and overall confusion to slip through the crowd, meandering on his bike, unnoticed, right up to the barrier at the checkpoint. The Russians and East German police were focused on the hundreds of motorized vehicles they were holding back, and the ever-increasing tension of the noisy protesters. Suddenly Norbert felt like a rebel with a cause—his impulse to defy the Eastern authorities grew moment by moment. Before sorting out his dangerous thoughts, he found himself on the eastern side of the checkpoint. Nobody had stopped him. *What now?* Should he try to sneak back, or should he just keep on going further west, crossing through the Soviet Zone? Quickly realizing that it was too dangerous to hang around the checkpoint even on the eastern side, he opted for pedaling deeper into the Eastern Zone, where he had not been since the end of the war.

"Stupid!" he mumbled. "Whatever I'm doing now is even more than stupid." Ahead of him he saw the rows of *Spandau* apartment houses thinning out, making room for family homes and patches of forest and weed-overgrown pastures. There was absolutely no traffic on this stretch of the autobahn. Is that all he had come to find out? Why was he taking such an idiotic chance?

"Stupid!" he yelled several times in English. Then he saw something that made him hit the brakes with full force. "NAUEN—18 Kilometer" a big traffic sign announced. Nauen? That was a town not even close to the two autobahn routes officially designated as connectors to either Hamburg in the north, or Braunschweig, due west of Berlin. This meant he really was in trouble! Norbert swung his bicycle around and hit the pedals.

Trouble met him just around the next bend. A Russian guard with a rifle casually slung across his shoulder and a big handgun in his holster looked up in surprise as Norbert came flying toward him. With a powerful growl the soldier shouted, *"Eh, stoy! STOY!"* Even as he yelled at the approaching bicycle, the Russian was not sure he was doing the right thing in commanding the cyclist to stop. After all, a man or boy on a bicycle *within* the Soviet Zone was allowed to travel in any direction, as long as he stayed in the Zone. On the other hand, now when there was absolutely no traffic to or from Berlin or Nauen, even an otherwise innocent-looking bicyclist in high speed could be a real danger to the Soviet Union and was suspicious enough to be stopped.

Norbert had no intention of obeying the command of Private Anatoly Chukov, even though this Russian looked as huge as a grizzly bear and was armed with deadly weapons. At first he stared straight at the Russian soldier. Then he looked past him and waved, as if to signal to somebody behind him. Chukov did not know what to make of it. Startled, he quickly turned his head, searching for something or somebody behind him. That was all the time Norbert needed to zip by the soldier. As he rode his bike with full force, he could hear the grizzly:

"*STOY!*" But even the loudest bellowed order would not stop Norbert now.

At last Private Chukov became focused, and with well-practiced motions he wrestled the rifle from his massive shoulder, aimed at the fast-disappearing cyclist and fired three shots. None of them hit Norbert, who rode in a zigzag pattern.

Hearing the shots, nearby comrades of Chukov came running into the street; however, Norbert was out of sight. Still, they had been ordered out as reinforcement in defense of their fatherland, and were burning to live up to their duty. Each of them fired five or six shots into the air or into the nearby bushes. When suddenly a frightened little Terrier—made nervous by the flying bullets—ran yelping from under the garden bushes into the street, they aimed at him. After a few shots the dog was lying dead at the edge of the street. The soldiers were jubilant.

"Better a dog than nobody," shouted Private Anatoly Chukov. His comrades formed a strange chorus repeating gleefully, "Better a dog than nobody."

Chapter 11

Major General Kotikov, the Commander of the Soviet Sector of Berlin, could not have made it clearer how important the mission was than by coming over in person to talk to Sergey Svertlov, early on June 22.

"Anything you have done in the army so far pales in importance compared to what we are called to do now," said Kotikov as he emptied the shot glass that Svertlov had offered him.

"*Nasdrovie!*"

"*Nasdrovie!*" Svertlov toasted in return.

"Look, comrade, we have to act fast—brutally fast—and in total secrecy," Kotikov said. "If the damned Yankees or Tommies or the West Germans find out what we are doing, the entire plan could blow up in our face. As you know, when we blocked the supply to the Western Allies back in March, we had to give in after ten days. This time we are going for the throat! We are cutting off any—and I mean *any* and *every*—supply going to the people in West Berlin, as of June 24."

"On June 24th? That is in two days, Comrade Major General."

"I know it is, Svertlov," answered Kotikov nervously. "We will show Moscow, that we can do things well and fast here in Berlin. As an American businessman once said: 'The impossible we do right away; miracles take a bit longer.' That's why Comrade Stalin gave us two days, not just two hours. And he has promised that many more Russian elite troops will take care of the checkpoints along the Western Zones."

Then Major General Kotikov gave Officer Svertlov piles and piles of printed detailed instructions on how to cut off the western part of Berlin from any life support via waterways, highways, and railroads.

"Are you surprised that I am asking you, an intelligence officer, to supervise the blockade of Berlin? Don't be! Your unit will report directly to me, the *Commandant.* That's how we keep the lid on the boiling pot and prevent a leak."

With that, the two officers saluted—and Kotikov was gone. Not a minute too soon, because to get the blockading job done in two days was more than any Soviet officer had ever been asked to do. Svertlov needed every single minute. To get it all started, he decided he needed another shot of vodka right away—and another one, and another ... *No, stop right here! You need a clear mind to get this hellish job done*, he told himself. With one swipe of his arm he cleared the corner of his desk of several shot glasses. Then he shook his head and mumbled,

"Talking to myself will not get the job done." He stood, gathered the heavy stack of documents from Kotikov, and cursed loudly as he slammed his apartment door behind him.

"Where to, Comrade Svertlov?" asked the still sleepy driver as Svertlov yanked the limo door open.

"Office! Office!" No greeting, no other words—just "Office." It took the military driver only seconds to understand that his boss was on an urgent mission and that even the shortest conversation would not be welcome.

Little did he know that the next 48 hours would be a whirlwind of activities, taking him and his boss from the military headquarters to the *Golpa-Zschornewitz Grosswerk Electricity Center,* to shipping complexes, to traffic control offices, to railroad yards, to the Berlin Main Water Works Center, and to the East German *Volks-Polizei Headquarters.* There was time neither for lunches nor for coffee breaks during those two days. Roads and streets had to be blocked, streetcars needed to be derailed, river junks had to be stopped from maneuvering into Berlin. Svertlov's instructions from his superiors always had been the same: "Should anybody ask about these blocking activities, just tell them that the East is short of coal supply and has to conserve energy."

On the second day, just when Svertlov thought that in spite of an aching, spinning head, he had not overlooked anything, he realized that he had forgotten to give shut-down instructions to Berlin's largest electricity producer, the *Klingenberg Elektrizitätswerk.* His exhausted chauffeur could not believe that his demanding and hard-working comrade and boss would have forgotten anything. When driving Svertlov to the electricity center, he dared to ask why all the shutdown orders had to be delivered in person instead of by telephone or telegram. Svertlov almost exploded.

"Have you ever heard of secret orders and secret actions?" Svertlov yelled. "Probably not, you numskull!"

When Svertlov finally arrived back at his office, he had only one thought on his mind: He needed to wash down all the trouble of the day with a bottle of vodka. He had stored several caviar sandwiches in his office cooler. He could almost taste the delicious caviar mixed with vodka that waited for him as he unlocked the apartment door and stepped into the dim room. But—but who was this big bear clad in a military uniform, sitting in the waiting room? And who had allowed this soldier of low rank, as he could see, to get into his office? With a mixture of disgust and irritation he approached his half-visible visitor, who suddenly jumped up and stood at attention.

"What brings your fat face into my office at such an hour?" he tore into the motionless soldier in front of him. Not waiting for an answer, Svertlov started to continue his tirade when he suddenly realized with whom he was dealing—it was his Berlin-stationed cousin from Tashkent, Anatoly Chukov. Again!

"Anatoly Svertlovich Chukov! Is that really you?"

"Yes, Sir, Lieutenant Svertlov," answered Chukov, on his best behavior. Svertlov flicked the light switch, which gave the small waiting room sufficient light to reveal that it was really his cousin who had come to see him. He grabbed Anatoly roughly and pulled him out of his attention pose.

"Come on! Come into my office, you son of a bear!" laughed Svertlov, a bit more relaxed. Anatoly still hesitated, so that Sergey almost had to push him into the more comfortable office.

"Comrade Svertlov," Anatoly started, while he was still standing.

"None of that formal stuff now, Cousin Anatoly!" interrupted Svertlov. "First sit down and have a gulp of vodka!" Sergey instantly produced a full vodka bottle along with the longed-for refrigerated caviar sandwiches.

At last, Anatoly relaxed a little, but he still was not sure his coming was not a stupid mistake. Perhaps he should have ignored the incident with the cyclist on the autobahn…but what if…?

"Well, then," the older cousin started the conversation, while drinking and chewing his sandwich at the same time. "What brings you here, Anatoly? And, by the way, how did you get into my apartment?"

"I told the guard that we are cousins, which made it alright."

"Did it really? Well, anyway, what is your coming all about?"

"Comrade, I mean, Sergey, let me be frank with you—I mean like cousin-to-cousin—I might have run into the person you have been searching for."

After this somewhat clumsy beginning to a meeting, Svertlov was suddenly alert and focused on the soldier in front of him. He nodded for Anatoly to continue.

"You see, I am stationed west of the *Heerstrasse/Staaken* checkpoint. As you well know, we were to control all traffic coming from Berlin. My platoon was on duty where the *Braunschweig* autobahn has an offshoot branch road leading to *Nauen*, which the Nazis had never completed. Even though this autobahn stretch is only five kilometers long, we were

101

told that some German or Western military trucks might travel on this otherwise unused road in order to bypass the heavily controlled regular autobahn."

Svertlov did not like his cousin's ponderous, heavy-footed reporting. He itched to push him to come to the point, but he quickly changed his mind. After all, he was from Uzbekistan in Central Asia, where everything moved at a slower pace—it was to be expected that the relaying of events would seem excruciatingly slow to most other people.

"I had been watching this totally deserted *Nauen* autobahn for hours. I walked and scanned the road and roadside, kilometer after kilometer. Then I turned around and quickly walked back, looking and listening for even a distant car or truck. Nothing. Not a single rabbit had crossed the concrete road, until all of a sudden a cyclist showed up."

"A motorcyclist?"

"No, Comrade, a regular bicyclist. I ordered him to stop. As much as I shouted, he did not listen—instead, he pumped the pedals that much harder."

"What are you trying to tell me, Anatoly? Did you finally get hold of him?"

"No, Sergey, nobody could!"

Bending the truth quite a bit in his favor, he continued, "I gathered my entire platoon and we blocked him...and then shot volley after volley as he disappeared in the direction of Berlin. Afterwards we found blood splattered along the autobahn, but there was no trace of him."

"What does that mean?" asked Svertlov, now stern and unsmiling.

"I wish I knew! I guess he made it back to Berlin—perhaps even West Berlin.

Being wounded, he may have gone to a hospital. Is there a way of searching for him in West Berlin's hospitals?"

"Have you lost your mind, Anatoly? How would we get a permission to search on the western side?! That is totally out of question, unless he is a spy."

"But he is a spy, Sergey."

"How do *you* know? How do *we* know? Our government might search this abominable hoodlum for who-knows-what reasons. By the way, is that all you have to tell me? Is that why you left your platoon in *Staaken* to report here of this wild goose chase—this wild cyclist chase?"

Anatoly felt dejected, but he was not ready to give up. He tried to regain the favor of his disgruntled cousin as he shared his interpretation of the cyclist encounter.

"I think the bicycle was a disguise to make us think that he was an innocent young man. He wanted to appear as only a youth who got lost on the wrong autobahn. Who knows where he has been snooping around, all over our Zone!"

There was a knock at the office door. At first Svertlov ignored it. Upon more knocking, the Lieutenant shouted, "If you are the cleaners, go away and come back tomorrow!"

Almost instantly he heard the shoveling sounds of moved cleaning equipment, and a German male voice answered, *"Schon gut! Schon gut!"* ("Okay! Okay!")

Both men had another shot of vodka. Then Lieutenant Sergey Iliavich Svertlov moved closer to his cousin and, in a guarded, lower voice, told him the entire story of the arrest of the journalist Dieter Friede at Dr. Peter Dau's medical office and the connection with the evasive German boy, whom they had been hunting ever since.

"Listen, Anatoly…some time ago you witnessed my phone call with Major General Kotikov. I told you then that he was the Commander of the Soviet Sector of Berlin. He is a *very* important man in Moscow. Everybody in the Kremlin seems to know him—or at least that is what he says.

"Anyway, in the fall of last year, Kotikov hunted an anti-communist journalist who worked for the daily *Der Abend.* His name is, or was, Dieter Friede. The Major General had the cooperation of several Soviet agencies, including the people from my office. This Mr. Friede was like a rabid fox—all our plans to catch him failed for several months. Then we discovered that one of Friede's friends was Otto Seiler, who worked for another western newspaper. Our agents also found out that Dieter Friede was a patient of the rather well-known Dr. Peter Dau, who lived and practiced in *Berlin-Friedrichshagen* in the Soviet Sector.

"At last we came up with a good plan—but, listen!" he said. "This is top secret. Should you repeat the story to anybody, you'll end up in Siberia. Well, around two in the afternoon, on the first of November, three KGB—or NKWD as the Germans say—three men in civilian clothes showed up at

Dr. Dau's practice at *Wilhelm-Bölsche-Strasse* 11. Incidentally, this house was also where the doctor resided.

"A young man—*our young man* !—opened the door to Dr. Dau's office. When Dr. Dau came out, he explained that the young man at the door was his wife's nephew, whom he had just treated for an infected wound.

"The three agents didn't really care who he was; they had come with a different goal, namely to catch Dieter Friede. One of the men spoke German and ordered Dr. Dau to sit at his desk and write what they would dictate—in essence, ...*a certain Otto Seiler has suffered a car accident on the Berliner Ring autobahn. He severely injured his knee. An ambulance brought him to my office here at Wilhelm-Bölsche-Strasse 11, and I have treated him. He asked that I call you to come and assist him in getting home to his apartment.*

You can imagine, Anatoly, that Dr. Dau at first refused to cooperate. Fortunately we Soviets know how to handle such cases. When the KGB discovered that Dr. Dau did not have a working telephone, one of the men took him to a public phone booth where—under strict supervision—he was forced to make the call to Dieter Friede."

"Did the journalist Friede suspect a trap?" asked Anatoly.

"Perhaps he did in the beginning, because he did not show up that day. KGB agents stayed in the Dau house throughout the night. The next day, November second, was a Sunday. Dr. Dau had to make his usual medical rounds at a nearby hospital.

"Shortly after he had come home, the doorbell rang twice. As she was instructed, Mrs. Dau opened the door and asked Mr. Friede to step into the doctor's office where I and two

105

other agents were waiting. Neither she nor her husband was permitted into the room, for obvious reasons. After close to an hour, Friede was escorted out to civilian car, never to be seen again.

I left the Daus a bit later in my own car."

Anatoly had listened to Svertlov's story with engrossed attention. He had heard of Soviet kidnapping cases before—but this was quite different.

"So our people arrested Dieter Friede. But what happened to the young man with the flesh wound, the nephew of the Daus?" he asked.

"You wouldn't believe it, Anatoly, but that kid got totally forgotten in the midst of closely managing the doctor and his wife, luring the journalist, hiding in wait, and finally arresting this Friede. And he was not so small or young to be overlooked like that. He was there, right outside the office. Believe me, not a day has passed since then that we have not cursed our idiotic neglect of not arresting the doctor, his wife, *and* their nephew—who is undoubtedly too inexperienced to know to keep his mouth shut.

"By the way, since you seem to be interested in the Daus, or at least in their rotten nephew, you should know that a few months after Friede's arrest, the Daus escaped the Berlin Soviet Sector. They now live incognito somewhere in West Germany. Their nephew, on the other hand, has continued to be a thorn in our flesh, wherever he shows up. His eyewitness story about Friede's arrest has made all the western newspapers. Now you know why we are after that scoundrel, who seems to have nine lives like an evil cat. But trust me—sooner or later we will catch that devil."

Instead of further discussing the case of the mysterious German "spy" who had avoided getting arrested for more than eight months, Anatoly Chukov excused himself a few minutes later and drove to his barracks in Staaken at the outskirts of East Berlin.

Chapter 12

On June 24, 1948, the inhumane goal of the Soviets to totally block the access to and from the city of Berlin had been accomplished. One day later, the first Dakota C-47 Skytrain landed by the Americans on the Tempelhof Airport with supplies of food for both the Allied occupiers and the starving civilian population.

The man in charge of getting the airlift going was General Lucius D. Clay, the chief commander of all US troops in Europe. His right-hand man in this unprecedented operation was Lieutenant General William Tunner, who for many years had promoted the idea of using big aircraft for transporting any cargo, in preference over trains or ships. Neither American nor other military commanders thought that such an airlift would ever be required or even possible.

Were they wrong!

Since March of 1948, General Clay had feared a possible Russian blockade of Berlin. Even he had never imagined the proportions of such a blockade. During the war, he had received orders to make the destroyed harbor of Cherbourg in Normandy, France, maneuverable in two weeks time. The Western world was stunned when this man of action accomplished this gigantic task in only two days! Thus, with

Clay and Tunner in command, Berlin had two excellent leaders and organizers to overcome the horrendous crisis.

Hundreds of US Air Force pilots and crewmen who were stationed in such distant places as the Panama Canal Zone, Hawaii, Alaska, and California, on June 26, received urgent orders to depart for Germany to participate in the Berlin Airlift. The same was true for British aircrews stationed in Australia, New Zealand, India and South Africa. (In England they called the airlift the "Air Bridge" or "Operation Vittles.")

Since General Clay was not certain that the life necessities of a city of almost two million West Berliners could be totally supplied by air, he sought counsel from the Air Force brass and local government leaders. A few hours before midnight of the fateful June 26, he met with Ernst Reuter, the Mayor-elect of Berlin, and his Aide, Willi Brandt.

General Clay told Reuter: "I am ready to try an airlift. I cannot guarantee it will work. I am sure that even at best, people are still going to be cold, and people are still going to be hungry. And if the people of Berlin won't stand that, it will fail. I do not want to go into this unless I have your assurance that the people will be totally in sync with us."

Mayor Reuter assured Clay that Berlin would make all the necessary sacrifices and would definitely support this action. Now convinced that he was making the right decision and, more importantly, having the support of the US President Harry Truman, Clay and Tunner ordered the airlift on a full-scale basis. Immediately, every available plane in the European Command was pressed into service, along with other Air Force units around the world. President Truman went so far in his vow to keep West Berliners supplied to say, "…even if it takes every Piper Club in the United States."

As excited as a great challenge could make General Clay, he also was a man of caution, clear analysis, and calculation. Once he gave the order to start the airlift, he then sat down to write a rough estimate of ALL available planes.

The Royal Air Force, Clay figured, could send only 150 planes. The French, who were busy fighting Ho Chi Minh in Indochina, could contribute ground personnel, but no aircraft.

The United States had only 102 usable transport planes in Europe. Clay determined that initially he would have to rely on several hundred relatively small planes, such as the two-engine Douglas C-47, to carry most of the cargo. These "gooney birds," as they were known, lumbered along at 160 miles-per-hour and carried just three tons each.

Clay's mathematically-skilled counselors had quickly determined that West Berlin would need 4,500 tons per day to support both its military and civilian populations with food and coal to heat homes and produce electricity. This meant that at least 225 planes as large at the four-engine C-54s would be needed right away—but they were not available!

Another piece of news disturbed General Clay just as much as the lack of planes: West Berlin had food supplies to last for only 36 days. While Great Britain had just announced the end of bread rationing, here in Berlin all bread supply was going to run out in a few weeks, and the outlook for a timely and permanent solution did not look good.

USAF Airman Fred Harrington's life to this point had been neither a cakewalk nor a particularly hard struggle. What really made him happy was the fact that his wish to be deployed to Europe had come true. After a few "detours" he had landed in Berlin. Thanks to USFA officer Harry Strong's instructions, Fred had a good grip of what Berlin was all about—at least he felt that way initially.

Fred regretted that during the last few days he not had time for reading. He had many questions occupying his mind. *How was the newly founded State of Israel doing? When would Ernst Reuter, the elected Lord Mayor of Berlin, be allowed to function in his job in spite of Russian protests? Would he and his buddies have the chance to see Cole Porter's new musical, "Kiss Me Kate," or at least read the printed version? How about seeing the movie "Bitter Rice," starring Miss Italy, Silvana Mangano?*

There was the constant demand of so many small and big military duties that the world of books and reading in general had to take a back seat. Now rumors were flying that there was a flurry of activity in Washington, London, and Paris over the issue of how to handle the increasingly hostile, growing demands by Moscow regarding how to govern Germany, preferably under Russian, communist administration and leadership. From various sources he had heard the unnerving whisper that sooner or later the Western Powers would be forced to withdraw from Berlin.

This morning, Airman Harrington felt a buzz of excitement in the air. The meeting hall, usually half-empty, was packed to overflowing. When Officer Strong, flanked by two high-ranking officers and a smiling Lieutenant, walked into the hall, everybody stood at attention.

"Gentlemen! It is my distinct honor to introduce to you General William Tunner, the newly-appointed head of the Berlin Airlift Operation, and also Captain Arthur Eve, Junior, Chief of Personnel Operations for the 7100 Support Wing 7120 Air Base Group, and the newly-arrived Lieutenant Gail Halvorsen.

"Let me start with the last mentioned first. Lieutenant Halvorsen is a veteran of the North African and Italian campaigns. Lately he has been stationed in Mobile, Alabama, assigned to the 17th Air Transport Squadron. Two days ago he got his orders to come to Berlin in such haste, he only had time to park his car under a tree in Mobile and hide the car keys. Let's give a hand to the continent-hopping, fast-flying lieutenant!"

The hall broke into a rousing applause. Most airmen sensed that Halvorsen's extremely fast move to Berlin also meant a quick call to action for them. Then General Tunner stepped to the podium and the room became silent as all the men gave the general their undivided attention.

"The Berlin Airlift is on! The Berlin Airlift is on!" he shouted. "The day has come to show our teeth and clenched fists to the Soviet bullies who have cut off all life supply to Berlin. As of a few hours ago, General Clay and I have given the signal to a non-stop supply action.

"Our own Captain Arthur Eve Junior, here, is the chief of all personnel operations. Until yesterday, he had an easy job in his luxurious office in *Wiesbaden*. Now he will be working with us from his office at the Tempelhof Airport. His job is to organize the needed flight personnel as well as recruit German nationals to work as loading and unloading crews.

"Men, you don't even want to know where I was and what I was doing when the order to fly immediately to Berlin reached me."

"Tell us anyway!" a voice from the back of the hall was heard.

"Not really!" General Tunner smiled. "Let me instead tell you about First Lieutenant Guy Dunn, Junior, who must be here somewhere among you."

"Here he is! He is here!" some soldiers shouted.

"Well, good old Guy Dunn, or *Dunny* as I call him, was en route to a golf course when the message reached him to immediately round up four aircraft, three crews per plane, and 62 maintenance people to form a squadron to be assigned to the 61st Military Transport Service of the Lift Division. Frankly, I don't know how and where he got the planes and crews. But I do know that one hour after the order reached him, he was flying somewhere between Alabama and the Rhein-Main Airport in Frankfurt, Germany, still on his phone and teletype, rounding up ten more aircraft to deploy to Berlin.

"Well, that's enough story for now. You were not called here to listen to long speeches. We are here to tell you: Let's roll! Or in your case, get flying!"

As the crowded hall emptied, the airmen almost stumbling over each other, Fred Harrington suddenly found himself next to Lieutenant Gail Halvorsen. In his excitement and admiration for the veteran flier, Fred forgot to introduce himself. He just shouted to Halvorsen, "I wish I could fly in your squadron!"

"Perhaps you will, son. What's your name?"

"Fred Harrington, sir."

"What planes can you fly?"

"The C-47, sir."

"Oh, that old, faithful *Dakota*—and I mean very old and faithful. Cheer up, Harrington, C-54s and over one hundred C-47s are on the way to Berlin."

Fred tried to keep step with Lieutenant Halvorsen, even though other airmen were jostling to talk to the famous pilot, too.

"Sir! One more question. Is there a way of finding out whether I might be in your squadron?"

"Sure…let's see!" Halvorsen reached into his flight jacket and pulled out a roughly folded piece of paper

"What was your name again?"

"Fred Harrington, sir." Fred's heart was pounding.

"Yes, here it is. Fred P. Harrington. Is that you, and what does the 'P'' stand for?"

"Yes, Sir! That's me. And 'P' stands for 'Pilot'—I added the 'P' as my middle initial at the recruiting center."

"I like that, son. Hopefully now and forever a pilot. We will be starting at thirteen-hundred sharp! Use the hours until then to check and recheck the navigational maps. We can never be too careful, with the Russians watching every move we make. For you it would be wise to know the German territory we are flying over like you know your bride." After a quick glance at Fred's empty ring finger, he added, "Like your bride you probably don't have—YET."

"Not yet, sir. Not yet."

Both men laughed, while their minds were already racing ahead. The day had arrived to stand up and be counted.

Chapter 13

After Saturday, June 26, when the airlift had started, there was an almost constant humming of engines over Berlin. The incoming, heavily-loaded planes had to land either in Tempelhof in the American Sector, or on the one runway at the Gatow Airport in the French Sector.

As a young boy, Norbert had walked many times to the St. Thomas Cemetery in *Neukölln's Hermann Strasse*, where he had watched the relatively few planes landing or taking off at the Tempelhof Airport. Before the war, his father occasionally had taken the entire family to the huge airport terminal building with its high observation tower where they watched the occasional planes come and go.

Toward the end of the war, Norbert had watched in fascination how small aircraft and single-pilot ME-109 fighter planes still managed to land on the bomb-damaged runway. Even the once glorious terminal buildings were in ruins. Nothing had come of Hitler's promise that the Tempelhof Airport one day would be the largest airport in Europe. Once the US Air Force had taken over the airport, Army engineers built a 12-foot thick rubber base runway, which they enforced with landing mats made out of steel. Heretofore this rather primitive runway solution may have served rather well. Now, with the airlift underway, it became clear that the anticipated continuous pounding by many more, and much heavier planes would require stronger steel or concrete reinforcement of the runway. That had to be done without delay, because after only a few days into the airlift operation, many of the steel landing mats had cracked, forming dangerous depressions in the runway.

One week after the airlift began, Norbert Anleger stood at daybreak at the war-battered *Karstadt* department store at the *Hermann Platz* in *Neukölln*. This was the third time he had come, hoping for a job offer. Suddenly two US Army trucks drove up to the large crowd of men looking for work. The driver in the first truck looked straight at Norbert and shouted, "Hey, you, do you speak English?"

"Soldier," Norbert shouted back in English, "is the Pope Catholic?"

The driver was surprised to hear a German use the American idiom, but at the same time relieved to have so quickly completed his search for workers and a possible bi-lingual assistant supervisor.

"Hop on, quickly! We need all of you for urgent repair work at Tempelhof!"

The beleaguered men quickly responded and eagerly climbed into the back of the trucks. To work for Americans was much more than they had hoped for—perhaps it even meant extra food or American cigarettes!

Less than an hour later, dozens of men were hard at work replacing the broken steel landing mats between incoming plane landings. Nothing seemed too difficult for Norbert and the other men because they knew that this job would last for many days, weeks, and perhaps even longer. They had known the Amis paid better than German employers, and they had better-working tools.

Also there was an element of excitement in this project because every other day the runway workers were taken to the hangars for unloading airlift cargo, while the previous unloading crews went to work on the runway repairs. Norbert was thrilled to board the C-47 and C-54 planes, even if it was only to help unload the many tons of cargo each carried, and not to fly. Norbert could not have wished for a better job. It was even rumored that sometime in the near future the giant four-engine C-74 transporters would land in Tempelhof.

In early July, construction on a second runway began at Tempelhof with a much larger crew than the repair crews on "Runway 1. This new runway construction was not interrupted by airlift traffic, which was limited to the old runway, enabling the workers to complete the second runway in record time. Now the massive C-74 giants were able to land.

Overjoyed by the fast master construction of Runway II, the jubilant workers were then told that plans were being made to construct an even stronger and wider third runway. This runway would be able to accommodate even B-29 bombers, which now were confined to airfields in England.

The B-29 was known for its capability of delivering the atomic bomb; thus Moscow would be in range, if action was necessary. Norbert had heard from airmen in-the-know that these B-29s no longer carried atomic bombs, but it was speculated that knowledge of their ability to carry such powerful weapons would keep the Soviets from becoming too brazen.

While the eyes of the world were on the planes and crews which transported all kinds of life-supporting cargo to Berlin, very few people knew of the heroic effort of collecting sufficient food in West Germany and in a few western nations. While supplies were flown into Berlin at a constant pace, the goal was to have a three-day supply warehoused at each railhead in West Germany. The cargo was then trucked to the airfield control points, where it was registered and loaded into waiting planes. Some fresh milk for babies came from farms as far away as Denmark. Soon, more weight-efficient supplies were used, such as condensed milk or milk powder. The idea of shipping *Trocken Nahrung* (dehydrated food) took hold like a firebrand.

The Germans in Berlin gladly and thankfully made the adjustment from real potatoes to dried potatoes, fresh fruit to fruit powder, and regular meat to meat *ersatz* surrogates. The most painful sacrifice for Berliners came when the use of electricity was reduced to one or two hours per day. Electricity had become of greater value than gold. Naturally, the fact that thousands of able-bodied Berliners lost their jobs because factories were closed was also an indescribable hardship. Subways and elevated trains (*S-Bahn*) as well as streetcars and buses operated on a minimal skeleton-schedule basis.

When it became painfully clear a few weeks into July that Berlin desperately needed more electricity but the power stations lacked coal to generate it, some airlift planes changed their cargo from food items to coal. From July of 1948 to September 30, 1949, more than 2,325,000 tons of food and

119

supplies were flown to Berlin on 277,500 flights. Of this total, the most (and heaviest) transported cargo was coal, with more than 1,500,000 tons—only 500,000 tons were food. It is little wonder that some of the airlift pilots sometimes referred to themselves as *peasants,* "because" they said, "we are hauling coal and potatoes." Additionally, airlift cargo included liquid fuel, raw material, industrial supplies, construction equipment, mail, newspapers, vehicles, and medical supplies.

The French Air Force had most of their planes tied up in the Indochina warfare.

The British, however, did their valiant part. On June 27, the RAF started out their support with only 16 C-47s. Soon they assigned 150 additional planes to the Berlin Airlift. The most dramatic (if not exotic) planes to participate were the Sunderland Flying Boats of the British Coastal Command. Taking off from an airfield near Hamburg, they landed on the *Havel See,* a large lake in the middle of Berlin, with nine tons of cargo. Upon landing, they were met by Berliner crews who came out in small boats to unload the desperately needed rations.

For Norbert Anlieger, the flurry of work all over Tempelhof, around the clock, was like an all-consuming surge. When the airlift flights expanded their schedule to include all night hours, Norbert was never too tired to watch (during his brief breaks) the incoming planes with their bright headlights, glistening in the oversize search lights mounted on both sides of the runways. These super lights illuminated not only the parking ramps but also served as navigation aid for pilots starting their return trip from Berlin.

By mid-August, most aircraft were making four to five trips each day to and from Berlin. All planes were carrying heavier loads and making more take-offs and landings than they were designed for. Soon the totally overworked Tempelhof Airport had one take-off every 62 seconds. In order to keep the planes in top condition, maintenance check-ups were performed every 50 flight hours. This maintenance work was done at the home-base airfield of each plane, around the clock, Sundays included.

How often Norbert regretted that he had never received his father's training as an engineer! It would have come handy, now, when the Western Allies searched for qualified engineers and mechanics. Still, he liked his job of building runways and unloading planes.

Just yesterday he had run into an American pilot resting next to his aircraft. Norbert's crew, like always, had done the unloading in record time. When he and his sweaty coworkers were taking a short break, the pilot came over to them, handing out cigarettes. When Norbert declined the offer, Airman Fred Harrington could not hide his surprise.

"You are the first German who ever refused to take my cigarettes. Why? I guess, smoking is not your thing."

"Never has been, sir. The only time I handle cigarettes is on the black market."

Harrington reached into his jacket.

"How about some candies? What's your name?"

"Norbert Anleger."

"Hi Norb. I'm Fred Harrington. I am from Sumner, Iowa. First I was stationed in France, but for a while I've been here in Berlin."

"Well, I was born here…and I like candies. Thanks!"

Fred took a candy, too. As both men savored the sweets, the American asked Norbert if he had heard of Gail Halvorsen, "The Chocolate Flier."

"Oh, I have heard of him—most of the kids in West Berlin have. Only we Germans call him the *Rosinenbomber*."

"Yeah, 'the raisin bomber' has gotten pretty famous—and it's well-deserved. You know, Lieutenant Halvorsen flies in my squadron. What a great guy!"

"Tell me more about him! Is there a chance of meeting him?"

"Naturally! We fly two or three times every day to Tempelhof. The Lieutenant got several of us into this candy-dropping-thing. My buddy, Captain Eugene Williams, for instance, is just as good as Halvorsen in dropping candies—but he doesn't use little handkerchief parachutes. He does it like I do…just before the landing, we pull the window open and throw out chocolate bars, letting them find their own way. And I guess, the smart and hungry little German kids find them all."

Harrington received a signal from his co-pilot that it was time to get back into the cockpit and start the engines for another flight. At first he wanted to get up, but then he leaned toward Norbert, showing him his loaded hands.

"Here are some more candies and chewing gum for you and the other workers. Before I go, let me quickly tell you how this whole candy business got started. I have it straight from the horse's mouth—from Gail—from Lieutenant Gail Halvorsen. He had flown many missions in World War II. Fate took him to North African and Italian war theaters. You need to know, he loves children. When he was stationed in war-torn countries, he had always seen desperate-looking children. What had amazed him was that most of these kids had not begged for food, but rather for chewing gum, candies and cigarettes.

"Things were different, when he came to Berlin. Again and again, when he was surrounded by young as well as older children, he was astonished how shy and reserved they were. He had expected them to jerk at his pants and beg with stretched-out hands. But instead of begging for much-needed food, these youngsters politely hoped for short conversations in English, the language they had begun to learn in Nazi Germany, and which they now wanted to try out on him. Halvorsen told me that sometimes their English was as bad as his German.

"Still, he could not figure out why these kids had not begged for food or things like the children in Africa and Italy. Then it came to him: It was not the lack of food or candies or gums that held them back from begging—they either were too timid, or they had given up hope."

Norbert nodded in agreement, and said, "Yes, I can see the children here being reserved, at first, anyway."

"So," Fred continued, "the Lieutenant told them that the next day they were to wait near the beginning of the runway, where a surprise would be waiting for them. That night, he got some of us to help him wrap candy bars and chewing gum

123

in handkerchiefs. His plan was for his co-pilot to sling the little parachutes from the low-flying plane to the children."

"Yes," interrupted Norbert, "I know what you are talking about. A few weeks before I got this job, I was sometimes among those kids, helping them find the dropped sweets."

"Good for you, Norb! Well, every day the crowd of anxious kids waiting for the chocolate drop got bigger, especially at the St. Thomas Cemetery, right at the edge of the runway. Myself and a few other pilots joined the effort. Frankly, there was no telling who got a bigger kick out of these candy drops, the chocolate fliers or the excited kids on the ground."

A quick glance at his watch told Fred Harrington he better shut up and get back into the plane. Less than two minutes later the engines revved and the now-empty plane rose quickly into the sky. In spite of looking into the blinding sun, Norbert waved, imagining that his new American friend waved back.

The world had never before seen a denser flight schedule than the one over Berlin. Planes were constantly either arriving or departing. Even during the few nights when Norbert did not work in Tempelhof and was sleeping in his uncle's apartment in *Neukölln,* the droning sound of plane engines was always in his ears. The only exception was the night of August 13, 1948, when thick fog and rain caused the Military Airlift Command to suspend all flights for three hours, the first time the project had ever paused since its beginning.

Two fatal accidents in July had been a warning to the Command not to press their luck too far. The sheer number of flights with fatigued aircraft and overworked crews was like an invitation for casualties. On July 30, 1948, The Berlin Observer reported: *The third accident and the second fatal crash of the 7,231 flights logged in "Operation Vittles" occurred early Sunday morning, when a C-47, piloted by Lieutenant Charles H. King of Britton, South Dakota, and Lieutenant Robert W. Stuber of Arlington, California, crashed into the street in front of an apartment building in the Berlin-Friedenau district. Both the pilot and copilot were killed instantly.*

With the US Air Force in Berlin-Tempelhof, the British Royal Air Force had opened its airport in Berlin-Gatow in the British Sector for airlift flights. This much smaller and less developed airport was located in the southwestern corner of Berlin. However, because of its location near the *Havel* River and the big *Wannsee* Lake, the British could use their Flying Boats of the British Coastal Command in addition to C-47s and Avro York transport planes. Gatow's runway was improved with a concrete surface and was lengthened to 1,800 meters by mid-July.

Near the end of July, the combined US/British tonnage being flown to Berlin was averaging 2,500 tons in about 600 daily flights. That was still short of the 4,500 tons estimated as the daily minimum requirement to feed and support the Western Allied military plus Berlin's civilian population.

After the first tragic accidents and fatal landings had happened, the need for additional airports in Berlin was apparent. The improvements in Tempelhof and Gatow were not enough to keep the airlift functioning properly. The search for a feasible site for a new airport led to a tract of land in the Berlin-Tegel area in the French Sector, where, during the war, the German *Luftwaffe* had a small pilot training ground.

French Military leaders stationed in Germany were consulted and it was agreed that the United States would construct a large airfield and operate it, while the French would maintain it and provide manpower to unload the airlift cargo.

Construction in Tegel began on August 5, 1948, with a target completion date for January 1, 1949. Estimating only five construction months was an unbelievably ambitious time frame, especially in light of the limitations—little available heavy equipment, almost no raw materials, and very few skilled laborers.

The airlift activity during the months of August through December resembled a huge and frenetic version of Santa's North Pole workshop. Large construction equipment (critical for rebuilding and bringing the city back to life) was cut up with acetylene torches in West Germany, then loaded into huge C-74s and jumbo-sized C-82s for the trip to Berlin. There it was unloaded and quickly welded together again. Some of the raw material shortage problems were solved by using brick rubble and rocks from the bombed-out streets and buildings. The manpower problem was solved by enlisting thousands of volunteer Berliners who gladly pitched in—often without pay—to save their city.

For Norbert Anleger, a little-educated and non-skilled worker, the job at the Tempelhof Airport was just perfect, and most fulfilling. He and his hardworking buddies knew that without their untiring labor, the airlift would slowly—or not so slowly—collapse.

While top athletes and spectators from 59 nations were enjoying the 1948 Olympic Games in London (to which German athletes had not been invited), thousands of American,

British and French soldiers along with 65,000 German workers labored with determination to keep the people of Berlin alive. Norbert loved sports, too, as did thousands of other workers, but in the summer of 1948 they had more important things to do than cheering on Olympic athletes at Wembley Stadium.

Occasionally during their work breaks, some of the older men would tell their younger co-workers of the glorious 1936 Olympic Games in Berlin, which they had attended. As hard as Norbert tried to find at least one athlete among his working crews who had competed in the Berlin Games, he could not find a single one. "What happened to our honored hero athletes of 1936?" he asked a group of men and women doing cement work on the runway. "It wasn't *that* long ago…I would think I could find at least one Olympian to talk with! Have they all gone—"

"They were all killed," somebody cut in. "They were killed fighting in Poland, France, Russia and Africa. As the saying goes: 'The best Jackboots die first.' I think that goes especially for soldiers with excellent athletic qualities."

Norbert was a bit surprised at the older man's words, but not shocked. "What about you?" he asked. "You look like a man in good physical condition. How did you manage to stay alive?"

"You mean, how did I survive the crazy war? Well, when the war broke out in 1939, the medical guys sent me home—I was already too old, or 'well-matured' as they put it. The inspector comforted me with: 'We need good workers also at the home front.' But then in 1944, when things looked very bad for Germany, they came and got me anyway, and this time even without a health inspection. They needed *kanonenfutter*.

But since I was past the regular military age, they drafted me into the *Volkssturm,* the Home Defense Army. The regular soldiers treated us like a bunch of losers, which we really were. My company was made up of high-school kids and 'well-matured" men. Perhaps we *Volkssturm* soldiers helped Hitler lose the war."

Norbert left the break area as he knew it was time to get back to work. He noticed an American officer with a notepad walking through the working crews, talking mainly to the younger workers and then, evidently, entering their names on his list. Soon he was facing Norbert.

"Name?" the officer asked.

"Norbert. Norbert Anleger."

"Do you speak English?"

Here it comes again, Norbert thought. Always the same tedious questions! However, the American did not ask other questions. After Norbert told him that his English was "pretty good," he just commanded, "See me in my terminal office tomorrow at 900 hours! Office 394." Then the officer continued working his way through the crews.

"Wow!" said one of Norbert's neighbors. "That guy acts and barks like one of the KGB. I hope he is a true American and not an Ivan in disguise. I have enough experiences with KGB agents to last me the rest of my life."

"Maybe he is looking for people to work on the big Tegel Airport project."

"I guess you are right, Norb. They started working in Tegel in August. Now they are talking of constructing the city's longest runway there, which will allow planes like the 707, 747, DC8 and even bigger jets to land. They are going to complete the entire job in five months."

Norbert too had heard rumors about Tegel's future airfield, but what his buddy told him now was baloney! Who ever heard of building an entire airport with runways, hangars and terminals in only five months? That had to be the craziest rumor ever, or—if true—the most exciting opportunity for work.

At 9 o'clock, sharp, the next morning, Norbert knocked at the office door number 394.

"The door is open!" he heard somebody yell. Norbert stepped into an office showing no sign of decorative effort. He saw a huge desk, two chairs, a small table overflowing with hand-written notes and two telephones, in addition to a red phone on the desk.

"Welcome to the United States Air Force!" the American greeted Norbert. "You must be wondering why I asked you to see me, right?"

"I should say so, sir! I thought you were signing up people to work on the new airport project in Tegel—so, here I am, ready to switch from Tempelhof to Tegel."

"Not so fast, young man! I need more information about you. Let's start with your age. How old are you?"

"Sixteen."

"Sixteen? You must be kidding me. I would have guessed 18 or 19. Shouldn't you be in school right now?"

"I probably should, but I am not. I haven't been in school for a few years. I went only to elementary school, and even that was with interruptions and gaps...you know, the war."

Captain Kalamai Giftos did not need a further explanation. The reference to war said it all.

"For a young man with only a grade-school education you seem to manage well. I can even hear that in your voice. Tell me, how many languages do you speak?"

"German and English."

"Any other?"

"Well, I can make myself understood in Russian. Actually I speak it fairly well, if I have to! But I have learned not to admit that—especially not to Russians."

"Who taught you Russian?"

"I picked it up in the street. You see, the streets are my university. There I have learned everything I know—even Russian."

Both laughed, starting to feel more at ease with one another.

"Seriously, Norman, I have a proposal to make," said Captain Giftos. "It is not about you working on the Tegel project. We have come up with a plan to help hungry and starving young people in Berlin."

"I wish such a plan had existed when I was really young and forever hungry. By the way, my name is Norbert, not Norman."

Without acknowledging Norbert's correction, Captain Giftos continued, "This program is called *Aktion Storch,* or,

Action Stork. Along with your German relief agencies, we will evacuate or relocate more than 50,000 kids, to free them from the stressful living in Berlin."

For a moment Norbert just stared at the American. Sure, living in Berlin was tough, especially now with all the complications and limitations caused by the Russian blockade.

But "stressful living"? All Berliners had lived with extreme stress for more than five years.

When Giftos looked at Norbert's puzzled face, he saw that his reaction was typical of many young Berliners who took the situation matter-of-factly, even though they lived in hardship as if on a lone island.

"You street boys are tough, Norb, but there are thousands of kids whose hunger has gnawed away on their health and nerves. We can help by bringing them to West Germany where food supply is not that meager."

Norbert understood. His siblings, now all dead, had been older than he. Therefore, his contact with children had been limited, except for the few times when he had helped them find the little candy parachutes which had gone astray after the Americans dropped them. Maybe here was a chance to show that he, too, loved children.

"Captain, how can I be of help in the *Aktion Storch*?"

Giftos had hoped that this young, quick-witted German would be willing and excited enough to work on this daunting but crucial project. "Norbert," he said. "You know that many people of all ages are busy either repairing the old, or constructing the new airports. For you, however, I have a more challenging job—work for us as an interpreter!"

Norbert could hardly trust his ears. Had this rough but kind American officer just said that he wanted him to work as an interpreter? He really had no idea what that job might demand from him, but it surely sounded like a dream come true. So he quickly clicked his heels, straightened up his body and said with a loud voice, "Yes, sir. I'll do it."

"You'll be paid by the US Air Force, Norbert."

"Thank you, sir! That sounds even better."

A few minutes later, Captain Giftos gave Norbert one of his used leather flight jackets and a pair of nearly-new shoes. "After all, we want our interpreter to look important, not like an occasional part-timer," the Captain explained with a laugh.

Norbert was totally overwhelmed. This officer, who just yesterday had called him away from the construction site and whom his buddy had called "a barking KGB agent," was a wonderful man after all, even though sometimes a bit short on explanations. Now, for instance, he asked Norbert to follow him to his Jeep without saying where he was taking him.

Giftos took Norbert to Gatow, the other available air field in West Berlin, located in the far southwest corner of Berlin and on the west side of Wannsee Lake. The construction work of lengthening and improving Gatow's one existing runway had just been completed. In addition, the British Royal Air Force was using the *Havel See* for their Sunderland Flying Boats, recruited for the airlift. Taking off from *Finkenwerder* on the Elbe River near Hamburg in northern Germany, these Flying

Boats landed on the *Havel* in Berlin, each plane carrying a respectable nine tons of cargo.

Norbert had seen these rather plump looking Flying Boats before, even though only from a distance. Now Captain Giftos took him right into the belly of the water-parked plane. Just when Giftos was about to give Norbert more information about his new job as interpreter, there was a powerful bump which made both men stumble. Their plane had been rammed by a small barge carrying about 30 screaming children and a few old people.

Giftos was the first to compose himself. Standing at the open door of the plane he yelled to the skipper of the barge, "Have you lost your brains, you incompetent midget captain? You could have smashed a hole into the hull and sunk the *Sunderling!* The British Coastal Command would have skinned you alive, you *dummkopf*!"

"Verzeihung! Enschuldigung! Ich verstehe kein Englisch."

The apologizing barge pilot shrugged his shoulders. He had not understood a single word except for *dummkopf.* Captain Giftos turned to Norbert.

"Come on, Mister Interpreter! It's your job to tell this careless imbecile that he is an idiot and that he better shape up when transporting his next ferry load."

Norbert quickly shouted a few admonishing words in German, which were not the exact translation. He also told the still-screaming kids to "cool it" and line up to start transferring from the barge to the plane. Shortly after, a second barge arrived with another load of German youngsters. Captain

Giftos took the lead again, this time assisted by Norbert's instant translation.

"Listen everybody! You are the lucky ones to have been selected for the *Aktion Storch* Evacuation Program. Flying from here to West Germany, you do not need passports or other transfer documents. Once you land in Hamburg-*Finkenwerder*, you will each receive 50 *Deutsche Marks*, which will help you get started in the West."

There were cheers of gratitude from the young and old travelers, who by now were seated tightly together.

"Oh…I must be getting old—I forgot to introduce myself," said the Captain. "I am US Air Force Captain Kalamai Giftos. And this young gentleman in the fine flight jacket is Norbert…" Giftos looked at Norbert and tried to remember his full name.

"Norbert Anleger," the new interpreter helped out.

"Yes, this is Norbert Anleger, the best interpreter we ever had, or more honestly, the only one we ever had." The travelers smiled, happy with their guides.

"One more thing. I will not be flying with you. My job is to arrange for your flight and make sure you take off for Hamburg. But Norbert Anleger here will fly with you and will make sure that you understand what we Americans might say to you."

Norbert stared at the captain in utter surprise. He had watched many planes fly over Berlin, and he had unloaded cargo from hundreds of them, but he had never flown in one. He had the thought that Giftos should have at least mentioned this part of his job to him before.

"Sir," he said, "did you say that I will be accompanying this plane-load of people? You were joking, right?"

"Far from it! Your job as interpreter requires that you are with your group from the beginning to the end—that is until you turn them over to the authorities in Hamburg-*Fuhlsbüttel*. By that time other Flying Boats will have received their cargo for Berlin, and hopefully will have enough space left for you for your return flight."

Most of the passengers had not understood the conversation between the captain and Norbert, and were only anxious to be on their way to West Germany where they would get food and rest, even though at this point they had no idea where they would be ending up and for how long.

Chapter 14

Major General Kotikov, Commander of the Soviet Troops in East Berlin, was fuming. For almost a year now it had become a devilish pattern—whatever he or his higher-ranking Moscow bosses suggested to the Western Allied leaders was voted down or, what was worse, laughed at.

Back in 1945, when the Americans and British were still absent from Berlin and the Soviets had unhindered control of Berlin, the SMAD (Soviet Military Administration Deutschland) had appointed a City Council to run day-to-day affairs. They had set up a communist-run German police cadre. Radio Berlin and affiliated neighboring stations were under unchallenged communist control.

The Soviets had even claimed the right to determine how much food the Berliners received. If they were communist public officials, they were assigned twice as many food stamps as non-communist citizens, or the elderly. By the time the Western Allied troops entered Berlin in July, 1945, the Soviets were the sole rulers of the communist-dominated city administration. That was also the time when trouble started—at least in the eyes of the Soviets.

Kotikov remembered when the Soviets had tried to merge the Communist Party with the Social Democratic Party to form the majority Socialist Unity Party (SED). Most Social Democrats had rebelled and formed their own non-communist Social Democratic Party (SPD). Kotikov's ultimate wish was that a communist government for all of war-torn, exhausted Germany would be installed, just as it had happened with Czechoslovakia in February, 1948, after a Soviet-backed coup-d'état.

Major General Kotikov was present on March 20, 1948, when the Allied Control Council (ACC) met. The mood shift from comradeship to hostility between the Western and Eastern Forces had happened many months before, and was increasingly apparent. On that day in March, however, the entire Soviet delegation, led by General Vassily Sokolovsky, walked out of the ACC, claiming that the Western Powers planned to form a provisional West German government. Actually, they were not too far from the truth. Three months later, the "Big Three" indeed revealed their plans both for a currency reform in their Zones, and for the establishment of a provisional West German government.

One week after the Russian "walk-out," the Soviets strengthened their anti-Western position by restricting Western military and passenger traffic between the American, British, and French Zones and Berlin. General Lucius Clay bypassed the restrictions by giving the order to supply all Western military garrisons by air. This program was called the "Little Lift" or "Little Vittle."

By April 10, Major General Kotikov had given up on the imposed restrictions. Annoying, periodic interruptions of rail and road traffic, however, did not stop, so the United States continued supplying its military forces by air, with an average of 20 flights each day.

By the end of June, by order from Moscow, West Berlin was totally cut off from Western food and material supplies, and Kotikov was satisfied—at least for a short time.

Soon after, the Western Allies launched the real airlift on June 28, hauling flour, salt, milk and medicine, this time mainly for the West Berliners.

At first, the Russian commandant had laughed at what he deemed futile attempts to supply a city of more than two million people by air. As the airlift not only continued but expanded by leaps and bounds, he had ordered more harassment and disruptions. By orders from "higher ups," Russian planes often were buzzing or flying too close to Western Allied planes, or the Soviet military held maneuvers with ground fire, explosions, rockets, and balloons. As a result, a few Western planes crashed or were severely damaged. Yet, none of the Soviet interferences brought a halt to the airlift.

Throughout the first few months of the airlift, Generals Sokolovsky and Kotikov, along with German communists, also subjected the West Berliners to intense psychological warfare. The communist Radio Berlin, for example, continually proclaimed the readiness of the Western Allies to abandon West Berlin.

Furthermore, Soviets, together with East German communists, regularly harassed the non-communist members of the democratically-elected city parliament, *Stadtverordnetenversammlung von Gross-Berlin.*

On September 6, 1948, a Soviet-organized *putsch* for control of ALL Berlin resulted in the takeover of the city hall by communist SED members. When the free radio station RIAS (*Rundfunk im Amerikanischen Sektor*) called on Berliners to protest against the actions of the communists on September 9, more than 500,000 demonstrators gathered near the Reichstag and the Brandenburg Gate in the British Sector, right at the border of the Soviet Sector.

Ernst Reuter, who in June of 1946 had been elected Lord Mayor of Berlin, but who had been hindered from assuming his position because of either Russian or Kotikov's personal opposition, was one of many speakers. Instead of inciting the crowd to rebel against the Soviets, he wisely appealed to the conscience of world opinion. Reuter stated:

"My wonderful people of Berlin! This demonstration gives Allied statesmen a good opportunity to find out what the Berlin people really stand for. We cannot be bartered; we cannot be negotiated; we cannot be sold. We Berliners are determined to maintain Berlin's freedom.

"Whoever would surrender this city, whoever would surrender the people of Berlin, would surrender the whole world—more, he would surrender himself...People of the world! Look upon this city! You cannot, you must not forsake us! There is only one possibility for all of us: To stand jointly together until the fight has been won."

The crowd of 500,000 was excited; some people were ecstatic. As the large gathering was peacefully dispersing, some youths became unruly, shouting obscenities at Soviet soldiers who were watching the event. Then a few youngsters scaled the *Brandenburger Tor* (Brandenburg Gate), tore down and burned the Red Flag, which had flown over Berlin since May, 1945. Shooting broke out in other locations where young people had thrown stones at East German police, who then shot and killed a 16-year-old Berliner.

As the crowd drifted away and Soviet Military Police arrived to support the East German *Volkspolizei*, five Berliner teenagers were arrested. They were taken to the Soviet Military Court on September 13, where each demonstrator was sentenced to 25 years of imprisonment for "Assault on the Occupation Forces" and "Disturbing Public Order."

The fact that General Kotikov had not been able to stop the airlift made him work that much harder to change at least the membership of the City Assembly. In September, 1948, when the non-communist Assembly members had experienced too many Soviet-inspired disruptions, they walked out of City Hall and moved to the Technical University campus in Berlin-Charlottenburg in the British Sector, which they made their provisional meeting place. Their communist colleagues had stayed behind, claiming to be in charge of the entire city, i.e., of all four sectors.

Now Berlin had two "de facto" governments—one for the communist East Sector, the other for the three Western Sectors. They worked in the same city, but their ideologies and working methods differed greatly. The Soviet Generals Kotikov and Sokolovsky were still hoping that the East Berlin communists would be the ruling city government, and the West Berlin government would somehow disappear. At one of the planning meetings of the Soviets and East Berlin leaders, General Sokolovsky turned to Kotikov and shouted, "Those damned so-called 'free' West Berliners and their Allied cohorts with their constant know-it-all attitude— one day they will make alcoholics out of us all!"

"I'll drink to that," replied his colleague and friend, and all conference participants broke into a roaring laughter.

Major General Kotikov, now East Berlin Commander, had to admit to himself that he really hated his job. Take for example his hostile encounters with his French counterpart, Jean Ganeval. The issue always was about the construction of the airfield in Berlin-Tegel, which was located in Ganeval's French Sector. All Soviet leaders, not just Kotikov, hated the unbelievably fast construction work done at Tegel. The Western Allies had estimated a total building time of five months. Now, not quite three months into it, the construction neared its completion.

No delaying tactics of Kotikov had been successful. The real bone of contention was a 200 foot tall radio tower in Tegel. Allied Air Force officials had visited Kotikov several times, pleading to have the Communist Radio Berlin transmitting tower either moved or dismantled, since it was an obstacle in the approach path of the future runway.

Each time, Kotikov had either ignored their requests or had given evasive, "crucial" reasons for the existence of this radio tower. Then the French did something totally unexpected. Having lost patience and being truly concerned for the safety of the planes and crews, which soon were to land there, French military specialists attached explosives to the base of the tower and blew it up.

That made Kotikov's blood boil. This time the French had pushed him too far. The next morning, he stormed into

General Ganeval's headquarters. He found his office door closed. Without knocking, Kotikov tore the door open and shouted at the still-seated Ganeval,

"How could you totally demolish the important Tegel Radio Tower !?!"

"With dynamite, General, with dynamite," was the sarcastic answer of General Ganeval.

Chapter 15

Each time Airman Harrington landed in Tempelhof or Gatow, he had been impressed with the zeal of the poorly-dressed German male and female working crews. He had never seen them taking a break. Neither the hottest sunshine nor freezing rain had kept them from working with the heavy cement or the stinking asphalt tar loads.

The week before, he and about 50 of his airlift buddies had been taken to Tegel where the intensely busy construction of Berlin's newest and largest airport was underway. The military buses had taken them directly to the feverishly working crews, made up of two-thirds men and one-third women. Spread along hundreds of feet, the partially-built runway looked like an anthill without a hill—there were busy workers everywhere!

A few days before, Fred Harrington had read in *Stars and Stripes* that a total of 20,000 Germans were employed in building Berlin's newest airport. When Fred first came to Berlin, his briefings instructor, Lt. Harry Strong, had talked about the unbelievable willingness of Berlin's population to help with the reconstruction of their destroyed city. Unfortunately, the able-bodied middle-aged generation was severely depleted, casualties of World War II. However, both the young and old, men and women, tried to fill the gap.

Lieutenant Strong also had taught the eager Air Force newcomers about the Marshall Plan, officially called the "European Recovery Program." General George C. Marshall, US Army Chief of Staff, had become the US Secretary of State in January, 1947, under President Truman. Together with President Truman and his most skilled economic advisors, Marshall had developed a recovery program of continental dimensions, which eventually contributed $ 12.5 billion to European countries in dire need.

The fact that the former enemy nation, Germany, was included in the recovery program was like a miracle. Germany did not even have its own government, but rather was ruled by the Four Powers Allied Control Council. Still, Marshall was convinced that Germany should be included. In a speech given in Chicago in November, 1947, Marshall proclaimed: "The restoration of Europe involves the restoration of Germany. Without revival of Germany's economy, there can be no revival of Europe's economy."

Marshall knew of the 35 million soldiers and civilians killed in Europe and Asia during the war. Now he wanted to give Europe, and especially Germany, a chance for healing and recovery. A total of $3.7 billion was given to West Germany and West Berlin, which was like a gift from heaven, especially during the Berlin Airlift with its huge expenses.

Naturally, all this infuriated the Soviets and their communist East German partners. Russian Foreign Minister Molotov openly denounced the Marshall Plan. Thus, neither East Germany nor the Russian Sector of Berlin was included in the plan.

At the time, Fred Harrington had not really understood Lieutenant Strong's political teaching regarding the Marshall Plan. Now when he saw the overwhelming work that was being done on Berlin and West Germany airports, he understood that the money for the costly airlift had to come from somewhere. He also found there was more and better food in West Berlin than anywhere in East Berlin or East Germany.

When he wanted to discuss some of these issues with his flight buddies, he usually drew blank stares. One of his squadron colleagues gave him a "thumbs down" sign and said, "Man, don't bother me with that political mush! I bet you that even most of our politicians in Washington have no idea what this is all about."

Fred's mind was not to be quieted. He was a compulsive puzzle-solver and sought them out—whether the ones he solved so easily in magazines, or complex, global-sized problems.

As the weather turned cooler in Germany and more days with heavy fog became a real problem for the airlift, all Allied pilots were extremely grateful that the Tegel Airport, constructed in only three months, was now in full operation. It had been built mostly by hand, by thousands of predominantly German laborers who worked day and night.

"That's how you get something big done in 90 days," was General William Tunner's new motto. Recognizing his outstanding organizational talent, the United States had made him the commander of the "Combined Air Lift Task Force" (CALTF) on October 15, 1948. Before he received this impressive title, he had experienced the taxing daily challenges of the airlift. The frequent 12- to 16-hour duties were exhausting for all involved, especially when the temporary marching orders for airlift pilots were extended for another 90 to 180 days.

General Tunner, a man of many talents and ideas, also arranged for a competition between the Air Force squadrons and units by establishing a "How-Goes-It" board at each airlift-participating airport, both in Berlin and West Germany. Each day, every flying unit was given a cargo quota. At the end of the 24-hour period, the cargo carried results were posted and the winners were declared. This unique idea caught on and led to a light-hearted yet energized rivalry between units, bases, and their loading and unloading crews. The contest among pilots, crewmen and German laborers gave them fresh excitement, much appreciated after five months of the steady hard work of operating the airlift.

In April, 1949, General Tunner came up with an especially invigorating idea. He informed his airlift officers and airmen that on April 17, Easter Sunday, there would be an "Easter Parade." For 24 hours, all units were to complete airlift missions with the most outstanding tonnage ever. It worked! The faithful American, British and French planes had been hauling 5,000 to 7,000 tons of cargo per day—on Easter Parade Sunday, 1,398 flights delivered close to 13,000 tons of coal (the heaviest cargo) to Berlin. This required the handling of an unprecedented density of air traffic with almost 2,800 incoming and outgoing flights at West Berlin's three airports.

General Tunner proudly reported to Washington: "The 24-hour Easter Parade went by and concluded without a glitch. We were tired and worn out, but we all felt more than conquerors."

Chapter 16

During the last month, the job as interpreter and unofficial chaperon had kept Norbert busier than ever before in his life. The work he had done at the Tempelhof Airport, building a new runway, had given him a better understanding of how valuable cement and asphalt were to form stable, solid foundations. However, working as an interpreter at the Gatow Airport kept him running—often 15 to 16 hours per day. No, it was not a sweaty job like the one in Tempelhof. Yet, he would never have imagined how complex the shipping of a planeload of people could be, and in his case it had been hundreds of plane loads he had processed.

The good thing about his seemingly never-ending interpreting duties was that one day Captain Kalamai Giftos, Norbert's Greek-American protégé, had arranged for him to live in the barracks of the American flight crews.

"Your life will be so much easier," Captain Giftos said. "You can start work early and stay until late at night, if need be, without having to worry how to get home after work. You won't ever again have to trudge an hour home because you've missed the last streetcar. You can always visit your uncle when you have time off —you'll enjoy being around the Americans more."

Norbert was excited, and relieved. "Yes, very good," he said.

"Another thing…when you have any time, you can polish up on your written French. When I asked you to help us with translating from English to German, and German to English, I had no idea that we would have need of you also as a French interpreter."

"Neither did I, Captain Giftos," said Norbert.

"Hey, Norb, why don't you call me Kal ! All that Giftos and Captain crap is too heavy between friends."

The invitation caught Norbert by surprise since the captain was more senior and older, but he especially liked the "between friends" —he smiled and said, "Okay, yes—Kal."

Norbert soon found that he, indeed, needed to be facile with French translation. Most of the "Action Stork" passengers were German-speaking people, however, some of the French Air Force personnel stationed in Tegel had been sent to the Gatow Airport to help process the thousands of (mainly young) people. Norbert was by far not the only interpreter, still, for him it often seemed that he was translating 24 hours a day. That left no real time for lunch and supper breaks, which he really regretted because he had found out how much he liked the American food.

When he had accepted Captain Giftos' offer to live in the military barracks, he had been afraid that Uncle Theo and Aunt Hanna would be disappointed. To his surprise they were anything but disappointed. His uncle praised the new situation over and over again.

"Norbi," he said one day, when his nephew had come by for a short surprise visit. "Not only are we glad that you have found a place of work, where they give you good food, but as you can tell, it has gotten very cold in our apartment. After all, this is winter. Our firewood supply is down to nothing. This worries us more than the shortage of food, which we have been used to for years."

"If I only had a bit more time, Uncle Theo, we both could go hunting for wood in the ruins."

"I know you would. Frankly, we would probably not succeed in finding anything. Our friends and neighbors have combed through every inch of the ruins; and all park bushes and most trees have been cut down by freezing poachers. What the *Trümmerfrauen* [rubble women] managed to find in the debris in 1945, is all gone, a long time ago. By the way, Norbi, did you know that last week Mrs. Radow in our neighbor house has died? She froze to death during the night."

Norbert did not know what to say. After a while he got over the shock and mumbled, "I knew her two boys, Holli and Moppel. Mrs. Radow had sent them to their grandparents in Hannover. Mister Radow was killed during the war in Stalingrad—poor woman! Where was she buried?"

"I don't know," answered Theo. "An unmarked truck came and hauled away her body, wrapped in a white bed sheet. God knows where!"

Norbert shuddered to think about the fact there was no wood to spare for coffins; not while people were freezing to death for lack of coal or firewood. He felt a wave of gratitude for the airlift, knowing that would have been the fate of many more thousands of Berliners if the airlift had not saved them by providing food, fuel, and medicine, among many other necessities. But how long could the airlift last?

In the course of the early winter months, even many West Berliners were afraid that the time might be near when the Western Allies would pull out of West Berlin and hand over that "bone of contention" area to the Russians. However, the construction of the large Tegel Airport had injected new life and hope into many tired and hungry Berliners. The Tegel airfield, with its record-long runways, could now accommodate more and bigger planes, such as the 707, 747, and DC8s, which meant more tonnage of life-saving provisions.

From the first C-54 landing at Tegel Airport on November 5, 1948, the airfield was so busy and dangerously overcrowded that the officials had to wait a full month until they found enough time for a Dedication Ceremony. Finally, a big banner proudly proclaimed: "TEGEL AIRPORT – Built in 90 Days." The new airport may not have been a "wonder of engineering," but most certainly it was a "wonder of cooperation" with regard to international participation and gender equality. For the workers, that meant the same pay regardless of nationality, faith orientation, gender, or skin color.

As spring arrived in Berlin, rumors were circulating about the blockade possibly being lifted soon. Norbert Anleger, along with two million West Berliners, was used to rumors of all kinds. However, on May 5, 1949, a Four Power communique announced that the blockade would end on May 12. This exciting piece of news raced around the world, bringing hundreds of reporters and news photographers to Berlin, where they wanted to witness and record every aspect of the end of the wretched blockade.

Even Norbert felt the urge to be among those who would experience the opening of the Berlin autobahn, or witness the arrival of the first *Interzonen* passenger and freight train. When he stopped at Captain Giftos' office, he found only the young secretary sitting in the captain's desk chair. He knew her well, and she had seen him many times.

"Can I help you, Norbert?" she asked, a bit embarrassed about her disrespectful behavior in her boss's office.

"I was looking for your boss."

"Who is also *your* boss, right?"

"Right! I wanted to ask him ... well ... I should really ask the captain in person."

"Tell me, Norb, what do you wish to ask him?"

"Whether he would release me for a few days, or a week, so that I can crisscross the city and see what is going on."

The uniformed secretary—Norbert did not know her rank—put on her most charming smile and said, "Why don't I try to reach the captain by phone, and then you can tell him what is on your mind!"

She made the call. Suddenly Norbert's courage left him. He felt like retreating through the still-open door, especially when the secretary was put on hold. When she saw Norbert turn toward the door, she waved for him to stay.

"Hello, yes this is Captain Giftos' office. Who? No, I need to talk to the captain. Who? No, nobody else will do. Yes, I'll wait." The secretary rolled her eyes in mock exhaustion.

"Hello! Hello! This is she," she said, when connected at last. "Captain, I have a young man here who is anxious to talk to you. Yes, it's our interpreter genius, Norbert. I will put him on. One moment." Norbert took the phone as she handed it up to him.

"*Guten Tag, mein Freund. Wie geht es dir?*" asked Captain Giftos.

"Wow! Your German is getting very good, *Kali mera*," said Norbert, ending with the greeting in Greek.

"*Ja, ja*, I learned two sentences! So, what's up?"

"Sir, you are aware what is about to happen in Berlin. I want to be there when the border crossings are opening up, and when the trains and streetcars begin operating like they used to, almost a year ago."

"I understand you, Norbert. You must be feeling great."

"Yes, sir, I am. Therefore, I thought you might be willing to grant me a short vacation time. After all, I've almost never taken a break since I've been working for you."

"What does your contract allow you?"

"My contract, sir? I have no contract. As you know, I just do whatever people want me to do, when they want me to do it—or what gets thrown my way," said Norbert, adding, "with all due respect, sir." He could hear his boss laughing.

152

"Okay, Norb. You are free to do as you please for the next two weeks. Enjoy the time, and don't get caught by the Russians!"

"Thank you, sir. I'll be back. You can count on that!"

As he hung up, Captain Giftos recalled, with some disbelief, how a simple request addressed to a German boy for help with German-speaking airlift passengers had developed into a full-blown interpreter job for the very capable young Norbert Anleger. But then, everything in this city had been crazy since June 25, 1948, when General Clay had given the order to launch the Berlin Airlift. And now, it seemed, the end of the blockade finally had come. "**Blockade Ends – Airlift Wins**" was the new slogan.

As soon as Norbert realized he really was going to get to take leave, he was jubilant. Using his bicycle, he wanted to experience all of the mind-blowing events he could get himself to. Luckily he made it just in time, even though the sun was barely rising, on May 12, when the first "Autobahn Courtesy Patrol Jeep" arrived from West Germany at the West Berlin checkpoint, followed by a convoy of food-carrying American military and German supply trucks.

He also managed to see the first *Interzonen Zug* (inter-zone train) at *Bahnhof Zoo*.

There were welcoming flowers and celebratory wreaths everywhere. More importantly, wherever Norbert looked, he saw happy faces and tears of joy of old and young Berliners.

"Why are you standing here, looking around?" shouted a middle-aged, bearded man to Norbert. "Get back on your steel horse and pedal to the *Schöneberg Rathaus*! There is something big going on."

Norbert did not need a second hint. With full force he pedaled in the direction of West Berlin's temporary city hall, the *Rathaus Schöneberg*. The closer he got to the square in front of the *Rathaus*, the more impassable the thick crowd made his travel. Finally he had to get off and push his bike, lest the shoving, shouting, cheering people would have stepped over him and wrecked his bicycle.

More than 200,000 ecstatic West Berliners gathered at City Hall to celebrate the newly gained freedom from the Russian blockade. Nobody had ordered them to meet here; they just knew where to find like-minded, celebratory fellow citizens. Most of the prominent city officials, among them Lord Mayor Ernst Reuter, had also come. Welcoming the end of the blockade, Reuter spoke for all freedom-loving Berliners, when he declared:

"The attempt of the Russians and their communist East German collaborators to force us to our knees has failed, frustrated by our steadfastness and firmness. It failed because the world heard our appeal and came to our assistance."

The excited crowd constantly interrupted the speech with victorious shouts. Reuter ended his speech with a familiar phrase for Berliners:

"*Berlin bleibt doch Berlin!*" (Berlin will always remain Berlin.) Norbert could hardly contain his joy. When the people stopped applauding Reuter's speech, Norbert found a slightly elevated base of a war-destroyed monument. With a few steps, he stood on it, shouting:

"*Hurra, wir leben noch!*" (Hooray, we are still alive!) The shout was first echoed by the people standing close to Norbert, then it spread like a wave and finally became a tsunami. "*Hurra, wir leben noch!*" the roaring crowd chanted. Many of the people demonstrating had lost relatives or friends to hunger and frost during the brutally cold winter months. But these people here, they had survived! Right now, they seemed to form the happiest city in the world.

After two weeks of exploring Berlin's new situation, when West Berliners could again buy fresh oranges and bananas, when most department stores sported fashionable clothes, and restaurants were re-opened and well-stocked, Norbert was back at work again. He told neither Captain Giftos nor his colleagues that he had also taken several trips to the Soviet Sector. There, he had been shocked how miserable and drab the stores looked, with mostly empty shelves. How could he have forgotten how that felt, so quickly?

The eastern side of the border was propped up with barricades and patrolling police.

What surprised him most were the formerly friendly East Berlin citizens, who had developed a strange shyness which held them back from talking to people "from the West." Soviet "Big Brother" had managed to intimidate the already fearful East Berliners to the point that Norbert no longer thought of them as being part of Berlin. He had to admit that there had been moments and situations across the border when he suddenly was overcome by a fear of being snatched off the street by Russian militia or East German *Volkspolizei.*

During Norbert's two weeks of so-called vacation, he had found out that General Clay, the Commander-in-Chief of all

US Forces in Europe and US Military Governor for Germany, who truly had become a friend of all Berliners, was scheduled to leave Germany and fly back to the United States on May 15. Norbert wanted to get access to Clay's farewell ceremony, to be held in the General's headquarters in Berlin-Dahlem.

Wearing his leather flight jacket and looking, acting, and speaking more and more like an American, Norbert hoped that the Military Police guards would admit him. The closer he came to the headquarters, he saw hundreds of US military personnel crowding the famous *Kronprinzen Allee*. There were also at least a thousand Germans, who as "outside spectators" hoped to get a glimpse of the famous general, whom they loved. When Norbert finally made it to the high steel gate, two Military Police stopped him.

"Where do you think you are going?" one demanded.

"To the farewell ceremony of General Clay, sir," Norbert answered in his best American accent, showing as much confidence as he could muster.

"And why would General Clay, or anybody here be interested in having you around?"

"I am the chief interpreter for Captain Kalamai Giftos," bragged Norbert. "I am sure he would want me to attend the ceremony."

"Do you really think the United States military has no better interpreters than you?"

Now the second MP stepped up to Norbert. "Just beat it, boy," he said. "If you came here to get some extra chewing gum, here—have some!" With that, he reached into his pocket for a pack of Wrigley's and held it out to Norbert.

"I didn't come for that!" Norbert spit out the words. "My orders are more important than your chewing gum. Why don't you call Captain Giftos and tell him that his …"

"Did you hear me, boy? I said beat it, and I mean it! You're just another German begging a meal or something off us." He stepped closer to Norbert's face. "Look at my name tag! My name is Isaacson. Does that mean anything to you? Yes, I'm Jewish. My parents were smart enough to send me to relatives in America in 1933. They ended up being killed in the furnaces of Auschwitz, without having done anything wrong! They were Jews. That was enough for you Nazis to kill them!"

The first MP tried to stop his wound-up buddy from continuing his tirade against anything and anybody German. Isaacson took one small step back, but continued to rant at Norbert.

"I grew up in America. In 1939, I got the news that my parents had died in a German 'rehabilitation center'—really just a concentration camp. When the war broke out against Germany in 1941, I was proud to volunteer to serve with the US infantry. I asked specifically to serve at the front, in Germany. For three years I saw action—by that I mean, I killed enough Germans to calm my angry soul."

Having thrown these harsh words into Norbert's face, the agitated man turned around and walked away. But suddenly he stopped and turned to look at Norbert.

"You lousy Germans," he hissed. "You have no business around here, anyway. You should be in one of your infamous camps, which you are world-famous for!"

Norbert was fighting back tears. The MP's verbal attack had come as such a surprise that he was speechless. He had a fleeting urge to tell the MP that his own dad, who had never been a Nazi, also had died in a concentration camp, that he had lost two brothers in the senseless defense of Berlin-Neukölln's city hall, that his mother and his oldest brother had been torn to pieces by a Russian grenade a few days before the end of the war. But why bother! A man harboring so much hatred toward Germans would not understand, and surely would not care about his suffering.

Norbert slowly turned away from the gate, looking for his bicycle. He spotted a group of Air Force officers approaching the headquarters entrance gate. Their confident strides showed that they were invited guests, and the two MPs saluted and waved them to pass through. As they were happily chatting and walking away, Norbert caught his breath as he recognized Lieutenant Gail Halvorson and the pilot, Harrington, among them.

"Hey, Lieutenant Halvorson! Hallo, Fred Harrington! Hey, it's me, Norbert Anleger— remember me?"

But the Air Force men just kept on going, and Norbert realized the military band had begun in earnest. As he saw the MPs walking quickly toward him, he didn't want to hang around until they were within earshot. He hated giving up after being so close to meeting General Clay in person, this famous American who had won the hearts of all Berliners. He told himself that some day he may still get a chance to meet the man he admired, the man who had said to the throngs of people he helped to liberate, "I entered Berlin as a conqueror, and I leave Berlin as a friend."

These recent memories flooded Norbert's mind as he sat in his unofficial office, next to the office of Captain Giftos. "Norbert! Hey, Norbert!" called the secretary, raising her voice. "Are you dreaming? The boss wants to talk to you right away." Her tone signaled urgency. "It is very important!" Within seconds Norbert stood in front of Captain Giftos.

"Here I am, Captain. What's up?"

"It's still hard for you to call me Kal, right?"

"Yes, sir, Kal, sir!" Norbert said with a big smile.

"Anyway, I hope you have no commitments for tomorrow. I need you in *Fassberg*."

"Is that the airport between Hamburg and Hannover? I remember that lots of C-54s heavy with coal came from there into Berlin-Gatow."

"You are absolutely right! Good memory! But now to the point! Tomorrow, July 29, there will be a big memorial ceremony at the Fassberg Airport, honoring the 61 Allied soldiers who died in the service of the airlift. Since Fassberg is in the British Occupation Zone, the Brits are in charge of the service. Just a few minutes ago, I got word that their German/ English interpreter was injured in a terrible car accident. I told them—without asking you—that you and I would be happy to help out."

"As you well know, sir, I am always glad to be of service," said Norbert quickly.

"Good! But there is a little problem. The car in the accident caught on fire, and the briefcase containing the speech manuscripts was destroyed. You would have to translate the speeches in real time, as they are being given."

"I would not call that a problem, Kal. I am ready when you are. When do we drive?"

"Drive? Man, you are working for the Air Force. Remember, we never drive or walk when we can fly!"

Early the next morning, Captain Giftos piloted a small plane, with a co-pilot, the Captain's secretary, and Norbert as the only passengers. When they landed in Fassberg, the airfield there resembled a beehive with British, American, and French officers and enlisted men and women flying and running around. They came from all over Germany: Lübeck, Hamburg, Celle, Hannover, Bückeburg, Wiesbaden, Frankfurt and Oberpfaffenhofen (the US Maintenance Depot near Munich). Add to those about 2,000 Allied soldiers and the 1,500 German airlift laborers, and one understands why a *Stars & Stripes* reporter called the gathering "the anthill of Fassberg."

The memorial ceremony started at noon. All military personnel were dressed in their finest. Norbert wore his "finest," too—the flight jacket he had received from his boss. As a military band played, the Allied Forces took their formation according to their nationalities. The civilian German workers comprised the largest block. The dignified ceremony was to honor the 31 Americans, 41 British, and 7 Germans who had sacrificed their lives in the airlift operations.

Silently, respectfully, the participants listened to the report of an American Air Force general, who told the international audience that the airlift had transported a total of 2.3 million tons in 227,000 flights at a cost of $253 million. In addition to the cargo, 227,655 passengers had been transported to or from Berlin.

While Norbert faithfully interpreted the statistic-filled speech of the general, he allowed his mind a quick detour, remembering the many days with *Action Stork*, when he had been privileged to help hundreds of youngsters fly to West Germany, where for a few weeks or months they found better living conditions.

Right from the outset here in Fassberg, Norbert had taken the liberty of translating the terms "airlift" and "vittle" with the German words *Die Brücke der Liebe* (The Bridge of Love). After all, that had been his own experience. While "airlift" in German was *Luftauftrieb*, Norbert had found a better understandable and more meaningful way to translate the word "airlift" into the German language: *Die Brücke der Liebe*.

Chapter 17

Of all the days in his young life, Fred Harrington would never forget May 12, 1949, when the hellish blockade of West Berlin finally came to an end. It almost came as a surprise since the airlift efforts were still in full force. Only a few weeks earlier, the Airlift Easter Parade on Easter Sunday, April 17, had been a spectacular highlight for the three Allied Air Forces involved. During a 24-hour period, 1,398 flights delivered a record 13,000 tons of cargo to Berlin. On that day, Fred, one of the youngest American pilots in Berlin, had been able to make five round-trip flights instead of the usual two or three trips. However, even the victorious Parade Day in April did not compare to the euphoric mood that spread across all of West Germany and West Berlin when, shortly after midnight on Thursday, May 12, the barriers for roads, rail, and barge traffic to Berlin were raised. Now supplies began again arriving in Berlin by means other than airplanes for the first time in almost eleven months. Berlin's blockade had ended!

Much earlier on that day, Fred's schedule called for a very early flight between Frankfurt/Main and Berlin. The plane assigned to him had been at the Maintenance Depot in *Oberpfaffenhofen* near Munich, and now was waiting for him at the Rhein-Main Airport in Frankfurt. Even though Fred had slept well the night before, winds and rain made the early flights in darkness often difficult. Actually ALL Berlin inbound night flights through the three Soviet-prescribed corridors were difficult because of the crowded flight schedules. Even on sunny days with clear vision, he sometimes had the impression that there were planes in the air wherever he looked.

Right when his plane was about to touch the dim Tempelhof Airport runway, he could make out ground personnel lined up along the runway, holding up white signs with something scrawled on them. When he opened the passenger door, he was greeted by both enlisted men and civilians happily pointing to their signs: **BLOCKADE ENDS—AIRLIFT WINS.** He was overcome with the surprise and joy of relief, as well as pride. "WOW!" he shouted as he practically leaped from the plane.

Russian saboteurs, summer heat, fall storms and hail, winter ice and snow—the airlift pilots had overcome them all! But this was the ultimate! Life here in Germany really was so much more exciting and fulfilling for Fred than it had been in France or—in Sumner, Iowa, for sure!

On the same day of the blockade removal, however, General Lucius Clay announced that the Berlin Airlift would continue for some months, just in case! General Clay believed the continuation of the airlift would build up sufficient reserves of food and fuel for Berlin to be better prepared for possible future blockades.

With the recent political developments in Germany and especially in Berlin, Fred regretted that he had never studied the German language, which now would have helped him keep informed through German newspapers. The American papers, including the military *Stars and Stripes,* reported a lot about sports, especially in the

163

USA. But of what use was it to know the scores of football or baseball games in Chicago when you had to tackle real-life political crises here in Germany?

For example, no sooner was the Russian blockade lifted when a new crisis struck Berlin on May 21, when the railroad workers went on strike. At first, Fred did not even understand who was striking against whom and why. The Berliners, on the other hand, felt the impact severely, and they knew the reason why.

Back in 1945, the Allied Control Council, unfortunately, had given the Soviets the authority to operate the railroads and the *S-Bahn* (Berlin's elevated commuter train that served the city and the suburbs). Thousands of East and West Berliners worked for these railroads. Those workers living in West Berlin, however, received their salaries in East Marks, when now (only two months after the Currency Reform in March) it took four East Marks to buy <u>one</u> West Mark. But living in West Berlin, the residents had to pay rent and utilities in West Marks. Confusing? Yes! Most of the West Berliners were bewildered and upset by living in a city with two separate, unequal currencies.

Furthermore, since most of the German domestic mail was transported by rail, the strike suddenly prevented all rail traffic from entering and leaving Berlin; thus all mail service was cut off. Even though most Berliners understood and agreed with the railroad strike, or *S-Bahn Strike* as the Berliners called it, it brought even greater hardship to most households.

Fortunately, this strike was soon settled on June 28 with the promise that the strikers would not be punished, and that railroad workers living in West Berlin would receive 60 percent of their wages in West Marks.

Now that all travel was moving again and import/export restrictions between West Berlin and West Germany had been lifted, the Allied Air Force officials announced that the airlift would be terminated in September or October, 1949.

On September 30, the last American C-54 made the run from Frankfurt/Main to Berlin. The British Royal Air Force made their last flight on October 6, bringing a truly important and unique chapter of air transportation strategy to an end.

Shortly after the official end of the blockade, Berlin's magistrate decided to erect an Airlift Memorial in a year or two, which would honor the 31 American and 39 British fliers who had sacrificed their lives in the airlift operation.

If anybody would have asked Fred Harrington to explain the military and civic happenings and implications of the last weeks or months, he would have drawn a blank. What he noticed, however, was that now he, his pilot buddies, and the airport crews were able to lead a more relaxed lifestyle. Most of the pressure he had become so used to was gone.

In recognition of Fred's outstanding flight skills and his untiring commitment during the airlift, he had been promoted to U.S. Air Force Captain, skipping the Lieutenant rankings. He could not deny that this had made him proud and gave him deep satisfaction.

Having a bit more time for himself, Fred looked for stores that offered good English reading material. When he shopped in two such stores at the *Kurfürstan Damm*, he found quite a bit of useful literature. To his surprise, the personnel in both book stores had given him the same hint: *If you want exceptionally good reading stuff, such as classic works by internationally-recognized authors, try the Alexander Platz International Bookstore.*

The *Alexander Platz*? In the heart of the Soviet Sector of Berlin? When he asked some of his buddies what they thought of such a trip to East Berlin, they gave him a puzzled look.

"You mean, you have not done any super-cheap shopping in the East Sector? Good man, get with it!"

"Can I drive there in my American uniform?"

"I don't know if you CAN, but you MAY—and you SHOULD," one of his friends answered. "I can assure you, you'll be much safer in your uniform than taking a chance they mistake you for a West Berlin citizen."

"Why a West Berliner?"

"Because the West Berliners wear better quality clothes. Just look around next time!"

The "next time" came on the following Saturday, when Fred had no flight duties. He and two of his buddies hopped into a Jeep and headed for East Berlin. Without being checked at the sector border, they landed in East Berlin. They knew they had reached the East Sector when they saw the many banners and posters with communist slogans. And they were absolutely sure that they were now in East Berlin when they encountered two gigantic posters declaring, "AMIS – GO HOME!" and "YANKEES – GO HOME!"

Yes, they were in the heart of the former German capital which, though badly bruised by the war, still had an air of its former noted prominence. Instead of driving straight to the bookstore on the *Alexander Platz,* they decided on a quick sightseeing tour. With a city guidebook, they were able to find East Berlin's landmarks. Traveling the famous *Friedrichstrasse,* they saw the Brandenburg Gate, then Hitler's *Reichskanzelei* (Chancellery) and Hitler's infamous bunker. It wasn't that hard to also find City Hall, the State Opera and State Library, Humboldt University, and the Memorial to the Victims of Fascism and Militarism (in pre-war times called the *Helden Ehrenhalle* or Hall of Fame) with its goose-stepping East German military guards.

When their Jeep finally reached the *Alexander Platz,* the square was filled with crowds of people as if a big open-air meeting or perhaps a parade was about to begin. Luckily, they found a parking spot. Then, mingling with the thick crowd, they were eager to find out what was going on.

"S-E-D! S-E-D!" two of the marchers shouted to them in English. Neither Fred nor his buddies knew what that meant. However, they soon saw the large posters:

Sozialistische Einheitspartei Deutschland – unsere Rettung!

They understood: "Socialist Unity Party of Germany – Our Salvation."

Also, *SED – Deutschland's Hoffnung,* which meant, "SED – Germany's Hope."

Now Fred and the other Americans remembered that back in April they had heard about the merger of two German parties into one Unity Party.

"I believe it was the Communist Party swallowing the Socialist Party," Fred's buddy said as he searched his memory of the news.

"Yea, you're right," said Fred. "Even our *Stars & Stripes* reported for three or four days about. As a matter of fact, it's all coming back to me now. I read that of the 16 million East Germans, more than 2 million instantly became SED members."

"I remember that, too," his buddy said, "because it really struck me how strange communist societies are. One article said that 75 percent of all lawyers became SED members almost overnight. Can you imagine that happening in the US?"

"No, absolutely not!" said Fred. "Even in West Germany—I mean in the new *Federal Republic of Germany*—the lawyers would have joined a new party more cautiously."

The pushing, noisy crowd on the Alexander Square was really not the right setting for that kind of conversation. Besides, Fred's buddies had no idea what to say. Therefore, Fred continued, "You guys should remember September 15, because on that day the US State Department officially took over the administration of Germany from the Department of the Army. I remember that date because it's also my father's birthday."

"You sound like it's such a big deal," said one of Fred's buddies, who by now was getting bored of all the political talk.

"Yes, it is a big deal, believe it or not! For you, and me, and thousands of American soldiers—it means that the military reign is over. *Finito!* Finished!"

"Really? Then why didn't we celebrate? Why didn't our government ship us home?"

"Because we Americans are the occupiers, and our duties here are not over."

Just in that moment, three young boys in their new Communist FDJ (*Freie Deutsche Jugend*, or, Free German Youth) uniforms placed themselves in front of Fred's group and shouted, "Ami go home! Go home, Amis!"

That was too much for the rather innocent, young American men, really just there as tourists and unsuccessful shoppers.

"Shut up, you little Nazis! You just changed the brown shirts for blue ones!" said one of the Americans. Apparently the new communists really had been brown-shirted Hitler Youth in the not-so-distant past, because they had no reply and turned to disappear into the crowd.

Realizing that this SED Celebration Parade Day was the wrong day for successful shopping or further sightseeing, Fred and the others turned around and pushed their way back to the Jeep. To their amazement, they saw a fairly large group of civilians standing around the army Jeep.

"Good car!" said one German in English, as his hand admiringly stroked the Jeep.

"America good!" said another.

"You Americans all good. Welcome to Berlin!"

Well, that sounded different than the hateful remarks by the FDJ youngsters. There were smiles all around. As the Americans got into the Jeep, Fred explained in intentionally simplified English, "We came to buy good books. International Bookstore. No open today. Too many people on Alexander Platz."

"Sorry, soldiers, all stores near the Alexander Square are closed today because of the SED rally," said a middle-aged German man.

"Oh, you speak English very well," one of the Americans replied.

"Why should I not? My parents were German diplomats in New York City, where I was born. That made me a US citizen for life." When the man saw the surprised faces of the Americans, he added, "Now I live in Leipzig, Thuringia, in southern East Germany. I am in Berlin on business. By the way, the victoriously fighting American troops should never have turned over Saxony and Thuringia to the Soviets...See you later, perhaps!"

Without any further words, the East German-American turned and joined others heading into the crowd. The soldiers were in good spirits despite the surprises of the day, or perhaps because of them. They decided to drive back to "the American Sector" for now, but they figured that sooner or later they would be back for shopping in East Berlin.

On the way back to their barracks, the Americans stopped at the PX. Actually, they could not think of anything they needed to buy; they just wanted to stroll through the aisles stocked full of all kinds of American goods, available to Western Allied Forces and related personnel only.

"You know, guys," Fred said. "Things didn't work out today at Alexander Square. I have heard that even the Communist

DDR government operated stores are mainly propaganda shops with big hats and no cattle. That means, even in those stores most of the shelves are empty. One of my former East German airport workers told me that in order to buy a good radio, he had to pay a deposit of half the price and then wait six months for delivery. Why don't we plan on a really big shopping trip in West Berlin next weekend?"

"Are you crazy, or are you going soft?" asked his buddy. "Since when do you care about shopping, anyway?"

Fred's other buddy thought the same, though he would not call the newly promoted Air Force Captain crazy. But Fred understood that these guys were not the right partners when it came to shopping. For him, having grown up in a small rural Iowa town, big stores in big cities had a bewildering fascination. Now the cosmopolitan city of Berlin with its 2 million West Berliners beckoned to be explored—and even used for a shopping spree.

A few days later, just when Fred had made up his mind to go shopping on his own, he bumped into Floyd Burke from Detroit, the Air Force soldier who had befriended him in his first days in Berlin. Since they had flown in different squadrons with different flight schedules, they hardly recognized each other after almost one year. Fred was just stepping away from the flight scheduling counter in the Tempelhof US Air Force Administration building when he suddenly faced Lieutenant Burke.

"Say, aren't you the Floyd from Detroit officer, my long-lost, or at least, long-ignored friend?"

"Well, hello, Senior Airman—or Senior Master Sergeant—or Second Lieutenant Harrington! No, hold it! I see your proper title is now Air Force Captain Harrington."

"Come on, you Lieutenant Mobster from Detroit!" laughed Fred, throwing his arm around his friend's shoulder as they walked. "Fred and Floyd seem to be the more appropriate titles for us two."

"So be it, Fred," said Floyd.

Even though both were in a hurry, they quickly exchanged as much information as needed to catch up on the news about each other.

"Listen, Floyd! Are you free on Saturday?"

"Yes, I am. Why? What's up?"

"I want to go on a shopping spree. Would be fun to have you along."

"Where are you going? East Berlin?"

"No, not this time. I was there with some guys a few days ago. It was a fiasco. We saw some of the city, but when it came to shopping at the *Alexander Platz* – nothing. All stores were closed. Besides the SED crowd was so thick, we could hardly move."

"What's the SED crowd?"

"Oh, you know, the new communist party that goes by the fancy name of *Socialist Unity Party of Germany*—the real fanatic commies."

"And the SED guys kept you from shopping?"

"You better believe it! There were several thousand of them. Many in uniforms, like the *Junge Pioniere,* the *FDJ* , et cetera, et cetera. Young and old. Hot and cold. They were celebrating their SED's birthday, while making it miserable for all other people in Alex Square."

"So, where would we go this Saturday, if you really want me to come along?"

"I thought we'd roam around West Berlin and have some strong German coffee and cakes and cookies."

"Stop right there, friend! If we can go to a good German bakery, I'm in!"

"Then it's a deal. I'll pick you up Saturday, oh-eight hundred."

Chapter 18

Long ago, Heidi Anleger had given up on counting the days she had been working as a *Trümmerfrau* (rubble-clearing woman). At the end of the war in May, 1945, life had been hell for her and thousands of Berliners, especially for women and girls. When a whole pack of Russian soldiers had gang-raped her on May 1, she thought her life had come to an end. Half-naked and crusted with blood and dirt, she had grabbed a few of her torn clothes and run away. In her panic, she took no time to linger over her beaten-up, unconscious brother—he looked dead to her. She only had the instinct to run, to get away from this horrible scene.

She ran, but had no idea where to run to, what to look for, or whom to ask for help.

Her life of 17 years seemed over. She stopped for a moment to catch her breath, then everything around her blurred into blackness and she knew she was dying. In one of the side streets of Neukölln, she collapsed, forming a little bundle of misery on the sidewalk. Many hours later she woke up, or at least her eyes opened. Her brain still did not function enough to register where she was, why she was in terrible pain, or, even, her name.

She noticed that people were coming and going, talking, asking her questions, but she had no strength to respond. "She is in shock," she heard a woman say.

"Perhaps she'll never regain consciousness," another female voice reached her ears. Then Heidi saw the shapes of the bystanders swirl around. She closed her eyes as she was pulled under, into a sea of molasses. In her half-conscious state she felt as if she were being pulled under deeper and deeper. When she hit the bottom of the molasses sea, she imagined her body breaking into hundreds of splinters.

That was also the moment when she suddenly gained full consciousness. Seeing everything around her clearly, she pushed her hands into the pavement to push herself up, but her muscles gave out on her. She moaned, then managed a soft cry, "Help me…"

"We are trying to help you, *fräulein*," said a woman wearing a blue head scarf, "but you must give us your name and address, so that we can take you home."

Heidi asked herself the questions, but no answers came to her. *Home? Address?*

"Hey, old man!" the woman with Heidi called out to an old man pushing a wheelbarrow.

"What do you want? I am on my way home after a hard day."

"I'm glad you have a home to go to. But look at this poor, bloody girl! All I want is your wheelbarrow for a little while—and if you have a Christian heart—to help me load up this girl and carry her to the Red Cross station."

"Red Cross station, here? I don't know of such a station around here. Why don't we take her to a hospital?"

"To what? Even old people like you must know that the war has not left a single working hospital in all of Neukölln, or the neighboring districts."

The man cleared his throat, spit into the palms of his hands and said, *"Schon gut. Schon gut!* Let's get her loaded up—and then you show me the Red Cross station!"

Heidi had been quietly listening to the conversation of her *Good Samaritans*. But when they reached to pick her up, she shrunk back and cried, "Nein!" Her entire body ached painfully. And, she never wanted to be touched by a man again.

"Come on, little blond angel," said the woman, leaning down so that her black bangs beneath the blue scarf fell over her right eye. "You have nothing to fear from us. Since you probably have no home anymore, we'll take you to the field hospital—if it survived the last Russian shelling." Now the old man came alive. He hit his forehead with his open hand.

"How could I forget? Our troops made a *Feld Lazarett* out of the school not far from here." Ignoring Heidi's shrieks of protest as she tried to fend them off unsuccessfully, they finally had the "patient" in the wheelbarrow.

"Let's roll!"

"Ja, let's roll!"

After 15 or 20 minutes of hard pushing and balancing the heavy, shaky wheelbarrow, they reached the badly damaged school, which did not even look like a building any longer. The steel-framed door was bullet riddled and had been partially ripped off its hinges. They tried to move the door in order to get inside. But inside, there was nothing but meter-high rubble and stinking debris.

"Oh!" said the woman, out of breath.

"Nothing!" echoed the man, wiping sweat from his forehead. But when he let go of the wheelbarrow he saw on the other side of the street a hand-painted wooden sign: *Not-Arzt – Bunker Hotel* (Emergency Doctor – Bunker Hotel).

"Do you see that, partner? Let's push her across the street! Perhaps she can get help there."

They made their way across and stared at the totally destroyed house. Beneath the sign was a four-foot-wide opening with a staircase leading downstairs. Carefully, they lifted the still struggling Heidi out of the wheelbarrow. To their amazement, they saw that some strength had come back into her body. Leaving the wheelbarrow outside, the three cautiously made their way down the slippery steps of the former air-raid shelter. When they reached the basement, suddenly a door opened and a surprised but smiling elderly man, dressed in a no-longer white coat, greeted them.

"Welcome to the Bunker Hotel! I am Doctor Horst Hamburg!" That is all Heidi heard before she blacked out, falling forward into the arms of the doctor.

Heidi never found out the name of the helpful woman with the blue scarf, or of the old man with the wheelbarrow. But she had found shelter and care for her broken body and spirit. Doctor Hamburg had given her a thorough examination. His diagnosis was that Heidi had been in such a fragile state from practically starving for so long, the painful shock of the brutal rape had pushed her over the edge.

After a few months of relative safety in the bunker, with two meals a day, Heidi regained most of her former strength, and even a bit of her beautiful smile. It bothered her, though, that she was living solely at the mercy of Dr. Hamburg's generosity.

"How can I expect you to keep treating me, even feeding me, while I cannot pay you and can't even be useful?" she asked him many times.

"Don't worry!" he always said. "God takes care of you and the other 24 bunker dwellers. In spite of the misery of the war, there are still lots of people around who help us survive. You all will continue to have food and clothing, even though sometimes it's thanks to the black market."

"But for how long? I want to stay…I feel safe here. But I want to at least help out."

"Listen to me, my child. First of all, I wish you would eat more and gain your strength back faster. Second, I was a rich doctor until I was drafted into the army. Now, I have learned how to survive in a place like this, with only bare essentials. All I have left is my gift for healing people, and people to heal. You are not a burden; in fact it is good for me to see you becoming well."

"Surely you were a well-respected doctor in the army, too. How did you end up here?"

The doctor motioned for Heidi to sit down, and he began to tell her his story. "My wife and three children were killed in the air-raids that wiped out Dresden in February of 1945—like you, I felt like my life had come to an end. For unknown reasons, the army discharged me one week after the Allied attacks on Dresden. But I had nowhere to go. The bodies of my wife and children, who had sought safety in a public shelter, had not been recovered. My big medical practice in Dresden's city center had been blown to bits during the bombing. You probably have heard that even our former Nazi government admitted that during those two nights, 12,000 buildings and houses were destroyed. Nobody will ever know how many civilians lost their lives, since the city of 650,000 citizens was overflowing at the time with more than a million refugees who had fled the onslaught of the Red Army in Eastern Europe. I firmly believe that more than 200,000 people were killed in 48 hours; most of them were women and children.

"In order to survive, I hitchhiked to Berlin, where hundreds of injured people were in desperate need of medical help. A former medical student buddy of mine hired me as assistant. One day, he just disappeared. As you well know, no one is really safe. Well, after some time, I ended up here, where I became the self-appointed *Boss of the Bunker Hotel*."

"My three brothers and my mother were also killed during the war," Heidi now dared to interrupt her doctor. "I still don't know the whereabouts of my father, who disappeared or was arrested at the end of 1943. And just a few months ago I lost my youngest brother."

"What do you mean by *lost*?"

"When the drunk Russian soldiers attacked me, my brother tried to defend me. I am not sure, but I think the soldiers bludgeoned him to death."

179

While Dr. Hamburg and Heidi fell into a long silence, Heidi suddenly started shaking uncontrollably. Then she looked at her benefactor and spoke quickly, "I am Heidi Anleger. I am Heidi Anleger! I was born in 1928 in Berlin. My parents were Karl and Gertrud Anleger!"

Dr. Hamburg looked at Heidi in utter amazement, but he knew what was happening. Her memory was suddenly flooding back like a tidal wave. He wanted to encourage this astonishing process, and asked, "And where did your family live in Berlin?" However, Heidi did not pay attention to his question. She was too busy welcoming her returning memory. As if in a trance, she continued with her family tree.

"I have—I mean, I had—four brothers: Hans, Kurt, Waldemar and Norbert. *O ja,* we lived at the *Weise Strasse* in Berlin-Neukölln."

The next few weeks were exceptional in the lives of Heidi and Dr. Hamburg. Heidi was back to life. Each day was another victory for her care-giving doctor, and especially for his special patient. With determination, Heidi hunted her thoughts and memories for clues and images from her past, trying desperately to put together the pieces of her life puzzle. Now she even remembered the tensions she had created for her family with her blind faith in Adolf Hitler and all the Nazi leaders.

She also remembered that as a 17-year-old teenager, she was obligated to work for free one day each week as a *Trümmerfrau* in her district (Neukölln) or somewhere else in Berlin. There was a seemingly endless amount of rubble to be cleared. But then she recalled that at the age of 15 she had become a middle-ranking leader in the BDM—*Bund Deutscher*

Mädchen, or, Union of German Girls—which, in the eyes of the Allied occupiers, made her a citizen with special Nazi connections. That meant she would have to work one year long without pay, six days a week as a *Trümmerfrau.*

She learned this when she registered her existence, as required, with the German city officials. "Miss Anleger, you will be working as a *Trümmerfrau* six days a week for one year. You understand that you will receive no pay for your work. Frankly, I wish I could sentence you to four years of free labor, which would be a more fitting treatment for Nazi lovers."

"If I don't get paid for my work, how am I going to exist? How can I buy groceries or clothing?"

"You should have thought of that, when you fell in love with your damned Adolf Hitler!"

Over the weeks, things fell into place, though. For example, the hard, rough labor required the wearing of protective gloves, but how would she get them, when she had no money? On one especially bad, cold day, when her hands were chafed and bleeding, one of her older coworkers took off her gloves and handed them to Heidi.

"Here, take these, you fool! Without gloves you could get blood poisoning!"

"What about you?"

"*Ach Quatsch!* [Dear me!] I am so old...see all these wrinkles? They make my skin tough. They will keep my blood from getting poisoned."

"Is that true, medically?"

"I don't know. But it helps when I tell myself that."

While both women were laughing, the older woman continued, "Don't worry about me, kid! I have another pair at home which I knitted myself and have been saving for better days—if they ever come!"

One year of hard labor was a long time, especially during the cold winter months.

Just when Heidi thought she could not take it any longer, she was offered the pitiful wage of one German Mark per hour. Measly as that was, it surely was better than nothing. She thought of buying gloves for the kind woman who had once had helped her, but rumor had it that she had died in her unheated apartment during a freezing cold January night.

Since the collapse of the German *Reich* had prevented Heidi from completing her high school education, she was not able to land a better job than working as an unskilled *Trümmerfrau*. In the fall of 1946, her salary had increased enough that she could afford to move from the Bunker Hotel to a bomb-damaged, but livable, apartment, which she shared with three young women.

When the frigid winter days made outdoor labor even more miserable, Heidi was glad of her job as a *Trümmerfrau* because that gave her a chance to find wood scraps in the ruins. At least she did not have to suffer ice-cold nights in an apartment with no heat as many other citizens in Berlin had to endure.

Still, after working for almost two years at the neck-breaking job, Heidi began looking seriously for an indoor job—anything to be out of the snow, rain, wind and hot sun.

Since she had never learned to type, she did not qualify for a secretarial job. But how about going into sales? At work she had been told that with her gift of persuasion she would be able to sell ice to people in Alaska. Chipping away at a small piece of ice-covered lumber, her found treasure of the day, she was reminded of her coworker's remark. Perhaps there was some truth to what they had seen in her.

One day in the fall of 1947, she put on her finest dress (actually her *only* dress), got her blond, unruly hair in order, put some coins in her wallet and took the *U-Bahn* to the *Schloss Strasse* in Berlin-Steglitz. Maybe she would be lucky in her job search if she started at the top of the line, like the famous Wertheim Department Store. As a young girl, she had been in this department store which the Nazis had confiscated as Jewish property and renamed AWAG. She had not given a thought or care about the store's history at the time; all she wanted then was to enjoy the grand Christmas decorations and lights.

Now she was back after many years, sadly discovering how badly the war had mutilated this once-magnificent store. A big banner proclaimed the original Jewish name again, WERTHEIM DEPARTMENT STORE. Giving herself a push in the right direction, she entered and asked her way to the Personnel Department. For the young woman coming out of "hell" not long before, it felt like she was entering the anteroom of heaven.

Heidi used her conversational skills to breeze through the job interview. She complemented the office décor, the store's excellent reputation, and the interviewer's smart attire. She politely answered all the standard questions. Yes, she was only 19 years old. No, she had never been a sales girl. Yes, she spoke English rather well. Yes, she was interested in a permanent employment—the longer, the better.

"When can you start?"

Heidi had not anticipated such a speedy employment offer.

"Well, I was thinking ...I mean...I could start next week." What had she to lose by giving up her crummy job as a *Trümmerfrau*? Nothing, absolutely nothing.

When Heidi was back on the street again, she neither sang nor danced for joy. Her eyes were searching for a special store. *Aha*, there! Without hesitation she directed her flimsy old sandals to cross the street where she stepped into the Salamander Shoe Store, a shop quite famous pre-war. Before a salesperson could address her, she rummaged in her bag, hoping to find the Ration Card coupon for shoes. Here it was! She quickly handed it to the approaching clerk.

"I want a nice pair of shoes. Here is my shoe coupon. But wait! First I have to get rid of these awful sandals." It took Heidi only seconds to slip out of her straw-soled sandals. As she was holding them in her hand, not knowing what to do with them, the saleswoman said, "Throw them as far as you can! The days for these ridiculous straw monsters are over—at least for you."

Heidi was warmed by the clerk's understanding smile, and noted how the woman had so quickly become her ally, sharing a victorious moment. This was exactly the kind of salesperson Heidi hoped to become.

Chapter 19

Some anonymous person had placed a translated article, clipped from the Canadian newspaper, *Spectrum*, on Kotikov's desk. In contrast to his big boss, General Vassily Sokolovsky, who was fluent in English and even knew some German, Major General A.G.Kotikov, the Commander of the Soviet troops in East Berlin, spoke only Russian. He enjoyed this kind of anonymity which did not expose his limited linguistic skills. The translated headline read: "The Human Cost of War." Underneath, in smaller print: "Estimated military and civilian deaths in the Second World War."

Twenty participating nations were listed. Brazil had the lowest number of military losses with 943. Canada listed 42,042 military deaths and no civilian casualties. The United States had 292,131 military and 6,000 civilian deaths. Germany was second highest, with 3,500,000 military and 780,000 civilians killed. The Soviet Union took the first place with 11,000,000 soldiers and 7,000,000 civilian deaths.

Reviewing the statistics made Kotikov slump deeper into his upholstered arm chair. For him, the Soviet statistics instantly turned from facts on paper into faces of friends and relatives whom he had lost in the war. And now in peacetime, he had been involved in making life miserable for millions of West German and West Berliners. What was it all about? Revenge? Hunger to annex more land for the already-largest nation in the world? Kotikov came from a huge country that had been dealing with internal problems since the Bolshevik Revolution in 1917. After the First World War of 1914–1918, the war that supposedly was to have ended the future of all war, the Second World War of 1939–1945 had been much more brutal and fatal than any before. Had his generation not learned from the horrific First World War? Did there always have to be strife and bloodshed?

Looking again at the statistical chart on his desk, which listed the combined total of 19,406,970 military and 17,346,614 civilian deaths, the Major General had to fight back chills. Yes, the defeat of war-happy, expansionist Germany had been a victory for the world, as was the overthrow of the militaristic Japanese regime. But with more than 36 million people being killed within six years, why was there no hope for peace, friendship and understanding among the nations now?

Overcome by cold shivers again, Kotikov climbed out of his chair and looked for something helpful to fight his oncoming depression. When he found a bottle of vodka, he knew from experience that even this would not help him very much. Still, he reached for it and drank one, and then another shot glass full.

When his phone rang, he was glad that the call saved him from drinking more. He was just not happy to hear the particular voice on the other end of the line. It was Sergey Svertlov!

"Yes, Lieutenant Svertlov, what is it this time?"

"Major General, forgive me for interrupting your important work. However, I need to inform you about a very pressing matter."

"And what would that be? I hope you will not report again that you still have not been able to arrest that young German idiot."

"Sorry, Comrade Kotikov, unfortunately it *is* about that damned German boy again."

Kotikov jumped to his feet, almost dropping the phone receiver. He caught it in midair and now used it like a hammer, as he let Svertlov have it.

"Listen, you genius! As long as you have to call this kid 'that German boy' because you still don't know his name, I don't want to hear anything else about him. Is that understood?"

Met only by silence, the general again barked, "Is that understood?"

"Yes, Major General Kotikov, I understand. But—"

"No 'buts'!"

"I do hear, and I will obey your order, comrade. It is just that this matter does not allow any delay."

"You are joking, Svertlov, are you not? How long has your failed search for this criminal youngster delayed other more important duties? Must I remind you of your Central Asian relative, Chukov, who allegedly saw him on the autobahn, and with his soldier friends shot at him?"

"I apologize again, Commandant Kotikov," Svertlov responded after another painful silence. "You are right, Anatoly

Chukov is my cousin, and you remember correctly that this dutiful soldier opened fire on the German kid—and it appears that he and his platoon failed to kill him. That is the reason, among other reasons, that I need to talk to you."

Today, however, Major General Kotikov was not in the mood for changing his mind. He had ordered Svertlov not to report anything about the maddeningly elusive German youngster until at least he knew his name. That was it! Without another word, he disconnected the telephone line.

After another vodka, Kotikov slowly eased into a better mood. He thought of the blockade of West Berlin, which in 1948 he had so skillfully orchestrated. He also remembered how much he had appreciated Sergey Svertlov's zeal and efforts to totally isolate the 2.5 million West Berliners. Secretly he had hoped that after 30 days, the West Berliners would not hold up.

Then West Berlin would have been ready for a Soviet takeover, like an over-ripe apple.

Who could have imagined that American and British planes, leaving every few minutes from nine different West German airfields, would deliver sufficient coal, food and medical supplies to sustain the West Berliners indefinitely, or at least until May of 1949? Kotikov just could not understand why the Western Allies kept their former German enemies alive, while his Soviets tried to strangle them.

What really made the Major General livid was what he had observed daily: the West Berliners could not do enough to show their grateful friendship with the Americans, while they had an unyielding disdain for the Russians. Kotikov was proud of how he had managed to cut off most of the life support for the West Berliners. They, however, always found new ways to keep going. And these crazy Americans never stopped helping them.

The general recalled the time he had been informed about how electricity was being shared. While he had successfully cut off all utilities running from East to West, the Germans agreed to a rationing scheme which allotted energy supplies to vital industries first. West Berlin citizens would receive only one or two hours of electricity daily, usually at night. So what did West Berliners do? Each family would leave a single switch turned on in the evening. Then, when the light bulb lit up, they would quickly do whatever had to be done. For instance, one family might use their one hour of electricity to boil potatoes for several households, while a neighbor cooked carrots or string beans for themselves and others.

In May, 1949, even Generalissimo Joseph Stalin had to admit that the Berlin Blockade had been a Cold War fiasco, because the Western forces had thrown in their lot with the Germans, and their unique and massive airlift had made all Russian blockade plans *kaput*.

After the end of the blockade in May, and the termination of the airlift in September, 1949, Kotikov arranged for Soviet agents to continuously disrupt the City Assembly at City Hall, which eventually led to the formation of two governments in Berlin.

Then, thanks in part to the Marshall Plan aid, the unexpected but most welcome economic progress started in West Germany and West Berlin. Once again, shoppers and tourists crowded West Berlin's refurbished boulevard, the

Kurfürsten Damm. East Berlin, on the other hand, where Kotikov's Soviet "brothers" and agents had stripped most of the manufacturing equipment and raw products, lagged pitifully behind.

General Kotikov had to admit that something in Moscow's planning for Germany had gone wrong. Still, as Commander of the Soviet troops, he had kept the propaganda machine running, telling the world how great life in East Germany was. Nevertheless, most embarrassing and humiliating to the East German (DDR) regime was the unrelenting exodus of East German citizens to the West via West Berlin. Most of those who tried to relocate from the Communist workers' paradise to the West were young and well-educated. Up to 1949 and 1950, the "fleeing trip" was neither expensive nor dangerous. Residents from Magdeburg or Potsdam merely had to take a train to East Berlin, then take the *U-Bahn* (subway) to West Berlin. There they would make their way to the Berlin-Marienfelde Refugee Center, where they received food, temporary shelter, and if they were lucky, a free airline ticket from Tempelhof Airport to the destination of their choice in the Free World, often Munich, Frankfurt, Hamburg, Paris or London. Or, once they were in East Berlin, they could simply walk into one of the three West sectors, as long as they did not carry too much luggage with them, which would have looked suspicious.

The loyal Commander knew that something drastic had to be done to stop the west-bound "youth drain" and "brain drain." He took a Din A-4 paper sheet and wrote in big letters:

1. Find a way to stop the East-West Exodus!

2. Grant East German Government to find more effective methods to cut off west-bound brain drain!

3. Enlarge *Volks-Polizei* troops, in order to make them more effective in stopping the East-West escapes!

4. Use all available media resources to proclaim that West Germany is the driving factor behind the East-West land flight.

5. Insist on support from highest ranking military and civilian Soviets to make the German Democratic Republic an attractive and inviting country.

6. Discontinue all press exchanges between East and West Germany— No exception!

Kotikov looked at his declarations. Why had not such guidelines been drawn up by anyone before? And why had he not thought to write such an impressive, assertive document before? Well, things would change from now on.

Chapter 20

Heidi loved her job at the Wertheim Department Store on the *Schloss Strasse* in the American Sector. Two years had passed since she had been accepted to work as a salesgirl. During West Berlin's blockade and airlift, there were days when she feared she would be fired. Often, too often, the store had no customers in the morning hours. Then, Wertheim closed at five in the afternoon to avoid the risk of a suddenly dark department store full of customers, a likely event because of the frequent power outages.

Heidi's exemplary dependability had not only kept her employed, but she had been promoted twice. Now, while she was still occasionally selling on the floor, most of the days she spent at the sales office or in the purchasing department. On difficult, gray days, when things were rather dim at Wertheim's, she only had to think back on her days as a penniless *Trümmerfrau*, and her mood would change for the better.

Back in fall of 1948 during the airlift, she suddenly had remembered the address of her Uncle Theo and Aunt Hanna. The long process of memory recovery brought new surprises almost daily. One week later, she knocked at the apartment door at *Hermann Strasse* 245. Both her aunt and her uncle gave her a very warm welcome. Over a cup of *Ersatzkaffee* (coffee substitute), they had told stories from the past which helped Heidi fill in more childhood memories, and they caught one another up on current experiences.

"Do you know if Norbi is alive?" Heidi asked her relatives, which made Theo and Hanna exchange strange looks. Could it be that Heidi had not seen her brother since that fateful first day of May in 1945?

"Well?" pursued Heidi when the couple just looked at one another without answering. "Tell me, I must know. Did he die on that day, when the Russian soldiers knocked him down?"

"No, Heidi, Norbert is very much alive. For a few months, he even lived here with us, until he started working for the American Air Force."

"Norbi worked for the Americans? But he is German!"

"Yes, he is, and always will be German," said Theo. "However, because of his superb English, he was hired as an interpreter for a captain in the United States Air Force. I think his name is Kalamity or Kalium or ..."

"Kalamai Giftos," Aunt Hanna helped out. "His family is from Greece."

"Kalamai Giftos? I can remember that name," Heidi said. "All I have to do is think of the author, Karl May, as a *gift* to the German youth."

"Hey, wait a minute, Heidi! Karl May is read not only by the young, but by old German boys like me. Almost all I know about America I learned from his books. The funny thing is that Karl May himself visited America only once in 1908 after he had written most of his 70 books about America's Old West and other regions."

Heidi shook her head and smiled. "I can't believe that I just found out that Norbi is alive, and now we are talking about Karl May, the famous author who died back in 1912, I believe. But I have to admit, that even I, a girl, enjoyed reading a number of his 'Old Shatterhand' books."

"He is still a topic of conversation. Our *Neuköllner Tageblatt* reported a few months ago that Karl May's books have been translated into more than 40 languages. Among his avid readers were such famous men as Albert Einstein and Albert Schweitzer. The article said that even though he is known to all Germans and his books have outsold all other German authors, he remains virtually unknown to the English-speaking world."

"Well, if my brother is an interpreter now, he might change America by translating Karl May's books for millions of English-speaking readers," said Heidi.

"Well said! And may the Great Spirit of Manitou rest upon Norbert and us all!"

Since then, Heidi had visited her uncle and aunt several times, always hoping that one day she might run into Norbert. It never happened, though.

"I wish I could call Norbi," Heidi sighed one day. "To be cut off from him in the same city is enough to drive me crazy."

"Well, we have no telephone," replied Uncle Theo. "But why don't you try a public phone booth?"

Heidi had to smile. This was 1949. Had her relatives never heard of the American Military Fraternization Law, which prohibited personal phone calls between German citizens and Western Allied military members? At first she wanted to explain to her otherwise very intelligent uncle how difficult it was, for example, at Wertheim's Department Store when an American military customer would say to a salesgirl, "Why don't you call me when the item I am interested in has arrived?" Even if the soldier would have given his phone number to the clerk, the switchboard would not have made the connection out of fear that this might be a "personal call." But then Heidi changed her mind. Why bother her lovely relatives with explaining a law that she did not understand herself! One day she would meet her brother. For now she was just grateful to know he was alive and that they lived in the same city, both in the American Sector.

What neither Uncle Theo nor Heidi knew was that Norbert Anleger's interpreter job with the US Air Force had come to an end on September 15, 1949, when the US State Department had taken over the administration of Germany from the Department of the Army. On that day, most of the military government offices and personnel were transferred from Berlin to Frankfurt-Main, with reduced responsibilities and staff. Norbert had received a *Certificate of Honorable Discharge*, normally given to military members only. But since he always wore an Air Force leather jacket and acted like an dedicated American, his superiors had decided to honor his service that way, even though they had to bend the military etiquette slightly.

Now that Norbert was unemployed, he applied for studies at the *Freie Universität Berlin,* which had opened in December of 1948, financed mainly by the Marshall Plan. To his disappointment, he was not accepted as a student. The reasons given were, first, his young age of not quite 18 years, and second, serious gaps in his educational background.

On the same day he received the rejection, he registered for evening courses at the popular *Volkshochschule* (People's High School), which had a flexible curriculum. Norbert took courses English, French, Political Science, and General Civic Administration & Law. He was convinced that Germany, with its American, British and French military administrators, would always be in need of properly trained interpreters and certainly English teachers whose English perhaps did not have such a strong American twang as he had picked up while working with the US Air Force.

Chapter 21

Fred Harrington picked up his buddy, Floyd, as promised, at the entrance to his barracks compound. When they greeted each other, Fred asked, "How's that for punctuality? We said let's meet at oh-eight hundred, and here I am."

"Good!" said Floyd. "But what do you do on a Saturday morning in a big city, where not everybody speaks English?"

"Cheer up, you jerk!" said Fred, with a big smile. "This is Berlin, not Detroit, or Sumner, Iowa. As badly as this city was destroyed during the war, four years later it is on the move 24/7. You don't even have to hire an expensive taxi for your city tour. I'll be your chauffeur, and the Jeep comes with compliments of Uncle Sam."

It did not take long for Fred to detect that Floyd had seen very little of Berlin to this point. Right away he decided to expand their original shopping spree to include some sightseeing in all three Western Sectors. The grown-up boy from Sumner, Iowa, was about to become a master of tourism.

Starting out from "Fort Dahlem," the American soldiers' nickname for their Air Force compound in Berlin-Dahlem, they traveled through the Grunewald Forest. At the *Teufelsberg* (Devil's Hill), they got out of the Jeep and jogged to the top. They had thought of Berlin as a gray, jungle-asphalt city—very bomb-damaged from the war, with neither grass nor trees. Now, standing on the *Teufelsberg,* overlooking the huge Grunewald and the Havel River, they discovered how wrong they had been. Somehow surviving the destruction of the war, this still looked like a piece of paradise.

Then they drove north to the Olympic Stadium where the games had been held in 1936.

The British Military Headquarters was close by, even though there was not much interesting to see. Driving west, they briefly visited the infamous Spandau Prison, where many top Nazi leaders had been imprisoned.

They maneuvered their Jeep south and turned east at the *Bismarck Strasse*, which took them to the *Siegesseule* (Victory Column), a memorial of an ancient German victory over the French. A few kilometers further east, they came to the bombed-out *Reichstag,* where the Russian troops had hoisted the Soviet flag of victory over Germany in 1945 at the end of the European part of World War II.

Leaving their Jeep parked in the American Sector, they walked the *Unter den Linden Strasse* and examined the historic *Brandenburger Tor* (Brandenburg Gate), a well-known landmark in Berlin. For a few minutes they visited City Hall, which had become a communist propaganda piece for East Berlin.

"Hey, Fred, across the street is Humboldt University," Floyd said. "Let's go there, too."

"Why? You feel like studying German with a communist twist?"

"No, Fred, we have no time for that! But believe it or not, my grandfather traveled all the way from the USA to Berlin when he was a young man, just to study at the Humboldt *Uni*. It's pretty famous, don't you know?"

"Yes, well, now it's in the Soviet sector, and it has a *much* different current claim to fame which started last year when the communists began ousting professors and students who did not conform to their ideology."

"Right! Now I remember that in 1948, the US helped West Berlin open the *Freie Universität Berlin,* located very close to the US Military Headquarters in Berlin-Zehlendorf of Dahlem. I've been there."

"You never stop amazing me, Floyd. How did you get there?"

"Walked. The new university is housed around a nucleus of buildings formerly belonging to the *Kaiser Wilhelm Akademie.* Really, it is a fairly short walk from our compound to the *Freie Universität.* How come you haven't been there yet, Fred?"

"I have been a little busy flying stuff from West Germany to the West Berliners, so that they could live another day to study."

"Touché!"

After visiting the drab, badly war-damaged and poorly repaired Humboldt University, Fred convinced Floyd to also take a look at the Dom close by (the entrance doors were locked anyway), and to walk "just a little bit further" to the *Alexander Platz.*

"Isn't that the square where you and your buddies got chased away a few days or weeks ago?" asked Floyd.

"Well, if you want to call our giving up on shopping at the overcrowded Alexander Square 'being chased away,' so be it!" After they had walked a bit more, Floyd took up the conversation again.

"Fred, for a guy used to flying most of the time, I think I have walked enough this morning. Besides, didn't we originally want to do some shopping, too?"

"I didn't say it, but I hoped we would find some time to check out what West Berlin's department stores have to offer."

"Good! Let's go! I mean, let's drive, if our Jeep is still where we left it parked illegally."

It took Fred and Floyd almost half an hour to walk back to the Jeep, and as much time to cruise through *Schöneberg* and *Friedenau,* until they came to a big intersection where *Rhein Strasse* merges with *Birkbusch Strasse* and flows into *Schloss Strasse,* not far from Berlin's Botanical Garden. There was their destination! Big black letters on an even bigger banner advertised: "WERTHEIM WARENHAUS BERLIN – *the Store for Young and Old, Men and Women, Rich and Poor—We sell what you want and need!"* Hopefully this store did not close on Saturday at noon, as most of the smaller shops did. They quickly parked their Jeep and walked to the entrance, relieved to find the store was open, after all.

Once inside, they slowed down enough to notice they were hungry, tired, and perhaps even a bit disoriented—at least they did not know what to look for. During all the morning hours they had been together, they had not discussed what they might buy. Suddenly a blond, blue-eyed, angel-like young woman caught sight of them and approached them with measured steps. Both men were stunned, not knowing who should address whom.

"Welcome to Wertheim's, gentlemen! May I be of assistance to you?"

The angel's almost perfect English confused them even more, even though she spoke the typical King's English taught in German high schools. To bridge the silence, she asked again with a sweet voice that made the Americans' hearts melt.

"Gentlemen, what are you looking for?"

"You!" both Air Force men answered simultaneously, as if they had rehearsed it. That broke the ice, and all three broke into laughter. When the laughter dwindled, they looked at each other in poorly-disguised embarrassment.

"I see on your ID badge that your name is Heidi Anleger and that you are the manager," Fred said, taking the lead. "My friend here is Lieutenant Floyd Burke, and I am Captain Fred Harrington." Well, that sounded a bit more fitting.

"Now that we know each other a bit better," said Heidi, "I still don't know what items I can show you. Just so that you two know, I am not for sale," Heidi said, smiling. Floyd glanced around the store as Fred continued the friendly banter, and was glad to see no other customers in their vicinity. The three continued the light-hearted chit-chat for several minutes.

Fred finally caught himself and asked, "Does your department store have a restaurant? Floyd and I have not eaten since really early this morning."

"I am so sorry that our store cannot help you with your hunger. Before the bloody war, when Wertheim operated under a different name and management, there was a large restaurant on the top floor. But now we have to be happy that at least most of the store has been rebuilt."

Both Americans smiled and wondered how this German, even though trained in the King's English, could make them feel so relaxed and happier than they had felt in a very long time. However, just talking would not get them anywhere. The fact remained that in spite all pleasantries, Fred and Floyd were very hungry.

"Look, Miss Heidi—may I call you that?" asked Fred.

"Just 'Heidi' is fine."

"Okay, Heidi! We really don't need anything in particular here. Perhaps we are only wasting your time—sorry. But, I just had a great idea. It is now two hours before closing time. Why don't we come back then— if by then we have not starved to death. All joking aside! Miss Heidi, we would be honored if you would join us for a nice evening meal. No strings attached. Is that a deal?"

"And where would you take me, if I may ask? I must first make sure that I have enough ration coupons, if we go to a restaurant."

"Oh, that will not be necessary! We know of a lovely restaurant in the Grunewald operated by the American military. Since most of its guests are non-Germans, no ration cards are required."

"You're sure that will be alright?" asked Heidi. "Will I not be kicked out? After all, I am German."

"Would anybody dare to kick out such a lovely person as you?" Floyd asked in honest surprise.

"You have no idea how much some of us Germans have been kicked around," said Heidi, shaking off a cold shiver. Nobody picked up the thought, instead agreeing to meet outside the store entrance at ten minutes past five.

"We'll be there, Miss Heidi— unless we get stuck in traffic," said Fred.

Later, as the American boys tried to kill two hours, Floyd asked Fred, "Why did you say, *unless we get stuck in traffic?* This is not Detroit with its lousy rush-hour traffic."

"I know, but this is Germany, where punctuality is like a sacred cow. I just wanted to be on the safe side. You never know!"

Very few people traveled by car (most took the *U-Bahn* or *S-Bahn* or streetcar) and so Fred and Floyd did not get stuck in traffic. Two minutes after five, they stood in front of the large entrance doors of Wertheim's. At precisely ten after five, a blonde angel appeared at the door. It had worked! Their plan was in motion. They were together. And close-by was the faithful Jeep. Heidi looked absolutely stunning, even after a long work day. Fred wanted to comment on her beauty, but then he thought better of it. He had to focus on driving. He chose the *Grunewald Strasse*, which became *Königin Luise Strasse* as they got closer to the Grunewald Forest. A small one-way path took them right to the *Jagdschloss Grunewald.*

"Oh, I have been here before!" Heidi said, pleasantly surprised. "With my schoolmates, quite a few years ago. Before and during the war, this used to be a museum and the residence of the Chief Forester."

"Yes," said Fred with a big smile, "and then the Americans came and turned it into a restaurant. We Americans know more about food than art."

Soon Heidi discovered the truth of Fred's statement. She was 21 years old and still hardly knew how to order from a menu. After all, ten of her years had been about nothing but surviving the war, both during and after. She could not remember when she had ever sat in a fancy restaurant or ordered exotic food. Reading the food item prices, she realized she did not even know how to pay for her meal, should the Americans not treat her.

"Excuse me, Miss Heidi," said Fred. "You look so worried. Please relax!"

As if he had read her mind, he added, "Please get whatever you like, and remember, you are our guest—we'll take care of the check, which will be paid in American dollars."

This was the first time Heidi had heard somebody use the word "check" when it had nothing to do with being stopped at the East German border or at a *razzia* roundup in East Berlin. And she thought she knew English well!

Apparently she did know it well enough to thoroughly enjoy the dinner conversation. They all agreed the food was excellent. They also drank Coca-Cola with the meal, which she loved!

Was it really true that she had accepted the dinner invitation from two American soldiers she had just met? Sure, these two young men looked startling handsome in their uniforms—especially Fred, with his full, dark hair, high forehead, and pronounced cheekbones. As Heidi looked more closely at him, trying to determine the exact color of his eyes, she realized she did not even know how old he was. Granted, Fred had introduced himself as an Air Force Captain, but was he single? Did he have a girlfriend back in the States, or perhaps here on the base? Up to now, she had never worried about such things because, frankly, she had never dated a man. Could she even call this a date?

Her curiosity and growing interest compelled her to make some things clear. At the Wertheim Department Store she had told them jokingly that she was not for sale. Should she go one step further and set a boundary, if this really was a date? She had to give herself an extra push, until her face looked serious enough to tell them what was troubling her mind.

"There is something I just have to tell you two."

"What? Did you have too much Coke?" joked Floyd.

"No, Floyd, I am very serious now."

They could see now that her serious face warranted attention to her words.

"Let me put it bluntly. I am not one of those girls who want to get picked up by American or French soldiers for free cigarettes, beer and a *good time*. As a matter of fact, my life has been so complicated, that I have never been on a date. Shocking, right? I love being here with you. I like our talk, jokes, and even silliness. But you need to know that I don't want to be one of those GI girlfriends who Germans call *Ami Huren* or whores. And that's all I wanted to say."

Heidi's table partners were shocked and speechless. Had their innocent dinner invitation been so badly misunderstood? Or had they behaved wrongly or perhaps said something insulting or suspicious?

There was a long silence. Heidi avoided looking at them. Floyd pretended to search for his wallet. Only Fred looked straight at Heidi, trying to make her look up to his face. Carefully and discreetly he put his hand on hers.

"Heidi, when our sightseeing today ended up at your store, and when you offered us your assistance in the most polite, English way, all I saw were your beautiful blue eyes. I was hooked! Immediately, I tried to think of some way to spend more time with you. The fact that Floyd and I were starving gave me the idea of having dinner with you. It was a great idea, because here we are, enjoying each other's company, as if we had known one another for a long time. As a matter of fact, I don't remember having had a better dinner ever—and I don't mean the wonderful food."

At first Heidi wanted to quickly withdraw her hand, but Fred's warm, tender touch felt so good! Besides, looking into his eyes, she believed and trusted him. Again, there was a fairly long moment of silence. When the waiter approached and presented Floyd with the check, the spell seemed to be broken. Heidi looked around, somewhat lost.

"After we—you—have paid, does that mean we have to leave now?" asked Heidi, slowly freeing her hand from Fred's touch.

"Is that what you would like us to do?" Fred asked.

"If it were up to me, we could sit here a bit longer," Heidi answered, lost in thought.

"No, no! We don't have to leave. We could either take a little hike along the Grunewald Lake shore, or we could talk some more here."

"Then let's talk! I really would like you to tell me about yourselves," said Heidi, to the amazement of her American hosts.

For the next hour, Heidi heard all about the US Air Force men at her table. They told her about Detroit, Michigan, and Sumner, Iowa. She enjoyed learning about their families, their enlisting with the Air Force and their training, and about being deployed to Germany to help in the Berlin Airlift. All of a sudden, Fred stopped.

"You must be thinking that we are crazy, and you may be right," he said. "For more than an hour we've been talking our heads off, telling everything about ourselves. If you were a spy, you would have us in your hands now."

"But I am not a spy," Heidi laughed. "I am just an over-grown girl, who has never been outside of Germany and who has never flown in an airplane. My much-younger brother, on the other hand, knows all of your different aircraft types and has been in the air many, many times."

"In the air? Jumping, flying, or being flown?" Floyd said, using his humor in his attempt to be charming, as usual.

"Come on, Floyd! You know what I mean. My brother, Norbert, has been working for the Allied Air Lift, at first with the construction crews building runways in Tempelhof and Tegel. Then he was asked to work with the *Storch Aktion Programm,* flying with children and other deportees from Berlin-Gatow Airport to West Germany."

"Did you work there, too?" Fred asked.

"No. Right when Berlin was collapsing under the Russian onslaught in 1945, I got quite sick for many months…and afterwards I worked for two years as a *Trümmerfrau,* digging Berlin out of the endless rubble. I was told that the war created 2.6 billion cubic feet of rubble in Germany."

"Wow! That must have been hard. But what about your brother? How did he get so closely involved with our airplanes?"

"One day an airlift Air Force officer made him his personal interpreter. Norbert was only 16 years old. His English must have been really good, because very soon the Amis used him for all kinds of interpreting and translating jobs. Then, I suppose so they could have him constantly at hand when needed, they moved him into your military barracks, where he received food and clothing, and even a small salary."

Fred cautiously interrupted Heidi. "When you talk about your brother, you sound a little detached, as if you hear about his life only second-hand."

"The reason may be that I was totally separated from Norbi for years. As a matter of fact, I thought he had been killed by Russian soldiers in 1945. Then, even though we lived in the same city, we did not know of each other until three years later." When Heidi saw the puzzled looks of her American friends, she said, "You lucky Americans never had to live in a totally destroyed big city. You don't know what it is like to have no mail service, no telephones, no cars, and not even bicycles to stay in touch with each other."

As the dinner date was drawing to a close, Fred was thinking of hundreds of questions he could, and perhaps should have asked. Too late for today! But there had to be more get-togethers with Heidi—preferably without Floyd.

When they walked out of the restaurant, Heidi was surprised how many military cars with various military license plates were filling the lot, even some Russian plates. Here at the lovely *Jagdschloss Restaurant* in the American Sector, all four Allied Powers seemed to get along well. Fred was driving again, but this time with Heidi sitting next to him.

"What happened to your co-pilot?" Heidi asked with a sly smile.

"Floyd preferred sitting in the back seat on the way home. That gives him the chance to write a letter to his girlfriend in Detroit."

"Oh, he has a girlfriend?"

"Yes, he has. A very steady one back home, as he told me."

"A very, very steady one!" came a voice from the back.

"Speaking of 'home,' we want to drive you home, but I have no idea where you live."

Heidi's quick come-back was, "Very few people know. Please just drop me off at the *Rathaus Steglitz U-Bahn* Station."

"Come on, Heidi, we had a wonderful time together, and now we want to take you right to your front door, as gentlemen should."

Heidi thought that was a nice gesture, but still she had to ask, "What about the American Military Fraternization Law? Aren't you asking for trouble?"

Fred quickly looked back at Floyd. Both men were shaking their heads. Then Fred answered firmly, "First of all, that is an absolutely stupid law. I have lovely grandparents, who immigrated from Germany. And, I have met the nicest German construction crew workers at the Tempelhof Airport and many, many German maintenance workers at several airports in West Germany. And now I have met you."

"So have I!" trumpeted Floyd from his back seat.

"I thought you are writing to your girlfriend," said Fred.

"Yes, I am. Still, I want to know what you are talking about, like a good chaperon should do."

"I thought of you as a friend and partner, not a chaperon," Fred said.

"Friends, yes —perhaps forever. But partners—perhaps no longer, at least not in our relationship to Heidi. I have the feeling you two would be better off without me."

"I think you may be right, Floyd. Don't you agree, Heidi?"

Instead of joining the conversation, Heidi touched Fred's hand on the steering wheel.

Fred looked straight at Heidi, as he said to Floyd, "Yes, you probably are right, my friend."

Chapter 22

Berlin was a tragically divided city. However, in 1949, all four power allied military members were still allowed to move freely between Sectors for sightseeing, shopping and restaurant visits. Major General Kotikov was extremely pleased with himself; his wish was finally fulfilled and he was dining at the legendary *Jagdschloss Grunewald.* Yes, it was located in what was for him the dreaded American Sector, but that meant nothing to the heroic Russian conquerors of all of Berlin. This was their town, and neither American nor British officials would ever stop them from dining wherever they wanted.

For such a "fine dining" experience, the general could even tolerate the company of his deputy, Lieutenant Sergey Svertlov, whom he often found to be a pain in the ass. Kotikov knew that his own nickname was "General Njet" (General No)—but his deputy Svertlov did not know that his boss had given him the nickname, "The Jew Lieutenant Maybe," a cruel reference to Svertlov's Jewish grandmother.

Years before Svertlov had been assigned to Kotikov's Division in Berlin, this young, idealistic and sophisticated Muscovite had constantly been the victim of bullying soldiers, most likely because of his Jewish background. Still, as he had been one of the young "liberators" of Berlin in 1945, Moscow had given this young lieutenant the questionable honor of supervising the so-called "Cattle Drive" from *Oranienburg* to Berlin immediately after the war had ended. He had never before heard of a cattle drive, and did fully grasp the reference to something most Americans would understand—as they would at least be familiar with the practice of herding cattle from Texas to Kansas, and then on to Chicago, where they ended up in the slaughterhouses.

Svertlov's job was to herd several thousand cows and bulls, collected from the rich grazing fields of central Germany, to *Oranienburg*, and from there to Berlin, where they were loaded on freight trains and shipped to various slaughterhouses in the Soviet Union. He had wondered why he, a decorated Berlin liberator and Moscow city-dweller who had attended university (never learning about cattle) had been selected for this job. But, he had learned as a "Young Pioneer" at age 10, never to doubt the wisdom of the Soviet Government.

Now, at the elegant *Jagdschloss Grunewald,* Sergey Svertlov almost spoiled the peaceful dining atmosphere. Just when Kotikov and his highly war-decorated female dining companion invited Svertlov to join them in a toast to the victorious and incomparably glorious Soviet Union, Svertlov brought up the young German, still at large, in spite of all Russian and East German efforts. Like a thunderbolt, General Kotikov came down on his deputy.

"Didn't I tell you *never* to bother me again with any stupid talk about that damned German kid until you have locked him up?!" Kotikov's loud outburst in Russian penetrated the other guests' quiet conversations in the calm restaurant. All eyes seemed to turn to the three uniformed Russians.

Kotikov was still sober enough to quickly realize his rude behavior. He stood up, looked around, and said, "Pardon! Excuse me! Pardon!" He raised his glass and said, "To our health!" The tension vanished and guests at nearby tables toasted their glasses, and somebody started applauding. Others in the back picked up the applause, without knowing what it was about. Even the two American soldiers sitting with a beautiful young German woman in a side alcove, who had heard nothing of the Russian officer's outburst, applauded.

Later that night, thinking back, Kotikov was not sorry for how he had acted. Actually, asking the people in the restaurant for pardon, and leading them in a toast, had given him a respectful edge. Yes, in moments of crisis, he was the right man to come out on top.

But the very next afternoon, his life took a turn for the worse. It was the call from the Kremlin that spoiled his mood for the rest of the day. Moscow's high-ranking brass had been in a meeting for many hours, discussing Kotikov's "Six Points of How to Handle the East–West Exodus," which he had cabled to Moscow. After a brief greeting, the unidentified voice at the other end of the line came to the point.

"Major General! We have studied your six-point guidelines."

"Thank you! So what did you think?" Kotikov asked confidently.

"Not much. General, were you drunk when you put those points on paper?"

"Drunk? No, sir, never!! Why would you think so?"

"Let me be very straight with you. Your guidelines contained absolutely nothing new. Except for number six, about discontinuing press exchanges between East and West, you have come up with nothing practical that could stop the flow of people from East to West Germany."

"You must be mistaken, comrade. My document suggests finding effective methods to cut off the west-bound brain drain; to enlarge the *Volkspolizei* cadre; to sharpen the propaganda—"

"Major General," the other officer interrupted. "Do you call those guidelines new? Just going over your repetitive and trite ideas can make the reader fall asleep."

Kotikov could hear chatter and even laughter in the background. He felt like throwing up. His brilliant plan on how to bring East Germany closer to the Soviet fold had seemed to him practical and possible.

"Sir," Kotikov said, "May I ask to whom I have the honor of speaking?"

"No, you may not! We are a committee of eight intelligent, experienced, and loyal Soviet leaders. Perhaps some of us fought with you in the same trenches in the last war. So, don't think that we are simple school teachers checking up on your homework!"

Kotikov, the respected and powerful Commandant of East Berlin, could not think of any more words right now, other than asking, "Is there anything else?"

"No, not for now! You'll hear from us soon."

The line went dead, and that is how Kotikov felt now, too. After all he had done during the Berlin Blockade! Now this?

You'll hear from us soon— hear what? And he had thought that the cattle drive in 1945 with thousands of stubborn animals had been a hard job. What should he call this? Was this perhaps another "drive," this time supervised by others, that would end in the slaughter of his reputation, power, and rank?

Chapter 23

When Norbert came back from his *Volkshochschule* where he had registered for the Summer Course in 1950, he saw a big Studebaker parked in front of his apartment house. An American GI leaned leisurely against the hood of his street cruiser, a cigarette dangling from his half-closed lips. As Norbert got closer, the American tossed the cigarette aside and got busy straightening his uniform.

"Are you Norbert Anleger?"

"Yes, I am—and who are you?" asked Norbert.

"I'm just an army driver, so the name makes no difference. More important is that you are Norbert."

"I told you so!"

"Well, Norbert, I hope you had nothing special planned, because I am to take you first to General Maxwell Taylor at his headquarters, and then to the *Schöneberg* City Hall."

"You want to take me to the US Commander of West Berlin, and then to our city hall?

What have I done this time?"

"I hope, nothing. My job is to deliver you to General Taylor's office. Ready to go?"

"I guess I have worked long enough for you Amis to know how quickly orders can be given and changed. Okay, I am yours. Let's roll!"

Norbert enjoyed the short ride from *Neukölln* to the US Military Headquarters in *Zehlendorf*. He marveled at the sound of the 8-cylinder engine, and as he shut the door he stopped a moment to stroke the shiny metal and admire the largest car he had ever ridden in.

"Man, this is a swell car!"

"Yep, I'll buy it when it gets old."

A uniformed orderly appeared and led Norbert to General Taylor's office. Taylor looked at Norbert with a fatherly smile. "I hope we didn't scare you by bringing you here," he said.

"I am used to surprises," answered Norbert quickly. "General Taylor, sir, I am Norbert Anleger. You wanted to talk to me."

"Indeed," the general said, thumbing through papers on his desk. "Ah, here it is! If you should accept our offer, then these are your marching orders for the next four months."

"Four months, sir?" Norbert asked. "What do you have in mind?"

"We want you to be our official German interpreter and translator for the *Crusade for Freedom*. You were highly recommended for this job, and you will be paid well."

Norbert looked at the general without a word. He had never heard of the *Kreuzzug der Freiheit*. Suddenly he realized he had, in his head, automatically translated the title of the crusade from English to German.

"If you accept the job, we will need to get you a passport ASAP and also an American visa," Taylor continued. Norbert still did not know what to say.

Finally, searching for the right words, he said, "General, sir, I thank you for the offer. For almost two years I have learned to trust the Americans. None of them has ever let me down. I get the impression that what you have in mind for me is rather urgent and important. You have my full cooperation." After a brief pause, he added, "I have only one concern. Perhaps you do not know that in April, I turned 18 years old. I hope my age does not disqualify me for the job you have in mind."

"You are only 18?" asked General Taylor in surprise. "Nobody mentioned your age when telling me what a terrific interpreter you are. This will involve considerable foreign travel. Should we ask your parents' permission first?"

"Sir, my parents are dead. I am on my own. My word must be enough for you."

"Then that settles it. Can you start in ten days?"

"I'll be happy to," Norbert quickly replied, even though he still had no idea what this lengthy assignment would require of him.

"Now remember, Norbert, first things first. In your case, that means to get yourself a passport—we will take care of your visa. You've never been to America, right?"

"No, sir!"

"I guarantee you'll like it. My deputy will brief you on the *Crusade of Freedom* background." The general reached for the phone, punched a few buttons and told his secretary,

"Dorothy, tell Major Blythe that Norbert Anleger is ready for his briefing. And please notify the Lord Mayor's office that Mr. Anleger will be at the city hall in about two hours."

When Norbert heard the name "Blythe," his memory started working in overdrive. He was nearly certain that was the name of the friendly officer from Illinois who had interrogated him in 1948, right after his escape from East Berlin.

Norbert was taken to a small conference room at the end of a long hallway. Before he could sit down to focus on additional memories, the door opened and in walked the highly decorated Major Robert Blythe. Norbert recognized him instantly, and with a big smile he took a step toward the officer.

"Major Blythe! Is it really you?"

Now Blythe recognized him, too. "Aren't you the crazy ruin-climber we picked up at the border between East and West Berlin about three years ago? With your extreme taste for adventure, it is good to see that you are still alive," the Major laughed, shaking Norbert's hand.

"Remember, I told you that I am like a cat with nine lives!" Norbert said, also laughing.

"Yes, but we don't know how many you've used up! Do you still live in Berlin?"

"Where else would I live? But don't ask me for my address! Again, like a cat, I move around a lot. Best of all, I liked living for a time in the US Air Force barracks in Zehlendorf or Dahlem. However, now my postal address—if anybody should ever write me—is in care of my uncle and aunt, in the Hermann Strasse in Berlin Neukölln."

"I have heard about your half-militarized or half-Americanized existence in Tempelhof and Tegel," Blythe said. "One time I even tried to contact you by phone. No luck!"

"That doesn't surprise me because I have no phone to this day," Norbert explained. "You see, I am not a government worker, nor a lawyer, pastor or shopkeeper."

"What about them?"

"Those people have better chances to get phone service in post-war Berlin. Others have to wait, who knows how long! That's what drives my sister crazy, that she can never reach me by phone."

"You told me once that your parents and all siblings were dead."

"That's correct, except for my sister Heidi, who miraculously survived. You see, on that terrible day in May of 1945, when she was gang-raped by Russians, the same soldiers also knocked me unconscious. When I woke up, nobody was around, and she was gone. I assumed she was dead, like the rest of my family."

"How did you discover she was still alive?"

"After nearly three years she finally connected with my relatives who live in Neukölln.

My Uncle Theo told her that I was alive. Since then we have seen each a few times, mostly just by chance."

Major Blythe looked at his wristwatch. "Listen, Norbert, I better get to telling you about the Crusade for Freedom before your appointment with Lord Mayor Reuter."

Norbert was anxious to hear about the project, which sounded like an adventure which would keep him busy for many months. Blythe told him how millions of Americans had collected sufficient funds for the casting of a huge bell, designed after the American Liberty Bell in Philadelphia. The 10-ton bell had been cast in England. From there, it was to be taken to New York City to begin its "Crusade for Freedom" through the USA.

"Your job will start when you fly to London's large military airport. The bell will be transported from Croydon to London Harbor to a ship which will take it to New York. Since the loading process will take less than 24 hours, you will not need a British visa. But you must have a visa for the United States! You take care of the passport, and we will get you the visa—both must be expedited. Understood, young man?"

All Norbert understood was that right after his city hall visit, his next urgent duty was to get a passport. The same American car that had brought him to the headquarters now took him to the *Schöneberg Rathaus,* the temporary city hall of West Berlin. There he was received like a dignitary. As a matter of fact, a beautifully-dressed, smiling secretary was waiting outside the massive front door entrance when the Studebaker sped up to the curb and abruptly stopped. Norbert quickly exited the car and walked toward her.

"*Guten Tag*, Herr Anleger!" she greeted him, shaking his hand. Then she rushed him through the ornate entrance hall and up a winding staircase to the second floor. She led him to the mayor's outer office.

"Please, wait here. Mayor Reuter will see you soon."

Then she was gone. As Norbert looked around, he noticed close to 50 framed photos covering two walls, depicting various facets of life in Berlin. As he scanned the familiar scenes, suddenly his gaze stopped—on his own face! He was surrounded by hundreds of happy-looking Berliners. Under the photo he saw the inscription: *HURRA, WIR LEBEN NOCH!* ("Hooray, we are still alive!") He remembered exactly when and where the photograph had been taken.

It was May 12, 1949, when the horrible blockade of West Berlin had ended and everyone gathered to share their relief and celebration. He recalled how his own shout, *"Hurra, wie leben noch!"* had been picked up—at first by hundreds, then by thousands of fellow citizens in front of the *Schöneberg Rathaus.* That had happened right after the Lord Mayor Ernst Reuter ended his speech with the familiar slogan of defiance: *"Berlin bleibt doch Berlin!"* And now—now he was to meet Mayor Reuter here at his office! Norbert quickly turned at the sound of a loud voice.

"Oh, there you are!" said the mayor, approaching Norbert with outstretched arms. "Thank you for coming!"

"It is my distinct pleasure," replied Norbert.

"I see you entertained yourself by looking at our 'Then and Now' photos."

"Yes, sir, a very nice display. I did make an interesting discovery."

"Tell me what you found!"

"Here..." Norbert pointed at the picture featuring him. "This was taken when thousands celebrated the end of the blockade, and when you ended your famous speech with '*Berlin bleibt doch Berlin!*'"

"Right!" Reuter said, moving close to view the photo. "And the crowd responded with an ear-splitting—wait, is that you? There—standing on that elevated, broken statue pedestal?" When Norbert nodded, the mayor said, "I was told that this young man—you!—started the cheer that became the chant of the crowd, the slogan of the entire celebration—'*Hurra, wie leben noch!*'"

"Yes, Mister Mayor, that was me. Actually, at first it was only my own expression of joy, but then it got picked up by everyone around me, and then by the crowd of thousands."

The mayor slapped Norbert on the back. "Good for you, my young friend. Now, come into my office, please!"

For the next half hour, Reuter and Norbert talked about the *Kreuzzug der Freiheit* and Norbert's role as the chief interpreter. "If this is your first trip to the USA, you will be overwhelmed with the vastness of the land," Reuter said. "In a way, I envy you. While I'll be studying papers and city proposals, you'll be traveling all over America, and at no expense to you. We will be happy to take care of your needs, trusting you will represent us well in the US."

"Yes, of course, sir. Thank you, sir!" said Norbert.

"Oh, and please give my regards to General Eisenhower and to President Truman, whom you certainly will meet.

And you better be good, Mister Interpreter, because the US President knows German, to some extent!"

Ten days later, Norbert flew from Berlin-Tempelhof to London. In his company were 20 GIs on an unidentified mission to England. "Why are so many of you Americans not flying to America, but rather to England?" Norbert asked naively.

"If you had ever served in the military, you would realize how stupid your question is."

"But I didn't ask you what you would be doing in Great Britain!"

"Even if you had asked, you would not have gotten an answer. The fact is that we don't know ourselves what we will be doing. That's the military for you!"

Norbert decided to turn his attention away from the unresponsive bunch of soldiers and instead focus on his papers regarding his own trip. But now the GI seated next to him asked in a loud voice, "What about you? This is a military plane, but you don't wear a uniform. We are used to not being checked when boarding—why were you civilians not monitored? Besides, I have been looking you over—can't figure out if you're Army, Air Force, or what."

Now another airman spoke up, without waiting for Norbert to answer.

"Your suit looks like an officer's outfit, but you're too young. So, what's the deal with you?"

Up to this point, Norbert had been proud of his brand new, custom-made suit, which really had the style worn by higher-ranking officers, but without any insignia. Now he felt embarrassed by the questions from his co-passengers. Still, he owed them at least an answer.

"Have you guys heard of the *Kreuzzug der Freiheit*?" A chorus of "Nos" was the answer.

"How about the Crusade of Freedom? Anybody?"

His travel companions still drew a blank. Norbert decided to explain, at least a bit.

"I am on my way to England to pick up a 10-ton alarm clock, which will help you to always report for duty on time."

The GIs looked at one another and met Norbert with blank looks and a few chuckles. Norbert had been right to guess they had no idea what he was talking about.

"Are you a spy on a secret mission?" a GI asked.

"Why do you ask?" responded Norbert.

"You speak with a German accent."

"If I were a spy, would I fly with you guys? Especially dressed in this mysterious officer's uniform?" Norbert hoped he sounded like he was kidding around, which he was. Even though he had worked around GIs for some time now, he still felt a little nervous around them.

"Give it a rest, boys!" interjected an Air Force Senior Master Sergeant. "Maybe this nice young man is a civilian policy coordination inspector from the State Department, or maybe he is with the Central Intelligence Agency."

"Sure, the CIA is in desperate need of greenhorn youngsters like him."

"As I said before, boys, give it a rest!"

It was a rather short flight from Berlin to London, yet it was long enough for Norbert to read some of his Crusade for Freedom material. He learned that one the Crusade's first actions had been to commission a "Freedom Bell" designed after the American Liberty Bell. This bell would travel through many US states, along with a "Freedom Scroll" for people to sign. Engraved on the bell were the words of President Abraham Lincoln:

"That this world under God shall have a new birth of freedom."

The Freedom Scroll, which Americans were asked to sign, had the following text:

IN THE BELIEF THAT FREEDOM IS THE MOST PRECIOUS OF HUMAN RIGHTS, I GLADLY SIGN MY NAME TO THIS FREEDOM SCROLL AS EVIDENCE OF MY PARTICIPATION AS A FREE CITIZEN IN THE CRUSADE FOR FREEDOM, SUPPORTING THE NATIONAL COMMITTEE FOR A FREE EUROPE AND ITS STRIKING ARM, RADIO FREE EUROPE. IN SO DOING, I JOIN HANDS WITH MILLIONS OF OTHER AMERICANS IN BRINGING TRUTH AND HOPE TO THE COURAGEOUS FREEDOM-HUNGRY PEOPLE BEHIND THE IRON CURTAIN.

The more Norbert read about the Crusade for Freedom, the more inadequate he felt about the role he was to play. Even Major Blythe had talked about the Crusade as a critical American propaganda campaign with the goal of raising funds for Radio Free Europe. The purpose was to air programs to Eastern Europe in several languages, and serve as a beacon of hope to people who had otherwise lost access to the outside world.

After reading his information and the Freedom Scroll, Norbert now understood that the entire Crusade was a powerful call to the world to take a stand for freedom and human rights. And he had been invited to play a part in this noble cause? More than ever, he was determined to give his best.

When the Vickers Viscount Transporter landed, Norbert could barely make out the name of the airfield: "Southern Municipal Airport – London." During World War II, the airport had been restricted to military use only. Today, as a civilian aviation field, it was used for many purposes. Norbert could not figure out why he had been directed to fly from Berlin to this primitive, small airport. What was to be his next move? And what did this place have to do with his mission? This certainly was not the spot where the transporting ship for the bell would dock. Confused, Norbert slowly got off the plane.

Next to the runway stood a table loaded with sandwiches, fruit, and juices. His American travel companions had discovered the table first and were helping themselves to the free food.

"Wow, look here, boys!" one of the Americans shouted. "We never had it so good! Free food for all Americans—with compliments of the Brits."

Not to be outdone, Norbert quickly added, "And free food also for the passengers who will be working for the Americans!"

Since he had no visa for England, and since the ship transporting the Freedom Bell and its companion interpreter was to sail to New York City with a midnight departure, Norbert did not get to sight-see in London. However, once he arrived in New York with his 10-ton "baby," that would change. He looked forward to feasting his eyes on all the marvelous sights the United States had to offer.

Norbert realized he did not have a prior arrangement of how to get to the dock where the *American Clipper* awaited with "his" bell. He quickly reached for his notebook to look up the address as he spied a nearby taxi. He wondered if the taxi was available; it seemed strange and against security rules that one would be parked here so close to the planes.

"Hello, mate. Where are you headed?" the taxi driver asked.

"I need to get quickly to my ship, the *American Clipper*. She is docked at the Londonderry Dock."

"In Ireland?"

"No, here in London. Why would you think Ireland?"

"Because that's where Londonderry is."

"The *American Clipper* is docked in Londonderry, and I need to get there as fast as possible."

"Now I know what you are talking about. Among the many docks in the London Harbor, there is one called Londonderry. I'll take you there. Just hand me your suitcase and hop in!"

Norbert was relieved, and glad that the driver had not asked for an advance fare because he had not a single British coin. Never mind that! Once he was at the *American Clipper*, there surely would be *Freedom Bell* officials who would help him out.

Well, after many detours and lots of inquiries, the taxi driver finally got to the right pier—not in Ireland, but in London. Norbert arrived with lots of time to spare. American officials on the ship who had been waiting anxiously for Norbert Anleger to arrive were happy to sweeten the taxi fare with a hefty tip. Everything was well. The ship could and did sail, leaving the port on time. Ahoy!

It was the twenty-seventh day of August, 1950.

Chapter 24

Finally another day off for Fred and Heidi! He could not wait to drive to the secluded, romantic place by a beautiful lake which he had discovered a few weeks ago. As much as he longed to put his arms around her again, now he was especially excited as he had some very good news for her about her brother.

As the Jeep approached the *Grosser Wannsee,* Fred could not wait any longer. He just had to tell Heidi the great news. He pulled over and stopped in the fire break lane.

"What's wrong?" asked Heidi. "You cannot park your Jeep on a fire break lane, which is strictly for emergencies!"

"Maybe my news is worth an emergency stop. Heidi! You wouldn't believe what I found out—Norbert is working for us again! There will be no *Volkshochschule* courses for a while. His fame as an interpreter has catapulted your brother back into full-time work."

Heidi, normally quick to respond to Fred's frequent off-the-wall remarks or jokes, was speechless.

"You mean there is a valid reason why I have not seen Norbert or heard from him in weeks? Not that my brother would need a reason for not staying in touch with me!"

"Heidi, your brother is busy dealing with really important people like US General Maxwell Taylor, and West Berlin's Lord Mayor Ernst Reuter. I am afraid he will be too busy to contact you for quite some time."

"How did you find out about Norbi's newest adventure?"

"For sure, not from the Soviets, who still are trying to catch him. No, I read it in yesterday's *Stars & Stripes*. The American officials who are organizing the Crusade for Freedom hired Norbert to be their chief interpreter for the entire tour all across the United States and back to Berlin in October. There was even a picture of him. Here, I cut it out for you."

Heidi got quite excited over the news, just as Fred had been for the last 24 hours. What better way to show her happiness than to lean over and give Fred a long-deserved kiss! They both forgot all about being parked illegally until a passing car honked. Heidi reluctantly sat back as Fred put the Jeep into gear and sped off to that perfect place by the water that he had in mind.

When he pulled up to the secluded area and turned off the Jeep, they were both quiet for a long time. "This really is a wonderful, little place," Heidi finally said. "You have a good eye for beauty."

"That's why I found you, Heidi." Such sweet words led to more kisses and embraces.

After a while they got out of the Jeep to walk to the water's edge. "Did I tell you that three or four weeks ago I actually met Norbert?" asked Fred. Heidi's eyes widened in surprise. "No, you never told me. When was that?"

"It was that week when we both had a day off. Since I could not phone you, I wanted to surprise you. You had told me once that you usually went to visit your uncle and aunt on your day off. I found their apartment in the *Hermann Strasse* and rang the doorbell."

"That must have been the day my schedule was changed at the last minute. I didn't get the day off after all. Oh, I'm so sorry I missed you!" said Heidi.

"That's right, you weren't there, but the young man who came to the door looked so much like you I was amazed! And he seemed surprised as well to see me, some guy in an Air Force uniform, and immediately spoke in perfect English with an American accent. There was something in his voice and mannerisms that reminded me of a boy on the work crew at Tempelhof Airport, whom I had met in 1948."

"Norbi worked at Tempelhof!" Heidi interrupted.

"Yes, it took me no time to figure out that the young man standing in the doorway was the very same boy I had met at the Tempelhof Airport. I even remembered his name—Norbert."

"How did you remember the name of one of the crew? He was just one of so many," said Heidi.

"He made an impression on me. I remember I told him all about the *Rosinenbomber*, Lieutenant Gail Halvorson. When he heard me say that Gail and I flew in the same squadron, he was full of questions. He would have asked me a hundred more questions but the tight schedule of the airlift did not permit any long conversation. I had to take off, but I did have the chance to tell him that besides Lieutenant Halvorsen there were quite a few other American pilots, including myself, who regularly dropped off candies and chocolates for Berliner kids before landing at Tempelhof."

Heidi was quiet and let Fred do the talking, not sure where this would take them.

"We quickly re-introduced ourselves. Then came his sixty-four-dollar question. He said, 'Okay, Fred, but what brings you to my uncle's—wait a minute, wait just a minute! Are you that Fred Harrington my sister raves about every time our paths cross?'"

Fred and Heidi enjoyed a laugh together, thinking how crazy it was that their three paths would cross like this.

"Since he and I had nothing else to do that morning, we just shared our life stories over one or two cups of *Ersatz-Kaffee*."

"Did Norbi tell you about our family...and about me?" asked Heidi, almost in a whisper.

"Yes, he did—how in your younger years you had admired Adolf Hitler, just like millions of other young Germans. And he told me how you tragically lost one after another family members."

"Was that all you talked about?"

"He also told me about that awful first day of May in 1945, when the drunk Russian soldiers knocked him unconscious and—and when a whole bunch of the boozed-up beasts pounced upon you."

Heidi's chest was heaving. She could hardly breathe. They both fell silent. When she finally turned to look at Fred, she saw that tears had washed over his entire face. She had been just about to leap up and run away into the forest, unable to face the shame this memory flooded her with. But now her heart caught in her throat. She longed to crawl into his loving, strong arms, while at the same time feeling empty and unworthy to even touch him. She managed to whisper, "I'm sorry."

"Heidi! Heidi, darling! There is nothing, nothing, to say you're sorry about. You are the love of my life! Whatever happened in the hell of post-war times did not destroy who you are now. You are lovely! You are strong! You are beautiful! Never forget, God created you in his image. That makes you magnificent. Oh, I forgot to mention also graceful, enchanting and gorgeous. Whether you agree with me or not, that's the truth." He hugged her tight.

There were more tears—did tears have the power to wash away painful memories forever? Only time would tell. For now, having the darkest hours and days of her life finally revealed, Heidi felt more happiness and wholeness than she had in a very long time. She felt safe with this man. She knew that facing this knowledge together had created even stronger bonds holding their hearts together.

Fred stoked her head, holding her to his chest. He noticed an old familiar tune playing in his head. It was the church hymn he had sung many times back in his home church in Sumner, Iowa, most memorably on the day he had left for military service.

Blest be the tie that binds
Our hearts in Christian love:
The fellowship of kindred minds
Is like to that above.

We share each other's woes
Each other's burdens bear,
And often for each other flows
The sympathizing tear.

Fred wondered whether to share this thought with Heidi, who was not raised in a church-going family. He decided to save such a discussion for a later date.

After a few more hours in the sun and a refreshing swim, it was time to drive home. That brought up the usual question, *Heidi, where do you live?* For the first time, Heidi had no hesitation to answer. Today she would not ask him, as usual, to be dropped off at the *Rathaus Schöneberg U-Bahn Station.*

"Fred, you know where my uncle and aunt live in Neukölln. What you don't know is that right after the war they had to give up the privacy of the three-room apartment. With 80 percent of Berlin's living quarters destroyed, they were asked to harbor six women in their apartment. Imagine, eight unrelated people living so closely together! It must have been like an asylum for shelter-less females."

"Well, I have heard that almost everyone had to double-up like that. But, eight! Wow!"

"A few years later, six of the forced renters had moved to different accommodations, so Uncle Theo invited Norbert and me to share their apartment 'whenever needed.'"

"I remember you telling me that Norbert was really happy when he lived at the Air Force barracks," said Fred. "Just as I have no complaints about living at the Andrews barracks in *Steglitz* or Berlin-*Lichterfelde*, or whatever the actual address is."

"Back to your question about my place…believe it or not, Fred, I share my apartment—not with eight—but with three single women plus the original owner couple. The couple put up a temporary partition wall. We four women use bedsheets hanging from wires to create small cubicles, which we call our *sub-apartments*. Now you know why I never wanted to bring you there. We have no privacy. Whenever I need a quiet place for writing my Wertheim reports or performance evaluations, I usually go to the *Lincoln Bibliotek* in Steglitz."

"Oh, now I know why I've never run into you at the *Amerika Haus* where I hang out, especially when I am searching for special reading material," said Fred.

"Why travel all the way to the *Amerika Haus* when I have the Lincoln Library, which is a branch of the *Amerika Haus,* closer by?"

She is always thinking, Fred marveled. He made a mental note that the next time he needed a library he would go to the *Lincoln Bibliotek.*

"So, which is it this time, Heidi? The *U-Bahn Station Rathaus Schöneberg* drop-off or your real address?"

"Relax, darling! I'll guide you close to my apartment, where the owners and their four spinsters live!"

As Fred removed his right hand from the steering wheel in order to caress Heidi's neck, he said in a jubilant tone, "Lady, you can guide or misguide me to wherever you want! I will always find you. I guess you are stuck with me forever!"

Heidi reached for his hand and kissed it, saying, "That would be my greatest joy!"

Chapter 25

The ten days at sea on the rugged *American Clipper* passed faster than Norbert had expected. He got enough rest and sleep and there was always plenty of food—and it was good! He had almost no duties other than occasionally giving the tightly-packed Freedom Bell a thorough look-over. However, his regular check-ups on the huge cargo piece caused suspicion from one of the security guards on board.

One day, when Norbert leaned against the massive cargo crate and even tried to push it to check on its proper anchoring, an armed security guard suddenly stepped up to him and grabbed him by the shoulder.

"What's up, Mr. Spy?" he asked Norbert. "You want to find out if the bell is still there?"

Norbert did not answer.

"Perhaps you are just attempting to find out what is written on the bell," the guard teased him. "In case you care, the text on this bell is not the same as the text on the Liberty Bell in Philadelphia."

"I know what's written on *this* bell," said Norbert.

"I bet you twenty dollars, you don't," the guard said, with a sneering smile. Norbert saw his chance to embarrass the loud-mouthed guy.

"It says: 'That this world under God shall have a new birth of freedom.' Now give me my twenty dollars!"

"How did you know what's written on the bell, smart-ass?"

"I read all the information about the bell and its background, while you were annoying other passengers, or were playing poker with your buddies," said Norbert.

That was too much for the guard. Without a word, he turned around and stomped off.

Norbert had not intended to insult him, but the man had called him a spy! That had hit Norbert's nerve. Actually this little nasty interlude had made the rather long voyage a bit more interesting for him, even though he never got his twenty dollars!

On September 6, the *American Clipper* steamed into New York's harbor, passing Ellis Island and the Statue of Liberty, which Norbert knew (along with other landmarks) from studying books about America. In awe as he viewed the skyline of the city, his heart raced. He had arrived! He had made it to America!

He felt sorry that he had just missed General Dwight Eisenhower's speech on September 4, the American Labor Day. Actually, Norbert had not missed it altogether, but the reception on his small radio had been very poor, since he had been still at sea.

Still, Norbert had been extremely interested to hear General Eisenhower speak about the Crusade of Freedom. In his speech, he introduced both the Freedom Bell and the Freedom Scroll, which Norbert very soon was to accompany all across America.

As Norbert stood on the ship's deck marveling at the vertical city before him, he saw two dignified-looking gentlemen come aboard, obviously looking for something or someone. They spoke to one of the uniformed security guards by the bell's giant crate. Then, a bit hesitantly, they approached Norbert. "Are you Norbert Anleger, the interpreter from Germany?"

"Yes, I just arrived, along with the Freedom Bell. How do you do, gentlemen?" "My name is Abbott Washburn, and my colleague here is Nate Crabtree. We are the ones who came up with the idea of using the Freedom Bell as the symbol for the Crusade for Freedom. No bragging intended! We came here to make sure that our "big baby" is well taken care of, and ready for its arduous journey across the country. In two days the Freedom Bell will be the centerpiece of a large parade in Manhattan. I bet you that thousands of Americans will want to touch it for good luck."

Nathan Crabtree quickly added to his colleague's introduction, "By the way, welcome to America!" Then he and Washburn had a long discussion with the ship's captain about how to get the monster bell safely on land, and then onto a flatbed truck for the rest of the Crusade for Freedom.

Since the entire transfer procedure was done using English, there was really no need for Norbert's interpreting skills. The two PR specialists were constantly on the phone, anyway.

When a call ended, they quickly were studying New York City maps, special street drawings, and weight charts of platforms to be used for the 10-ton bell. Then a whole string of other phone calls captured their attention again.

Norbert was disappointed that nobody seemed to care about what happened to him. He left the ship and wandered over to a building near the dock. When he scanned his official papers, he came across a New York emergency number. But how could he phone anyone, when he had no American currency? Somebody was supposed to have met him with US dollars, lodging information, and other helpful instructions. But where was that person?

"Hallo, sir!" A port security officer walked up to him. "I've been watching you for a while. You are either lost or a total nut-case. Which is it?"

"Why am I a nut-case?" asked Norbert

"Because you should know that you cannot walk around here in the restricted area all by yourself."

Norbert quickly explained that he had just arrived in New York on the *American Clipper*, which had transported the Freedom Bell from London.

"The what?" the security guard asked, even more suspicious.

"I'm a German interpreter and have to stay with the Freedom Bell as it travels all over the country," explained Norbert. He was a little nervous, as he didn't know if he should expect uniformed security guards in America to act more like his American military friends in Europe or like ruthless Russians.

"Are you sure you aren't looking for a way to get to Philadelphia to steal the Liberty Bell?" the guard asked, quite sarcastically. Norbert was not eager for this interaction to continue another minute.

"I tell you what. Why don't you phone your superior and ask him if anybody is meeting Norbert Anleger, the United States Air Force interpreter for the Crusade for Freedom campaign. That's me, whether you believe it or not!"

"Oh, you are with the military? They are known for messing up things, before they make them work," the guard said as he started to walk the few steps to the building where the office telephone was.

"Just make the call. Please!"

Within minutes, a Jeep with security markings pulled up. IDs were checked out. Things looked okay, and the Jeep took Norbert to a nearby hotel which had no sign out front except one which said, "FOR MILITARY PERSONNEL ONLY!" Perhaps he was in luck after all!

Then Norbert checked in at the front desk. His luck indeed was changing for the better. The US Air Force had prepared for his coming. He saw his name listed in the "Arriving Guests" book. He also could read (even though upside down for him) the remark in red ink: "Free Accommodations and Meals." The desk manager checked his book again, then looked at Norbert and said, "Welcome to the US Short-Term Accommodations Center!"

That's what it was! Not a Best Western or other hotel name Norbert might have recognized— just a Short-Term Accommodations Center. Norbert really did not care one way or another, as long as there was a bed for him. One time he had lived for some weeks in a wet, stinky, rat-infested, rubble-filled basement in Berlin—and he had survived.

The next morning, he expected a phone call from somebody who would clue him in to the plan for his day. Nobody phoned. At noon he ordered a hearty meal and took a swim in the large pool. On the way back to his room, he stopped at the front desk.

"Any messages for Norbert Anleger?"

"No, sir. Nothing!"

In good military tradition, Norbert decided if nobody contacted him, he would play deaf and blind, too. Just when he thought of changing into a comfortable track suit to go for a run, the phone rang. It was housekeeping, asking if everything was to his satisfaction. What could he say? He had gotten here yesterday after a long journey from London. The Freedom Bell had arrived safely, too. So—yes, everything was to his satisfaction. Thank you!

The radio in the room automatically played soft, boring instrumentals. He tuned it to jazz, which would give him more energy, or so he thought. After about 10 minutes he still felt tired, which was very unusual for him. Then he remembered that the time difference between London and New York might be the cause of his feeling so droopy.

The phone rang again. Half-amused and half-annoyed, he answered with, "Everything is still to my satisfaction."

"What? Who is this on the line?" a gruff male voice said on the other end.

"This is Norbert Anleger speaking."

"Norbert Anleger! Where have you been all day?" the man said, raising his voice.

"Excuse me, but it is now only shortly after noon."

"I don't care what time it is! The question is why you didn't report to our office right after landing in New York?"

"*My* question is, whose office and what are you talking about," said Norbert.

"The Office of Policy Coordination—OPC. We were expecting you yesterday."

"Good. I was here yesterday. But nobody met me from the OPC."

"The NCFE, the National Committee for a Free Europe, sent their top PR experts, Washburn and Crabtree, to meet you and give you further instructions."

"Ah, now I remember two gentlemen by those names. Unfortunately for me, they were much more interested in the Freedom Bell than in its accompanying interpreter."

"Cut the crap!" shouted the rather unpleasant voice from some NCFE office somewhere in NYC. "Have you read the text of the 'Freedom Scroll'? If you did, you would know that the NCFE has a striking arm, Radio Free Europe. That is us! We expected you in our studio for an interview this morning. You were a no-show. Don't let us down again, German boy!"

Wow! Norbert had not encountered such strange hostility coming from Americans for a long time. "I am working for the US Air Force and am getting my orders from them. My itinerary relating to the Crusade for Freedom did not list an interview with Radio Free Europe for today. I am sorry!"

"So am I!" The phone line went dead. Norbert threw himself on the bed, thinking, *I hope they don't have any more of such rude jerks in their NCFE organization.*

After a few minutes rest, Norbert's low energy got a tremendous boost. It was the phone call from the US Air Force Field Officer for the New York City area that changed Norbert's mood and early impressions of America.

"Hi, kid! This is Colonel Bruce Hardford. Ever heard of me?"

Norbert did not know what to make of this strange telephone introduction, so he decided to simply answer truthfully. "No, sir, I have not."

"Well, I don't blame you. You guys in Germany had more important things to tackle like the Berlin Blockade and the airlift—and especially those pesky Ruskies, who are worse than a swarm of mosquitoes in a nudist camp."

"Sir, are you talking of nudist camps in Berlin?"

"Hey, that's a good one! Nah, I don't know anything about nudist camps anywhere. I just like that ...what do you call it?"

"Metaphor, sir?"

"That's it! Since you don't know who I am and what my job has to do with you, I better introduce myself properly. So here it goes again! I am Colonel Bruce Hardford, spelled with two D's—one D before 'for' and one D after 'for.'"

Norbert had to hold on, not to break out into laughter.

"I am the Air Force Field Officer for Greater New York City. I have known about this Crusade for Freedom and the Freedom Bell for many weeks. Very recently I was informed about your coming, Norbert, as the accompanying civilian interpreter. Welcome to America!"

"Thank you, Colonel!"

"You know, my young friend, I hate to continue our conversation over the phone. There are at least a hundred important things we need to discuss. Why don't we meet in two hours in my office—let me see—at 1600 hours. My driver will pick you up at there at the Center about 45 minutes before that. Okay with you?"

"Could not be better, sir! See you at 1600 hours."

Suddenly all fatigue left Norbert. He was ready for action! But he had no time to lose. He showered, dressed, and reviewed his papers. Just when he was about to leave his room, the radio reported the arrival of the Freedom Bell and Freedom Scroll in New York City. The reporter even mentioned Norbert Anleger's name and praised "this young German interpreter for his active involvement in the Berlin Airlift." Norbert had no time to listen to the end of the report. He had to run for his appointment with Colonel Hardford.

Hardford was exactly the man Norbert had imagined him to be: humorous, relaxed, full of energy, sensible and practical. Recalling his first contact with any military officers as a young boy, Norbert was struck by the contrast—unfortunately, those had been Hitler's stiff and stern army officers, never smiling, always correct. This Colonel, on the other hand, could have been his long-lost friend, in spite of their age difference. After a few words of greeting, Hardford immediately focused on the jobs ahead, though.

Without a doubt, tomorrow, the eighth of September, would be the make-or-break-day of the Crusade for Freedom celebrations. Hardford went over with Norbert every detail of the schedule for that day. The Freedom Bell would be transported through the streets of New York City on a flatbed truck that was richly decorated with American and many European flags, plus hundreds of flower garlands. Arrangements had been made for blocking off traffic, probably for quite a long time, since several school and military marching bands were part of the parade.

Norbert hardly dared to interrupt the flow of words and ideas by the colonel, but after several failed attempts, his question finally got through. "Will there be any official speakers at the parade?"

"No, Norbert, not tomorrow. As you might know, General Eisenhower spoke on Labor Day. Was that a great speech!"

"I know. I listened to it on the way to New York, even though the radio reception on the Atlantic was very bad."

"Bad?" asked the colonel, a bit distracted. "The speech? Ah, I see, you meant the radio signal reception was terrible. You know, I might still have a copy of a New York paper somewhere. The text of Eisenhower's speech appeared in all the major newspapers and magazines. They had received advance copies of the speech. Remind me to give you a copy!"

From the first minute of their meeting, Norbert and Hardford planned, strategized and plotted how to make the first appearance of the Freedom Bell a super success. With the occasional help of two advisors, a good portion of time had also been spent on how to make the Freedom Scroll accessible to thousands of Americans for their signatures and, hopefully, for their donations. Norbert felt that he was dealing with an officer who wanted to be on top of every detail in planning and effect.

All of a sudden, Colonel Hardford jumped up from his chair, stretched his body, and said,

"Okay, guys! It's 1900 hours. Time to go home, for you married men! And you, my boy, and I—we have earned ourselves a first-class dinner. Where would you like to eat? And don't tell me at the US Short-Term Accommodations Center!"

Norbert had no idea what to say since he had never been to a real American restaurant.

Field Officer Hardford, however, knew his city well. Half an hour later, they walked into the Copacabana on East 60th Street, the perfect place for the two to enjoy great food and music as they talked, joked and relaxed before a day that was sure to prove especially demanding.

Early the next morning, a military taxi picked up Norbert. When the taxi reached the office building of Colonel Hardford, he was already waiting at the curb. "Don't bother getting the door for me! I am still fit enough to do that myself,"

Hardford said to the driver as he hopped into the backseat next to Norbert.

"So, how was your first night without an ocean under you?" he asked, smiling.

"Actually, Colonel, that was my second night on land. And thanks to you, I slept much better, now that you have given me a clear picture of what will be expected from me for the next several weeks."

"I'm glad to hear that. Just remember—whatever we do and wherever you'll go, we need to have you back in New York City in one month—that is on October eighth. On the ninth, the bell will be crated and stored securely on the ship which will transport the bell, the scroll, and you to Germany."

"Do we already know what ship it might be?" Norbert asked.

"I thought you knew how the military works. If you are told something specific too soon, the answer might be changed five times before it's over."

"So it might be the *American Clipper* again?"

"Norbert, don't worry what ship you will be on, as long as it's not the *Titanic*!"

Right now it was not the *Titanic*, but rather their ability to get to their destination that they started to worry about. Most of the major streets were blocked off to vehicle traffic, and no military ID would move New York's policemen to allow the taxi to get close to where the big flatbed truck with the Freedom Bell was stationed.

"But I am in charge of the event!" Hardford said, trying to keep his temper in check.

"Sorry, sir, but I have my orders."

The driver took one, then another, detour as the streets were filling up more by the minute. Sweating profusely, Norbert turned to Colonel Hardford.

"I am really sorry, Colonel, there is no way of getting to the bell. I think you better—"

"What?" Hardford interrupted. "Come on, Norbert!" By the time Norbert got out of the taxi behind him, the colonel had jogged almost half a block ahead. It took them ten minutes to plow their way through the thick crowd until they got to the big truck with the giant bell. Hardford was shocked to see 15 or 20 children who had climbed onto the flatbed truck and were banging with small rocks on the bell. Mortified, he yelled to Norbert, "No children! Do you hear me, Norbert! Absolutely no children on the truck or near the bell! Not now, and not ever!"

In seconds, Norbert was up on the truck, asking the children to get down. Any bystander could see that Norbert had never dealt with kids from the streets of New York. At first they looked surprised, then they booed loudly. But not a single kid moved off the truck. He was trying to think of what would work when he was startled by a shout right behind his ear.

"Get down, you little devils! Beat it, before I beat your brains out! By the count of ten!"

Hardford had jumped on the truck, ready to take on the unruly kids. Now the screaming children jumped off and fled in all directions.

"That's how it's done in New York, Mr. Anleger," said the Colonel.

The rest of the day went as planned. Everything ran like clockwork. Some of the spectators had heard on the radio about the Freedom Crusade. Many just came because others had come. The sound of the marching bands brought thousands more who curiously looked at the Freedom Bell and signed the Freedom Scroll. Norbert was not called on as interpreter all day, but he and the colonel gave six interviews for the press and also for city officials. When all the celebrations were over, it was hard to tell who was happier and more satisfied—the colonel or the interpreter.

Again, Hardford took Norbert to the Copa where they were greeted by New York City's mayor and deputy mayor, who would dine with them. The food was even better than the night before, even though neither Hardford nor Norbert had much time for eating in peace. The mayors and their support staff had endless questions about the Crusade: Where would the bell be taken from here? To how many American cities? What would happen to the signed Freedom Scrolls? How would the donated money be allocated;? And, where in Berlin would the Freedom Bell be housed permanently?

Finally it was all over. Tonight Norbert would sleep in a hotel close to the Freedom Bell rather than having to make his way through the still overcrowded and partially-blocked streets in order to get to the Short Term Accommodations

Center. As Hardford and Norbert waited outside the restaurant for their driver, they were tired but in high spirits.

"Well, Norbert, one down—25 to go! Right?"

"I guess you are telling me that the bell and I will visit 25 more cities with a similar program like today."

"Right again, except for the *similar program* part. I suppose each city has planned a different program, which will be shorter or longer depending on circumstances. And the convoy will have several vehicles in addition to the flatbed truck carrying the bell. By the way, I found out today that after your next stop you will be traveling, sleeping, and living in a comfortable bus."

"Will you be the conductor collecting the bus fare?" asked Norbert, jokingly.

"No, I will be the bus *driver*," the colonel joked back.

On the following day, the Freedom caravan was on its way. Most of the time, Norbert rode on the big flatbed truck that carried the Freedom Bell, though he was glad to be able to ride in the bus when it rained or he needed a rest. The press had named the convoy the "Freedom Train." Even Norbert considered "train" more fitting than convoy or caravan.

Even in his wildest dreams, Norbert never would have imagined how exciting the Crusade for Freedom across the USA would be. At first he kept a detailed diary of the dates and events of the cities visited. He noted the names of important people who had come out to greet and interview him. Soon, however, he discovered that he just had no time for all that. The moment their "train" stopped in one of the scheduled cities, he was overtaken by city officials, photographers, and reporters, all clamoring for a share of his time. After a few city stops, the bell train's own press agents printed flyers with detailed information about the history and purpose of the Crusade for Freedom, to be handed out by volunteers in each city and in bigger towns.

Among other duties, Norbert constantly had to tell reporters about his own family—or the loss of it—at the end of World War II. He was asked about his survival in post-war Berlin, and especially about his experience during the Russian blockade and the Western Allied airlift in 1948-49. Since his English was so fluent, some of the reporters had a hard time believing that Norbert was German and had been an eyewitness to what he was talking about. One of the skeptic reporters cornered him in Chicago.

"Say, how come you know so much about the World War II theater? Have you read a good book about it?"

Norbert did not smile when he replied. "I didn't have to read about it—I lived it! And for me it was not a *theater*, as you call it."

"But you are too young to remember all the fear, misery, starvation and survival tricks that supposedly kept you alive!"

Norbert reminded himself that he must remain calm and diplomatic, that he was like an ambassador for the bell and all it stood for. "What you lucky Americans don't understand," said Norbert, "is that during a war, people in the middle of it age faster. When the war ended in 1945, I was 13 years old. That's what my birth certificate said! But I felt at least 20—I had experienced so much horror, bombings, bloodshed and death. I had to grow up fast, or I would not have survived."

One week into the Crusade, they were leaving Kansas City, Missouri, where people had been exceptionally generous with their contributions to the Freedom Bell and signatures for the Freedom Scroll. Norbert checked his tour schedule and saw that the next stop would be in Denver, Colorado, where he would stay for only two hours.

"Driving about 600 miles from Kansas City to Denver, and then we stay there for only two hours? That's crazy!" said Norbert to the bus driver.

"Not so loud!" the driver cautioned him. "Can't you see everyone is trying to get some sleep after that marathon ceremony in Kansas City?"

"Sorry—but, if we drive that far and then have only two hours for a large city like Denver, what's the big rush?"

"The reason for the rush, young man, is that America is a big country! We have to go to many more cities, but have to be back in New York by October 8. *Verstehen Sie mich?*" The bus driver threw in the German term for "do you understand?" to impress, or perhaps to comfort Norbert. Before Norbert could continue complaining about the brief stay, the bus driver continued, "Yes, our stay in the Mile High City will be brief, but it will have character."

"Character?" Norbert asked.

"Well, perhaps character is the wrong word—I should have said *quality*. If you had studied your schedule a bit more thoroughly, you might have noticed that there will be no interviews and no long photo opportunities in Denver. The reason? General Dwight Eisenhower, most likely the future U.S. President, will be the speaker. Remember, he gave the first Crusade speech on Labor Day before you arrived. His fantastic speech was broadcast to millions of people, over all major radio networks. The same will happen in Denver. People will be nearly delirious when he gives a speech. Don't miss a word of it!"

"I won't!"

The bus driver had been right. The large crowd listening to General Eisenhower's speech went crazy afterwards. This was one of the early major speeches of the Cold War, when a top leader of the United States did not mince words, but dared to call a spade a spade! His speech was interrupted constantly by roaring applause, especially when he said, as he had on Labor Day:

"To destroy human liberty and to control the world, the communists use every conceivable weapon – subversion, bribery, corruption and military attack… this Crusade for Freedom is a campaign sponsored by private American citizens to fight the big lie, Communism, with the big truth, Democracy."

When the Freedom Train was moving again on September 16, it had to cover the slightly shorter distance from Denver to Salt Lake City. In Salt Lake City, however, the Freedom Bell and its crew were to stay for two full days. The trip between Colorado and Utah may not have looked far on the map, but the steep mountain roads were a challenge to the flatbed truck, the bus, and even the smaller military vehicles.

The day of arrival in Salt Lake City was a rest day. The citizens of Salt Lake City (the capital of the "Beehive State") really lived up to their state's nickname. For many days, if not weeks, they had been busy as bees with plans and preparations to make the visit of the Freedom Bell and the Scroll a great success.

They received permission to re-broadcast General Eisenhower's Denver speech here in the heart of the patriotic Salt Lake City. By now, Norbert was used to enthusiastic applause being given for General Eisenhower's speeches, and praise for the Freedom Crusade idea. It warmed his heart when he saw thousands standing in line to sign the Freedom Scroll and to drop their donations into large collection buckets.

Downtown streets and shops were decorated with flowers and banners. The well-dressed citizens impressed him, too. He just could not figure out the inscription on some of the banners displayed mainly near the State Capitol and the Temple Square. Finally he asked a group of young men, dressed in white shirts and black pants, for the meaning of one banner, "LDS of SLC for LWP." At first these youngsters were surprised that anybody would not know the obvious answer they were so familiar with. Then, spontaneously, they formed a speaking chorus:

"LDS of SLC for LWP!"

"Latter Day Saints of Salt Lake City for Lasting World Peace!"

"LDS—SLC—LWP!"

The city had planned an exciting excursion for the personnel of the Crusade to the Antelope Island State Park, located in the Great Salt Lake, connected by a causeway. Their sightseeing trip started at the Tourist Information Center, but they soon found themselves at the water's edge of the giant lake. Many took off their shoes and socks, rolled their pant-legs up, and waded into the super-salty lake water. Other visitors came better prepared, wearing swim trunks, so they could let their bodies float on the water surface. No chance of drowning here! The extreme salty water kept the bathers from going under.

Had they not been told at the Visitors Center that the Great Salt Lake was 4,212 feet above sea level, they would never have guessed it. However, once the tour bus stopped at the foot of Antelope Island's tallest mountain, which, with lots of sweat and energy they managed to climb, they read with self-congratulation: "Frary Peak – 6,596 ft." Norbert had never been that high in his life. Berlin's highest "mountain" was the *Kreuzberg*, 218 feet (66 meters) high.

Coming down from the Frary Peak was almost as challenging as going up, but they made it. When the bus took them to the south end of the island, they came across bison and they even saw pronghorns sticking their heads out of the high grass.

The day went by so fast that there was no time left for seeing any of the many colorful canyons Utah is famous for. But the great Creator had another treat for them on the way back to Salt Lake City: the setting sun had spread gold over the peaks of the Uinta Mountains, a mountain range where at least three of the many peaks reached over 13,000 feet.

When the group returned to the city, they began to split up to go their own ways to find their hotel, a place for dinner, or, for Norbert, a ride to his bus where he would sleep overnight.

"Hey, German boy!" someone called out as Norbert turned to see who. "Have you told your family in Germany how beautiful Colorado and Utah are?"

"No, I haven't. I have no time for writing letters."

"Why don't you telephone them?" asked the friendly coworker, whom he had not met before.

"Telephone them? Overseas? Do you mean telegraph?"

Now the man who had called out turned away from the hotel door and walked up to Norbert.

"Come on! Don't play dumb with me! You know how to make phone calls to Germany, England, or wherever."

"No, I don't!" said the embarrassed Norbert, "and I have never done it before."

"Well, then it's high time for you to find out. First of all, all military calls to anywhere in the world are free. Did you hear me? I said FREE. But you have to limit them to 15 minutes.

Second, you pick up the receiver and tell the operator your name, serial number, and the military outfit you are serving. Then you give the operator the name and number you want to talk to.

That's it!"

"And when can these calls be made?"

"24 hours a day—at least between America and Germany."

"But I am not in the military," said Norbert.

"Man, you might as well be. Listen, just call them tonight—no, wait, you would reach your people in the middle of the night! But if you call tomorrow morning at 700 hours, that should ring in Germany at three in the afternoon." He looked at his fingers like an abacus. "Seven plus six—no, we're on Mountain Time. Okay then—seven plus eight equals 15. That's 1500 hours, or 3 PM. Call them, OK? You can use my Outfit ID—Pioneer Battalion 347/12."

The man left before Norbert knew his name or could tell him how much he appreciated this information. Norbert felt as if a new world had opened up for him. He had never even thought of phoning Heidi across the ocean, especially since neither one of them were in the military. And now he had learned he can call her easily—and free! Tomorrow was a regular work day. She would be in her office at the Wertheim Department Store.

Chapter 26

Major Kotikov was one of those early-risers who always showed up as the first one to the office. He loved the extra hour in the morning when everything was quiet around him. He did not necessarily use that time to get a head start on work; more often than not, he would just stare out of his office window, or aimlessly thumb through the stack of mail to be answered. Inevitably, his thoughts would turn to his *Six Points How to Handle the East-West Exodus* guidelines, which had been ridiculed by his colleagues in Moscow. His telephone conversation with the cryptic "Committee of Eight" had ended abruptly, with the nearly threatening words, "You'll hear from us soon!"

He had never heard from them since. He did not know whether this was good or bad. His secret attempts to find out who comprised this committee had brought no results. Frankly, he was not surprised about the lack of action, because those military bosses who made it to Moscow usually worked underhandedly. Once he had compared them publicly (fortunately, only one time) to an underwater current, which often runs in the opposite direction of the surface current, called "undertow."

This morning when Kotikov entered his quiet office, he found a sealed letter on his desk. The envelope was propped up by paper clips so that he would not overlook it. He quickly ripped it open and read: "Commander Kotikov: Urgent! There will be a short but important meeting at 0900. All Allied commanders of the four sectors of Berlin are expected to attend. To guarantee the presence of the Western commanders, the meeting will be held at the *Schöneberg Rathaus*. Parking available at *Innsbrucker Strasse*, corner *Freiherr von Stein Strasse*. It is mandatory that you be there, and on time.

P.S. Bundespräsident Heuß from Bonn will be honored with a short reception after the session of the commanders."

Instead of ringing for the chauffeur, Kotikov reached for his car keys and slipped out of his office. He needed to talk to his deputy, Svertlov, even at this early hour. Perhaps "Lieutenant Maybe" had a better idea what this meeting was all about.

Kotikov took a shortcut through the *Treptower Park*. As he was passing the *Schlessischer Bahnhof*, a thought struck him. A few weeks ago, somebody had leaked to the press that he intended to rename the *Schlesischer Bahnhof* (station) to *Ost* Bahnhof, and the *Stettiner Bahnhof* to *Nord Bahnhof*. Since the former German province, *Schlesien*, and the city of *Stettin*, were now Polish, these names no longer fit Berlin and would forever stir up bad memories. Yet even many East Berliners had protested against such change of names. Would this controversy warrant such a meeting?

Or perhaps the discussion would deal with Kotikov's idea to demolish the badly war-damaged *Berliner Schloss* (castle) in order to create a big open square for future mass parades.

260

As a matter of fact, the demolition of the *Schloss* had already started.

When Kotikov reached his deputy's house, he discovered that Sergey Svertlov had absolutely no idea what might have prompted the hurriedly-called meeting of the Big Four.

In order to make up for his ignorance in this case, Sergey invited his boss to a quick breakfast.

"My wife is the best chef in Moscow—well, at least on our street *Perulok Stanislavski*. Now she has brought her cooking skills to Berlin. Comrade, you just have to stay for breakfast.

It is still almost two hours until your meeting in *Schöneberg*."

Kotikov had heard what a great cook Luba Svertlov was, even though Soviet military officers hardly ever talk about their wives. What did he have to lose? Besides, the reception for the West German *Bundespräsident* after the Big Four meeting would certainly only offer those dry American crackers and cheese.

"Okay, then, Tovarish. Let's have a quick bite!"

"No quick bites in our house when Luba cooks!" protested Sergey.

In no time, Luba whipped up a hearty breakfast: nine eggs, bacon, sausages, cream, crusted white bread, shredded cheddar cheese, lots of mustard, and a dash of cayenne pepper.

When Sergey came to the dining table with a bottle of fine red wine, Kotikov waved him off.

"Thanks, but no wine this morning for me! Meeting with those Western leaders, I don't want to smell like a drunk."

"*Charasho*, General! I have something with no stench," said Sergey as he hurried into his food cooler room, only to reappear with two flasks of vodka.

"Here! These will warm your body and soul—and without any odor."

The rare get-together of these three had a good effect on all. Sergey felt honored that his boss had come to seek his advice, and Luba Svertlov was proud of the general's compliments on her cooking. And for a few minutes, Kotikov relaxed a little, feeling more at home here with his generous hosts than with the starchy generals in Moscow who had become so critical. A quick glance at his wristwatch made the slightly inebriated Kotikov jump to his feet.

"Sorry, my dear friends, but I have to run!"

"Where is your chauffeur, sir? Do you want me to call him?" asked Sergey.

"No, I drove myself. Some things an officer has to handle without help. Besides, with my driver not being here, there was more of Luba's wonderful food for the three of us."

A few bear hugs as farewell were totally acceptable. Then General Kotikov took off in his big Russian limousine. He should have broken up the breakfast party a bit earlier—and he certainly should not have touched the second vodka!

Still, he knew his city well. During the morning hours, traffic was very light, anyway.

He chose the wide, almost-deserted *Prenzlauer Allee,* which took him from the *Prenzlauer Berg* district to the *Alexander Platz.* Because of a construction detour, he had to take the *Rathaus Strasse.* He screeched the car brakes to a halt as he suddenly found the road in front of the *Rathaus* (city hall) blocked by six buses. Dozens of East German tourists were taking pictures of the historic buildings and of each other, and they paid no attention to his loud honking.

By now, Kotikov was getting worried that he might arrive late for his meeting in *Schöneberg.* He yanked the steering wheel to the right, which took him to the *Friedrichstrasse* and then to the six-lane *Unter-den-Linden Strasse.* As he raced toward the *Brandenburger Tor,* an East German policeman standing in the middle of the street held up both hands to stop him. The speeding car had no option but to stop, nearly hitting the officer. The anxious (and slightly intoxicated) Kotikov was outraged. No *Volkspolizist* had the right to stop a Soviet Major General! Now the approaching policeman discovered his mistake. With an apologizing gesture, he waved Kotikov's limo to proceed.

Right after passing through the Brandenburg Gate, Kotikov was in the British Sector. He chose the first street going south. It was the once prominent *Potsdamer Strasse,* which he now used like a race track. When he finally saw the sign for *Bezirk Schöneberg* and recognized the Four Power Control Council Building in the *Kleist Park* to his right, he knew that he would make it to the meeting on time. Just when he took his foot off the gas pedal, there was a deafening crash, and the limo exploded in fire. Kotikov never saw the huge fire truck with two student drivers which failed to stop at the intersection.

Now the limousine and the fire truck formed a blazing inferno with no hope of survival for either the Russian officer or for the two firemen.

Word of the fatal accident spread quickly throughout both West and East Berlin. Since the crash had killed the highest ranking Soviet officer in Berlin, and two West Berlin government workers, the accident site soon became a jumble of East and West Berlin cars and trucks with reporters and investigators swarming all over the place.

The next morning, the Soviet newspapers—including the otherwise fairly neutral *Soviet Voice*, the paper for the Soviet military in East Germany—proclaimed:

"...the veteran commander of Soviet troops in Berlin, Major General A.G.Kotikov, met a violent death at the hands of West Berlin villains, who were assisted by anti- Russian American and Zionist fanatics."

Since neither the Soviet nor East German newspapers had any proof to back up their outrageous accusations, the articles were kept suspiciously short. Most affected by Kotikov's sudden death were Sergey and Luba Svertlov. They heard the tragic news soon after the crash, just a few hours after they had enjoyed breakfast with Kotikov. Immediately, they drove to *Schöneberg*, where at the intersection of *Potsdamer Strasse* and *Grunewald Strasse*, all traffic had come to a stop. Hundreds of German spectators had gathered. Even though the Svertlovs did not understand what the Germans were saying, they sensed that the death of the three people had touched the Berliners' hearts. People had already put flowers at the accident scene.

Sergey Svertlov stood motionless, completely overwhelmed by the events of the last few hours. Tears were running down his cheeks. Most Berliners had never before seen a uniformed Russian cry. Luba held on to her usually-strong husband, quietly saying something to herself.

"What are you mumbling?" Sergey finally asked.

"It cannot be true! It cannot be! It cannot be!"

What amazed the Soviets and Berliners alike was how quickly a successor to General Kotikov showed up in Berlin. There had been no press releases regarding what had happened to the body of Kotikov, or concerning the whereabouts of his family. Rumors had it that within 48 hours, they were flown to the Soviet Union where the Major General was buried with full military honors at one of Moscow's many cemeteries. For the time being, his grave had been identified with a hand-carved marker, showing just his name but devoid of any dates or military rankings.

A new man was on the scene now. His name was Andrey V. Molotov, and he was a major general, also. "Any relationship to the famous Soviet Foreign Minister Vyacheslav Molotov?" people asked.

"Yes, in a way. Instead of having his mother's maiden name, as we Russians all do, he has taken the initial of his uncle's given name, Vyachslav. That was sufficient for him. His rank is major general, but 'General' is how he likes to be addressed."

"So he really is a nephew of the foreign minister?" a reporter asked at a quickly arranged press conference.

"Yes, he is." The Soviet press secretary shifted in his chair, not sure what else he could tell the assembled journalists. "Off the record, I can tell you that he has accompanied his Uncle Vyacheslav to important international meetings as—as a kind of body guard. For example, when 16 countries met in Paris in 1947 to discuss the feasibility of the European Recovery Program, known as the *Marshall Plan,* Molotov flew to Paris, too. The foreign minister vehemently denounced the plan as another form of imperialism. Andrey V. Molotov agreed with his uncle 100 percent."

Another reporter, who wanted to shine with his knowledge of history, asked the press secretary, "Of the two Molotovs, who said, 'What happens to Berlin, happens to Germany; what happens to Germany, happens to Europe'"?

"The older and wiser Vyacheslav Molotov! But this younger Molotov follows the same line, if you know what I mean."

Now this younger Andrey V. Molotov had come to Berlin to fill the shoes of the battle-proven Soviet Commander of Soviet Troops in East Berlin, the late Major General Kotikov.

Chapter 27

Even though Norbert did not have his own telephone, he had used this marvelous invention since he was young. However, what was about to happen now was different. He, a civilian, was to make an overseas phone call to another civilian, his sister Heidi. The wall clock above Norbert showed 7 AM. Pushing aside the fear of possibly creating problems for himself, he reached for the phone. He gave his name and the borrowed battalion identity number to the operator.

"Thank you, sir!" a friendly voice responded. "Now please give me the number of the party you want to reach."

That was easy enough. After five rings, he heard Heidi's familiar voice.

"Good afternoon, Wertheim's Department Store. This is Heidi Anleger speaking—may I help you?"

Norbert had planned on starting the conversation with a joke or with a disguised voice, but when he heard Heidi's voice, all he wanted was to talk to his sister – finally!

"Heidi? This is Norbi."

There was silence on the other end of the line across the Atlantic.

"Hello, Heidi! This is your brother Norbert speaking. *Wie geht es dir?*"

"Oh, Norbi! I am fine! How good to hear your voice! How are you? Where are you calling from?"

Norbert had a hard time slowing down the flow of Heidi's words, and the beat of his heart.

"I am calling you as a freshly-recruited member of the US Battalion 347, presently stationed in Salt Lake City, Utah."

"Cut the crap, you wisecrack! The telephone time is too precious to talk to a comedian."

"But Heidi, I am so happy that I don't know what to say. Besides, thanks to Uncle Sam we have 15 minutes of free talk."

Every second of the free time was used as the siblings caught one another up on their lives. Norbert told her about picking up the Freedom Bell in London and about the USA Freedom Celebrations so far. Heidi told her brother about her work in both the purchasing department and the sales office at Wertheim's.

"And how are our folks at *Hermann Strasse* 245?" asked Norbert.

"Oh, Uncle Theo is fine—like always. Aunt Hanna is also good, if you want to call her sad condition good."

Norbert took a deep breath before asking the most important question.

"Seeing that our minutes are almost up, tell me, how is the American boyfriend?"

"Listen, Norbi, for you he may be 'the American boyfriend'—for me, Fred Harrington is the love of my life."

"Wow! That sounds pretty convincing. Are you sure, Heidi, that he is the one?"

"As sure as I can be! By the way, you would not believe how much German he has learned."

"Fred knew some German from his Schweigert grandparents, he told me."

"That may be so—as little as it might have been! But from our first date on, he constantly asked me for German translations of hundreds of words."

"And I thought I was the interpreter!" Norbert laughed.

"Hey, Norbi, before I forget to ask—Fred has an older brother, Jim, who married Cindy, a Mormon girl from Utah. Now that you are in Utah, have you per chance run into a Jim or Cindy Harrington?"

Norbert could not help but laugh.

"Darling sister! There are thousands and thousands of Mormons in Utah and Colorado—perhaps some even by the name of Harrington. My tour bosses are keeping me so busy here that even if I had looked for them I would not have a minute to talk to a long-lost relative of your boyfr—I mean, of Fred's. Like today—I have the Freedom Bell Ceremony, which sometimes can draw out over three hours. Then I have to persuade as many people as possible to sign the Freedom Scroll. Then I will have several interviews. I tell you, Sis, some of these radio journalists can be real pests if you don't respond to their questions—"

"Good, good! It's alright, Norbert! I was just asking. I have no idea what Utah is like."

"Maybe one day we should come back here for an extensive trip?"

"You and I and Fred, okay?"

"Naturally! I'll join you two on your honeymoon to America."

"Ha!"

"Your fifteen minutes is up," the detached voice of the operator interrupted.

"Til next time, then!" Heidi quickly said.

"Okay. Talk to you soon. Take care."

After the uplifting talk with his sister, Norbert was ready for a full day of activities in Salt Lake City. Norbert just hoped that his sister's falling in love with Captain Fred Harrington, actually her first real love, would last a lifetime. After all, she was born in 1928. That made her 22 years old, old enough to know what she was doing! The difficult years after the war had also matured her beyond her age.

Heidi, on the other hand, was close to the end of her work day. Her heart was filled with overflowing joy because of her talk with Norbert. The trouble was that she knew of nobody she could share her happiness with—other than Fred. Forgetting about the Fraternization Law, she reached for her phone and dialed Fred's office number. The call worked without an operator's assistance! That was the second big surprise of the day.

"So how are you doing today, Heidi?" asked Fred, casually.

"How am I doing today? That's all you can think of when you first hear my voice over the phone?"

"Your real voice sounds much nicer than through this machine," answered Fred diplomatically.

"Fred, I just had to tell you that a few minutes ago I talked to Norbert in Salt Lake City."

"That is indeed some interesting news. How did that happen?"

"That crazy brother of mine made the connection through a military exchange and reached me here at Wertheim's. We talked for 15 minutes."

"There goes somebody's weekly salary!"

"No. The call via the military was free. Darling, it felt so good talking to Norbi."

"Heidi, I share your joy with all of my heart."

Fred was so used to making and receiving phone calls every day—many even overseas— he could not help but marvel at Heidi's excitement. The highly-developed Germans had lost so much because of World War II. Now, five years later, it was still a rarity for a private party to have a phone connection.

Two weeks ago, when he made a business flight to Stockholm, he had mentioned the German telephone dilemma to two businessmen over a cup of strong coffee. The Swedes, who had grown up with "a telephone in their cradle," as they say in Sweden, thought that Fred was pulling their leg.

271

"No, I am not joking," said Fred.

"I cannot even imagine life without a telephone," one said. "And of course you Americans wouldn't think of it. You know, one time I worked for *Stockholms Allmänna Telefonaktiebolag*—before they came on the scene every bit of our telephone materials and engineering came from America."

Fred and Heidi were on the phone much longer than 15 minutes. They cherished their face-to-face meetings, but at least now they could talk over the phone in spite of the Fraternization Law, which Americans and Germans alike detested and thus ignored—except for the communist East German officials. Whenever Heidi and Fred met somewhere in Berlin, time seemed to race by too fast. Still, sometimes Heidi felt guilty that she claimed too much of Fred's free time, especially when he had mentioned once that reading was no longer his main hobby, since there never seemed to be enough time for it. Just to support his "former" reading habit, she would ask Fred what he was reading.

"Let's see. I read an interesting article about the United Nations Secretariat being constructed in New York City. It will be a 39-story building of white marble with lots of green glass. And I just started reading A.B. Guthrie's new Pulitzer-prize-winning book, *The Way West.*"

"Who is A.B.Guthrie?" asked Heidi.

"In 1947, he wrote the novel *The Big Sky.* But let's talk about Guthrie another time! What are you reading these days, darling?"

"Having very little private time with the three roommates around when I come home from work, I don't even dare to start reading a thick book. So I read magazines that customers or colleagues leave for me."

Heidi hesitated to divulge more about her present reading choices. Fred waited for her to continue.

"Right now I am reading—I don't even remember the title of the magazine—an article about the very first *Kriegsbraut*—war bride—Charlotte Petty, from Ladenburg. She married an American soldier in December of 1945. She had to wait for two years until she was reunited with her husband in America. Her one-year old baby had never seen her daddy before."

Carefully, very carefully, Fred asked, "Are you reading my mind, darling? Some nights, when sleep will not come, I lie awake and dream what it would be like to be married."

"You, too?" Heidi asked in surprise.

"Yes, me too! When the Air Force shipped me over to Germany a few years ago, my secret plan was to buy a Porsche. I have never told anybody of that far-fetched dream. But when I met you and really, really fell in love with you, you became the focus of all my dreams. First you—the Porsche can wait!"

"Are we still on the phone, Fred? Please forgive me for taking up so much of your time!"

"Forgive you for what? Maybe I owe you a bigger apology. I work for the military, but you work *for a living.* But let's not forget about this topic. When can we meet? We need to look for better living quarters for you. You have endured long enough living with three-plus-two people in that little apartment."

"I'll be off this Friday. How about you?"

"I have a meeting, but I can change the time and be done by 10 o'clock. May I pick you up at 10:30—or as you would say in German, *halb elf*?"

"I will be waiting for you at 10:30, and always!" said Heidi, in the most enchanting tone.

Chapter 28

Since everything had happened so fast in his life due to the sudden death of Major General Kotikov, Andrey V. Molotov felt like a fish taken out of the Moscow Red Sea and thrown on the dry and hostile land in Berlin. He really should have been proud for having accomplished at a young age what many older and more experienced officers were still only dreaming about. Most likely, his famous family name and relationship to the Soviet Foreign Minister Molotov had influenced the committee's hasty decision to make him Kotikov's successor.

Now he was the Commander of the Soviet Troops in East Berlin. What he was lacking in experience, he could make up for with an extra amount of confidence. He would prove to his jealous colleagues in Moscow that the right man had been sent to Berlin at the right time. His official first two days were spent composing directive ordinances for his troops.

Ordinance # 1: New business cards would have to be printed, spelling his given name with a "y", not with a "j"; i.e. Andrey.

Ordinance # 2: Always use the French spelling of "troupes" over the American-sounding "troops" on all official documents, including the new business card.

Ordinance # 3: He was to be addressed "General" instead of "Major General."

Ordinance # 4: Discontinue the hunt for the young "no-name spy" from West Berlin. Explanation: Far too much money and time had been spent to catch a rather insignificant youngster, who most likely was not even a spy. Resources will be put to better use.

The "Ordinance of the Day" list contained many more points, including the admonition to the Soviet occupation force to show respect to each other, regardless of military rank, and to the German population. General Molotov would not tolerate the "hate all Germans" attitude which had been fueled by campaigns led by Ilja Ehrenburg, Aleksey Surkov, and other high-profile Soviet literary figures. Typical of this campaign were slogans such as, "Germans are no human beings. Kill the Germans!" and, "It should be an honor for every Russian to kill a German." This new commander, who intended to speed up spreading the communist ideal of international peace and understanding under Soviet domination, knew this extreme intolerance would be counterproductive.

At the end of his second day, Molotov ordered his secretary to get the message to Lieutenant Sergey Iliavitch Svertlov to be ready for his first meeting with Molotov the next day.

"Where would the Major General like to meet Lieutenant Svertlov—in your office or in his?" asked the secretary.

"In *my* office, of course! And you will address me as 'General,' understood?"

The Russian army private understood clearly. He instantly noticed that a new wind of authority was blowing, and he better sail along with it.

Lieutenant Svertlov also noticed the change of atmosphere the moment he stepped into the commander's office. "Good morning, Major General Molotov!" Svertlov greeted his new boss.

"General, please! Understood?"

This admonition surprised the good-natured but well-educated Russian officer.

"*Da*, Comrade Molotov!"

"General Molotov! Understood?"

These were the first two times Svertlov heard Molotov use the word "understood." Over the next two years, though, he would have to tolerate this condescension thousands of times.

Since Molotov had not offered Svertlov a seat, he moved a chair over from against the wall to in front of the commander's desk and sat down. After all, he had been in this office hundreds of times before to meet with the previous commander. He was one of the most respected liberators of Berlin, had a civil engineering degree from Moscow University, and now he was this newcomer's deputy!

Molotov came right to the point, his flaming words flying like arrows. "Lieutenant Svertlov! I have studied your job evaluation written by the late A. G. Kotikov. You did well enough with the task of blocking West Berlin in 1948, but you and Kotikov completely failed to prevent the Berlin Airlift."

Svertlov sat up straight in his chair, his mind racing with words to defend himself and his former commander, but he knew better than to speak until the General was finished—and he clearly had more to say.

"Furthermore, you had no success in hindering the brain drain from East to West Berlin. Your 'Six Points of How to Handle the East-West Exodus' are ridiculous and made us laugh in Moscow."

"Excuse me, General Molotov. The 'Six Points' document was not from me! Major General Kotikov composed them. I had not even read them until after Moscow denounced them."

"Well, you could have stopped him from looking like a fool."

Svertlov decided to keep his mouth shut. This young officer without any international experience seemed to be full of himself and his new rank.

"There is another very important item we need to disc—I mean, I need to tell you.

Stop this absurd waste of resources hunting the young German! By the way, he is not nameless any longer. My immediate staff and I are convinced that this youngster, who you and other Soviet officers have failed to arrest, is a young interpreter working for the US Air Force. His name is Norbert Anleger. By now he is known too well, and is too popular with many Americans and Germans to be snatched off the street and thrown into a Russian dungeon or an East German prison. You blew your chance to find this troublemaker."

"General, how did you find out that his name is Norbert Anleger?"

"I thought that *you* are the one working for the Intelligence Unit. You want a hint? This man's gangster activities go back to 1947, when KGB agents arrested the anti-communist reporter of *Der Abend*, Dieter Friede. Friede was hiding at the office of his doctor, Peter Dau. Norbert, a relative of the doctor but also his patient, opened the door and admitted our agents to Dau's practice.

"General, sir, please tell me a little more. We worked on this case a long time," said Svertlov.

"Why did Dieter Friede come to Dr. Dau's practice, you must be wondering? The *Komitet Gossudarstvennor Bezopatnost*—KGB—lured him there to help his friend and colleague, Seiler, who allegedly had been hurt in a car accident. However, there was no Otto Seiler at the doctor's. A bit later, Friede left Dr. Dau's practice as a handcuffed prisoner. Unfortunately, Norbert Anleger witnessed the entire incident. During the following months he leaked the details of this arrest to the Western press. Since the KGB had failed to also arrest Dr. Dau and Anleger, they later tried everything to at least catch the witness, Anleger, since Dr. and Mrs. Dau had already fled to West Germany."

Svertlov started to interrupt with a question but the commander held up his hand to cut him off, and continued, "Why do I tell you all these details? Because you were personally involved in the botched Friede affair. Just so you know, Svertlov, this Anleger was not worth stirring up so much trouble then, nor worth your continued idiotic chasing after him all this time. Understood? So what that he had witnessed Friede's arrest! Since then, Soviet agents have captured hundreds of East and West Germans! Anleger is history! Understood?!"

Oh yes, Lieutenant Svertlov had understood his boss well. No more chasing after this

German spy, or gangster, or potentially threatening witness—or whatever he was! *Rest in peace, Norbert Anleger,* Svertlov thought, as he also wished his former boss were alive so he could finally tell him the German boy's name.

Chapter 29

When Fred saw Heidi walk through her apartment door, he jumped from his Jeep—right into her loving arms. Had there ever been a time in his life when he had been so happy? There had been many highlights, like when he had won sports trophies in school, or when he became one of America's youngest pilots, or when he was promoted to captain. Now happiness had taken on a different perspective; it was the overwhelming feeling of loving and being loved.

"So, how is my baby today?" Fred asked, still holding Heidi in his strong arms. He had never before called her "baby" and she was a little surprised.

"Baby? Did you say baby?"

"Well, I could have called you 'darling' or 'love.' You know we Americans use the word 'baby' much more casually than you Germans."

"Aha! Now it's 'we Americans' and 'you Germans'? Is that how it will be from now on?"

"Well, there is nothing wrong with 'you Germans' and 'we Americans' until the day when we both will be Americans. I did fall in love with you, right?" said Fred.

"Oh, Fred! You are so wonderful! You would make a good German, too."

"Sure, sure, after all the *Bratkartoffel* and *Kartoffelpuffer* my grandparents stuffed me with. Come to think of it, you are going to love my grandparents, Alex and Hedwig Schweigert, too."

"Help me out again, Fred—the Schweigerts are your mother's parents, right?"

"Yes, and they raised my mother and then my father to be the best turkey farmers in Sumner, Iowa—maybe in all of Iowa."

Detecting the enormous pride in his voice, Heidi could not help but ask, "And the Harrington side were the ones who kept you humble?"

"I don't know about that. All I can say is that I bet you a thousand dollars that you'll like my parents, George and Anna Harrington, with all of your heart."

"Why are you so sure about that? Don't forget, they will be my in-laws."

"Much better than if they were your out-laws!" laughed Fred. Then he looked deeply into her eyes and his tone became serious. "I can honestly say that my God-fearing parents are the loveliest people in the world, and I am positive they will make you feel very, very loved."

Some people in the street had stopped walking, wondering why an American officer was holding on to a young German woman for what seemed forever. When they caught a glimpse of their eyes, they knew that these two were in love. Most of them smiled when they saw the couple finally let go of each other and take off in the Jeep.

They were floating on air as always when together, however, today business was number one on Fred and Heidi's agenda. Fred was right; it really was time for her to find a small apartment where she could live by herself. Fortunately, she had gotten along well all this time with her landlord and her three roommates, but now she had earned promotions at work and the ability to spend a bit more money on her own comfort.

Before meeting Fred, Heidi had studied the "For Rent or Sale" ads in the newspaper. It had been a quick study, because only very few ads offered an apartment to single occupants. The shortage of living quarters was still a major problem in 1950 Berlin. Fred, living in military barracks, had no idea about any of that, thus he let Heidi take the lead. As they were driving, Heidi shared with Fred how hard it was to find a decent place with adequate repairs and no water leaks.

"I never talked about it, Fred, but do you know what the greatest hardship was living in one apartment with so many occupants?"

Fred did not even dare to guess.

"That we lived with the constant worry of how to control our electricity usage. Thinking back on the months during the blockade, they were the worst of all. Our electricity allowance had been reduced to two hours per day, or night. In our kitchen we had a stove with gas burners, but no gas! In spite of our best attempt to live within our electric allowance, our landlord was fined 10,000 marks during the coldest month in 1948."

"What? That is impossible!" interrupted Fred.

"It may sound impossible, but it happened to us. Naturally, we split the fine equally between the apartment owner and us renters. Actually, our landlord was relieved because he could have been sentenced to 12 months imprisonment on top of the 10,000 marks."

"That sounds totally ludicrous."

"You are right. But even more preposterous was that our ration cards granted us, per person, only two pounds of bread and 200 grams of meat per week. We were also entitled to half a pound of sugar per month, but it was almost never available!"

"How in God's name were you able to survive?"

"Many people did not survive…and God must have been weeping. One neighbor family had a break-in. Thieves robbed them of the family's ration cards. In despair, the father sealed the kitchen door, turned the gas stove on and poisoned his family of four. So sad. God must have wept especially hard."

Fred did not want to show his tears of sympathy and pulled the Jeep over to the curb while looking away from Heidi. She saw what was happening anyway. She tenderly put her arm around his neck and whispered in his ear, "It's alright, Fred. It is okay to cry, even for a man."

For a while nobody moved and nobody said anything. Then Fred found the first words.

"Heidi, you and thousands of women and men in Berlin have looked into the furnace of hell. But you have survived. Praise God for that!"

"There were many days, weeks, and months in my life when I had *nothing* to thank God for. I wondered if there was a god who cared at all, especially when I felt like I was being swallowed up by the devil." Now she, too, felt the sting of tears in her eyes.

Fred put his hand on Heidi's shoulder. With the other hand, he pressed her left hand and said, "There *is* a God who cares. Trust me! I have talked to Him most of my life. And sometimes He talks back to me."

"Okay," said Heidi. "Why don't we ask God to find the right apartment for me."

"Let's do that right now!" answered Fred, and addressed God audibly with the very same petition, to the absolute surprise of Heidi. Fred's prayer was short, like a son talking to his father, which indeed it was. Then he ended his prayer with a loud "Amen!"

"Fred, you really meant that, didn't you?" Heidi asked.

"Yes, I really meant it, because I have experienced God at work, answering the petitions of his children, many times before."

Heidi had no words to respond. She was even more speechless when, in less than two hours of searching, they found an adorable little 2-bedroom apartment in Berlin-Tempelhof, close to Fred's barracks, and with a good U-*Bahn* connection both to her work place and to her uncle's apartment in *Neukölln.*

The apartment owner was a former, highly-respected architect who had just completed the first half of a reconstruction project. The gray-haired gentleman with pleasant manners was happy to have found his first renters. Heidi quickly agreed to the asking price and signed a contract which stipulated a moving-in period within seven days.

"Seven days is a fair time for such a move," Heidi said to the architect. "Besides, seven is my lucky number."

"Are you superstitious, *mein Fräulein?*" the man asked Heidi, with a charming smile.

"Actually, no," Heidi said, hesitantly. "I am not superstitious, not even about the proverbial lucky number seven. But Captain Harrington here, my dear friend, asked God to help us find the right apartment for me. Perhaps there was more than luck at work."

"How are you, Captain Harrington!" said the man, excitedly and in fluent English. "Are you stationed in Berlin?" Fred had purposefully kept quiet until now.

"No, *ich bin ein Berliner!*" Fred answered, saying "I am a Berliner" in his joking way.

"Thank you for the compliment, Captain! Incidentally, I have cousins and aunts who emigrated from Germany to the USA many years before the wretched war. We were able to stay in touch with them, even during the war, via Switzerland, where a friend translated my German letters into English. With all German and our German names omitted, he then mailed the letters to California and Wisconsin."

"Wisconsin, you said?" Fred asked. "That is next to the state where I was born, Iowa."

"I know where Iowa is, sir. As a matter of fact I still remember all states and their capitals. Our high school teacher made us memorize and identify them geographically, before our Nazi government discouraged us from knowing too much about America."

"The Nazis did not manage to suppress you learning fluent English. You must be gifted in languages," Fred said.

"That could well be so. I speak five, which is not that unusual for many German businessmen. Actually, I don't even include two of the ancient languages I had to study during high school many, many years ago, Latin and Greek."

"So you really speak seven languages?" Heidi asked.

"No, dear, I know nobody who can claim to *speak* Latin or Greek. But—but I know what I should have done more than 30 minutes ago—introduced myself properly! My name is Wolfram Siemens," he said, with a polite nod to Heidi and then to Fred.

That name was instantly of interest to Fred, who asked, "Do you belong to the Siemens Dynasty? Have you been accused of any war crimes?"

"No. My family belongs to the not-so-rich Siemens side, which nobody could accuse of being war profiteers. The war did draw many other Siemens into the quest for the fortunes of war, which changed our highly respected pre-war reputation into a maligned death-causing industry infamy."

"As a famous architect, you were never recruited by Adolf Hitler to build his German

Fantasy Cities?"

"No! For Hitler's crazy building projects, he needed people who agreed with his political philosophies and plans. My colleague, Albert Speer, was such a man. In 1942, Hitler made him the Minister of Armament and Ammunition. I never could understand what that had to do with architecture, and I told him so. That was the end of my relationship with Speer."

"You'll please forgive my curiosity, Mr. Siemens," said Fred. "I've read a lot about the Nazis, but there is so much more I'd like to learn—not that I will ever understand their thinking."

"Nor I," said Siemens. "The crisis for Speer came with Hitler's order to melt down every single church bell in Germany into material for casting cannons. That was too much, even for the Hitler-follower, Albert Speer. Naturally, in the battle to prevent this insane order from being carried out, Speer lost. Even though he succeeded in avoiding Hitler's wrath, after the war the Allied Forces sentenced him to 20 years imprisonment at the Spandau Prison, where he will serve every single day of his sentence."

"Forgive me, friends, I always have talked too much in my life. This time I just wanted you to know that not all people named 'Siemens' are war criminals. As I mentioned before, some of my relatives were on Hitler's side, some were sitting on the fence; and some worked against him at the sacrifice of their lives."

It really was time to say goodbye, and as they were shaking hands in good German fashion, Mr. Siemens said casually, "You two seem to like each other quite a bit."

"Yes, and we are getting married," Fred said, matter-of-factly.

Mr. Siemens didn't let on if he noticed Heidi's little gasp as her eyes grew wide, and she bit her lip. "May I ask when and where the wedding will take place?" he asked, politely.

"We'll let you know, Mr. Siemens," said Fred. "Bye!"

Once they were back in the Jeep, Heidi turned to Fred. "What have you done, my love? You told Mr. Siemens that we are getting married. Did I miss something? When did we discuss that seriously?"

Fred headed the Jeep down the road, wearing a big smile. "But we have discussed it, darling—perhaps without words. Whenever I kiss you—really kiss you—that's me asking for your full, loving commitment. I wish I could ask your parents' permission to marry you, but you've lost them. All I can do now—wait just a minute!"

Fred brought the Jeep to a halt, jumped out and rushed around to her side. Heidi was just opening her door, when she saw Fred getting down on one knee. He pulled a small, cloth-wrapped package out of his breast pocket. He bought a friendship ring a few weeks ago and had been waiting for an opportune time—perhaps like now!

"Heidi, you are the love of my life! No long speech when I am kneeling on the side of the road, so, I just ask you: Darling, will you marry me?"

"Yes, you crazy lover! I will marry you to have and to hold forever! And now, please, get up, before some fast car ends your precious life!"

Chapter 30

There had been a lot of flag-waving and marching band music in Salt Lake City. Most citizens seemed to be very happy living there in the Desert State, which their forefathers had built with their own sweat and pioneer zeal.

It would have been fun if Norbert could have located Fred Harrington's brother while in Utah. Jim Harrington, and his wife Cindy, could have told Norbert a lot about what it was like to move to, and live in, Utah. And Norbert imagined he would learn a lot about his future brother-in-law, Fred, if he got Jim talking about his younger brother what it was like growing up in rural Iowa. But who knew where Jim and Cindy were now, or if they were still alive? Fifteen years was a long time, even in America.

Now, when the Crusade Train was ready to continue its journey across the West, Norbert was looking forward to not only getting to know different types of people and see new areas of the United States, but also to being an effective witness to the privilege of living in western freedom, in contrast to existing under communist suppression.

Next stop for the Freedom Bell was San Francisco. What a magnificent city! Walking across the sunny, but wind-swept

Golden Gate Bridge was a totally different experience for Norbert than what he had imagined from reading about it.

A similarly exciting experience awaited him in Los Angeles. This huge city spread out over hundreds of acres and seemed to have no beginning or end. Studying the southern California map, Norbert's finger cruised from Santa Monica in the north, to Newport Beach in the south. He saw that Oceanside and San Diego seemed to belong to "greater Los Angeles" and even the Mexican border town of Tijuana acted as if it belonged to Los Angeles. He would have loved to explore Hollywood and Beverly Hills, however, his duty to the Freedom Bell came first. He did take time to record in his notebook some of the places he now could only pass by, but wanted to return to visit some day in the future.

From Crusade stops in Phoenix, Albuquerque, Dallas and Houston, to stops in Atlanta, Raleigh and Richmond, the desire to spend more time in each place became overwhelmingly stronger. The Crusade schedule was purposefully tight in order to expose the bell to as many Americans as possible, to raise awareness and funds. Resigned to the rigid time line, Norbert comforted himself by remembering that his main reason for coming to the US was not to sightsee, but to help bring the message about the often abominable conditions in communist Eastern Europe, and especially about the dilemma of the divided German nation.

At last, there were only three Crusade stops left: Washington, DC; Philadelphia, PA; and New York City. These three important cities were outdoing each other to make the celebrations memorable. Musical bands were giving their best. In each city, several speakers were giving inspiring, short speeches which caused frequent applause. Civilians and uniformed volunteers collected signatures and donations from the vast crowds gathered around the Freedom Bell.

By now, close to 16 million Americans had joined the Crusade for Freedom by signing the Freedom Scroll, which proclaimed:

<u>I BELIE</u>VE IN THE SACREDNESS AND DIGNITY OF THE INDIVIDUAL

<u>I BELIEVE</u> THAT ALL MEN DERIVE THE RIGHT TO FREEDOM EQUALLY FROM GOD

<u>I PLEDGE</u> TO RESIST AGGRESSION AND TYRANNY WHEREVER THEY APPEAR ON EARTH

<u>I AM PROUD</u> TO ENLIST IN THE CRUSADE FOR FREEDOM

<u>I AM PROUD</u> TO HELP MAKE THE Freedom Bell possible, to be a signer of the declaration of freedom, to have my name included as a permanent part of the Freedom shrine in Berlin, and to join with the millions of men and women through the world, who hold the cause of freedom sacred.

Norbert expected a large and impressive welcome for the Crusade in Washington, DC, this absolutely beautiful capital of the United States, and he was not disappointed. People came by the thousands to see the Freedom Bell, which by now had been displayed in 23 different states. There were delegations of senators and groups of congressmen who came to see the bell, but also to be seen by as many voters as possible.

There were bands from schools and universities, and organized groups from sports clubs and historic societies, just as Norbert had anticipated. What he could not have imagined happened on the second day on the Capitol grounds. The President and his entourage had just left the highly-secured location where the decorated bell rested on its big flatbed truck, when somebody threw a Molotov cocktail against the bell. As the explosive bounced off, white smoke quickly swept across the truck and engulfed some spectators. A few people were screaming; others covered their faces in shock or perhaps in shame. Then one loud voice could be heard above all: "People of America! What are you doing? Are you celebrating the people who killed your sons who were fighting for freedom in Poland, France and Norway? Get rid of this fake Liberty Bell! Drown it in the Potomac! Down with Germany, Italy, and all the other Germany-sympathizing nations!"

Norbert watched as a few bystanders tried to get hold of the bullhorn which the raving man used. Within minutes, police were able to silence the outraged protester who had interrupted the peaceful celebration. As they led him to a patrol car, the man continued his rant, now shouting out, "Death to all Germans! We should have bombed them to hell! Why are we coddling those devils? To hell with the Marshall Plan! Damned be also all Soviet satellite nations who licked the Russian boots! Now they are stretching out their greedy hands for our hard-earned money, while—"

The squad car door slammed shut. Norbert was stunned. Had it taken 23 major stops across America, plus 20 short stops in additional cities, only to run into such an incredibly foul situation here in the capital? While Norbert still stood in shock, he felt a tug at his sleeve.

"Come with me, young man! Please follow me! Somebody wants to talk to you," a neatly dressed, middle-aged man urged. What was he to do? Did someone try to trap him? Did this have a connection with the shouting maniac, with his cohort now attempting to lead him away and drown him along with the Freedom Bell in the Potomac River?

When the tugging and pulling got stronger, Norbert decided to face the challenge head-on. He followed the man to a news mobile unit and was asked to wait outside. Wait for what? After a quick ID clearance, Norbert was waved in. He started to relax when he saw that this was a legitimate news trailer. Looking around, he saw two technicians behind a large recording control board getting ready for action. Before Norbert could ask a question, a young man introduced himself as Samuel Goldberg, the news anchor of WNSI, the Washington News Service International.

"I apologize for dragging you over here like that, but after that guy with the Molotov cocktail, we were afraid for your safety. You are a German citizen, right?"

"Yes, I am."

"We want you to know that you are safe here with us."

"Safe from what?" asked Norbert. "What do you mean? I have traveled all across your country and have met hundreds of people, and I always have felt safe."

"Good, good! What I meant to say is that in our country there is still a lot of racism against Latinos, Negroes, Asians, and even Germans."

"But my race is the same as your American race, Caucasian."

"That's true. Perhaps I used the wrong word. Look, I told you that my name is Samuel Goldberg. I personally know many Jewish families who are not willing or ready to forgive what you Germans did to our parents and grandparents."

Norbert had to bite his tongue which was eager to defend his own innocence with regard to the Jewish suffering and the Holocaust. He remained silent, though, waiting to see where the conversation was going. Goldberg, who easily was ten years Norbert's senior, reached behind him for a Coca-Cola bottle and opener.

"I hope you drink this stuff," he said as he handed the bottle to Norbert.

"Not only do I drink this *stuff*, I really like it—and occasionally use it to clean the tires of my boss's car."

"I do that too," laughed Goldberg. "Now let's see what else we have in common. You mentioned your boss. Now, who would that be?"

"Over the years I have had quite a few American bosses," Norbert quickly responded.

"First there was Major Robert Blythe, then Captain Kalamai Giftos."

"I don't know them."

"Then there was General Lucius D. Clay, the US Military Governor for Germany."

"I know who General Clay is. Was he really your boss?"

"No, not really! He was my friend, just as he was a real friend of all German people, especially in West Berlin."

"Then why did you claim him as your boss?"

"Just to impress you!" laughed Norbert sheepishly.

"Great! Go on with your reference list."

"General Maxwell Taylor, the US Commander of West Berlin. He sent me on the Crusade for Freedom."

"Wow! That's a short but impressive list. Tell me, did you have enemies, too – just for balance?"

"Yes, I do. For some reason I am the declared arch enemy of the Soviet Major General Kotikov, the Commandant of Soviet Troops in East Germany and East Berlin, and his Deputy Sergey Svertlov."

"Did you say Major General Kotikov?"

"Yes. Why?"

"He was killed a few days ago."

"He was killed?"

"He died in a fatal car collision on the West Berlin side. His successor is Andrey V. Molotov."

A strange silence followed, which made the recording crew even more nervous. They had been waiting for a signal by Goldberg to start the recording. Until now they had witnessed only the private conversation between the interpreter and the reporter. To break the silence and to get the interview going, they gave Goldberg the starting signal.

After the wordless admonition by his recording crew, Goldberg now focused on the Crusade for Freedom issues. He was fairly young but also extremely skilled, so he could quickly identify and discuss the matters of the Freedom Bell tour. Norbert easily matched Goldberg's skill of dealing with the history, purpose, and experiences up to the disturbing last hour. Neither Goldberg nor his watchful crew could believe how fast the one-hour interview slipped by.

Relieved, Sam Goldberg leaned closer to Norbert.

"Norbert Anleger, we are done! Thank you for a very informative interview. Now, please give me a few minutes of totally *off the record* time."

As the crew checked the recordings they had just made, the two men moved to a side table. "Well, Norbert, when I got the assignment to interview you—a German—I was upset. Why had they picked me—a Jew—for the interview? There are many senior reporters who would have jumped at the chance. When I told my girlfriend, who is also Jewish, she told me to refuse the assignment, to stay out of trouble. I guess she knows my temper. She knows of my hatred of Nazi Germany, and my weakness of treating all Germans alike. If you knew my family's history, you would understand."

Looking straight into Goldberg's eyes, Norbert spoke slowly and very deliberately.

"If you knew my family's story, you would understand me better, too." Again there was an odd silence between them.

They had talked freely about the Crusade for Freedom and the bell's travel across the country. But now, they were touching each other's heart and nerves—and they were treading cautiously. Norbert continued, carefully, "You have told me that you are a Jew, Mr. Goldberg."

"Please, call me Sam."

"Thank you, Sam. We both were born in Germany, am I right?"

"How did you know?"

Norbert shrugged, as if to say he was only guessing.

"But that's where the similarity of our families ends," said Sam. "I was shipped as a little baby, via Holland, to relatives in America. You grew up with the Nazis."

"You know, Sam, not all Germans of our age were automatically Nazis. Granted, some children had parents and older siblings who were members of the Nazi Party, but by far, not all!"

"Listen, Norbert, weren't you and your brothers members of the Hitler Youth?"

"At the age of ten, all German boys and girls were automatically enrolled for eight years as Hitler Youth members. It was not a matter of choice. The only exceptions were if you had Jewish blood, or if your parents were either homosexuals or convicted criminals."

"What, then?"

"Those boys and girls suffered, and were shamed into feeling unworthy to be part of the constantly-praised *Third Reich* of Adolf Hitler."

"I really did not know that," admitted Sam, with a mixture of surprise and apology.

"Don't worry, Sam. Many people living outside of Germany during the fateful years from 1933, when Hitler became the *Führer*, and 1945, when he committed suicide and plunged Germany into the deepest hellhole, really do not know what life was like in Nazi Germany."

"What about your family?"

"Neither my father nor my mother were party members. After the war ended, we found out that my father had died in a German concentration camp in December of 1943, where he had been incarcerated for allegedly disclosing important war secrets that helped the enemies."

"That's awful, to not even know his fate until after he died."

"Yes, it was one of many awful things. My oldest brother, Hans, after having lost one arm and a bit later, also one leg, was discharged from military service and sent home to Berlin. He and my mother were killed in the same air raid on April 28, 1945. To top off this tragedy, I need to tell you that my 15- and 16-year old brothers had been killed one day before, while defending a city hall in Berlin against the Russian troops.

"Even my pro-Hitler sister, Heidi, never was a Nazi Party member, even though she enjoyed her leadership role in the female branch of the Hitler Youth, the *Bund Deutscher Mädel*.

Don't you think, Sam, that this is enough news for one day about one family living and dying in Nazi Germany?"

After clearing his throat several times, Sam Goldberg asked, "What was wrong with the world our parents had before? My family consisted of law-abiding, well-educated, loyal Germans. They were neither upper nor lower class. Well-respected in their community, they belonged to the stable, affluent middle class. What my grandparents had accumulated through hard labor, my parents considered a blessing from God to prosper and share with others. They were normal Jews happily living in Berlin and caring very little about their forefathers from Jerusalem, if that is where they came from.

"My grandfather served with distinction as an officer in World War I. The economic depression of the 1920s robbed them of much of their hard-earned wealth. They managed well through all crises, until National Socialists like Hitler, Göhring, Himmler and Goebels *destroyed* their existence—" Sam's voice was choked with emotion as he finished, saying, "In their own beloved homeland!"

Sam's heartfelt story moved Norbert to get up and put his arms around Sam. Sam then told how his family felt that in the future, Jews would be the constant victims of Nazi hubris and hate. Thus, even before Hitler planned for the total extermination of the Jews, they sent their baby, Samuel, to family members in America.

A few years later, Sam's parents tried to get to America, escaping Germany through Spain. Somebody there reported to the German Consulate in Madrid about their possible plan to flee much further west to the US. Their passports were confiscated, to be picked up in Berlin. When they did so, his parents were detained and then taken to the Buchenwald Concentration Camp near Munich. His grandparents, taken to Auschwitz, suffered the same fate, along with millions of other innocents.

Two men, originally from the same country but living in two different worlds, had painfully recollected the insanity and destructive force of misguided pride, arrogance, and evil. They had been thrown together in the most unlikely one-on-one encounter, only to discover the common, blood-stained ground they shared. The Freedom Scroll did not yet bear their signatures, but with their hearts they pledged *to resist aggression and tyranny wherever they appear on earth.*

Chapter 31

When Norbert and the Crusade for Freedom convoy arrived in Philadelphia, their next to last stop, they confronted a split audience. At least half the Philadelphians were proud that their famous Liberty Bell had served as model for the new Freedom Bell, to be hung in Berlin, Germany. The other half was jealous, if not angry, that their historic bell had been abused by being cast into an anti-communist symbol, having nothing to do with American history.

Norbert Anleger and other bell officials sensed that the most important job awaiting them was to clearly explain to Philadelphia's divided population the mission of the Crusade for Freedom. In his presentations, Norbert made a word-game of the Philadelphia's Liberty and Berlin's Freedom Bells. Most listeners got the point right away, and their frequent laughter indicated that they were in agreement with how "their" bell had been used. In one of his interviews, Norbert even used the image of cloning the famous bell to create a precious "offspring" – thanks to the Philadelphia original. The generous donations and thousands of Scroll signatures proved that most people in the *City of Brotherly Love* were at peace.

On October 8, 1950, the Freedom Bell, on its extra-wide flatbed truck, arrived in New York City. Norbert had seen

Manhattan's breathtaking silhouette from the ocean-side before, having crossed the Atlantic nearly a month ago. Now he was approaching it on land from suburb to suburb, until the Freedom Train reached the heart of the city.

In his mind, he could not thank General Maxwell Taylor enough for having given him the chance of a lifetime to assist with interpretation jobs during the Crusade, and especially for the privilege of representing Germany when expressing her deep appreciation for the help and kindness West Germany had received from America. Norbert was filled with emotion as his bus approached the crowds which had already gathered. He reached for his last city itinerary. He would have plenty of time later to reflect on his experiences in the magnificent country of America.

In metropolitan New York's bustling city energy, neither Norbert nor his coworkers were surprised that the celebrations began the moment the Freedom Bell's truck was securely anchored in place.

On October 9, these celebrations reached their peak when 19 "Displaced Persons" (DPs), originally from Poland, Russia, Ukraine, Latvia, Estonia and East Germany, gave beautiful and heart-warming performances in dance, poetry and song. When the mayor of the city announced that the goal of securing 16 million "Declaration of Freedom" signatures had been reached, the crowd got carried away, dancing around the bell and in all available spaces. Bands played and even more people came out to join in, street vendors busy serving cold drinks, hot-dogs and other crowd-pleasers. Then suddenly it was all over! Now hundreds of sanitation crews moved on the scene, washing, sweeping and carting away the tons of trash. The

Freedom Bell was transported to the port, and in less than 24 hours the 10-ton bell was loaded onto the *USNS General R. M .Blatchford.* Its American tour complete, the now-famous Freedom Bell was headed home to Germany.

After arriving in Bremerhaven, it was unloaded to be delivered to the Berlin-*Schöneberg* City Hall on October 21. An unforgettable event for all Berliners was in the making! Even General Clay was scheduled to be at the celebration. As a special friend to all Berliners, he had been selected to dedicate the Freedom Bell on October 24. The American "Fathers of the Crusade for Freedom," Abbott Washington and Nate Crabtree, would also be present.

Norbert Anleger had lived with the illusion that once the bell was aboard the *R. M. Blatchford*, a restful period would begin for him, but that was not to be. Thinking back on the ten-day journey from London to New York City, those days had been pure vacation. Frankly, even the month-long USA tour with the Crusade had been much more enjoyable than exhausting. He had found that his "ambassador" role was often called for, and only rarely had he needed to serve as interpreter. And, in spite of many interviews with the American and international press, there always had been a string of hours when he could plan his own short side-trips.

None of that was the case now! Just before the ship had pulled up anchor, a small group of Army communications specialists came aboard. As skilled as they might have been in their field, none of them spoke German, yet they were on the way to install the Freedom Bell in Berlin. Norbert just shook his head. How would these "communications specialists" communicate with German work crews? He had to think of his Greek-American Air Force boss and friend, Kalamai Giftos, who would have had the fitting explanation for this snafu: *"Hey, man, keep in mind that you are dealing with the Army. Don't expect perfection!"*

Approaching the European continent, Norbert began receiving more teletypes and telephone messages. Most were in English, but many were in German. If needed, Norbert had to translate them both ways, as soon as they reached him.

When the ship sailed into Bremerhaven, he tried to phone his sister, Heidi. This time, however, his faked military connection did not move the operator to put the call through to Berlin. Norbert had to wait until the bell and most of the ship's crew (and the Army communications specialists) were on land. Then he rushed to the first public phone booth on the pier, and this time he had success. Heidi was overjoyed to hear from him. He told her that the US tour had gone well, and that he hoped to be back in Berlin in one or two days. Just when he wanted to ask her how it was going with her boyfriend, Fred, two bell crew members frantically waved him to quickly drop everything and come back to the truck.

"Sorry, Heidi! I have to go now. Talk to you once I have my ten-ton baby in Berlin." That was all the time he had; he ran to catch up with the already-moving truck.

"What's the hurry, guys?" Norbert asked, out of breath, as he jumped onto the truck.

"Are you scolding us, when you are the deserter?" one of the crew yelled back. "Look, even our new truck driver can't speak English."

Norbert quickly saw that it was his turn to apologize.

"Sorry, guys! It will not happen again. I just wanted to let my sister in Berlin know that our ship had … ."

"Sure, sure! You had to tell your sister—you said YOUR SISTER, right?—that soon you would be in her arms again."

"Come on! I really did phone my sister. I've had no time for a girlfriend."

Actually, nobody on the flatbed truck had time for debating Norbert's personal life. Since no vehicles other than the big truck met them at the Bremerhaven pier, they had placed their personal luggage next to the bell, barely leaving sufficient space for themselves. Supposedly other cars would be available for them at their hotel in Bremen.

"Do you know where Bremen is?"

"I sure do!" said Norbert, "South of Bremerhaven."

"South of Bremerhaven? So is Zürich and Rome. I need to know how far Bremen is from here."

"About 75 kilometers—or less than 50 miles. Why?"

"Bremen is the place where our import papers will be checked, and where we will stay overnight. And you better stay close to us when we have to deal with German customs!"

That's what Norbert planned to do, anyway. The big truck had just enough room for the Freedom Bell, for the military engineers and their luggage, and for Norbert. With Norbert forcibly in command again, even though he had never before traveled here by truck or any other vehicle, things were looking up. He was able to explain to the German driver where to go and for what reason.

The customs process took a bit longer than expected. One of the officials insisted that he had to inspect the bell, declaring that the crew had to remove all protective packing materials. Before a small revolution broke out, Norbert went to work, using his most convincing words and smiles to change the official's mind. They were permitted to proceed.

The truck had to make several stops so that Norbert could ask for directions to the hotel. Since it was so new, he got no help until he finally spotted a postman in uniform.

"I know where it is," he told Norbert. "Right by the *Radio Bremen Building.* Tomorrow, when you continue your trip to Berlin, take the *Kurfürsten Allee,* which is the tributary street to the Hannover autobahn. Then you drive east through Hannover and Braunschweig. In Helmstedt you will cross into the Eastern Zone of Germany, or as the East Germans call it, the *Deutsche Demokratische Republik.* As Americans, you should have no problem with the border crossing and driving through the Russian Zone."

Norbert thanked the man and signaled the truck driver to go. Unexpectedly, the postman got hold of Norbert again.

"I forgot to mention—don't break the speed limit in the Eastern Zone! All vehicles must drive 100 kilometers per hour, or less. And one more thing—make sure to get better vehicles for you and your men! What worked for you on the short stretch from Bremerhaven to Bremen will not be sufficient once you are on the fast autobahn. Trust me! I know how we Germans feel once we drive on the autobahn. Good luck!"

"Have you seen anything like that?" asked one of the American crew. "You ask a German what time it is, and he tells you a long story of how to fabricate a watch."

"*Ja, so sind die Deutschen,*" said Norbert, "but they mean well, and want to be of help."

The next morning, Norbert asked at the hotel desk for the location of the closest car rental. "The closest? Bremen has only two car rental places. One is close to the port in West Bremen. The other is in East Bremen, right at the entry to the autobahn. I suggest you take that."

"Could you order four cars for us?" asked Norbert.

"Four cars just for your group? That might take three to four days advance reservation."

"Well, we need the cars today. Please find a way to get them for us."

"Young man, you must be joking! First of all, hotels do not get involved in making car reservations because of too many currency difficulties. Secondly, in case of military clients, you will be better off to make your own reservations through military channels."

"And where would I do that?" asked Norbert, now a bit irritated by the unhelpful clerk.

"I have no idea! I am a civilian."

One of the crew who had witnessed Norbert's attempt to rent four cars saved the situation. He had a large pack on his back, a military field telephone. Without asking Norbert, he went into a side room, set up the phone and called his contact there in the British Zone.

"Yes, that's what I said! Army Pioneers, and we need four Jeeps, or any other passenger vehicles—today! …Yes, four! … We have to pick them up in Hannover? That is about 100 kilometers from here…Okay, we'll be there in two hours."

He hung up and turned to Norbert. "You may have learned to speak English well, but you have a lot to learn about cutting through the crap. You have to be more demanding than diplomatic to get things done."

"I'll try to remember. Still, thanks for getting the bell moving again, even though the trip to Hannover will be crowded, dirty, and very windy."

Norbert was relieved to see that when the bell truck with its "overweight load" arrived in Hannover, four cars were waiting for them. The transition of the crew from the truck to cars was smooth and fast. Finally things were going well, until they came to the East German/Russian checkpoint in Helmstedt.

There had been no trouble at all on the West German/British side, but when they pulled up to the Allied Military Checkpoint, a red-painted Jeep, flying a Soviet flag, came to a screeching halt behind them. Two armed Russian soldiers posted themselves in front of the truck with the bell. The third soldier climbed onto the truck, and a fourth soldier ran into the barricaded checkpoint barrack.

After a noisy, lengthy palaver at the Allied Checkpoint, the Americans driving the four Jeeps could not believe that the Soviets were powerful enough to require them to realign their vehicles so that they could drive through the West/East German Checkpoint. Once they had arrived there, Norbert did everything in his power to convince the Eastern checkpoint personnel that this was an American shipment, not subject to East German inspection. Since the transport of the bell was considered a regular action, nobody had bothered to apply for a Cargo Interzone Transport Permit. The unyielding East German answer was: This shipment comes from Bremerhaven, a West German port, and will be taken to Berlin-*Schöneberg*, in West Berlin. Thus, taking the cargo through the German Democratic Republic makes it subject to GDR rules—*basta*!

Norbert helped the leader of the Army Pioneer crew fill out the transfer forms, which were all in German. His attention was interrupted by the loud voice of a man approaching him.

"You! Young civilian man, please hand me your passport!"

"No, you may not have my passport," answered Norbert in English. In the past he had flown many times between West Berlin and West Germany when working for the US Air Force, especially for "Action Stork" during the airlift. He knew that he should never surrender any personal Western IDs or documents to Eastern authorities. Now, being so close to Berlin and under enormous time pressure to get the Freedom Bell delivered on schedule, he would not give in to any East German or Soviet demands.

Some of the American soldiers formed a circle around Norbert. "No papers from us! No papers from Norbert! No papers from us American now or ever!"

This very loud show of solidarity seemed to have an immediate effect on the pig-headed East German custom officials, who exchanged glances of uncertainty with one another. The high point of the hostile stand-off came when the American Lieutenant of the Pioneers spoke up. Looking straight at the East Germans he said, "Maybe this young Airman First Class, or *young man* as you called him, prefers to travel in civilian clothes because he sweats more and works harder than any of us—but he is one of us! And he even speaks your language, while none of us do. So, leave him alone—and us! Okay?"

Norbert did not have to translate what the brave soldier said. His tone and gestures had said it all. The bell truck and the four military cars were waved through, though without a smile by the checkpoint "robots." The passengers in the borrowed military cars, however, could not help but laugh and discuss the border control interlude all the way to West Berlin. When this strange-looking convoy eventually arrived at the *Rathaus Schöneberg* and the crew peeled out of their cars, the American Lieutenant who had spoken defiantly to the checkpoint guards patted Norbert on the back. "I said that you sweat a lot and work harder than we do, and that you are one of us," he said. "That was the truth, wasn't it? I said it then, and I'll say it again now— you are a *first class man.* Thank you for your service!"

Today was October 21, three days before the dedication of the Freedom Bell was scheduled. However, judging by the hundreds of Berliners milling around on the *Rathaus Platz,* one would have thought that the ceremonies were to begin any minute. There really was not much time left to get the construction work completed and the heavy bell in place. Norbert got little sleep during those days. His interpreter skills

311

were requested here, there, and everywhere— not to mention all the German reporters who tried to find out all about the success of the Freedom Crusade across America. When Norbert finally got a few minutes to phone his sister at Wertheim's, the call had to be brief—as usual! Heidi quickly promised Norbert that she would be present at the Bell Dedication— along with Fred.

"Oh, Fred will come along with you?" Norbert asked.

"Naturally! We are family!"

On October 24, all schools were closed to give students the chance of participating in this historical event. All children of West Berlin were smiling on that day. Even though the ringing of the Freedom Bell was scheduled for noon, more than 500,000 Berliners from both parts of the city streamed into the *Rathaus* Square from early morning on. Reporters of 2,000 radio stations from around the world were on the scene. Even Konrad Adenauer, the Chancellor of the Federal Republic of Germany, had come from Bonn, along with four government ministers.

Incidentally, or perhaps by design, October 24 was the international United Nations Day, first observed in 1948. Norbert, one of the first to show up at the *Rathaus*, felt very proud that the eyes of the world were on Berlin that day for a good and noble reason. He quickly got to work, assisting the event's organizers and officials in any way he could as all the last-minute details came together.

Around 10 a.m., at a brief break which all Germans call the *"Zweit-Frühstückspause"* (second breakfast break), Norbert looked up and could not believe his eyes. In front of him stood his friend, the field officer for the New York area, Colonel Bruce Hardford. He had flown to Berlin to be part of the Freedom Bell Dedication, too.

"Norbert, here you are chewing away on a sandwich," Hardford said, with a twinkle in his eye. "And I was afraid you would be too busy to even recognize me."

"Colonel! Colonel Hardford! How did you get here?"

"By plane! Remember: Air Force members always fly, or fly always, even if just to check the mail box on the neighbor's lot. That is—that is except for a few members who had to guard a brand new bell on an old ship—ha, ha! Seems you are happy to see me again, Norbert?"

"The word 'happy' is not strong enough to express my feeling when I see you, Colonel."

"Wow! I can hear that you have continued polishing your English—not that it was bad before."

"You will have a chance to judge my English in a few hours, when I will interpret Berlin's Mayor Ernst Reuter's speech into English, and General Lucius Clay's dedication speech into German," Norbert replied, with unmistakable pride in his voice.

"They could not have found a more capable man for this job than you!"

"Thank you, sir! You are always complimenting me."

"That's what keeps the world turning, when we compliment somebody, from whom we expect the best performance. By

313

the way, will we have some time for dinner, like in New York? This time, however, you will have to choose the restaurant."

"Sorry, sir, these days I have no idea what is being expected from me from hour to hour—often until midnight."

"That's alright, busy man! Next time then—if there is a next time."

They hugged each other and parted. Norbert threw the leftover pieces of his sandwich to the nearby pigeons and hurried to City Hall. It was high time to meet the dignitaries whose speeches he was to interpret.

The Lord Mayor Ernst Reuter was the first to address the half-million-strong crowd. Organizers estimated that of the 500,000 in attendance, about 100,000 had come from East Berlin. Reuter declared that, "Germany will never rest or relax until freedom will shine over the countries of Eastern Europe, which at present are forced to live in slavery."

Then it was General Clay's turn to speak. He began telling how the Freedom Bell, which had been financed by American donors and had just completed a month-long tour through the USA, had quickly become a symbol of American-German friendship. Norbert had not been given the opportunity to read Clay's speech in advance, yet he knew that what would come from the lips of this General, the dear friend of most Berliners, would be good. Norbert's heart pounded as he translated: "It is in the spirit of deep reverence that we dedicate the world freedom bell today. We dedicate it to the eternal honor of all those who have given their lives in the cause of freedom."

The roaring applause of the Berliners almost drowned out the General's words, when he summed up his speech by categorically stating:

"From this day forward, as it rings, may it strike a note of warning to all oppressors, a sound of confidence and courage to those who are called upon to defend their freedom, a message of hope and sympathy to those who are enslaved!"

Clay's hand traveled across the speakers' podium and reached for the button, which supposedly was to electronically signal the bell to ring. However, a fuse had blown, so that nothing happened.

In the midst of interpreting General Clay's final words, Norbert had simultaneously seen Clay's hand press the button. No sound of the bell! Norbert finished his translated German sentence and then—without an explanation to the startled speaker—he raced to the staircase that led to the belfry in the tower of the city hall. He had been there the night before when the crew who had installed the bell tried out the ringing mechanism, and were satisfied it worked.

Desperately, he pulled and pushed several wires, hoping to make an electric contact. Nothing! What a humiliation for the general and the US, and what a fiasco for the hosting nation, Germany! Where was everyone?! He could not believe no crew members had been assigned to the bell tower in case of a glitch.

With unflinching determination, Norbert threw his jacket into a corner and put all his weight against the bottom lip of the suspended bell, pushing with his legs and flattening his back against the belfry wall for support. Slowly, slowly the huge bell moved a fraction of an inch, but gained momentum as it swung back. Norbert pushed harder and harder and the clapper moved as well. Then he heard the bell tongue hit the bell stronger and stronger. Eventually the full sound created by the swinging bell and the hitting clapper almost overwhelmed him.

The Freedom Bell rang out for the first time—and was heard around the world, including in Eastern Europe over *Radio Free Europe*. Nobody had told Norbert how long the bell was to ring. He pushed until exhaustion set in and perspiration ran down his face. Let freedom ring! Let freedom ring!

Chapter 32

If Major General Andrey V. Molotov had hoped that being the Commander over the Soviet Troops in East Berlin would be a position of honor and glory with lots of free time for European travel, he soon found out how wrong he had been. Each day the workload seemed to increase. It looked as if his predecessor, A. G. Kotikov, had not been fond of work, at least not as fond as of his stock of vodka.

With the help of two military secretaries, Molotov uncovered hundreds of files that should have been processed years ago. Some of the paper documents literally had a bad stench since they had not been looked at for months or years. One day, Molotov gave the secretaries an unexpected leave so that he had the offices and all the filing cabinets to himself. After ten hours of concentrated work, even the cleaning personnel would not have recognized the two rooms.

Instead of just discarding outdated files of prosecuted or suspicious individuals (many of whom by now had escaped to the West) he made it a point of first reading each and every one before tossing them. At the end of this extra-long and lonely day, he felt more like a snooping file clerk than a member of Moscow's elite.

When, at his rather young age, he had been given the honorable position over the Soviet troops in Germany, he had reconfirmed his vow to himself to never drink vodka or any other strong alcohol. He had experienced what the alcohol demon had done to his father and to some of his friends.

With shame, he remembered the day of his graduation from the prestigious Leningrad Academy. After a lengthy, boring ceremony with lots of flag-waving and endless praises of the glorious Motherland, his Academy buddies had challenged him to drink with them in as many bars as they could, without passing out. The drinking tour had started in two bars in downtown Leningrad. Since one of his colleagues had received a 5-seater *Volga* as graduation gift from his rich father, five of the new officers decided to do their serious drinking outside of Leningrad, where nobody would recognize them.

In the old town of Pushkin, south of Leningrad, they found the most hospitable and romantic bars. After each emptied bottle of wine or beer or whatever the bottles contained, the five graduates felt more and more celebratory. However, when all the bars in Pushkin finally closed, they searched for more fun in the neighboring town of Kolpino. There they found a hangout still open long after midnight, with drinks being served by scantily-dressed waitresses. Soon all were so drunk that nothing mattered any longer; not the kind of drinks they had, not how much the drinks cost, how they were served, nor who served them.

Eventually they all agreed that it was time to head home. As they staggered to the *Volga*, it was clear its owner was not going to be able to drive. He sat on the sidewalk, waiting to be helped into the back seat. When they were looking at each other to see who might be the fittest survivor of the drinking spree, Andrey said, "I'll do it! I still feel good, and I know the road from Moscow to Zagorsk."

Why was Andrey talking of Moscow and Zagorsk? Had the drinking tour taken them that far east—all the way from Leningrad to Moscow? Everything and everybody seemed to be completely dazed. But they agreed, if Andrey knew the way to Moscow or Zagorsk, let him be the driver! Andrey's drunk-driving skill, however, was soon put to the test. When he backed out the fairly large *Volga* from its parking spot, he hit a concrete post behind him with full force. While Andrey rested his alcohol-loaded head on the steering wheel, his other four passengers jumped out of the car to inspect the damage. It was too dark to see anything.

"I think nothing happened to the car, from what I can see," one of them said in self-comfort.

Andrey lifted his head, foggy and embarrassed, and wondered what his buddies were doing outside the car. In a slurry voice he called out, "The engine is still running, brothers!"

"Yes, but you will no longer be the driver," threatened the *Volga* owner. "I will be driving."

Andrey's heavy head had started to throb. "Here," he said, as he opened the driver's door, "it's all yours!" Then he just let his body slide to the October-cool ground. His equally inebriated buddies pushed him back into the car—but this time into the back seat!

Sitting behind the wheel of his car, the owner at least remembered that their Academy was in Leningrad and not in

Moscow! When he reached the big highway between Kolpino and Pushkin, he stopped the car, looked to the left, then to the right, and again to the left and right, left and right, suppressing the urge to throw up.

"Get going, you lousy turtle!' his comrades yelled. After that remark, he revved up the motor and sped all the way to Leningrad without saying a word. The others were asleep anyway. With his window down, the chilly wind was the only help he had to stay conscious. When he passed Leningrad's large main station, he brought his car to a body-jerking halt.

"Hey, guys! I have a great idea," he said. "Why don't we send our snoring friend, Andrey, on a long train ride he will never forget? Understood?" with the last word he imitated Andrey's ridiculous habit of using this term. His friends just stared at him, and Andrey only grunted and was dead to the world.

"Besides having fun, this prank will not cost us a single *Ruble*. Just help me get him into the station!"

The Academy graduates had built up their muscles over many years and, though staggering a bit, they had no problem carrying their by-now-unconscious drinking partner into the station. They decided to just put him on one of the platform benches and leave him to sleep it off. At least one of them was considerate enough to take Andrey's wallet and ID for safekeeping. It could be disastrous if someone lifted these off him while he was passed out. Then the boys discovered that the sleeping car train next to them was ready to leave the station in twelve minutes.

"That's just enough time for us to put him to bed," one of them laughed—and all four knew what was coming! This was their buddy's punishment for backing the new car into a concrete post in Kolpino.

"Here in 'Wagon #5' is a good place. There seems to be some vacancies. Let's heave him in here and give him a good ride!"

"Guys! I just saw that this is an express train with no stops between Leningrad and Tallinn, in Estonia!"

"So what? The further—the better!"

Their loud laughter alarmed the train conductor who rushed up to them. When he saw that he was dealing with uniformed Academy officers, he slowed down and approached them with the typical Russian respect for the military.

"Can I help you with something, comrades?"

The four pranksters looked up in surprise. "Perhaps you can, sir. Our friend here, the top graduate of the Leningrad Academy, had a bit too much to drink, as you can see. Since he has a very important meeting with the mayor of Tallinn tomorrow, we were helping him to get on the train. His future is depending on a good outcome of tomorrow's meeting."

"But where is his luggage?" the conductor asked.

"It has been sent ahead with a government courier."

"And what about his train ticket and other IDs?"

"The courier will have all of that. His important departure came up so suddenly that planning blunders have been made. Sorry for that! In the meantime, kind comrade, help us to find a worthy sleeper-compartment for our friend. We don't know which one he has paid for, but we do know that it was in Wagon # 5. Everything will be cleared up when your train reaches Tallinn. *Charasho?*"

"Otchin charasho, Tovarishi!" The zealous conductor clicked his heals, then helped the pranksters put Andrey into a vacant First Class compartment, where they laid him fully-dressed on the white-sheeted bed. With not even one minute to spare, the young men lined up on the platform with serious faces, saluting the conductor, while he gave the signal to get the express train rolling. Two long whistle blows gave the assurance that everything was well.

On the way back to the Academy, the hazy brains of the graduates slowly worked a bit more clearly, showing the first signs of a bad conscience. Perhaps they had gone a bit too far with their prank—perhaps even more than a bit! But Andrey Molotov had none of these sober thoughts. The sound and motion of the fast-moving train made his alcohol-induced sleep even deeper.

The still-puzzled conductor was wise enough to let the drunken officer sleep. He looked at his watch and saw that it would take the train another four hours to reach Tallinn. He was one of those citizens who loved to live in the mammoth-sized Soviet Union, even though he had been born in Central Asia—more precisely, in Uzbekistan's capital, Tashkent, now a part of the Soviet Union. A conscientious employee, the conductor had never allowed himself to fall asleep on duty, even though some of the train routes had been through the most boring tundra. However, mostly when riding night trains with sleeper wagons, he had been able to cultivate his hobby:

reading books. Both his grandfather and father had loved books at a time when books were not easy to come by.

Tonight he was too nervous to read anything. The image of the four Academy officers placing their drunken comrade on his train was still vivid in his mind. He was extremely anxious to find out who this allegedly important fifth soldier was.

Following his required routine of many years, the conductor silently walked from wagon to wagon through the entire train. In the small caboose at the end of the train, he signed a chart and marked the time of his inspection round. As he walked back, he announced with a voice loud enough to wake up the passengers: "Next stop, Tallinn! Get ready for the next stop, Tallinn!"

When he came to the First Class compartment where he had allowed the anonymous Academy officer to be placed, he knocked at the door. Then he knocked again. When he still got no response, he reached for his master key and carefully opened the compartment door.

There he was, the Academy officer from Leningrad, lying sprawled across the bed—just the way he had left him several hours ago. Some dried vomit was sticking to his one cheek. Even his otherwise stunning-looking uniform was soiled around the neck.

"Get up, comrade! We are approaching Tallinn. Get ready!"

Finally, after several attempts to wake him up, the conductor saw Andrey Molotov force his eyes open. With a still drunk-sounding voice, Molotov asked anxiously, "What is going on here? What do you want from me? Who are you?"

When the conductor just looked at him reprovingly, without saying anything, Andrey said in a sharply, "Get out of my room – whoever you are!"

"Comrade, this is not your room. You are in the First Class compartment in Wagon # 5 on the Leningrad–Tallinn Express. Understood?"

The last remark by the uniformed conductor shocked Andrey back to reality, and into silence. As hard as he tried to remember, he had no idea how he had gotten on this train. His splitting headache did not help his memory either. And, where in the world was *Tallinn*?

In spite of an almost blind respect for the military— especially for officers—the conductor suddenly suspected foul play.

"I will be back," he said to Andrey, quickly continuing his walk through the remaining train wagons to announce the impending arrival in Tallinn. Then he was back in Andrey's compartment.

"So, you don't remember anything about how you got here?"

"I have absolutely no idea!"

"That should tell you how blind drunk you were when four young officers, wearing the same uniform as you, brought you to the train in Leningrad and put you into the sleeping car of the night train to Tallinn. They claimed that you had paid for it and that you had to get to a meeting with Tallinn's mayor."

"What? I don't even know exactly where Tallinn is."

Now the conductor's voice took on a sharp tone.

"If you were a marine officer, I would have you arrested for *free booting*. By riding one of our trains and not paying for it, you have deprived the government of its rightful income. The law calls that criminal. Over the years as a conductor, I have jailed many freeloaders like you. That's where you belong, too, in spite of your fancy uniform—which, by the way, no longer looks at all decent."

"Sir! That would ruin my future as an officer. I beg for your forgiveness, comrade. I would never decide to do such a thing. My buddies have pulled a very foolish prank, though I was foolish to get so drunk. But please—have mercy and let me go free this time. It will never happen again!"

The conductor took Andrey to the open wagon door, waited only a moment to be sure the train had completely stopped, and gave him a hefty push. Still somewhat shaky in his bones, Andrey landed on his feet, but then fell flat on his belly. When he pulled himself up, he saw that he had added many more dirty scrapes to his uniform. But—he was free! No jail time for an accidental freeloader like him!

But what now? Never before in his life had he faced such a degrading situation. He was far from his base. He had no money for food or travel. He knew of no friends in this strange city. The worst challenge was that his legs still did not want to carry him properly, and his head hurt so much his eyes burned. Why had he given in to that crazy drinking contest of his so-called friends?

Looking for a secluded spot away from the railroad station where he could sit or lie down, he saw a tall church steeple in the far distance. In the past, he had never wanted anything to do with churches. Now, he knew that next to a church he would find enough privacy. These days, many people walked long detours to avoid being identified with religious buildings.

On the way to the church, he had to pass the former Estonian Parliament and the Office of the President. He walked past it on the opposite side of the street because he knew that this official Soviet Government building would not be a source of help for him. He even passed the Canadian Embassy without asking for help there. He had been thoroughly brainwashed—NEVER trust a Westerner or Western organization.

Tallinn's cathedral, with its four towering, onion-shaped steeples, had been shut down as a place of worship. All entrances were blocked off by solid wooden beams. Here, Andrey did not find the rest and privacy he had hoped for. People were constantly rushing by. When they passed him, many shook their heads at him as if they were looking at a strange bird with a grimy face and an even dirtier uniform.

With great effort, Andrey reached the other church with the towering steeple. There he dropped to the ground in exhaustion. After catching his breath, a large plaque on one of the church walls caught his attention. He stood to walk closer in order to read the inscription, which appeared in both German and Russian. Andrey read that this colossal Olevista Lutheran Church had been built by German settlers over one hundred years ago. During World War II, and later under the Soviet rule, most German-speaking members had either fled to the West or had been "relocated" to Siberia. The church was now "Baptist" but, for all practical purposes, this was no longer a functioning church. He realized that he would get no help here, either.

Sitting down on the cold stone floor with an empty, growling stomach made his mood- thermometer sink dangerously low. Looking up at the imposing church spire, he had to ask himself what had happened in such a short time to him—a proud Russian officer, fresh out of the Academy, full of high aspirations? Now he was here, with nothing, appearing in public like a dirty, homeless vagabond.

All of a sudden a slightly bent-over, old woman touched his shoulder. She asked him something in a language he did not understand. When Andrey gave her only a silent, sad smile, she realized that a young Russian officer would not understand Estonian, the complex Finno-Ugric language spoken only by Estonians. Out of curiosity, she asked, "*Sprechen Sie Deutsch?*"

Again Andrey just smiled at her faintly. He recognized her words were German, and that she was making every effort to communicate with him. He could tell from her kind eyes that she was also trying to be helpful.

"You look as if you need something to eat," the woman said, now using Russian.

"Yes," answered Andrey in a soft but eager voice. "I am really hungry."

"But, sir, we have several good eating places in Tallinn. Why don't you buy yourself a hearty breakfast?"

"I have no money."

The woman's jaw dropped. Never would she have expected such an answer from an army officer. She did not dare to ask another question, but Andrey added, "Ah, it's a long story, *Babushka!*"

Just then, a plain but beautiful girl of about 18 joined the strange couple. She greeted Andrey in Russian, with "*Dobri den*" ("Good Day").

"*Dobri den!*" he answered, getting up from the ground. "My name is Andrey V. Molotov. I am from Leningrad—and please don't ask me why I was sitting here on a cold stone floor in a dirty uniform!"

The girl laughed. "I was just about to ask you why you were sitting on the cold stone floor, and why your uniform is dirty."

"You want my honest answer? Because I was very, very stupid. The alcohol demon got to me yesterday." Neither the old nor the young woman knew what to say. To break the silence the girl then said, "My name is Katharina Gargusha. And this is my grandmother, Elsbieta Marshevki. My grandmother was a member of this former German-speaking Lutheran church of more than 2,000 members. Now all the members are gone except for a few who survived the war and have found their way back to the church, and to God."

Andrey thought that this was quite a unique introduction. Perhaps his brain was still "off track" and he wasn't understanding Katharina clearly.

"When the members who are left come for worship, is the sermon preached in German? And what about the songs and prayers?"

"Oh, no! The German days are over. Everything is in Russian now, except when some members give a testimony or say a prayer in Estonian. That is fully accepted and not forbidden by the Soviet authorities."

Andrey's stomach made a frighteningly loud sound.

"Oh, forgive me. I forgot how hungry you might be," Katharina said. When she looked at her grandmother, she received an approving nod. She quickly disappeared through a small side door, to reappear after a few minutes with three paper-wrapped sandwiches, which she handed to Elsbieta.

"Before we thank God for the food," said Elsbieta, "we should do something equally important—wash the soiled hands and face of our friend, Andrey."

As much as the (still) alcohol-reeking Leningrad officer protested, the women had made up their minds. Katharina and her grandmother managed to find a bucket, soap, and cold water. Before long, Andrey's hands, neck, face and hair smelled and shined like new. He had not experienced such a treat since early childhood—the two women's care and kindness did wonders for his hangover. Then, since the autumn days were already cool, they decided to go inside the church to have their breakfast.

Elsbieta spoke an Estonian blessing over the sandwiches, and then they enjoyed their simple meal as if it had been a special dinner in a fancy restaurant. While they were "breaking bread together" in a church—a first for Andrey—they talked about their lives. Andrey even told them about his post-graduation binge-drinking with his colleagues, and how he had become the victim of their prank.

"From now on, no alcohol for me—ever again!" declared Andrey.

"Good for you!" said Katharina, smiling.

Grandmother Elsbieta nodded her head, "God bless you, young man! May God bless you, and keep you safe, now and always!"

It was soon time for the women to get busy with their work of cleaning the church, and certainly time for Andrey to be on his way for the long journey back to the academy—hopefully arriving before his absence was noticed by his superiors.

"How will you do it?" asked Katharina.

"I will try to hitchhike." Elsbieta and her granddaughter laughed out loud.

"You must never have tried to hitchhike in Estonia since the occupation by the Russians," said Katharina, her tone now serious. "What at one time was the most common means of transportation for poor people, and especially students, has become a real security problem."

"Wait a minute," said Andrey, "we are talking here about the Soviet Union."

"That is correct. However, when it comes to hitchhiking, we are still the old Estonian nation. Estonians will pick up Estonians, but never a Russian. Just like the Russians don't pick up Estonian hitchhikers."

Molotov had heard of similar situations in the Central Asian Republic. Did that happen also here in the Baltics, which Russian troops had liberated from the Germans?

"She is right," said Grandma Elsbieta. "You may not like it, but it is a fact. Don't even try it! But listen, dear friend—our small church has built up an emergency fund to help people in need. I think we just found a man in need. If you promise to pay back all, or part of what we will give you for the train, then we are in business—or better put, in God's business."

"But I am neither Lutheran nor Orthodox. To be honest, I never go to church. You should not use your church funds on a man who does not even believe in God—" Elsbieta cut into Andrey's words.

"It is not a question whether you believe in God. We know that God believes in *you*! It is in God's name, and for his sake, that we will provide you with the travel money. Katharina, go and get the key to the office, and bring me back the metal box from the top shelf. Our brothers and sisters will certainly agree with our decision when we tell them about it on Sunday."

While Katharina left to get the money, Andrey thanked Elsbieta, and told her that he was stunned by such kindness to a stranger. "Who are these brothers and sisters, with whom you will meet on Sunday?"

"Oh, they are all God's children. Some call themselves Lutherans, some Baptists, or Evangelical Christians, some Pentecostals, or Orthodox. But most call themselves just *Believers.*"

Andrey was quiet with his thoughts a minute before he spoke. "If I could belong to *this* church, I would call myself a Believer, too."

"May God make that happen one day!" replied Elsbieta Marshevski.

"Here is the money," said Katharina, as she came back into the small side room where they had eaten. "I have been busy finding out the cost of a one-way ticket to Leningrad. We have just enough in our emergency fund. Take it and, if possible, send some of it back, so that we can help others in need."

"But now," said Elsbieta, "we must get back to work, Kathushka. And you, young man, get your ticket for the next train to Leningrad. And keep your promise—*Never again alcohol!* God heard it, and so did we, as His unworthy witnesses."

Unexpectedly, Andrey walked up to Grandmother Elsbieta, reached for her hand and said, "Please permit me to kiss you on your forehead, my dear Believer and helper of people in need. Just so you know, this kiss is also for your lovely granddaughter, Katharina."

The old woman bowed her head, ever so slightly. Andrey kissed her forehead, with no hurry, only with gratitude. Then he turned around and walked away, blinking back tears.

General Major Andrey V. Molotov sighed deeply, as if waking from a long dream about an event that had happened many years before, which he had never forgotten. The totally unexpected encounter with the wise, slightly bent-over grandmother, Elsbieta, and her young granddaughter, Katharina, had not been a dream. In spite of their visible poverty and simple lifestyle, they seemed to be more content than his ambitions allowed him to be. Was there perhaps something really meaningful missing in his life, that neither his alcoholic father nor his God-denying mother had never passed on to him? What was so compelling about those two uneducated, yet wise, women? He could not even answer for himself—why did he not immediately throw away the pocket-sized New Testament he had found in his uniform while riding the train back to Leningrad from Tallinn? He had never opened it, but still, he had it—and had spent more time than he cared to admit wondering if Katharina was the one who slipped it into his jacket. Forcing himself to put such disturbing thoughts back into the corners of his secret past, Andrey used all of his energy to deal with the tasks and issues of the day.

Chapter 33

Heidi was bursting with pride as she saw her younger brother acting as the interpreter at such an enormously important occasion as the Dedication of the Freedom Bell in Berlin-*Schöneberg*. She could hardly believe how fluent Norbert's English was. Even the extent of his German language knowledge was exceptional for a boy without any linguistic studies at a university. That was her little brother, four years younger than she, but mature beyond his age.

Heidi and Fred had planned to take Norbert to a nice restaurant after the dedication celebrations in front of the *Schöneberg Rathaus* were over. Then, when General Lucius Clay brought to a close his brilliant speech and Norbert had interpreted Clay's last sentence, the huge crowd waited for the Freedom Bell to ring, but nothing happened!

When Heidi saw Norbert jump off the speaker's platform and run into the city hall, she was utterly startled. However, as she knew her brother, she figured he must have had a good reason for bolting away. Still, she had no idea that Norbert would think that he could get the huge bell to ring all by himself—which he did, as Fred and Heidi found out one hour later, when they hugged the sweaty hero of the day.

"Are you free now to go with us to a nice place for dinner?" Heidi asked.

"I am afraid not now, and perhaps not at all today. The crew that installed the bell will want to know how I managed to override the blown fuse."

"And how *did* you do it?" asked Fred, always curious about technical problem-solving.

Norbert flexed his arm and laughed. "With sheer, old-fashioned muscle power!"

Heidi glanced at Fred. "*Ja*, that's my baby brother, if you forgive the expression."

"As long as she used the word 'baby' in English, I don't mind," Norbert said to Fred. "In German, it would mean like tiny, weak or helpless."

"Wow! That boy knows his language stuff well!" is all Fred could think of saying. Then Norbert was gone again. Time for Fred to put his arm around Heidi and ask, "And how do you want to spend the rest of the day? Any place you would like to go? Grunewald? The zoo? A movie house?" Even though Heidi had a plan where they should be going, she pretended to consider some options.

"I think on this sunny afternoon," she finally said, "it would be perfect spending a few hours in the Botanical Garden."

"Ah, you mean that place in *Dahlem* with the 18,000 species of plants?"

"Exactly! I know we have been there before, but since neither you nor I know less than 1,000 species, it would be a nice educational excursion."

"Educational? Is that what you have in mind for this sunny day?"

"Yes, education—and a bit of kissing, and perhaps something else I will tell you about when we get there."

Fred did not let on that Heidi's remark about *something else* really caught his attention. Soon they were in Berlin's world-famous *Botanischer Garten*. Fred bought two *Alcolats*, which, in spite of its name, was a popular non-alcohol soft drink.

They both loved the sounds of singing birds, which were still active even that late in the season. Most trees had exchanged their green leaves with stunning multi-colored leaves. The warm sunshine made it an exceptionally beautiful afternoon. Next to an artificial waterfall they found an empty park bench.

"Just for us!" they both said at the same time, which made them laugh.

"Have we reached the point when we can read each other's thoughts?"

"Wouldn't that be nice?" Heidi responded.

"Like for instance now?"

"Yes, Fred, like for instance now. I was thinking that it would be so special for a person like me who has no parents, to get to know your parents and grandparents. I have pictured them in my mind, in some place called 'Iowa,' so many times. Perhaps you will take me to meet them."

Fred was amazed that this conversation had not come up before. It seemed they had purposely postponed it to *sometime later*. Yet, the thought of traveling together to America, and having Heidi meet his family, seemed like the perfect idea for right now, not later. He quickly pushed the thought away when he felt a twinge of sadness that Heidi would not meet *all* his family—his brother had not been back home since he married his Mormon wife and moved to Utah. Fred thought this a little sad, but mostly he felt bad for his mother who had always been devoted to her sons and family, above all. He made a mental note to pray about it later.

"Heidi, that is a splendid idea," he said. "I hope you mean soon! If you can get a few weeks off from your Wertheim's job, we could use our transatlantic military plane from Berlin to New York, and then to Chicago. From there, a smaller plane would take us to our Air Force base in Waterloo, Iowa. My parents would gladly drive the 40 miles to pick us up from there. Hey, we could have Christmas in Iowa! How about that?"

Heidi snuggled up to Fred to kiss him, even though a few Botanical Garden visitors gave them some disapproving looks. Neither Heidi nor Fred cared what they were thinking. Suddenly Fred let go of Heidi's embrace, giving her a distressing look.

"There is only one problem with that time table. In order to qualify for free military flight transportation, we have to be married or engaged. What do you say now, my darling?"

"Then let's get engaged, my love!" answered Heidi, throwing her arms around Fred's neck with no thought of

337

onlookers. Naturally, after such an unusual proposal, there had to be another exchange of hugs and kisses. When they finally left, Heidi didn't walk to the car—she skipped along, singing "Christmas in Iowa! Christmas in the USA!"

"Yes, and as a couple engaged to be married," added Fred, just as happy.

A few days later, Fred phoned Heidi to discuss the details of their travel plans. "Flying overseas before Christmas is very crowded," he said. "Most GIs want to spend their leave with their families over the holidays if they can. We need to make our flight reservations very soon, to get a flight."

"Did you have a date in mind for our engagement?"

"In America, an engagement usually is a matter of surprise."

"Like when you proposed to me in the middle of the street here in Berlin?"

"Something like that! But seriously, if we were to get engaged the weekend of November 9, we would stand a good chance to get a plane for the USA."

"Please, Fred, not on that weekend!" Heidi said, her voice almost frantic.

"Okay, darling. What's the matter? Tell me why you seem upset about that weekend."

"That was the weekend, in 1938, when Hitler's brown-shirted shock-troopers killed over 100 Jews and destroyed almost every synagogue. They burned down or destroyed over 7,000 Jewish stores and offices, and sent 30,000 people to concentration camps."

"I didn't know that you were into historical statistics."

"Fred," said Heidi seriously, "there is nothing to joke about Crystal Night. The name *Kristallnacht* comes from the shards of broken glass that littered the streets after the rampage on Jewish-owned buildings."

"You were so young, then," said Fred, now serious, as well. "Did you actually see those streets?"

"Oh, yes, you can't imagine. I had just turned ten years old, and so had been required to join the BDM, the *Bund Deutscher Mädel*, or for the ages between 10 and 14, called *Jungmädelbund* (Young Girls Union).

"I might have told you before that in a hyped-up *Verpflichtungsfeier*—swearing-in ceremony—I, along with 250 other 10-year old girls from our Berlin District, spoke the so-called sacred oath to *faithfully and selflessly serve our Führer Adolf Hitler*...and so on! Then when our BDM leader put a black kerchief around my neck, I was shaking with excitement and felt that I was now part of something really big and important. That ridiculous ceremony had been awe-inspiring for me.

"On November 9, our *Jungmädelbund* was asked to assemble to witness how *the new Germany would finally teach the Jews that they were no longer considered equal citizens in our country.* Oh, Fred! I am so ashamed to think back how brainwashed we were to swallow all the insane slogans about Germany's superiority, and Jewish second-class human ranking."

"Darling, please. You were, as you said, brainwashed. Such a horrible thing to do to a child. But, please, finish your story," Fred encouraged her.

"We marched through the streets of Berlin until we came to a burning synagogue. Two fire trucks stood about 100 meters to the side, doing *nothing* to put the fire out. People were standing around. Some were laughing, some shouted for water, others just looked on and said nothing. We had stopped marching. Then a young Hitler Youth leader walked up to our BDM leader and told her to have us sing the Nazi song, *Flammen empor*—flames rise up. But we were the youngest group of the BDM, and we had not yet learned this song. Desperate to make a good impression, our leader told us to sing *The Horst Wessel Lied* instead, which all of us knew since it was always sung as an addendum to the national anthem. Dumb and immature as we were, we sang: '*Die Fahne hoch, die Reihen fest geschlossen*' while high flames were shooting from the first and second floor of the synagogue—" Heidi's voice cracked with emotion as she relived the scene, still vivid in her mind.

"Wow, that must have been so surreal," said Fred, giving her a moment to steady herself. "What does '*Die Fahne hoch*'—the words you had to sing—mean?"

"I've never thought of it in English. It was just another Nazi-glorification song—'the flag flies high, the ranks tightly closed.' Nobody thought of explaining to us why the fire department was not quenching the flames. A few hours later, when I was back home, the radio broadcast the news that nearly all synagogues in Berlin had been torched that day, and that hundreds of Jewish stores had been ransacked. It took several weeks until it leaked out that on that same night, 30,000 Jews of all ages had been sent to 'Re-Education Camps'—Germany's attempt to turn them into noble, Führer-loving, 'real' Germans. That I did not understand at all, because some of my Jewish school friends were 'real' Germans, who spoke German, attended German schools, and acted in all ways German—whatever that meant!"

Fred asked cautiously, "Didn't your school teachers talk to you about what was happening?"

"No. Perhaps the teachers of the older classes discussed it, but my teachers said nothing.

Anyway, Fred, I hope you understand now why I would prefer a different date for our engagement."

"Sorry, Heidi, of course. I did not realize it was still so painful for you."

"Hopefully, those memories will fade, but—" Suddenly Heidi heard voices of men in the background, sounding like they had come into to Fred's office and were speaking to him.

"Heidi, I have to go!" Fred told her. "There is something going on with the commander of the UN troops in Korea. Heidi, I hate to have to hang up, but I really do have to go now. But listen—let's agree on our engagement date. How about the second of November? We'll have an engagement party. Is that okay with you?"

"That day is very much okay with me, my love. Thank you for your kind understanding."

In spite of the broken-off phone call, Heidi sympathized with Fred's situation. After all: duty was duty! She looked at the date of November 2 on her calendar. Her mood lifted completely out of her haunting past and into her exciting and happy future. She began gathering phone numbers and addresses of the people she intended to invite to her engagement party, and as she did so, she happily sang to herself a German folksong she had learned as a child.

First of all, there was her brother, Norbert. Then Fred's "military brother," Floyd, from Detroit. Next, her landlord, Wolfram Siemens, and his wife. Last, but not least, her four former roommates. That made eight guests, unless Fred could think of additional people.

Ten people they were, when they met on the first Saturday in November at the *Jagdschloss Grunewald* Restaurant, where Heidi and Fred's love story had begun. What a great time they had! Heidi showed off her new engagement ring, which replaced the friendship ring she had received from her "boyfriend" Fred. She told the story to all the party guests of how he had knelt in the middle of a street in Berlin when he gave her that first ring. Fred told the story of how he had first seen her at Wertheim's and thought he had "died and gone to heaven."

Fred had hired a trio to entertain them with English and German songs and comedy while they enjoyed their delicious meals. At the end of a wonderful evening, Fred stood up and surprised them all with an announcement. Even before he got a chance to thank his guests for coming, he was bursting with news to share.

"Friends, hold on to your chairs. In a little more than a month from now, when you will be freezing here in Berlin, Heidi and I will—" He stopped, looking at each guest during his dramatic pause. "—NOT be on a warm, romantic beach in Italy, since we also will be freezing…in America!" After being briefly interrupted by lots of "oohs" and "ahs," Fred continued, while holding up two flight tickets. "I got these today! We fly from Berlin to New York, to Chicago, then into Waterloo—only 40 miles from where I was born in Sumner, Iowa."

That was the moment when Heidi could no longer sit still. She pushed back her chair and flung herself at her now officially-recognized fiancé. Nobody could have come up with a more dramatic ending of the engagement party of two lovebirds, whom all the guests loved, too.

Chapter 34

The Korean War began for the United States on June 25, 1950, when North Korean forces commenced an invasion across the 38th Parallel into South Korea. The United Nations requested an immediate cease-fire and the withdrawal of invading troops. Two days later, President Harry Truman ordered American troops to South Korea, where they were to repel the North Korean invasion. On June 30, President Truman authorized both a naval blockade of the Korean coast and the use of US ground forces, which arrived the following day.

US General Douglas MacArthur was named Commander of all U.N. forces in Korea.

But since Korea was geographically so far from the United States, not many Americans cared about happenings on the small Korean peninsula. As a matter of fact, at one Washington, DC, press conference, a reporter was asked to describe the exact location of Korea—he could say a lot about the Chinese province, Manchuria, and he could even locate Vladivostok, the Soviet city a stone's throw north of the Korean border, but his knowledge of Korea was very limited.

The lives of Fred Harrington and Heidi Anleger, however, were to be greatly influenced by the political developments in Korea few months later. At first, after the capital of South

Korea had fallen to North Korean forces, the US troops proved their military superiority by recapturing Seoul in September, 1950. The successful U S push to the north was stopped when Chinese communist forces got involved in Korea's fighting. Soon, American and U.N. forces were on the run. The newly conquered capital, Seoul, was abandoned again.

To stop the negative war development in South Korea, President Truman declared a State of National Emergency on December 16, 1950. However, the week before, Fred Harrington had received an urgent cable announcing that all military flights between Europe and the USA had been canceled, effective immediately.

It was early in the morning, and Fred knew that Heidi was already on the way to work.

Fred jumped into his Jeep and raced to the Wertheim Department Store where he found Heidi in her office. He burst into her office, then tried to catch his breath. "Heidi, darling! You will not believe what has happened. We cannot fly to the States tomorrow!"

"What? Please do not tease me! My things are all packed, and all arrangements have been made. We have to go!"

"No, we can't go! The president has blocked all non-essential flights for military personnel going to the USA, as of today. I am so sorry, Heidi. I just had to tell you in person."

Suddenly the little-discussed Korean War in the Far East had become an important issue—certainly for Fred and Heidi. Three days later, however, the ban was lifted, at least for planes flying to the US. The moment he got the news, Fred called Heidi on the phone.

"Darling, start packing again! Our plane leaves tomorrow at 10 a.m.!"

Heidi was speechless. But knowing about the military's style, she had never unpacked her suitcase. Quickly she informed her boss about the changed vacation plan. He agreed that she should drop everything and go home to make the final travel preparations. As Heidi was leaving her office, the boss showed up again.

"I am really happy that it worked out for you after all, Miss Anleger," he said with a big smile. "And don't forget to phone your fiancé's parents about your changed arrival time!"

"That's my fiancé's job!" Heidi answered confidently. She had to admit to herself that it felt good to say *that's my fiancé's job.*

Dressed in his best US Air Force Captain's uniform, Fred rang much too early at Heidi's apartment door. "I thought you would not mind me showing up so early, darling. I could not sleep, anyway. Perhaps we can have a cup of coffee before we leave for the airport."

Heidi made sure that she looked just as good as her fiancé. Forgotten was the shock over the "no-flight ban." It was happening! Soon she would be on the way to America!

A few hours later, she looked out of the window as the plane lifted off from the Berlin-Tempelhof Airport, flying right over Neukölln, the district where she had grown up. She recognized the Hermann Strasse with its half-destroyed Karstadt building. When low-lying clouds swallowed up the plane, she leaned back with a relieved smile that would not go away.

As she moved very close to Fred, she whispered into his ear: "Saint Nicholas. *Weihnachtsbaum.* Christmas in America. Thank you, Fred!"

The quick cup of coffee in her apartment was followed by many more cups between Berlin, New York, and Chicago. Even though Heidi had never flown before, there was not an ounce of fear or anxiety in her. The man she loved more than anybody and anything else was sitting right next to her—and he was an experienced pilot. Nothing could go wrong.

Still, when after a few plane changes they finally landed in Waterloo, she was more than tired. Even her tough fiancé seemed to be exhausted. However, the moment their feet touched Iowa soil, a surge of energy bolted through their fatigued bodies.

It was sunset in flatland Iowa. The airport light had just come on as if to welcome them.

Fred looked around. Nothing had changed here since he had left Waterloo Air Force Base in 1948. The months of flight training, and then his time as a pilot during the Berlin Airlift had not given him a chance to be back here.

Fred spotted his parents as they stood behind a high wire fence. A military policeman guarded the iron gate. Fred's parents could not see the disembarking passengers because of the blinding floodlights, but they waved frantically, nevertheless. Fred took Heidi's hand, and together they started running toward the gate. The MP just saluted and smiled.

Joy all around, and tears from Fred's mother, greeted the ecstatic couple who were no longer groggy or fatigued. Greeting his parents, introducing Heidi to them, searching for their luggage—all made for a swirling, happy occasion, typical for airport arrivals. Soon they were loading into the car as Fred gave his parents admiring compliments and his dad told the story of how he got a great deal on their beautiful new Cadillac.

Heidi felt as if she were in a dream, a dream so full of happiness she did not ever want to come out of it. She snuggled close to Fred in the back seat, not having anything to add to the nonstop conversation between him and his parents—just enjoying the ride as she said to herself over and over, *I am really here, in America. I am with the love of my life, here, in America.* As the car approached their farm in Sumner, Anna Harrington said, "You should have come during daylight, Fred, to show Heidi our beautiful turkey farm!"

"Be glad that we made it at all, Mom! For several days it looked as if we would have to scratch the entire trip."

Fred's mother then turned around and met Fred's eyes with hers. She was overcome with a mixture of relief that he was home safely, and amazement that he had really found *the one* and seemed so confident and happy that this girl was going to soon be part of their family.

"I almost had forgotten what a handsome son I have," she said.

Fred waved off the compliment, as he typically would. "Like you said, there's no daylight, yet. Just wait—I am still the plain turkey farmer from Sumner."

"I hate to correct you, Fred," said his dad, "but you really never had time to be much of a turkey farmer. To skip a year of high school, you were studying harder than any of your school buddies. After graduating, you ran off to the air force—again, having no time for turkeys."

"But I joined the military with your blessing, Dad!"

"I know, son. What is a father to do? And look at you! I am very proud you made something of yourself, Captain."

For breakfast the next morning, Fred's grandparents, Alex and Hedwig Scheigert, had been invited. When Heidi came downstairs from her room, she had no trouble finding everyone as she made her way to the noisy voices and happy laughter coming from the kitchen. Fred introduced her and Grandma Schweigert even dared to kiss her future granddaughter-in-law.

"That's how we did it in Germany," she said, somewhat apologetic. "Once people are engaged, they are family, and you may kiss them."

Her husband patted her hand. "As long as you don't stop kissing also your old flame, Alex, *ja?*" Everyone laughed. Fred was pleased how his parents and grandparents made Heidi feel at home. He had been sure she would be welcomed with open arms, and he was glad to see she already seemed at ease. He felt his heart would burst with happiness as he now looked at Heidi's beautiful, smiling face as she talked with his mom about the German sausages being cooked on the stove.

Early the next morning, Fred's proud father gave an extensive tour of the farm. Then he handed Fred the keys to his brand new car. "The Hawkeye State is a big state, even though its population is only about the same as you have in greater Berlin," he said to Fred and Heidi. "Since we do not have any Jeeps here, we thought you could make do with our car. Drive around! See the sights! Visit wherever you want—and enjoy yourselves."

Just when Fred thought life couldn't get any better, his father's generosity and Heidi's obvious delight in the plan to tour the state made him even more excited. Before he would take off, however, Fred insisted on helping his father with all the farm's morning chores. From thousands of miles away, he had often pictured his dad, hard at work and with no sons around to help. He was determined to do what he could at least every time he came home to the farm.

Later, Fred and Heidi took their first day trip to satisfy Heidi's desire to see the famous Mississippi River, which she had been surprised to learn flowed all the way up through Iowa. The next day, they visited the capital, Des Moines, including Boone's Wildlife and Research Exhibit Station north of the city. But then a severe snowstorm crippled most of the traffic in Central Iowa and kept them from venturing out.

Instead of fighting the slippery roads, Fred suggested they spend the whole day with his grandparents, which turned into an exciting and informative visit. Breakfast, lunch and dinner—all meals were big productions that day, giving Heidi and *Oma* (Grandmother) Hedwig ample opportunity to bond as they worked together in the kitchen, often slipping into speaking German to one another.

Oma Hedwig told Heidi the Schweigert story. Alex and Hedwig had emigrated from Germany to America in 1905. They had traveled on a slow, but large steamboat that allowed passengers to travel with no luggage-weight limitations. After saying goodbye to their friends and neighbors, they had packed all of their earthly belongings into huge crates.

Once they decided where to settle in the United States —in a small rural town called Sumner—they never were plagued by homesickness. That surprised nobody, because all the "stuff" they had lugged across the Atlantic filled every room of their house and made it look and feel like a "little Germany."

While Fred's parents felt that he was a bit too young to consider marriage, the Schweigerts were absolutely delighted that their grandson had reconnected the family ties with Germany by wanting to marry a German woman. Mainly to surprise and delight Heidi, they opened boxes and crates filled with German Christmas decorations they had not used for several decades.

Oma, covering her no-longer-slim hips with an embroidered German apron, was inspired to bake *deutsche Kekse* (German cookies) and cakes she had not baked for many years, and Heidi was most of the time at her side—learning, tasting and complimenting.

Fred on the other hand, helped his grandfather to free the yard, shed, and sidewalk from the high snow drifts. The two dogs with whom he had played as a youngster, instantly recognized and re-adopted Fred as their "running buddy," though they were not as full of energy as they once were.

On Christmas Eve, the families Harrington and Schweigert attended the candlelight service at their Baptist Church. George and Anna sang in the choir. Heidi sat next to Fred, listening to the singing, prayers, and the short sermon by the preacher. The sanctuary seemed to be filled with a warmth and love she had never experienced before. As a "non-religious person," as she had called herself during her growing-up years in Nazi Germany, she never had religious education nor was

351

she confirmed at the age of 14; some of her schoolmates and BDM friends, even though they claimed no belief in God, had nevertheless followed the Lutheran tradition of being confirmed at a church. What Heidi experienced here was totally different than what she remembered from any church before. These people knew why they were here, and they lived what they believed.

On Christmas Day, the celebrations shifted from the Schweigert to the Harrington house. After exchanging modest gifts, there was plenty of food for everyone—even for the tail-wagging dogs. Mother Harrington served the jams she had made and preserved from her own garden strawberries and raspberries. There was not only one roasted turkey, there were two. There were so many bowls of side-dishes they didn't all fit on the table at once. This abundance was overwhelming for Heidi, the city girl who had lived in food-rationed, wartime Germany. Even after the war, living in Berlin often had been like a trial of survival on an "island in the Red Sea." When Fred paused between mouthfuls to ask her how she liked it so far, Heidi said, "So wonderful—and so much! Celebrating Christmas with your family, the most loving people I have ever met, is like a foretaste of heaven—if there is a heaven."

Heidi liked Fred's parents a lot, but she already felt a special bond with *Oma*. At the end of the day, *Oma* told her goodbye and Heidi replied that they would see each other soon, on *dem zweiten Weihnachtstag* (the "Second Day of Christmas"). Fred was glad to see that Heidi and his dear grandmother were such kindred spirits.

The next day, the postman brought an airmail letter addressed to "Captain Fred Harrington c/a George Harrington,

Sumner, Iowa." The family held its breath. What news would the official letter from the *U.S. Air Force Military Headquarters Berlin* bring?

In few short sentences the letter commanded Captain Fred Harrington to return to Berlin at the earliest possible time, where he would receive further orders about an impending deployment to Korea. From that moment on, the joyful mood at the Harringtons' faded away.

The following day, Fred decided he would make a call just to be sure this disappointing news was real, and still valid. It was good that the Harrington Turkey Farm had a private versus "party" telephone line, so that Fred could make a long distance phone call to his headquarter in Berlin without having neighbors listening in, as was the unpleasant custom.

"Yes, Captain Harrington," his commander told him, "you have to report back to Berlin within the next four days. I will make the flight arrangements for you and your fiancée. Sorry to cut short your US visit, but remember, we are now operating under President Truman's *State of National Emergency.* Frankly, we could be at the brink of a third world war with the involvement of the Chinese and the Soviets."

"Sir, with your permission, may I ask—will the Chinese troops recapture Seoul?"

"Yes, Harrington, we will have to abandon the South Korean capital within few weeks.

I cannot tell you more over this unsecured telephone line."

"Yes, sir, I understand. We will be ready to leave as you arrange."

The return flight information reached Fred two days later. Instead of making preparations for a fun family New Year's Eve and Day, the Harrington parents drove Fred and Heidi back to the Waterloo Air Force Base. From there, a small plane took them to Chicago. The flights back to Berlin felt even longer and more tiring for the couple, since they did not have the family Christmas to look forward to any more. Neither of them knew what was in store, and they reminisced about their time in Iowa for hours just to keep their growing anxiety in check.

In spite of the fact the vacation had been cut so short, Fred and Heidi were extremely grateful for their visits with parents and grandparents. The delightful days in Sumner gave them the strength to stomach the unpleasant news waiting for them: Fred was to leave his position in Berlin immediately. He would receive more detailed orders when arriving in Tokyo, Japan.

"How can they do that to you, Fred?" asked Heidi, revealing her disappointment.

"Please, darling, you know I am in the military. We can get sent to hot-spots anywhere in the world at any time. That is the commitment I made when I joined the Air Force."

Heidi buried her tearful face in his embrace. "But please know, my love," said Fred, holding her tightly, "I will come back as soon as circumstances permit."

"When do you think that will be?"

"Only the Lord knows!" Fred answered seriously, and Heidi knew that her fiancé spoke the truth.

Chapter 35

All the way from Berlin to Tokyo, Fred wondered why he had been sent to the Japanese capital. With the war raging in Korea, why was he not sent there? Once he was in Japan, and when he had studied the Pacific Ocean Area Military maps, he had to admit that his deployment to Japan had not been a mistake. South Korea had one big airport in Seoul/Inchon, and another small airfield in Kimpo. Both airports and Seoul itself had been occupied by Chinese communist troops early in January 1951. There was no safe place in Korea to land an American troop transporter, especially with the constant flux of changing ownership and occupiers.

Fred and several hundred US Air Force pilots and ground personnel had to wait for the right time to move from Tokyo to Korea. Though not without considerable risk, on April 1, 1951, Fred and 120 other pilots carefully maneuvered their planes to the safest landing area in South Korea. American General Douglas MacArthur was the commander of the United Nations forces in Korea, and had realized that instead of having more boots on the ground, the air force should be used more effectively in the battle for Korea.

However, President Truman relieved MacArthur of all his commands on April 11, 1951, creating something like an earthquake among the American military. Irreconcilable differences in leadership and strategic planning, compounded by MacArthur's public statements which contradicted the administration's policies, brought President Truman to this drastic step.

Even so, firing MacArthur did not strengthen the American position there. Soon, Fred was flying almost daily sorties across the 38th Parallel.

Each week Fred wrote a letter to Heidi in Berlin, and he always received a weekly letter from her at mail call. She wanted to know how he was doing. What could he write? That he had just killed about 10 or 15 North Korean soldiers in a low-flying attack? Or that he and his flying buddies had destroyed a weapons arsenal, causing explosive fireworks for hours?

Fred loved Heidi's letters which reminded him of simple, happy, day-to-day things in the world he had to miss out on for now. She told him she had just been to see the musical, *South Pacific,* by Richard Rogers and Oscar Hammerstein. She had a new neighbor, a very nice older woman from Austria who had already come over to introduce herself. In one letter, he read two pages just about her meeting a 19-year-old Berliner, Soraya Esfandiary, and her mother, Eva Esfandiary, at Wertheim's, where they were shopping for Soraya's "Thousand-and-One-Night" wedding to the Shah of Persia. Sharing such things helped to bridge the distance between Berlin and Seoul, separated by thousands of kilometers. Fred and Heidi both felt, at times, like they were living on two different planets. Each dreamed only of "being home, together."

Norbert Anleger, on the other hand, who had explored the USA on his Freedom Bell Crusade Tour, and who was still full of excitement over the things he had seen and experienced on that trip, yearned for even more adventures—he wanted "to see the world!" Thus, when several of his air force friends were sent to Korea, he tried to find employment there, too. However, what would a civilian German-English interpreter do in a country where the language was Korean, of which he spoke only five or ten words?

In order to avoid being unemployed, he went back to take evening courses at the *Volkshochschule* where he had tried to study last year, before he was snatched up by the Americans who sent him on the tour through the United States. Now he was 19 years old and needed a firm direction for his life.

The *Crusade* experience had matured Norbert in ways he did not yet fully appreciate. He was a little surprised at how much he enjoyed his studies now, and he registered right away for several courses. In spite of a heavy course-load, he managed to climb to the top of each class.

He spent many hours each morning in the library, completed his class assignments in the afternoon, and was at his classes in the evening. He had no friends to help him with his studies. Even his smart sister, Heidi, was not around to help. This only made him more determined to reach his goals on his own. He loved especially his Political Science course. From now on he wanted to stay informed about what was going on in the world, not just in Germany, the USA, and Korea.

His school colleagues did not understand Norbert's disinterest in movies. While they sometimes skipped class to see a new film, Norbert did not have much good to say about

Hollywood or the movie world. His growing interest was reading true stories about spies and traitors, like for example, the German-born Klaus Fuchs. Norbert told his classmate that if a movie came out about Dr. Fuchs, he'd be glad to go to see it with him. Dr. Fuchs, after studying theoretical physics in England, went to Los Alamos in New Mexico to work under Robert Oppenheimer on the further development of the atomic bomb. There he passed on important nuclear secrets to a Russian spy who also worked in Los Alamos. Fuchs' treacherous activities were discovered, and he was sentenced to prison.

It was a hot day in July of 1951, and Norbert was resting on his couch, soothing a terrific sunburn he had gotten while boating the day before. He heard the doorbell, but he didn't feel like getting up to answer the door. It rang again, and Norbert gingerly lifted himself off the couch and went to the door, finding a uniformed military messenger who presented him with a large envelope with the US Air Force seal. Back on the couch, he tried to read the letter, but his swollen eyes were not able to clearly focus on the typed words.

"Please arrive two hours before the dedication in case of unforeseen complications!" He tried rubbing his eyes to better see and understand what he was reading, but when this did not help, he put the letter aside, closed his eyes, and went to sleep. Later, he woke up and suddenly remembered that somebody had told him to expect an invitation to serve as interpreter at the Airlift Memorial Dedication in July. He reached for the letter again, and this time he read clearly about a dedication in Berlin-Tempelhof. The *Nord Deutscher Rundfunk* planned to transmit the entire ceremony, both on radio and television.

"Please do not wear a striped suit or a checked shirt, as such patterns have a negative effect on the television picture!"

Norbert could not believe how pedantic military planners could be. But then, he thought of the blown fuse during the dedication of the Freedom Bell in *Schöneberg*. He had to admit: *better to be warned before, than to be cursed afterwards.*

On July 10, 1951, Norbert arrived at the Airlift Memorial two hours ahead of time, as requested. A friendly but nervous technical sergeant handed Norbert a list of the event schedule, procedures, and protocol. Norbert recognized none of the scheduled American speakers. He noticed, however, that Berlin's Mayor Ernst Reuter was one of the featured speakers. Norbert had come to love and admire this man, even though he knew how unpredictable he could occasionally be. Twice, he had been told to be ready to interpret Reuter from German to English, and stood by just to hear the mayor make use of his good knowledge of the English language, requiring no go-between. Would he surprise Norbert again, today?

Having some extra time before the ceremony, Norbert took a good look at the Memorial structure, which the Berliners already had humorously nicknamed "The Hunger Claw." The 79-foot tall, 3-pronged, white shaft flared into the sky from a black basalt base. On the base were inscribed the 79 names of Americans, British, and Germans who had died performing their duties during the Berlin Airlift.

When the ceremony started, everything went as planned. The competent German TV crew of the NDR was thrilled with how well and dignified the dedication came off. The Berliner crowd was pleased for the chance of saying *thank you* to the thousands of men and women whose airlift effort had kept them from starving to death.

As always, Norbert's interpreting was flawless. After the ceremony, he was approached by many American soldiers and German citizens, including Mayor Reuter, thanking him for having contributed so well to the ceremony. Norbert was pleased with the outcome of his assignment.

Now, however, Norbert was already thinking of another event he would not miss under any circumstances: the SPARTAKAD—The *Weltjugend Festspiele* (World Youth Games) in East Berlin, August 5–19, 1951. Organized by and for the communist *Freie Deutsche Jugend* (Free German Youth), about two million youngsters from East Germany and East Berlin made this sports spectacle an endless celebration to the glory of the German Democratic Republic and the Soviet Union. Flags, banners, music bands, sport events, and loyalty speeches created the image as if the communist GDR and its Free German Youth represented paradise on earth and had the answers to all the world's problems.

What was never mentioned, or heard by one single participant of the Games, was the latest count of the number of East Germans who had fled to the West: in 1950—197,788 people had fled East Germany, and in 1951 (up to the time of the games in August)—155,500. In order to protect their precious FDJ members from the decadent West, 28,000 *VOPOS* (Folk Police) and 50,000 *Volksarmisten* (Folk Army and Border Police), along with 18,000 special Red Army Soviet soldiers, had descended upon East Berlin. Mixing their uniforms with the blue shirts of the FDJ, East Berlin looked like a colorful gypsy camp.

Norbert wanted to be at the Games on the opening day. Heidi had refused to go along, even when Norbert pleaded with her to at least come with him on the days when she was not working.

"Doing what? Looking at the young commies going crazy? No way, brother! If you want to go, do it by yourself—you're on your own!"

After spending several hours at the opening of the masterfully orchestrated *Weltjugend Festspiele,* Norbert had to admit that he was more impressed than he had expected to be. Originally, he had planned to be there only on the first day. However, to experience more of the impressive hoopla, he went back on Tuesday, Friday, and on the second Sunday of the Games. The grandeur wore off, and the robotic pro-communist chants began to really get on his nerves. Being surrounded by hyped-up, brain washed fanatics, he soon changed his positive opinion about the FDJ gathering.

These *Weltjugend Festspiele,* in spite of their strong emphasis on athletic competition, began to resemble an increasingly mammoth-sized human meat market. Boys met girls; girls met boys. Even the elite State Security Police (STASI) "played along" with the often-intoxicated FDJ girls.

When some blue-shirted *Spartakists* (a name given to FDJ members honored for victories in sport) discovered how easy it was to travel by streetcar or subway, or just by walking to West Berlin, a real avalanche of visitors started. By the end of the *Festspiele*, it was estimated that more than one million FDJ members had visited well-off, fascinating West Berlin, much to the anger of the Games organizers.

Norbert Anleger moved in the opposite direction. He pedaled to East Berlin, where he locked his bicycle to a streetlight. Then he headed for the Marx-Engels Square, the former *Berliner Schloss* Square, where hundreds of FDJ youngsters were either marching, debating, listening to speakers, or were just sunning themselves on the banks of the nearby river *Spree*. Norbert was drawn to the area where the most debating seemed to be going on. Soon he discovered that he was not the only West Berliner who had come here to snare or confuse naive Eastern debaters. While the Easterners continually praised life in East Germany and applauded the noble work of the *Freie Deutsche Jugend,* the critical Western visitors mocked the "Blue Shirts," especially their Hitler Youth type of military style.

For a short while, Norbert just listened. Then he had to get involved in the verbal combat.

"Listen, guys," Norbert began, "if life is so-o-o wonderful in your German Democratic Republic, why did almost 200,000 East Germans flee to the West last year?" The Westerners nodded and cheered approvingly, but most of the crowd was silent, seemingly stunned by this number Norbert had thrown out. But Norbert wasn't finished yet.

"Also think of the kidnapping cases!"

Several gasps came from the group; even some West Berliners could not believe that Norbert would bring up this explosive topic, considering where he and they stood—in the heart of communist East Berlin.

"You don't know what you are talking about," said one of the higher-ranking FDJ leaders. "We do not grab people in the West and bring them to the East."

"You don't?" asked Norbert in a harsh tone. "I suggest that you start reading other newspapers besides your *Neues Deutschland* to find out what really is going on."

"You mean your truth-twisting and lying West German papers?"

"You call them liars. I call them the free press—a source of truth and facts— like the *Frankfurter Allgemeine Zeitung.* Even the Swiss *Baseler National Zeitung* has reported about several kidnapping cases organized by your government."

"No, you are wrong! You are listening to lies. You have no proof!" several of the crowd shouted at Norbert, who ignored them.

"Take for instance, the most recent kidnapping on July 8, in West Berlin!" said Norbert.

"The victim was Dr. Walter Linse, who I personally know. He was a business reporter here in Berlin."

"I read about this bandit in *Neues Deutschland, "* somebody interrupted Norbert. "He worked as a spy for the Americans!"

"Let me finish! He was not a spy. Believe me! On the way to his office, Walter Linse was approached by a stranger who asked him for a light for his cigarette. While Linse offered him his lighter, the man knocked him down and, with the help of two known criminals, dragged him into his car. Witnesses say the car, an Opel, was disguised as a West Berliner taxi, and disappeared at high speed toward East Berlin. No one has heard from him since."

"If that really happened, then that trouble-maker probably deserved it," was the stoic answer of a *Volkspolizist* (VOPO). Norbert looked and felt frustrated.

"What can I do to make you believe me? Let me tell you of another case, which I know much better. This kidnapping happened back in November of 1947, but I remember it as if it happened yesterday—because I was right there!"

Norbert had their attention now. He told the group about the kidnapping of the journalist, Dieter Friede, which took place in the medical practice of his uncle, Dr. Peter Dau. "You may say what you want in defense of your Eastern regime, but I was there! I was an eyewitness. Just thinking of it, makes me shiver to this day."

Admitting publicly (in East Berlin, no less) that he had witnessed a kidnapping by authorities—what was Norbert thinking? It was one thing to talk about the recent Linse case, but why had Norbert been so naive to admit first-hand knowledge of the Dieter Friede kidnapping? That made it much too dangerously personal, as Norbert found out within seconds. Three uniformed VOPO grabbed his arms, crossing his wrists behind him as they forced him to the ground, all in one swift motion. They held him down until a squad car showed up. The so-called debating group had dispersed immediately, leaving Norbert alone with the police.

Norbert was taken to the nearest VOPO station and interrogated for three hours. Then he was hand-cuffed and shackled like a dangerous criminal and taken to Berlin's

Volkpolizei Headquarters, which was operated by East German police and Russian KGB.

The interrogations there were tedious, irrational, and increasingly unbearable because of their repetitive nature. Since Norbert claimed to understand no Russian, all interviews and interrogations were done in German. For two days, he was given no food, no water, no light, no outdoor breaks! The only exercise he got was when every three hours a KGB soldier took him to another interrogation, done by equally incompetent interrogators.

Hungry, thirsty, and extremely frustrated, Norbert decided to hold back nothing. He told the interrogators everything, and even more than was true, as long as he would get back his freedom. He even mentioned the real names of Russian agents and officers who had hunted him the most. Naturally, Lieutenant Svertlov was the number one "hunter." Since he was Major General Kotikov's deputy, Kotikov's name was also mentioned.

"Kotokov, the Commander of Soviet Troops in Berlin? Do you realize, Anleger, that Major General is no longer alive?"

Norbert pretended that he was not aware of Kotikov's death. "I am sorry to hear that *General Njet* is dead. Will Lieutenant Svertlov take over his position?"

The snappy-cold reply of the interrogator put Norbert in place. "That is none of your business, Anleger! But since you asked, I might as well tell you that his replacement has been in Berlin for quite some time. After all, Kotikov was killed one year ago."

Norbert did not like the interrogator's sneering chuckle that followed his remark. To him, death never was a laughing matter.

On the third day after his arrest, Norbert's conditions changed for the better. A young guard silently served him breakfast. A large jar of water stood ready to be refilled upon his request. Before sunrise, he was moved to a cell with a high window with opaque glass. Now he had what normal jailbirds would wish for. He still was not permitted to walk or exercise in the prison yard inside the Police Headquarter complex.

When his new cell door opened with an ear-piercing, shrill sound, he did not know what to expect. *"Bitte folgen!"* said a tall prison guard wearing a Russian uniform, motioning for Norbert to follow him.

"Oh, you speak German?" asked Norbert.

"Bitte folgen!" the guard commanded, but then he continued in German, telling Norbert that he had a visitor. *A visitor?* Norbert could not think of anybody it could possibly be, other than Heidi. Had she heard about his arrest? Had she come to bail him out? Norbert followed the guard from the prison section to the more civil-looking police wing. The guard opened the door to a large room containing only two chairs. On one chair sat a youthful-looking, highly-decorated Soviet officer.

"Sit!" the officer spit out the order, pointing to the empty chair. "I am General Andrey V. Molotov, the Commandant of Soviet Troops in Berlin." Molotov stood, now in position to talk down to Norbert as he continued. "With the death of my colleague, Major General Kotikov, the honor of commanding

Soviet soldiers here in Berlin and in part of Germany has fallen on me. And who are you?"

Norbert stood up and faced the Russian officer. "I am sure that you, General Molotov, know my name and why I am here."

Just when Molotov wanted to answer, Norbert quickly added, "General, my name is Norbert Anleger, but I do not know why I am here."

Only now the officer and Norbert realized that they both had been speaking in Russian.

"Interesting that you speak Russian," said Molotov.

"I try, when it is necessary."

"Well, then keep trying, because I speak no German. Now, to the point of my being here. The *Volkspolizei* reported you to my office for having given seditious speeches on the Marx-Engels Square, three days ago."

"Yes, I was there, by myself. Then I walked up to a small group of people and we were just talking to each other," said Norbert.

"The report says that you were *speaking*."

"Speaking, yes. Giving speeches, no!"

"You are an agitator and a liar. You spoke to a crowd, denouncing both the Soviet Union and the German Democratic Republic, which is an act that calls for severe punishment."

"Is that the reason why I was treated like a major criminal?"

"Watch your words, Anleger! I have the power to keep you here forever, if I don't like what you are saying."

Both men stopped speaking for a while. Norbert stood like a statue, staring straight ahead. Molotov slowly walked around him, circling him like a shark keen on its prey. Then he walked up to Norbert so close that their noses almost touched.

"You are not as innocent as you claim to be. You talked about the kidnapping of Walter Linse and Dieter Friede. Do not deny that! Understood?"

"You are correct. I do not deny that," answered Norbert, disarming the Russian officer with his honesty. "I just wanted to dispel the pro-East argument of the *Freie Deutsche Jugend* boys, who thought ... "

"Shut up!" Molotov ordered. "The more you talk, the deeper you make yourself sink into your own shit!"

Again, a long silence followed. Then Andrey Molotov said slowly, very slowly: "If my Uncle Vyacheslav Molotov, the Soviet Foreign Minister, had been informed of your case, he would have skinned you alive. Believe me!"

"And why is my case so criminal?"

"As I said before—shut up! Shut up for your own good!"

Something in Molotov's voice gave Norbert a sudden shiver. He kept his mouth closed. Then Molotov, again speaking dramatically slowly, said: "This may come as a surprise to you. I have come here today to grant you freedom."

For a moment, Norbert thought that he had not understood the Russian-speaking officer.

"Yes, I intend to set you free, Norbert Anleger. I have examined your thick portfolio and have concluded that you no longer pose a danger to us. But you should keep your mouth shut. Understood? That means that as of now I let you go back to your rotten, Anglo-American, monopole-capitalistic friends. *Dobri den!*"

Molotov straightened up, clicked his heals and walked to the door, where he addressed the Russian guard. "Get rid of this German skunk. His stink is offensive to me."

The guard hurried over to Norbert and asked, in Russian: "Where are your chains?"

"In my cell."

"And your personal belongings?"

"I have none, except for the clothes on my back."

"And where are your ID documents?"

"They were taken away when I got here—many years ago."

The puzzled guard asked, "Have you been here that long?"

"It sure feels that way!" answered Norbert, laughing for the first time in three days.

Chapter 36

When US President Harry Truman declared on October 24, 1951, that the *State of War* with Germany had officially ended, this meant nothing to Norbert. For him, there had been no war with the USA since May, 1945. The politicians were always a bit slower than the normal citizens in assessing the world situation correctly.

For Heidi Anleger, on the other hand, it was truly worrisome that the United States seemed to be drawn deeper and deeper into military combat with North Korea. Norbert felt sorry for his sister since she had not seen her fiancé, Fred, for almost a year. However, at least she knew Fred was alive! American casualties in mid-1951 had reached 100,000 in a war which the politicians did not even dare to call a war. Attempts to have a cease-fire in Korea had failed, as had several truce talks, so that both ground and air actions by the US continued and even intensified in 1952.

While American soldiers were fighting in Korea, Republicans and Democrats in America were battling for dominance in the November presidential election. General Dwight D. Eisenhower was elected president. He had promised, if elected president, to go to Korea in order to seek an early and honorable conclusion to the conflict. Once elected, Eisenhower flew to Korea less than a month later, fulfilling his campaign promise.

Only the White House knew that once his huge Air Force plane landed in Korea, the President-elect would switch to a much smaller plane, which he would navigate himself. Eisenhower's plan was to inspect the UN Forces and visit front-line positions. The three-day tour was to be kept secret until he returned from the danger zone. Naturally, in spite of not informing the press about this risky trip, the higher-ranking Air Force officers had been put on high alert and a co-pilot had been chosen—just in case! Fred Harrington could hardly believe that he had been the lucky one ordered to accompany the president-elect on this mission.

Fred was determined to talk as little as possible in order not to distract the future president, with whom he shared the small cockpit. Eisenhower had a different idea about the flight. After Fred had introduced himself, Eisenhower concentrated on the instrument board and the many control levers above his head. But once the plane was in the air, Eisenhower relaxed and started a conversation with Fred which was to continue, off-and-on, for the next three days.

"I did not introduce myself," Eisenhower said, "because I assume you know who I am."

"Do I ever, sir!" Fred tried to sound less giddy than he felt, sitting as co-pilot to a famous five-star general, now the newly elected next President of the United States.

After a few moments of silence, Eisenhower started talking again while he kept his eyes on the control panels. "Actually, I wanted to make this flight all by myself. However, some big-shot security officer in Washington insisted that I take along a *babysitter.*"

Fred looked up in surprised mock-hurt, and Eisenhower continued, "No insult intended, Captain! I was informed that you have a stellar record of service and top-notch skills as a pilot. Perhaps I should be grateful that you are my *just-in-case-backup-pilot,*" Eisenhower laughed.

"It is my privilege, sir," said Fred.

"Listen, Harrington—sorry, but I cannot share with you the exact flight route, and where we will make stops. You know that ours is an extremely secret mission."

"Don't worry, sir. You don't have to tell me where you will fly and land. I know South Korea better than my home state of Iowa."

"How is that?"

"Because I have been in this god-forsaken country for twenty months, sir."

"Are you counting the *days* of your service here, as well?"

"No, sir—but my fiancée in Germany does. I have not seen her for two years."

"You mean you've had no leave for such a long time?"

"Our leaves are spread over a year or more—a day here and there—whenever the Chinese or North Koreans seem to give us a break."

Since their first flight was a rather short hop, both pilots had to stop talking and concentrate on the landing information they now were receiving from flight engineers on the ground.

When the door of the plane opened up, there were excited murmurs from the ground personnel as they recognized their Commander-in-Chief. Then everybody stood at attention and saluted. Eisenhower now switched into his important role as the General visiting his troops.

After four hours, Eisenhower and Fred were in the air again, flying to their next surprise stop. Again, it was Eisenhower who started a conversation.

"Even though you are quite young, I see that you made *Captain.* Congratulations!"

"Thank you, sir! Sometimes I can hardly believe it myself. Shortly before the end of the Berlin Airlift, I was promoted to Captain," explained Fred.

"This morning you were telling me that you have a fiancée in Berlin. Where is she from—Iowa?"

"No, sir. She is from Berlin."

"You don't say! My co-pilot is marrying a German! And you have security clearance for this top-secret mission?"

"Yes, sir," said Fred, now unsure if the general was seriously concerned, or kidding him.

"Well, well—and I thought a German fiancée might disqualify you from being the future president's co-pilot."

"I don't see why, sir," is all Fred could think of saying.

"Now then, Captain, let me be the one testing you for your patriotism and loyalty," said General Eisenhower, as more of a jest than a threat.

"When did the Star-Spangled-Banner become our National Anthem?"

"President Herbert Hoover declared it the National Anthem on March 3, 1931—but Francis Scott Key wrote it in 1814 during the bombardment of Fort McHenry."

"Good! Next question: who won the heavyweight boxing championship this past September?"

"Rocky Marciano, who knocked out Jerry Joe Walcott in Pittsburgh."

"Wait a minute, Captain! You know *that* and you've been here in Korea?"

"Yes, sir. Occasionally we can listen to the armed forces radio. Besides, I read a lot."

"Okay. Tell me who won the World Series this year."

"The New York Yankees, defeating the Brooklyn Dodgers, four games to three," Fred answered without any hesitation.

"Man, you are like a walking lexicon!"

"Correction, sir! Perhaps more like a *flying* lexicon."

Fred was relieved to hear the President-elect break into good-natured laughter.

After three hectic, but very interesting days with Eisenhower, the mission was over. A small press conference in Seoul gave reporters a chance to gather information and report to the world about Eisenhower's secret fact-finding trip.

Before they parted at the Seoul Airport, Eisenhower took Fred aside.

"Fred!" the future President said, using his first name for the first time. "Damn fine job, son. Our mission was flawless. Listen, you mentioned your uninterrupted 20-month duty 'in this god-forsaken country' as you called it. Do you like your job here?"

"Sir, I am honored to serve my country, and I do really like being a pilot—but, can anybody really like war?" asked Fred. "Warfare looks exciting in the movies and in the brochures of military recruiters. The reality is different here in this hell, as it also was in World War II, and before, in World War I, I suppose."

"Right you are, my captain friend!" replied Eisenhower with great warmth in his voice.

"Life is the greatest teacher for all of us. I am 63 years old—an *old war horse*, some call me behind my back. How old are you, anyway? And how did you make captain so soon?"

"I was born in 1929, sir. That makes me 23 years old. I started out early, enlisting with the Air Force right after high school graduation. At 19, I was one of the youngest US pilots, and just in time to work my butt off in the Berlin Airlift. The promotion to captain came at the end of the airlift. I believe I mentioned that the promotion came as a real surprise to me, sir."

"I'm sure it was well-deserved."

"Thank you, sir!"

"But now listen to me—I think you're more than just a hotshot fly boy from Iowa! I may have another surprise for you. You are young, but not invincible. You need a change

375

of pace. Not to mention, you have a fiancée waiting for you in Berlin."

Fred had no idea where Eisenhower's talk was leading.

"In about one month, I will be the president of our great country. In the meantime, I am busy putting the most trustworthy and capable people into my cabinet and administration. How would you, Captain Harrington, like to become the Chief Pilot of Air Force One?"

Fred could not find any fitting words for a response. Was he dreaming, or had that been a real job offer from President-elect Dwight Eisenhower?

"Hey Fred! Wake up! I have no time to stand here and wait for your answer. Is it a *yes* or a *no*?"

"But, sir, I am only 23—well, soon, 24 years old. The present Air Force One Chief Pilot is in his late 40s and his rank is Lieutenant Colonel or Colonel."

"So what!" replied the veteran General. "In a war, we all age faster. Even promotions come up faster when you work for a high-enough chief in Washington, as long as he can trust you with his life. Now, do you accept the job?"

General Eisenhower looked at his watch, then at Fred.

"Before you give me your answer, note that being at the controls of Air Force One means you will make 100 to 150 flights in the States and to more than 50 foreign countries every year.

If that is okay with you and your fiancée, hopefully soon your wife, then give me your answer now!"

Fred came to attention and saluted. "Sir, it will be my honor to be Chief Pilot of Air Force One as soon as I have your official word."

Eisenhower returned the salute and reached out, shaking hands firmly with Fred, which for both men had the same value as a formally-written agreement. Then the general was escorted to a large military plane, and Fred was left behind with his mind racing with what the President-elect had just promised, and what the future might have in store for Heidi and him.

Chapter 37

In 1953, the US inaugurated its 34th president, a Republican for the first time in 24 years: General Dwight D. Eisenhower. Captain Fred Harrington received orders to report to the White House in early January. There, the President himself introduced him to the press corps as the new Chief Pilot of Air Force One.

Heidi Anleger had submitted her application papers for immigration to the United States. Main reason given: "To marry the American citizen, Fred Harrington, my fiancé since November, 1950." There was no guaranteed time line for when everything would be processed. She waited, doing her best to remain patient, trying to focus on the wonderful life which would soon come to be.

It was Norbert Anleger and his Uncle Theo and Aunt Hanna who experienced the shock of the year. One day the doorbell rang at their apartment in Berlin-Neukölln. Norbert, who just happened to be at home, opened the door and saw a scrawny, emaciated stranger.

"Yes?" asked Norbert, thinking that this was one of the usual beggars. "Do you need money or some food?" The scraggly man supported his shaky body by holding on to the door frame.

"No, not money, not food," he said, his voice so weak it was nearly inaudible. "I am trying to find Karl Anleger and his wife Gertrud."

"What is your name?" asked the skeptical Norbert.

"Fritz—Fritz Brenner. I think I am your uncle. Are you Norbi? If you are, then your mother is my sister, Gertrud Brenner Anleger."

Norbert felt suddenly transported back in time. In order to overcome the tragedies in his family, neither he nor Heidi nor Uncle Theo had talked much about their dead or missing relatives. They were like forgotten treasures kept in one's heart but kept out of current thoughts. But here was his uncle he had not seen in years, a face he now fully recognized.

This hunched-over, wrinkled man standing in front of him, the brother of his late mother, was indeed his favorite Uncle Fritz. It was strange for Norbert to see him as he was now, at the same time recalling the fond childhood memories. Only 12 years older than Norbert, he had been full of silly pranks and practical jokes. Was this spent, burned-out man the same person Norbert's family had once visited in his hometown, where they built the *Volkswagen?*

"Yes, I am Norbi. Come on in and rest a while!" Norbert said, opening the door fully. "This is my Aunt Hanna. Uncle Theo must be on the way home." Fritz nodded politely to Hanna and walked straight to a chair to sit down. Hanna went into the kitchen to get some juice for their guest.

Just then Norbert heard the apartment door being opened. "Speaking of the devil! Here is Uncle Theo now!"

Naturally, Theo recognized his relative, Fritz, even though with some difficulty. "Where have you been all those years, Fritz? I was afraid you had taken one of those Volkswagen Beetles and driven right to heaven or hell, wherever you had more friends waiting." Fritz did not even have the strength to laugh at Theo's joke. He just stared, and then he spoke in his thin voice.

"Yes, Theo, I remember you and your wife, Hanni. When I finished my Auto Mechanic training in 1938, you told me to get married."

"You remember that?" asked Theo. "I only made fun of you because you were the one who always joked with everyone else. You even teased me about Hanna and I having no children."

Norbert wondered when Uncle Theo would get around to telling Fritz that Karl and Gertrud were dead. For now, it seemed Fritz was in dire need of more comforting talk. Norbert was amazed at how the reunion of these two men had such an invigorating effect on both of them. However, it was the usually quiet Hanna who took over the reins.

"Enough with all that teasing! It is time to offer our guest a good coffee or perhaps a real meal."

"That is very kind of you, Hanni, but I came to ask you a much bigger favor than coffee or *Abendessen.*" Feeling embarrassed about what he was about to say, Fritz fell silent. Theo prompted him to speak.

"Let's have it, Fritz! What is on your mind?"

"I come directly from the Rehabilitation Center for former prisoners of war. Since I never had a family, would it be alright if I stayed with you for a few days or weeks until I am back on my feet?"

"Listen, Fritz!" said Theo. "My Hanni and Norbert's mother and you all have or had the same last name, Brenner. What does that make you?"

"I guess, family," answered Fritz in a weak voice.

"Right you are! Fritz Brenner, welcome home!"

Norbert looked at his watch. "Sorry, guys, I am late for my classes. I hate to leave you, but I see that Uncle Fritz is in good hands now. Just promise me, that after feeding this certainly hungry man and allowing him many hours of sleep, you will ask him not to tell his life story until I am back again. Okay?"

After his last class, Norbert literally ran from the *U-Bahn* station to the apartment, hoping to find his Uncle Fritz awake after a refreshing rest. Theo had let Fritz use his tub, shaving cream and razor. He also had pulled a brand new shirt and a pair of worn, but clean, slacks out of his wardrobe. The only item missing was a pair of better-fitting shoes. The ones Fritz had were a gift from an American border guard, but they were several sizes too large.

Now that Norbert was home, they all sat back with steaming coffee, begging Fritz to tell them about the past eight years.

"First of all, I promise that I will tell you nothing but the truth," began Fritz. "You probably remember that I finished school when I was 14— that was in 1934. I found a shop in *Braunschweig* that was willing to give me a four-year training in Auto Mechanics. It was especially nice that I could room with the family of my boss, who had only one adopted little son. After four good years, I was a 'Journeyman'—but I wanted to continue my education for another two years, which would have given me the Auto Mechanics Master Certificate. But circumstances changed."

Fritz sipped his coffee. He needed a moment to gather enough energy to go on. Theo asked, "So it was 1938, then?"

"Yes, it was 1938. Only about 30 kilometers southwest of *Braunschweig,* a giant factory was being built in a rural area known only for its hundreds of asparagus fields. The call had gone out to auto mechanics all over Germany to come to the factory close to *'Fallersleben next to no-where'* and be part of the giant work-force that would build thousands of small cars, which every German family could afford.

"I packed my few belongings, said goodbye to my lovely host family, and pedaled my bicycle from *Braunschweig* to *the place with no name,* close to Fallersleben. I had expected nothing but green asparagus fields, but I was totally wrong. The place was swarming with well dressed, impressive looking and acting men in uniforms and civilian suits. There were lots of swastika flags in all sizes, music bands, and *Kraft durch Freude,* or 'KDF, Strength through Joy' female athletes performing all kinds of floor exercises.

"On the next day, the first of July, this place got its official name: *Stadt – des – KDF Wagens – bei – Fallersleben*—city of the KDF car, near Fallersleben."

Norbert, always curious about the history of everything, asked his uncle to say more about this unusual event—a huge spectacle of festivities just because a plant was opening?

"You cannot imagine the atmosphere. Everyone was excited! No government ever had pulled off such a dazzling display of mixed entertainment and business. The wide factory doors were open to all visitors. Beer was flowing freely. Every few hundred meters stood a *Bratwurst* tent that also offered pretzels and *Wiener Würstchen*. It felt like I had died and gone to food heaven.

"Behind flower-decorated long tables sat KDF-dressed secretaries, helping to fill out the work application forms for the hundreds of people waiting in long lines. Naturally, I signed up, too! The promised pay was excellent and the three weeks of holiday sounded good. For the first three months, newcomers qualified for free housing in government-built barracks.

"I found out right away that I had the job, and, to my amazement, the very next day we newcomers received free work clothes and an advance paycheck of 100 *Reichsmark*. Every one of us was proud to be part of the greatest car-building project the world had ever seen.

Fritz paused, giving Norbert a chance to jump in. "Uncle Fritz, you are talking about the *Volkswagen*, the 'people's car,' right?"

"Yes, you are right. Hitler's dream come true—an excellent little car which was within the means of almost every German. During the second year of working there, we were offered to be able to buy a *Volkswagen* for 1,000 *Reichsmark*. But in September, 1939, when World War II broke out against Poland, England and France, the 1,000 *Reichsmark* promise changed. It was announced that all who had paid 1,000 marks for a *Volkswagen* would have to wait for its delivery until *after* the war had been won victoriously. We were all convinced that this would happen soon, especially after the *Blitzkrieg* victory against Poland."

"Some more coffee?" Hanna asked everyone.

All remained silent except for Fritz, who held up his empty cup and said, "I would not mind a bit more coffee for my tongue. I have not talked this much in many years. Sorry!"

"No! Don't be sorry!" said the captivated Norbert. "Keep on talking! Aunt Hanni will keep soothing your vocal chords with more coffee or beer or whatever you need to finish telling your story." Fritz managed a small smile, and nodded to Norbert as he continued.

"Because of the ongoing war, I still was pedaling my old bicycle every day to work instead of driving a shiny new *Volkswagen.* But no one was, because the production of the VW took second-place to producing trucks, guns, ammunition, and even small planes for the military. As a trained and certified mechanic, I was classified *Unabkömmlich*—indispensable— like my brother-in-law Karl Anleger was, until he was drafted in October of 1943 anyway. I was never drafted into the military.

"With Germany at war with the US, Soviet Union, Great Britain, Canada, France, Greece, and even countries in North Africa, many factory workers were sent to fight at the front. Their replacements were prisoners-of-war from Poland,

Yugoslavia, France, Holland, Russia and 'forced workers' from many other German-occupied countries in Europe.

"I worked as a civilian to the very end of the war. Then in 1945, when Germany had surrendered, was *kaput,* our huge factory also went *kaput.* Now that the Germans had lost the war, civil order was also lost. The German foremen and bosses no longer had any control over the foreign workers. I remember, because I was one of the hundreds of foremen who got spit at when I asked the laborers to be sensible so that we could get our bomb-damaged machines working again. All authorities and procedures were ignored. Our brilliant and well-functioning system was now *kaput.*

"It wasn't long before the Soviets took advantage of the chaotic situation in Wolfsburg, as we called our town unofficially, after the Castle Wolfsburg, owned by the Graf von Schulenburg whose family lived there. One day, when most workers were ready to go home, three military buses—actually American school buses painted over with war colors—drove up to the *Volkswagen* Administrative Building. Eight or ten Russian soldiers armed with heavy-caliber rifles jumped out of each bus, grabbing German civilians and shoving them into the buses.

"When one of the Ruskies stopped me and reached for my bicycle, I fought back. Dumb idea! While one soldier pointed his gun at me, another one came up from behind me and hit my head with the butt of his rifle. I screamed and let go of the bike. I was practically thrown into the bus, along with my co-workers who were packed in until the bus was absolutely full. Nobody cared that I was bleeding profusely. A few British soldiers tried to block the buses from leaving.

Russian and English soldiers and German factory workers were yelling, swearing, and cursing each other. Nevertheless, the buses started their engines and drove us right through the mass of frenzied remaining workers.

"Uncle Fritz!" Norbert interrupted. "We had no idea you were kidnapped! That is horrible!"

"It got worse. In less than half an hour our buses reached the town of *Helmstedt* and crossed the border into the Soviet Zone. None of us knew what was going on. But instinctively we knew that we were in trouble—that *something* really bad was happening."

Norbert, Theo, and Hanna saw that Fritz's hands were shaking. Had the lengthy account exhausted him that much, or was it the recalling of the events which led to his imprisonment in the Soviet Union that made Fritz lose his composure?

"Perhaps we should take a break here," Theo suggested. "You can always tell us more tomorrow."

Fritz wiped his brow, then his whole face with his table napkin. It was obvious that the gesture was an attempt to wipe away the vivid memories and pain he still felt as he recalled and re-lived the ordeal.

"No, Theo," Fritz said. "I want to continue telling you now—and then never again. To have been robbed of eight years of my life is not a small fate."

The rest of the family remained silent and waited until Fritz had gathered enough strength to continue.

"In Magdeburg, we were loaded into a cattle wagon and shipped off to the Soviet Union. At the Russian border we had to exchange our train with a Russian broad gauge liner. From then on, my memory is unclear. You see, we were traveling many days and nights without stopping, with no water or food, and without toilet facilities. That treatment was to prepare us for what was to come, once we arrived in Alma Ata, the capital of the Kirgheez Steppe in Siberia."

"Yes, Uncle Fritz, we know where that is," said Norbert. "Today Alma Ata is the capital of the Kazakh Soviet Republic, north of China."

"Well, you know more than we did at that time. After trying to stay alive on the train for two weeks, we had no idea where we were until we heard a loud whistle and a command, given in Russian, to get off the train.

"In oxen-drawn carts we were transported to a quicksilver mine outside of Alma Ata. You would not believe the hard labor we were forced to do. I had to work there for seven years with primitive tools, hacking away on the ore-bearing rock, the most hazardous mineral to be exposed to. We worked ten hours every day, seven days a week. Our food consisted of cabbage soup for five weeks, then it changed for five weeks to coarsely ground barley soup, then back to cabbage soup, and so on!

"On our arrival day at the mine—I have no date—we were told that the camp had 50,000 workers. And don't even think of escaping from down there in the southern-most corner of Central Asia! You have nowhere to go, unless you commit suicide. Then you would *go to hell faster than we could transport you there,* our commandant told us. To scare us even more, we received the daily statistic of fatalities, always around 100. By 1948, most of us suffered severely from mercurial poisoning.

"We were forbidden to write anything at all. Nobody ever received any mail. Sometimes we saw our Russian guards eating German *Bahlsen Kekse*—cookies which had been sent to us by relatives or the German Red Cross, we suspected.

"At the end of 1950, just when we could not take it any longer and thought that death would be far better than this life of hell, the Soviet government began sending prisoners back to Germany. After a few months our camp population was down to 20,000. For those of us who remained at the mine, life became nothing but a daily torment. In December of 1952, all prisoners 40 and younger were taken away—we hoped they were going home, but we did not know, really. After Christmas, which we had been forbidden to celebrate in any form, about 800 prisoners were put on horse-drawn carriages and transported to the railroad station in Novosibirsk. Finally, I was one of the selected POWs to leave that horrible, horrible place. The transport took three weeks. By the time we had covered that long distance, our group had shrunk to 600; 200 had not survived the harsh and freezing journey.

"In Novosibirsk, we dragged ourselves into the freight cars. We felt like we had moved into a luxury hotel simply by being out of the icy wind and snow. Heading through Russian East Poland, the closer we got to Warsaw, the more Polish partisans attacked our train. They searched us for valuables, which we did not have. Once we traveled west of Warsaw, the attacks were worse, and even our clothes were stolen as we were stripped down to our underwear."

Fritz reached for the hot coffee, now, perhaps remembering too well the bone-chilling trip he nearly didn't survive. Hanna refilled everyone's cup, but no one spoke; Fritz's tale had them in awe. Encouraged by their silent attentiveness, Fritz continued his story.

"On February 8, 1953, our train reached the German city, *Frankfurt an der Oder*. From there, most of us were sent to a former military hospital in East Berlin. All of us, but especially we 'older' prisoners, needed medical care. I weighed 90 pounds! Some fellow prisoners had relatives in what was now West Germany. We all hoped to be sent there—but we soon learned the devastating news that we would be sent to the East German Uranium Mine in Aue, close to the Czechoslovakian border, for one year of probation. Probation? Had we not suffered enough?

"When we arrived at the primitive mine in Aue, our *Alma Ata* prison group formed a non-political pact: under no circumstance would we work here for one year! We would try anything to escape to West Germany. One of us had to get through to the West to tell them that we were still alive. When everyone looked at me as their possible messenger, I told them that I was too weak for the job. Well, they did not think so! One of them even shouted, 'You are the strongest of all of us!' Can you imagine that he was speaking of me?

"Thus, on a cold, snowy night in February, I started out with neither a compass nor a map, and with little food reserves. I walked by night. During the daytime I hid in barns or haystacks. It took me almost three weeks to get to the West German border—a distance I could have made in two hours or less by car. When I came to a big, white sign announcing,

389

'*Achtung! Sie betreten die Amerikanische Zone!*' I kissed the ground over and over.

"I do not remember how, but I ended up in a hospital in Bayreuth in the *Fichtel Gebirge,* where I must have fallen into a death-like sleep for two days. When an orderly tried to wake me up, I could not even speak. I had very good care and nourishing food and finally, after many days, I felt like a human being again. They gave me some used military clothing and helped me walk up and down the hospital halls and gain some strength back."

Theo took a deep breath, exhaling slowly, as if he had not dared to breathe during this harrowing tale until the part where Fritz was finally free and safe. Norbert stared at his Uncle Fritz with newfound respect, as well as amazement. "Where did they send you after the hospital, Uncle Fritz?" Norbert asked.

"Ha!" said Fritz. "I was back to being a free man! No one could *send* me anywhere! But they did ask me where I wanted to go—where was my family, where was my home, what town should they arrange for me to travel to. So I told them—*just sent me to Berlin, where my sister and her husband are living.* After some searching, they could not find a 'Karl Anleger' in Berlin-Neukölln, but they discovered a 'Theo Anleger' address here in Neukölln – and here I am."

Chapter 38

Brimful with world-changing events, the year 1953 was one no one predicted, and no one would forget.

On January 20, the USA inaugurated a new President, the 63-year old Five Star General, Dwight D. Eisenhower.

On January 28, a one-day-record number of 2,000 asylum-seekers from the East was registered in West Berlin.

On March 5, Generalissimos Joseph Stalin died in Moscow without much government fanfare, since he was no longer the admired leader of the Soviets.

On June 2, Elizabeth II became Great Britain's new Queen.

For Norbert Anleger, the unforgettable highlight of the year (as of March) was the homecoming of his uncle, Fritz Brenner, finally free after a total of eight years imprisonment in the USSR and East Germany. But even more personally impactful experiences were in store for Norbert.

It was June, and something very important was brewing in East Berlin. The communist East German government had proposed a ten-percent increase for individual production quotas. For the blue-color workers, this was the last straw. Several thousand construction workers marched to the East German House of Ministries, demanding higher wages, the resignation of their government, and free elections. Neither the *Volkspolizei* nor the SED agents were able to break up the demonstration by the angry workers.

Word of the East Berlin protest spread quickly. By the following morning, twelve thousand workers across the city had gone on strike. Hundreds of strikers from East Germany had come to Berlin overnight. In radical moves, they burned communist banners along *Unter den Linden*, East Berlin's main boulevard, stormed local Communist Party offices, smashed the windows of state-owned grocery stores, set fire to police stations and to the huge *Columbia Haus* complex. The sparks of freedom quickly ignited other East German cities, where striking workers destroyed hundreds of communist properties.

That was the day when Norbert Anleger left his bicycle at home and took the *U-Bahn* to the center of Berlin where the demonstrations were in full swing. There were excited people everywhere. As Norbert walked through the *Brandenburger Tor,* he saw a white-shirted young man climb up a long wooden pole.

"What's going on?" Norbert asked the cheering bystanders.

"The Red Flag has to come down! Come on! Help us stabilize the pole!"

Norbert did not need a second invitation. He saw that three young guys were already on top of the Brandenberg Gate. The Red Flag, the symbol of Soviet dictatorial rule over half of Germany, was still flying in the wind. Norbert looked up and shouted, "One of you guys needs to tear down the flag, or I will climb up and do it myself!" Just then the pole climber had reached the upper edge of the 60-foot-high gate. That freed two of those standing on top to pull down the Russian flag and throw it to the applauding masses below, where it was held by one man while another lit it on fire. That was also the moment when Soviet tanks and troops moved onto the scene.

While the young men on top of the Brandenburg Gate tried to hoist a "Berliner Bear" flag as replacement for the Red Flag, Soviet soldiers began shooting at them and the demonstrators below. The crowd's cheers turned to screams and the protesters became even more enraged. The fact that Soviet troops now were fighting the unarmed demonstrators was an admission by the East German Regime that they were unable to cope with the situation, which had developed into a popular uprising.

Major General Andrey V. Molotov had been itching to send his soldiers to squelch the demonstration and get the unruly protesters under control. It had been his deputy, Lieutenant Sergey Svertlov, who attempted to convince Molotov not to get the Russian military involved in the East/West German revolt. But when the fearless demonstrators covered the entire area from the *Brandenburger Tor* south to the *Potsdamer Platz* and east to the *Alexander Platz,* Molotov had given the order to send in armed troops.

"And you, my loyal deputy," he said to Svertlov, "will be in charge of our attack.

Understood? Now get going and don't come back until every last demonstrator either has gone home or has been killed! We are at war, Lieutenant. Understood!"

Not without difficulty, Svertlov shoved his opinions and judgment aside, got the tanks rolling and soldiers firing their rifles at the East Germans. When the Soviet tanks erupted unto the *Potsdamer Platz,* the thick crowd scattered. Hundreds of young workers, not at all intimidated, ripped up the sidewalks and used small paver stones as ammunition against the tanks. Stones against tanks!

Other demonstrators risked their lives running toward the tanks, sticking crowbars into the tank chains, disabling them at least for a short while. Still, the primitive warfare methods of the opposition had forced the Soviet soldiers to leave the turrets and seek shelter inside the armored tanks. From there they continued aiming their rifles at the most daring demonstrators.

Norbert, a true West Berliner, but now showing his solidarity with the East Berliners, suddenly spotted his friend, Willi Göttling.

"What are you doing here, Norbert?" asked Willi.

"I was about to ask you the same question," replied Norbert, ducking rifle shots. "Norbert, you know that I live in West Berlin but I work in East Berlin, where my company has its headquarters," Willi said, scanning the area as he spoke. "Come on—let's move over there before we get killed!"

The two men raced to the edge of the fracas and away from the tanks' line of fire.

"Willi, you told me that you had lost your job and were unemployed."

"Yes, I got fired by my communist foreman—you are right. But I am on my way to my former company to arrange for my Unemployment Assistance. After all, I have worked for them for six years—I am entitled to relief payments."

"I thought you were demonstrating against the existing regime in favor of free and secret elections," said Norbert to his friend.

"No, I leave that to the East Berliners and East Germans. Remember, I am a married man with two small children. This time the younger workers will have to bail out us older ones."

"Come on, Willi! You are not too old to throw a few pavement stones at the Russian tanks."

"Like I saw *you* doing just a few minutes ago? Do you really think demonstrations like these will make a difference in this rotten DDR?"

"I do!" said Norbert, firmly. "Do you see any East German Party officials here? They are hiding in their offices with their pants full of shit. As to the Russians—look around! They might be shooting at us, but they are scared as hell."

The word *hell* had hardly left Norbert's lips when Willi reached for his chest. An explosive bullet had just ripped into him, mangling his clothes, flesh and bone. Norbert dropped the paving stone in his hand and bent over the bleeding body of his friend. *Had these bastards really killed his friend, this totally innocent young father, who in order to support his family, had to work in East Berlin?* The huge and gaping wound told Norbert that Willi was dead, but he still called to him, and bent to check his pulse and breath. *They killed this thoroughly good man, who had not even dared to speak out against the communist regime?*

Looking at his dead friend, Norbert could hardly breathe. He knew he had to get Willi out of the fangs of these killers. Some of the demonstrators around Norbert helped him lift up the body. They disguised the corpse with several pieces of clothing and Norbert dragged the heavy load across the near-by border into West Berlin.

When the West Berlin police took over, they assumed that Norbert had also been wounded, because his shirt and jacket were badly stained with blood, his friend's blood. He quickly told them that nothing was wrong with him. "Just take care of my friend! His name is Willi Göttling. I will inform his wife of his death. Where will you take Willi's body?"

"Did you know this man well?" Norbert thought for a moment.

"I would not say very well, but well enough to call him my friend."

"Then you need to give us your name, and his name and particulars, before we take him to the morgue. For whatever reason, there are no identification papers on the body."

After Norbert gave the police Willi's name, area of residence, and age, the police granted him his request to be the bearer of the tragic news. In about twenty minutes he stood in front of Mrs. Göttling's apartment door. As he reached for the doorbell, he saw his bloody sleeve. *I cannot face her like this!* Since he had nothing to wipe the crusted blood from his clothes, he quickly ran back down the street where he had passed a water-fountain. There he ripped off both his jacket and shirt and submerged them in the fountain basin, directing the water-spout onto the worst blood spots.

Even though his clothes were far from clean, he put them on again and walked slowly back to the Göttling apartment. How could he face Willi's wife? What would he tell her? When he rang the bell, he heard a woman's voice behind the closed door. "Is that you, Willi? Darling, did you forget your key? What took you so long?" When she opened the door and saw Norbert standing there in his dripping wet clothes, she quickly jumped back a step, startled.

"Oh, it's you, Norbert! Come on in! Willi should be here soon. Is it raining outside, or did you fall into the pond at the park?" she asked jokingly. When she looked closer at Norbert's sad, cheerless face, she asked in a more sober tone, "What happened to you? What's wrong?"

Norbert could not get any words to come out. Finally, after she asked him to come in and sit down, he said, "No, thank you. I am too wet to sit on your nice furniture. But I will talk to you, even though I don't have much to say except that Willi is not coming home—not now, not ever."

Instantly the young wife and mother grasped what Norbert was saying and her hand flew to her mouth as she uttered a sharp cry. The moment of anguish became even more painful when Mrs. Göttling's two little children came from behind her and ran up to the unexpected guest.

"Uncle Norbert! Uncle Norbert is here!"

"Hush, children! I know. Now go back into your room and play!"

What else could the new widow have said to her little ones, without knowing anything at all about her husband's death? True, the brutal war and the difficult years afterwards had made most Berliners tough and strong. But the shocking loss of her husband and children's father was too much. She barely made it to a chair before her legs folded. "Tell me what happened, Norbert. Tell me how my Willi—" She choked on her words, but had no tears as her eyes implored Norbert to explain.

After Norbert had shared the full story of Willi's death and had given all possible comfort to the children and their young mother, he excused himself and left the apartment. He wore a clean, white shirt which Willi had owned until this morning, and which Willi's widow had handed to him. Instead of rejoining the demonstrators, Norbert took the *U-Bahn* to his Uncle Theo's apartment. More than rest, Norbert needed time to think.

Two days later, when the family was eating breakfast, the radio announced the horrid results of the *Aufstand* (uprising): all of Germany was under Martial Law. During the few days of unrest, 267 demonstrators had been brutally shot and killed. Even 116 functionaries of the Communist SED had lost their lives, as had 18 Soviet soldiers. After a brief court-martial, 92 "perpetrators" had been executed. Fourteen more workers had received the death sentence to be executed at a later time. The announcer's voice broke when he reported that the number of injured was not firm yet, but at least 1,900 young and old citizens had sought help in hospitals and emergency clinics.

Not only had Norbert and the demonstrators around him witnessed the killing of Willi Göttling, another man had seen it, too. On June 20, this man had stood on top of a Soviet tank, shouting encouragement to the Russian troops. When East and West German protesters returned the Russian gunfire with a hail of pavement stones and other dangerous projectiles, Lieutenant Sergey Svertlov, only 29 years old, lost his composure. He had been surprised that his show of force—the soldiers with rifles, the large and imposing tanks— had not immediately subdued and dispersed the crowd. The more they resisted, the angrier and more frustrated he had become.

When a rock glanced off his kneecap, his feet had stamped and pounded the tank steel plate as he screamed, "SHOOT! Shoot them all!" When he surveyed his outnumbered yet much better-armed soldiers, who seemed to be paralyzed by fear, he had shouted even louder:

"SHOOT! Shoot, comrades! Don't spare the ammunition! Kill those ungrateful bastards!"

Even Svertlov's own soldiers hardly recognized their Lieutenant. Sure, he had been part of evil "acts of war" during the blockade, but never before had they seen him on a furious killing rampage.

When Svertlov came home late that evening, he felt totally spent and exhausted. Even his voice had given out, which was no surprise, considering how, for many hours, he had yelled at his troops to wipe out the stubborn Germans. His wife, Luba, was waiting with a delicious meal.

"What is it, my dear Sergey? You look as if somebody pulled you out of a mud bath!"

Svertlov had no energy to answer. He grunted and sat on the bench by the door to take off his boots. Luba, more concerned now, said, "Your face is red, your cheeks and lips are swollen, your full hair has gone wild—and your always beautiful, dark-brown eyes look like death. Am I really looking at my heroic liberator of Berlin?"

"Oh, Luba, you don't want to know what I have experienced today," he said in his extremely hoarse voice. "Had you been with me, your face would be as red as mine. I had a horrible day, fighting Germans."

"But you have fought Germans before—for years, defending our motherland."

"That was different, my sweet Luba. Today, in Berlin, and all over the DDR, we fought with tanks, guns, rifles and pistols against *civilians*, who had nothing to fight back with other than stones, a few crowbars, and a lot of guts—if I may say so."

Luba had no reply; she helped him off with his boots.

"It was upon my command that our soldiers aimed their weapons at thousands of people. Men, and women, too, who were demonstrating, demanding better pay and free elections. It was I who cheered on our troops to shoot and *kill*. I—I will never forgive myself for this day. Never!"

The next day, a courier delivered a letter to Norbert from the Chairman of the City Council of Berlin, Dr. Otto Suhr; Willi Göttling's funeral would be held on Sunday, June 21.

Göttling's funeral will stand as a representative memorial for the hundreds East German victims who will be buried in the Deutsche Demokratische Republik as a result of the disgraceful conduct of the Soviets and their senseless murders. We anticipate that hundreds of Berliners will attend the funeral and that a number of American mourners will join them. We know of two U.S. officers, who asked to speak.

Mr. Anleger, we ask that you attend, and please be prepared to translate any remarks or speeches made in English. Thank you for your cooperation! No need to reply.

Gratefully, Dr. Otto Suhr, Stadt-Verordneten Vorsteher von Berlin

Of course Norbert was very willing to function as interpreter at the funeral of his friend.

There was nothing else he could do for Willi. Norbert was used being called on with short notice. His only surprise came during the funeral ceremony, which was attended by at least 1,000 mourners. Willi Göttling had been neither a government official nor a community leader—just a painter, a husband and a father, like many other Berliners. It was not the overwhelming outpouring of sympathy from his fellow citizens that startled Norbert the most. His surprise came when he discovered the face of Lieutenant Sergey Iliavitch Svertlov among the hundreds of faces gathered at the grave site.

At first he had not recognized him, because Svertlov wore no uniform. Why was the Russian officer attending the funeral of a man who had been killed most likely as the result of his own orders? Norbert was tempted to approach Svertlov, whom he knew from the period of time the Soviet authorities had been hunting for him. Svertlov had been in charge of the search, until Major General Andrey Molotov, the new Commander of Berlin's Soviet Troops, had ordered an end to the hunting craze.

However, Norbert could not just walk over to Svertlov who stood at the back of the assembly; he had to stay close to the speaker's podium. The American Commander of Berlin was about to say a few words. The moment Norbert completed the translation, he excused himself and squeezed through the thick crowd. But the closer he got to the Russian officer in civilian disguise, the more that man moved further back, finally disappearing.

About one week later it was apparent that in the battle between East and West, the Soviets had won this round. The dead were buried. The injured received medical treatment, and the demonstrators had gone, and stayed home. The Communist clique was still in power. The East German press was removing the last traces of truth about the causes for the uprising.

For now, see you later, freedom! Rest in peace, if your conscience can tolerate seeing the hardships and distress of East Germans living in a suppressive dictatorial society!

Chapter 39

The signing of the 1953 Korean Armistice by the United Nations, North Korea, and China on July 27, at Korea's North-South border town of Panmunjom, was another historic milestone for improving international relations. Judging the positive development rather critically, US President Eisenhower stated: "We have won an armistice on a simple battleground, not peace in the world."

Since Eisenhower was not traveling that day, Chief Pilot Fred Harrington was resting in his quarters, listening by radio to the President's entire speech. Fred, who had personally experienced the calamity the Korean War had brought on the US and the world, felt as if warm waves and sunshine were washing over him. Even though only an armistice had been reached and not a permanent peace, all involved nations still had reasons for rejoicing. The dark cloud that would not go away for some time, however, was the shocking fact that the US Armed Forces had suffered 137,051 casualties, and 25,604 had died.

Fred thanked God daily that his life had been spared when President Eisenhower had ordered him back to the United States and appointed him Chief Pilot of Air Force One.

His equally great joy was that his fiancée, Heidi Anleger, had been able to clear US Immigration and move to Alexandria, Virginia, close to Washington, DC's National Airport. If they only had more free time, they would have been married already. Each time they had agreed on a possible wedding date, they had to cancel because Fred had to fly the President to "who knows where." The world was a big round globe for the political "marathoners" on Air Force One.

Heidi and Fred used their rare off-duty hours for discussing all the details of the wedding, other than the actual date. They had not yet decided the most important detail—civil or church? Each time the question came up, they had to think hard. A civil wedding did not require much preparation other than hiring a person authorized to officiate, enlisting two witnesses, and having the wedding rings handy. Fred told Heidi the official was the easy part—they could ask any Air Force officer with the rank of Captain or higher.

A church wedding, on the other hand, called for formal invitations, a church and minister, a bridal gown and groom's tuxedo, a wedding rehearsal with dinner, a wedding cake, flowers, and many more wedding trappings.

Heidi assured Fred that she didn't "need" a formal church wedding by any means. It had not been her lifelong dream— she told him her dream had come true when he asked her to be his wife. They decided on a simple, civil marriage in Washington, DC, on October 2, 1953. In addition to the two witnesses, they created a small guest list.

Then, the totally unexpected death of West Berlin's Mayor Ernst Reuter and his funeral scheduled for October 2, forced them to postpone the wedding date. Heidi's brother, Norbert, would be tied up with interpreting duties from morning to night, two days before, during, and even after the state funeral. Heidi, who had lost most of her close family during the war, would not even think of getting married without Norbert being present. Norbert had been booked by the West Berlin Magistrate to be the sole interpreter for the Reuter funeral.

Nearly all of West Berlin had come to know Norbert as the one who had started the "*Hurra, wie leben noch!*" shout on March 12, 1949, in front of the Berlin-*Schöneberg* City Hall.

And, many Berliners had heard Norbert interpreting for Mayor Ernst Reuter and General Lucius Clay, when the famous Freedom Bell was dedicated on October 24, 1950.

To miss Mayor Reuter's funeral was out of question for Norbert. Not only did he not want to let down the Berliners who expected him to be the interpreter, he knew he would want to attend the funeral even if it was not his job to be there. He very much wanted to pay his respects to this man he had grown to admire more than any other Berliner.

Chapter 40

After getting word that he soon would have to fly the President to Belgium, and then to Italy, Fred made a dinner date with Heidi. Before flying overseas, Fred wanted to set a new wedding date with her. They met at a quiet restaurant in Alexandria, where they could eat and privately discuss their plans. When they entered the restaurant, heads turned to admire—not the distinguished Air Force One Chief Pilot, but rather the poised, beautiful blond woman at his side. Fred was used to such a reaction, and it thrilled him every time he was reminded that this gorgeous woman belonged to him, and he to her.

"Well, Heidi, what's the scoop for our wedding day?" Fred came right out with his question as he wanted her to reveal her ideas first.

"Quite frankly, my new executive job at Macy's has kept me so busy that I've only had a little time to come up with a plan. So why don't you show me what you've come up with!"

"Now that both of us have such demanding jobs, I guess we should have eloped," replied Fred. "Just kidding! Listen, darling, here is what I came up with. As it stands, there is no wartime emergency I need to plan for, and the President and his family will spend the Christmas holidays in Gettysburg on his farm. My deputy chief will be flying them. That will give me about three weeks free time."

"Three weeks sounds great!" said Heidi. "Have you thought about a location?"

"Well, Heidi, I was thinking—no, let me start with a question. Do you remember the wonderful Christmas we had in Iowa in 1950?"

"How could I forget? That time with your parents and grandparents, and with each other, was the best Christmas celebration of my life."

"I am glad to hear you say that. You remember our holiday was cut short when my leave was canceled and I had to report for duty? There's so much more I want to share with you there. I really feel it would be wonderful to fly to Iowa and have our wedding ceremony and reception at our little Baptist Church in Sumner. How about it?"

Ignoring the other restaurant patrons, Heidi jumped up from her chair, squealing with delight. "Yes!" she shouted. She threw her arms around the surprised Fred. Naturally, such a moment called for several kisses and hugs.

"Are you really, honestly, *that* excited, Heidi?" asked Fred, sheepishly.

"Should I have yodeled instead of shouting to let you know how happy this makes me?"

It was settled. The wedding would be on Saturday, December 19, in Sumner. From then on, the telephone lines between Washington and Sumner were working overtime. Heidi had only her brother to invite. But the Harringtons and

Schweigerts had to contact many, many close and distant relatives and friends. Even Jim Harrington, Fred's brother in Utah, and his wife Cindy had accepted the invitation to attend.

Fred was able to arrange free military flights for himself and Heidi. In a long phone call with Norbert, Fred gave his future brother-in-law several hints about which American agencies overseas to approach which could possibly grant a free flight for him, too. Very soon Norbert found out that the days of free flights were over for him, unless he signed up for US military service. Such a plan was not in his future.

Heidi and Fred lived only a half hour's driving distance from each other, so they got together whenever time off allowed. In addition, they talked to each other over the phone every day. Before they knew it, the day for their departure for Iowa had arrived. It was December 16, and even though many flights had been delayed due to weather and heavy holiday travel, their plane departed right on time from Andrews Air Force Base in Maryland. They took this as a good omen for both their journey and marriage.

"Ladies and gentlemen!" the Captain's voice came over the loud speaker. "Welcome to our flight to Waterloo, Iowa. We are on schedule. Today, I have a special announcement. It gives me great pleasure to tell you that we have passengers on board who deserve special recognition. May I introduce to you Captain Fred Harrington, Chief Pilot of Air Force One, and his lovely fiancée, Heidi Anleger, soon to be Mrs. Fred Harrington!"

A roaring applause rose through the plane. The stewardess made it clear which couple was being recognized by standing by their seats and leading the applause. Fred felt like a celebrity, and tried to think who could have told the pilot about them. Heidi just beamed.

As for Norbert's flight to America, he could find nothing pleasant, comfortable or interesting about it except he felt confident he would eventually get to Iowa. His late booking had not given him a good seat for the long stretch from Berlin to New York, and the seat assignment from there to Chicago was even worse. In front, behind, and next to him sat a group of 10-year-old rowdy children from Brooklyn. Finally he caught his last connection and was on his way to Waterloo, hopefully arriving on time, nearly simultaneous with Heidi and Fred.

When Norbert saw Heidi and Fred waiting for him, all his tiredness disappeared. Walking quickly toward them, Norbert wondered who the handsome stranger was standing next to Heidi. Heidi hugged Norbert's neck so hard, he joked that she was breaking it. Rather than the usual handshake, Fred hugged Norbert as well. Then the other man put out his hand to Norbert.

"Welcome, I'm Jim Harrington, your future brother-in-law," said Jim, greeting Norbert with the biggest smile. "Let me help you with your luggage!"

A few minutes later, the four sat in the Harrington Cadillac, heading for Sumner.

"Sorry that my wife Cindy could not come to greet you all. The ladies were too busy with the endless wedding preparations, I guess."

Jim had not seen his brother Fred since his wedding to Cindy in 1935, when Fred had been only six years old. "Man, oh man! To think that my baby brother is 25 years old, a decorated Air Force officer, and the Chief Captain of Air Force One!" "And don't forget—'about to get married to the most beautiful girl in the world,'" added Fred, as everyone laughed. The trip to Sumner flew by with all the excitement and joking going on. For a moment, Heidi thought back to the years when her brothers—Hans, Kurt, Waldemar, and Norbi—had still all been at home. How many verbal battles and loads of teasing had she endured with her older brothers, and even with the younger Norbi! The terrible war had ripped them all, including her parents, from her, except for Norbert. She was nearly overwhelmed, feeling so happy and relieved Norbert was there, sitting right in front of her. She reached out and hugged him from behind.

"What was that for?" asked the surprised Norbert.

"Oh, nothing, Norbi—I am just so glad you are here!"

"So am I, Sis, really!"

The joyous mood reached its peak when they arrived at the Harrington farm. Even the hundreds of turkeys greeted them with their loud gobbling. There were no young children around since Cindy and Jim had left their four children at home in Utah. The happy reunion and first-time meeting of the adults, however, was as noisy as an outing of teenagers.

The next day, a sleek, new rental car pulled up to the farm and stopped right in front of Heidi, who was giving Norbert a tour of the Harrington property. Out stepped Mr. and Mrs. Wolfram Siemens, from Berlin. Only Fred had known there was a chance they could come to the wedding. Heidi was completely surprised and overjoyed.

"*Herr Siemens! Was machen Sie denn hier* in Iowa?" she asked Wolfram Siemens, after having hugged Mrs. Siemens first.

"We hope we are at the right place," said Mr. Siemens. "A little bird told us that there would be a wedding here in two days. Is that correct?"

More infectious laughter followed. Heidi could not believe that her prominent business friends from Berlin had come to her wedding in little Sumner.

"To be honest, Heidi—by the way, please call me Wolfram, and my wife Dora or Theodora—well, I had important business in Chicago, which, as you know, is just around the corner from here, ha! Since it was such a long trip from Berlin to Illinois, Dora and I decided she would come along. Then, when we heard of your wedding plans, we realized the timing would work out well for us to—well—just swing by! We hope it's okay with everyone. We promise that we will not be in your way. We are staying at a hotel in Cedar Falls."

Instead of treating the Siemens as welcome surprise guests, the Harringtons opened their hearts to them. The same reaction came from Fred's grandparents, the Schweigerts. "*Kommen Sie bitte rein!*" welcomed Grandpa Schweigert, "*und füehlen Sie sich wie Zuhause.*"

"We already feel at home," replied Dora Siemens, as Anna Harrington held both her hands in a tight embrace.

The day before the wedding, Fred, Heidi, and members of the wedding party drove to the First Baptist Church in Sumner, a small church with only 55 members. Fred had made an appointment with the relatively new pastor, whom he had not met before. The pastor had the tradition of not only interviewing the wedding couple, but also rehearsing the entire ceremony, except for the ceremonial prayers and his meditation.

Fred and Heidi were escorted into the pastor's office while the others visited out in the small foyer, enjoying the lemonade that Fred's grandmother had thought to bring for everyone. After the pastor introduced himself briefly, he focused on getting to know the engaged couple who were about to enter into Holy Matrimony.

"Actually, I usually require pre-marital counseling over several weeks," he told Fred and Heidi. "In your case, I understand you can only be here for this short meeting, but I will ask you all the important questions, yes?"

Fred and Heidi both nodded. "Yes, sir!" said Fred, revealing his ingrained military manners.

"Since you desire to have a church wedding, it is only proper to ask what your relationship is to God and His Son Jesus Christ. To ask for God's blessing, and to pray to Jesus without believing in God would be a travesty.

"So let me ask you first, Fred Harrington, do you believe in the almighty God, who created heaven and earth, and have you accepted Jesus, the Son of the Living God, as your Savior?"

"Yes, Pastor, I do so with all of my heart," answered Fred. "Perhaps I should tell you that I grew up in this church, to which my parents have belonged most of their lives."

"Have they been instrumental in showing you the way to God?"

"Yes, sir, they have. I could not have wished for more understanding and spiritually solid parents than George and Anna Harrington. When I was 16 years old, I was baptized as a believer in this church."

"That is wonderful, Captain!" said the pastor, his face beaming. "Did I say your military rank correctly?"

"You did, sir. My Brigadier General has recommended me for promotion to major, perhaps as soon as January."

"Congratulations! And now to you, Miss Anleger. Tell me about your relationship with God."

"I wish I had several hours to tell you about my life's path. To say the most important thing first—yes, I believe in God the Father, the Son, and the Holy Spirit. I grew up in a Lutheran family, where we attended church on Easter, and Christmas, for baptisms, and a few other times during the year."

"Yes, that sounds like the church attendance of all too many families, whether they are Lutherans, Baptists or other denominations. But I am glad to hear you grew up in a Christian family—though I was saddened to hear you have lost so many of them. The Harringtons told me that your parents were killed during the war, as were three of your four brothers."

Heidi nodded, then rested her face in the open palm of her hand for a minute before she spoke.

"To be totally frank," she said, "religion meant very little to me when growing up, especially when I became more and more involved with the *Bund Deutscher Mädel* movement during the Hitler years. This group increasingly swallowed up my free time and interest. Their schedule saw to it that there was not much time left for church and religion."

The pastor stole a quick glance at his wristwatch.

"I wish we had lots of time for you to tell me how you found your way back to God, if you ever left him."

"Oh yes, I had turned my back on God—and for sure on 'Jesus the Jew,' as we were taught to call Christ by our Nazi leaders."

"Your female Nazi leaders called him the *Jewish Jesus?* You certainly know that Jesus indeed was born a Jew."

"Yes, but I did not tell you all the other mocking and degrading names they gave Jesus.

"The tragedy was that in spite of absolutely horrible happenings in my life, I did not know that I had left God and Jesus. They just no longer fit into my life in the BDM.

"But you want to know where I am standing with God now. It all started with falling in love with this man." Heidi took Fred's hand and held it lovingly.

"We met in Berlin. He, an American, and I, a German. Two former enemies! On our very first date I noticed that Fred was so wonderfully different. He was not after my body. He disliked cheap and dubious entertainment. We loved to look at each other and to tenderly stroke each other's hair. After a few dates, we kissed and slowly fell in love.

"But you really don't have the time to listen to my sentimental ramblings. In 1950, we got engaged and visited Fred's parents here in Sumner over Christmas. Then suddenly the marvelous, dreamy life was over. Fred was deployed to Korea for two years.

"But our bond and love only grew stronger. Fred and I feel that God kept him safe and led him to the miraculous opportunity of becoming President Eisenhower's Chief Pilot on Air Force One. In January, 1953, he moved to Washington, DC, where I joined him as a legal immigrant in March."

Fred interrupted Heidi to explain that he lived in military quarters near the Andrews Air Force Base, while Heidi had an apartment in Alexandria, close to Washington's National Airport. The Pastor, nodded thoughtfully, and then asked Heidi to continue.

"If Fred was not flying for the President, we would spend all day together on Sundays. Since I loved him so much I wanted to be with him as much as possible—if that meant attending church, I attended church. In fact, we went together every Sunday we could."

"What church did you attend?" asked the pastor.

"Fred had started attending the Columbia First Baptist Church in Falls Church, Virginia, so I joined him. Very, very soon I detected that this was *the place where God lived,* as I called it."

Heidi stopped talking for a moment and looked into Fred's eyes, where she found love and gentle encouragement. She turned back to the pastor, saying, "And I made the decision, if there was a God who was alive and lived here, I wanted to believe in Him with all my heart. I had already been reading the New Testament for about three years—without telling Fred or anybody else about it.

415

"One Sunday, with Fred sitting next to me, the pastor gave an invitation to take a stand for God. I stood up and felt I just had to go forward, to indicate my desire to make God the Lord of my life. When I turned a bit sideways, I saw that Fred had followed me to the altar. He was kneeling in prayer behind me, and tears were rolling off his cheeks. This, and my wish to belong to the Lord, pushed me into the full commitment of being a Christian for the rest of my life."

"Wow, young lady! That is quite a testimony. I wish you could share it on Sunday with our congregation," said the pastor, who was deeply moved. During the balance of their time, the pastor gave Fred and Heidi pointers for a healthy and lasting marriage, with God at the center.

The wedding party had patiently waited for the pastor's session to end. Finally the rehearsal got underway. Everything went very smoothly and in a short time the pastor ended the evening with a short prayer and best wishes for a successful wedding day.

Minutes later, the Harrington convoy of six cars was on the way to a nice restaurant in Cedar Falls, next to the hotel where the Siemens had checked in. Naturally, they were included in the rehearsal dinner. Everyone was in a great mood, full of joy and anticipation of the big day. By the end of the night everyone, even if they had just met, felt like members of the same family.

Wedding day! This was Iowa, not Germany, where wedding bells would have been ringing for the last half hour. The small Sumner Baptist congregation faced a different challenge. When the church building had been constructed, they had planned for a seating capacity of 150. With the present membership of

416

only 55, the congregation still had plenty of space for regular worship events.

But today was not a regular event! The entire congregation, along with many Sumner citizens belonging to other churches, and even the volunteer fire department, had made it their personal commitment to attend. The Schweigert grandparents had invited their many friends from areas spread out over half of Iowa. A decorated temporary parking lot on one of the harvested fields next to the church looked like a huge used-car lot, occupied by at least 100 cars.

Wolfram and Dora Siemens, the city-slickers from Berlin, had never before seen such an unusual wedding congregation. When Wolfram spotted Norbert in the crowd, slowly moving toward the church, he joined him.

"Shouldn't you be in the church already, Norbert? I understand that you are the Best Man," said Wolfram.

"Yes, I am the Best Man, if only I *can make it to the church on time*."

"Too bad I did not bring my camera with me! I could have snapped an interesting shot of the parking lot and sold it to your *Neuköllner Tageblatt*."

"Always a business man!" was Norbert's absent-minded reply. His challenge right now was to plow through the thick crowd without being rude.

Heidi had asked Anna Harrington, Fred's mother, to be her Matron of Honor. She admitted it was unusual, but assured her future mother-in-law that she thought of her as a dear loved one. She had no one closer, especially in her new life in America.

Anna's husband George could not have been happier with Heidi's choice. When his oldest son, Jim, had married a young lady who was Mormon, he and Jim's mother had not been permitted to enter the *Wedding Palace Room* on account of them being Baptists, not Mormons. The beautiful wedding of their son Fred, to Heidi, made up for what seemed to have been missing in George and Anna's lives.

Chapter 41

It did not begin immediately after the uprising of East German workers in June 1953; the exodus to the West by East Germans and East Berliners had been going on for several years. But when the number of people fleeing after the brutally suppressed *Aufstand* (uprising) passed the 300,000 mark, Major General Andrey V, Molotov knew that he had to do something drastic.

In his eyes, his late predecessor Kotikov, as well as his deputy Svertlov, had been colossal failures. Molotov felt that he could not trust Svertlov, now deputy under his command. The way he had acted after the uprising in June, when Molotov had put him in charge of the Russian defense of East Berlin, had revealed again what a coward Svertlov was.

At first Svertlov had seemed very reluctant to follow orders. Then, he did an about-face, bravely standing on top of a Russian tank shouting "Shoot! Shoot them all!" and "Shoot, comrades! Don't spare the ammunition!" Then he disappeared, later to be found at home with his wife, who said he was resting and could not be disturbed. The Soviet Army had no room for such inconsistency, lack of discipline, and avoidance of duty. If Svertlov had been from Tashkent in Central Asia, like his backward cousin Anatoly Chukov, Molotov would have understood his deputy's ineptness. But, no! Lieutenant Svertlov came from a highly-trained, academically accomplished family; he was born in Moscow and had earned a Moscow University degree in Civil Engineering! Was his weakness perhaps the result of having been raised by a Jewish or half-Jewish mother?

Whatever the reason, Molotov could no longer tolerate it. As he was searching for fitting stationary, which showed his title and the proper spelling of his name with a "y" and not a "j," he remembered how he had been informed that Sergey Svertlov had attended the funeral of the West Berliner, Willi Göttling, who allegedly had been killed by Russian bullets. That news had shaken his last bit of confidence in his deputy.

When Molotov finally sat at his typewriter, his fingers hammered the text of a devastating evaluation regarding his deputy for whom he no longer had use. So what if Svertlov had seen this Göttling being shot and killed in direct response to his command to shoot! Officially, Germany was still at war with the Soviet Union, and in every war there are fatalities. Understood?

Molotov's stinging letter ended with: "There could be more uprisings in the German Democratic Republic. We do not need weak Soviet leaders anywhere—certainly not here in Germany. Please see to it that Lieutenant Svertlov is removed from his present position as my deputy. I could see him doing a more effective job as the director of a prison camp in Siberia. Please give his removal your urgent consideration!

"Thank you, Comrade Malenko, for hearing my concerns and acting upon them promptly. I ask this only in the best interest of our glorious Soviet Union Republic."

Molotov quickly reread his letter and was pleased. He carefully addressed the express letter to "The USSR Prime Minister Georgi Malenko, Kremlin, Moscow, USSR."

The request was granted rather soon, even though perhaps not soon enough for General Molotov. He ordered Svertlov to come to his office, where he informed him that based on a direct command from the Kremlin, he was being recalled by Moscow to possibly take over *domestic responsibilities matching his organizational skills.* The surprise announcement left Svertlov speechless.

"I am as shocked as you are, Comrade Lieutenant," Molotov broke the silence. "I have no idea what brought about this change for you. All I know is that I will miss you."

Instead of formerly dismissing his deputy, Molotov stepped up closely to hug him. Svertlov stood erect like a statue. However, when Molotov's face came close, he turned slightly away and spoke in a slow voice as cold as ice.

"General – you – are – a – terrible – liar."

Now both men were standing totally still until Molotov hissed, "Lieutenant! You are a disgrace! I will see to it that soon you will no longer wear the Soviet uniform—never again!"

Without looking back, Svertlov walked out of Molotov's office for the last time. The general disappeared through a private exit. Outside, Sergey Svertlov waved to his chauffeur to take the car back to where they had come from, but without him. He walked briskly away from the headquarters building he had known so well for many years. Sergey needed fresh air. He needed to think clearly about what was coming his way—and how to face the future.

But what about Luba? How could he face her? What would he tell her? He turned the corner and continued his fast walk, feeling the holster of his *Mauser* knock against his leg with every step. Was that black metal monster hanging from his belt perhaps the answer to the misery he would have to face from now on?

When he came to a park bench, he sat down. Slowly his hand touched the leather of the holster. He opened it and removed his pistol. Without a trace of fear he looked into the barrel.

Carefully he slid open the safety lock. Then he closed his eyes and let his mind dig deeper.

No, the answer to his life or death questions would not be found by pulling the trigger of his revolver. Even though he had no children to think of, what would happen to his beloved wife without him? Yet, if he stayed alive and lived in utter disgrace, would such a life be tolerable for his Luba?

In all their discussions over the years, they had never considered the possibility of committing suicide if things would go wrong for them, be it a war situation or a serious family issue. He had never failed Luba, and she had never failed him. He knew neither of them were cowards, and he knew that together, they were incredibly resilient.

Just as carefully as Sergey had removed the gun from its holster, he now put it back. There must be more to life than giving his military superior an opportunity to drive him to killing himself! Though not religious, he knew full well that suicide was a sin. Perhaps there was a God in heaven, after all, even though his government officially denied His existence.

But if there was a God, how would he, the insignificant little Sergey, explain to the omnipotent Lord of the universe why he chose to cut short his life? Because he had a cruel, egotistic boss, who tolerated no equally-capable competitors stealing his thunder? What a weak argument that would be, when standing before God!

Sergey got up from the bench, straightened out his uniform and walked in the direction of his house, a good three miles away. As if his eyes had been opened to a better world, he suddenly noticed that some East German pedestrians strolling along the promenade were greeting him with an almost-friendly smile. He also noticed the chirping of the always present, legendary *Berliner Spatzen* (sparrows), and he heard the melodious singing of other birds.

He was alive! To be 30 years old was not really old. The world was so much older, and yet each spring experienced a renewed drive for growth, warmth, and flowering beauty. Sergey felt new energy flooding through his body, quickening his step and making him reach his house sooner than he had anticipated.

He saw his car parked in the driveway, even though there was no trace of his chauffeur.

Parked behind his car was a black limousine with curtain-drawn windows. Could it be that the news of his ousting had already reached the KGB and they had gotten to his house before him? His new feeling of inner strength and freedom helped him discard the thought before he stepped into his house.

"Lieutenant Svertlov is already here?" asked his wife, jokingly. "What happened? I hope it is good news."

Sergey gave his wife a quick kiss. Without saying a word, he then pulled her into the living room. Putting his index finger to his lips as a warning sign to be silent, he checked all four walls for possible electronic listening devices. Then he walked over to the big West German radio and turned it on to full volume.

"No good news, my dear Luba," Sergey whispered in spite of the loud radio. "The news could not be worse. I am about to be fired and sent back to Russia, or perhaps to Siberia."

Luba suppressed a spontaneous shriek of horror. Sergey quickly took her in his arms, bending her ear close to his mouth. Then he spoke in an even softer whisper. "We have to leave here. I mean today, the sooner, the better! Let us put our most important things into one or two suitcases and a few duffel bags. Then we'll wait until dark. I'll put the car into the garage, so that we can load our few belongings—and I really mean FEW. Remember, this is not a picnic trip to *Wannsee*. It is a very risky attempt to escape the communist claws of the Soviet military and the East German *Vopos*."

"But where will we go?"

"We will drive to the American Military Headquarters just a few miles away from here. There we will ask for asylum."

"What if they catch us?"

"They won't!"

"What if they shoot us?"

"They might! As you well know, military officers and their families do not have diplomatic immunity. But don't worry, I know my way to the US Headquarters even in the dark.

"Now let us very quietly and quickly get our things together! Do not answer the phone or door today—we cannot afford to have anyone become suspicious of our plan." Luba just nodded her head silently, holding back the tears.

Rain started at sunset, which made for a dark night. No moonlight illuminated the Svertlov house when Sergey moved his car into the garage. After they had loaded their car, they were ready to leave.

"This running away at night reminds me of my Russian grandfather's attempt to avoid deportation to Siberia in 1917," said Sergey. "It failed miserably. He was gone for ten years. But we will not fail—we only have to make it from here to the Americans in West Berlin, and we will not come back here."

The car ride was painstakingly slow on that dark, rainy night. Sergey noticed that Luba was shaking, and he tried to lift the mood a little. "Isn't this the best luck?" he said as if gleeful.

"What?" Luba looked up at him.

"We have been given this cloak of darkness, and a curtain of rain to keep our enemies from noticing us. We are the two luckiest people on earth!" Luba had to share a small laugh, and managed to stop shaking. She knew they must be getting close now.

They arrived at the US Military Headquarters less than 30 minutes after sneaking away from their home. The rain stopped as if on cue, and Sergey rolled down the car window. He and Luba identified themselves to the guards and told them that they had come to ask for asylum.

"We are Soviet defectors. For us there is no turning back, once you let us enter your headquarters."

The military police guards opened the high gate of iron. Lieutenant Svertlov drove right to the front entrance. He opened the car door and stepped onto West Berlin's *free soil.* Like all the citizens of West Berlin, they were still surrounded by Soviet-occupied East Germany, but here in the American Sector, the Russians no longer were a threat to them.

"How do you feel now, my Luba darling?" asked Sergey. Tears were running down her cheeks. Luba put her arms around her husband's neck.

"Had we stayed, I would have lost you," she said, softly. "Now we have lost just about everything, but we still have each other. Should they accept our request for asylum, will we be going to America?"

"Yes, to our new life in America." Sergey had to wipe tears from his face. Had the new life already started? When Sergey rang the doorbell, a sergeant opened the door.

"Welcome to the US Military Headquarters! We have been expecting you, Lieutenant Svertlov."

"You have?" asked the surprised Svertlov.

"Yes, sir! News in Berlin travels fast, even on a dark, rainy night. Please make yourselves comfortable! Lieutenant Colonel Schubert is on his way and will be here shortly. Again, welcome, and make yourselves feel at home! Now, excuse me."

"Did he really say we should make ourselves feel at home?" asked Luba.

"Yes, but that is just an American expression, darling."

"No, I think he meant it," insisted Sergey's wife.

"Let's see, let's see! The future will tell," said Sergey. "Like I said, darling, we are the two luckiest people on earth!"

Chapter 42

Soviet Major General Andrey V. Molotov no longer had his deputy Sergey Svertlov around to blame for the increasing exodus of East Germans to the West. Svertlov and his wife had defected to West Berlin in early 1954. Without meaning to, they had become the prime "show-and-tell" Soviets, proving that occasionally even high-ranking Russian officers were glad to escape from the East to the West. In 1954 and in 1956, Molotov had mustered all of his energy to keep his troops in good shape for a possible fight against the West. He spent even more time planning how to stop the refugee flow. Whatever methods and control strategies he employed, thousands of disenchanted East Germans continued finding ways to get across the border and reach West Germany, "the Promised Land."

Molotov would never have admitted it, but he could almost understand the thousands of East Germans who were willing to leave everything behind and flee their underdeveloped land for the more prosperous West. There, the people enjoyed a clearly higher standard of living. East German leaders, prompted by their Soviet real bosses, gleefully proclaimed to the world how wonderful it was to live and work in the German Democratic Republic. Their brainwashing worked best on East German youngsters up to eighteen years of age. With the exception of party and governmental leaders, the rest of the population knew that they were the victims of lies and deception. Didn't the fact that just about all people in East Germany would have preferred to live in West Germany speak for itself?

West Germany offered a totally different image to the neutral observer. Recovering from a brutal war and a devastated economy, most citizens were eager to give it a new try. Because many male workers lost their lives during the war, West Germany's employment soon reached one hundred percent. True, there were risks along the recovery way, but risk-takers always received their reward.

Norbert Anleger was one of those ambitious businessmen with hopes for the future who had ignored the constant pressure and repression coming from the Russians and East Germans. With rather limited funds, but lots of enthusiasm, he rented a downtown office space close to Berlin's famous Philharmonic Hall. He hired a former university professor of linguistics, who was fluent in French, Spanish and Italian; he also employed a certified Russian interpreter. Two competent secretaries with excellent typing skills completed his enterprise, which he gave the English name, *Center for Interpretation and Translation (Dolmetscher)*.

On the first day of his operation, when Norbert was still busy with hammer and nails mounting the large business sign, he had three customers requesting the services of the Center. Each week, he and his employees dealt with a growing number of clients. After six months, his total staff numbered eight certified and well-qualified workers. Immigrants from Eastern European countries seeking legal residence in Berlin, war brides with American, British or French military partners needing documentation in several languages, and Deported Persons (DPs) wishing to emigrate to Canada or the US formed the never-ending stream of people looking for quick help and processing.

Toward the end of the first year, Norbert had to open a second office, which he strategically placed in *Berlin-Kreuzberg* close to the border of *Friedrichshain* in East Berlin.

This office was only a stone's throw away from the official East/West crossing *Oberbaum Brücke*, a crossing limited to West Berliners only. The political East/West tensions were still a daily challenge, even though major crises had been diverted.

Norbert now felt that the time had come to open a third office in order to handle the heavy workload. It would be in Berlin's northern District *Wedding* in the French Sector. To get there from his apartment in *Neukölln*, or from his second office in *Kreuzberg*, he had to take the *U-Bahn* from West Berlin's American Sector through East Berlin into the French Sector in the north.

With the exception of the *Friedrichstrasse* station in the heart of Berlin, the *U-Bahn* did not stop on any other station located in East Berlin. The East German police used this stop to get on and off the subway, to control passengers. Even though for outsiders this arrangement looked complicated, the West Berliners who had to travel by *U-Bahn* had gotten used to this. Norbert had traveled this stretch many times before, without having been concerned. Today, however, traveling this route to his third office (nearly ready for its grand opening) was to have catastrophic consequences.

For Norbert, work was never anything but enjoyable and stimulating. Even if a problem came up, he enthusiastically set about solving it. He could not believe how successful his idea of opening a *Dolmetscher Zentrum* (Interpretation Center) had turned out. Sitting at his desk in *Kreuzberg*, he leafed through the documents he would need for the opening of the *Wedding* office. He had come here early in the morning to sort out the names and addresses of his previous clients. To protect client confidentiality, he wanted to copy these documents himself, and then take the material to the brand new office in *Berlin-Wedding.* It would be convenient to have reference copies in all three centers.

Denying himself the pleasure of having a cup of instant coffee, he filled his big attaché case with the files along with a few other documents. Light-heartedly he left his office. Breathing the invigorating *Berliner Luft* helped him overcome the feeling of being tired.

He caught the *U-Bahn* at the *Schlesischer Tor* station, then changed to the north subway at *Hallisches Tor,* sat down on a nearly empty bench with his attaché case next to him—and fell asleep! He meant to close his eyes for only a moment, but was abruptly awakened when a rough hand shook his shoulder.

"Come on, man, I don't have all day," a sharp German voice commanded. "I said, open the case!"

I hope I am still dreaming, was all Norbert could think. But neither the green police uniform in front of him nor the piercing sound in his ears were part of a dream. He also realized that the subway train was still traveling under East Berlin, and that the man shaking him was a strict Inter-Sector Controller. The control agent had pulled the train emergency brake and

431

brought the train to a violent stop. The doors opened, but Norbert did not move. The two men stared at each other. Then the policeman reached for his gun and pointed to the door.

"Out there! Go ahead. I will bring the attaché case." Seeing that there was no chance of escaping, Norbert decided to play it cool.

"Why in the world did you stop the train?" Norbert asked innocently. "I am on the way to my office in *Wedding*. My case contains nothing of interest to you. I am an interpreter. I am only carrying copies of translated speeches and Berlin residency applications."

"Get out!" the policeman shouted, becoming more irritated by Norbert's delay in obeying his order. "And don't bother me with your story. We will see who you really are. Get going!"

Just then another passenger approached the uniformed controller and addressed him politely. "Please, officer! I know this man. He worked on my application papers to visit the Soviet Union. I believe his name is Anleger or Anlieger. There is no reason to detain him."

"Get out of my way!" thundered the controller, "Or I will arrest you, too!" Norbert and the gun-wielding controller made their way on foot through the dimly lit train tunnel. The overzealous Inter-Sector Controller , who could have waited for the train to stop at the *Friedrichstrasse* Station, had foolishly pulled the emergency brake far from the station, perhaps to make a name for himself for his "heroic" action. When he and Norbert finally reached the official station, a police squad was waiting and took them to the large police station near the Charité Medical Complex.

Norbert was taken inside and, without having signed the arrest register, was ordered to strip off all his clothing. A male guard made sure that Norbert had no hidden knife or pistol in his armpits or between his legs. Then he was handed badly-worn jail garb and led to a small, dirty cell. The guard gave Norbert a final push before he slid the steel door shut. Norbert threw himself on the hard bed in disgust. What bothered him more than anything was how careless he had been to fill his attaché case with client information and carry it openly through high-risk areas. Now the very sensitive information had fallen into East German or Russian hands.

For most of the day it seemed that, here in the jail, nobody cared who Norbert was or why he had been imprisoned. He could not know that specially-trained secret service people were spending many hours going over all the documents they had found in his case. His translation offices, a natural mecca for foreigners, had been under suspicion for some time, and now they were determined to find impeachable, indictable material against him and his "entire defection and spy operation."

Norbert knew that if they interpreted his documents as "help to escape the DDR" he would be in deep trouble. He knew of several cases where East German authorities had discovered ordinary DDR citizens or religious leaders who had aided fleeing persons with helpful information or finances.

They had been arrested and fined hundreds of East German Marks and sentenced to up to ten years in prison.

On the second day of his imprisonment, Norbert finally received a plate with two slices of bread and three radishes—no butter, no margarine, no jam!

"Hey, don't I get some coffee?"

"No! Criminals get their drink from the water faucet in their cells. *Prost!"*

Norbert did not like being called a criminal. "Do I at least have the right to make a phone call?"

"You shut up, now, or I may not turn on your water for drinking and washing for a long time!" Being plagued by torturing thirst, Norbert thought it best to keep quiet.

In the afternoon, Norbert was taken to an interrogation. Actually, it was more like a one-way lecture, typical for Russian and Eastern European prisons. The interrogating captain made it clear to Norbert that the documents they had examined proved that he had broken the DDR laws more than a hundred times, by helping East Germans to escape to the West.

"What were you thinking, Anleger?"

"Actually, not much. I just translated their document papers from one language into another," replied Norbert with faked calmness.

Just when the interrogator was about to dismiss Norbert for the day, Norbert asked, "By the way, does Major General Andrey Molotov know that I am in prison?"

"No, he does not. Why should he?"

"Because we know each other! He might want to look at my case. Would you inform him, please?"

"Why would a Soviet General care what is happening to a civilian German punk like you?"

"Just tell him. He might want to come and interrogate me himself," answered Norbert, managing to put a light smile on his face. "Understood?"

"That's what the General always says: '*Understood – understood – understood.*'"

"Yes. You see now I also know the General. He would not be pleased to know I was here and he was not informed."

In spite of his feigned confidence about Molotov wanting to see him, Norbert really was not sure that such a visit would happen. One positive outcome of the interrogation was that he got a decent evening meal pushed into his cell, and the next morning his breakfast plate with sliced bread and radishes also included a cup of hot coffee. It looked as if the prison personnel wanted to make a good impression in case the Soviet General did show up.

Two days later, Charité Prison welcomed Major General Andrey Molotov, and they assumed he would be anxious to begin his usual tour of inspection. "I have very little time today," he explained. "Just bring me this Anleger boy, with or without the documents you have examined. Understood?"

"Yes, sir, I understand."

When a prison guard returned with Norbert, Molotov signaled that he wanted to be alone with the convict.

"*Dobre den!*" Norbert greeted Molotov in Russian.

"*Dobre den, Anleger!*" responded Molotov. "So, we meet again! What crime have you committed this time?"

"I can assure you, General, that I have not committed any crime—this time. It all is a big misunderstanding."

"Go ahead! Tell me more! By the way, your Russian has improved greatly, since we last met."

"You are too kind, General! I know that the way I speak your beautiful language is more like torturing it."

"Did you just call Russian a beautiful language? I have never heard that coming from a German."

"You would have before the war, General. Educated people always had a great respect for Russian language, music, and art. Just ask my teachers and the friends of my parents! Unfortunately, the war has destroyed the good feeling for each other on both sides."

"Now tell me why you ended up here!"

"Well, I operate two—and soon, three—translation bureaus, or centers, as I call them. Together with my employees we supply interpreters for special international speaking events in all four Sectors of Berlin and, if requested, in the DDR and FRG. I am glad that things have worked out well so far, even in this city with its complex political structure."

There was a knock at the door. "*Da!*" said Molotov. A smartly-dressed secretary carried Norbert's attaché case into the room and placed it in front of the General.

"Please, Comrade General," she said, and left the room. Molotov pushed the case aside.

"I don't need papers. I want to hear from you what happened."

Norbert took a deep breath, convinced that the next few minutes would determine his fate. "With your permission, General Molotov, I remember the term you used for me in 1951. You called me a *German skunk.*" When Norbert laughed, Molotov had to laugh, too. Norbert spoke again.

"I have worked extremely hard and slept very little for the past two or three weeks. Exhausted, I was on my way to my office in *Wedding* when I fell asleep on the *U-Bahn.* The train traveled from the American Sector to the French Sector, passing through the Soviet Sector. I must have been sleeping deeply, with my attaché case and its innocent contents next to me, when a *Vopo* shook me awake, grabbed my case, and shouted to follow him.

"We scrambled through the dark tunnel until we reached the *Friedrichstrasse* station. From there I was taken here to the Charité Police Station, where I was put into a prison cell—no questions asked."

"This time you made no derogatory remarks about East Berlin or the DDR?"

"No, not a word! I remember the lesson you gave me at the *FDJ World Youth Festival* years back."

"Can you honestly—and I mean honestly—say that none of the papers in your attaché reveal that you have helped East German citizens to flee to the West?"

"Yes, General, that is so—and that is the full truth."

"You know, Anleger, there are things about you which are not so bad. You would perhaps have made a good Soviet citizen. Understood?"

437

"Had I been born in the Soviet Union, sir, I probably would have. But I was born in Germany, and I don't mind being German. Right now I am a prisoner in Germany put here by Germans—but I am most certainly not a criminal."

Molotov looked intensely at Norbert. Then he spoke slowly, deliberately.

"Yes, 1951—you owe me for letting you off for your seditious comments. People say that lightning does not strike twice in the same place. I have a *lightning announcement* for you. In your case, lightning is striking twice. Considering all circumstances and based on the collected evidence, my verdict upon you is *not guilty*. Norbert Anleger, you are free to go!"

The usually talkative Norbert sat speechless. He looked at Major General Molotov, searching for words to express his gratitude. As Molotov started to turn to leave, Norbert finally spoke.

"Thank you, General, for being 'lightning number two' in my life. I hope one day I can pay you back."

"Next time, keep your fancy leather attaché case at the office," Molotov warned. "You don't see anyone carrying such a thing on the *U-Bahn*. It would look suspicious to any inspector or controller, and even to me. Good bye!"

Chapter 43

The defection of Lieutenant Sergey Svertlov and his wife Luba in 1954 was a first for the US Military Headquarters. Lieutenant Colonel Paul Schubert was the Duty Officer that day. He had arrived a few hours after the Svertlovs had successfully escaped the East and had been welcomed by other American officers at the headquarters. Now it was Schubert's turn to function as the couple's liaison to the West.

"Hi!" he called out when he stepped into the reception room where he saw a man and woman sitting on a velvet-covered antique bench, looking absolutely exhausted. "Welcome, Sergey and Luba Svertlov! I hope you speak English."

"We speak Russian and some English, and we can make ourselves understood in German, too," said Sergey.

"Good, because I speak no Russian," said the Lieutenant Colonel, as he invited his guests to sit with him around a mahogany table, where a late dinner was about to be served.

"You must be very tired by now," said Schubert.

"Normally we would be tired, but more than anything, we are anxious as well as extremely relieved to be here. Rest, or eating a meal, has not been on our mind." answered the Russian officer in English.

As military orderlies carried in various containers with steaming hot food items, Schubert introduced himself. "Somebody around here certainly must have told you that I am Lieutenant Colonel Paul Schubert. Today is my lucky day as Duty Officer."

"Why is this day lucky for you, sir?" asked Luba Svertlov.

"To welcome you. It is very gratifying to assist those who see the light and come over to our side," said Schubert.

"We had not planned on this," said Sergey. "But after my talk with my boss, General Molotov, this afternoon—"

"Your coming to us might have saved your life, Lieutenant."

"Or banishment to a prison camp in Siberia," added Svertlov.

While they enjoyed the late but very delicious meal, Schubert said, "Actually, we should celebrate your arrival in West Berlin properly, with a glass of wine. Don't you agree?"

The wine was excellent and helped the Svertlovs to relax. "So, you said that you speak German, too. Your name *Svertlov* indicates no German origin," said Schubert.

"No, it's Russian. My father took some of his studies at a university in Germany, and my mother majored in German at the University of Odessa."

"Odessa by the Black Sea?"

"Yes, in Russia. Both of my parents loved languages and saw to it that we learned to speak German, too."

"That sounds like an interesting family history. I am sorry that my family tree is not that colorful, unless you are music lovers."

"Has your name a connection with the composer, Schubert?"

"Ah, you have heard of him! Yes, the famous Austrian composer, Schubert, was my great-great-great uncle. My father had me learn all about him—Franz Peter Schubert, 1797 to 1828."

"Was Schubert only 31 years old when he died?"

"I guess so. In Germany most people seem to know of him and his music. But in America I always have to spell our family name, saying 'you know, Schubert with a SCH.'"

Dinner conversation continued with surprising ease, everyone finding common ground or sharing interesting differences in cultures. Sergey, especially, was in awe that by the end of dinner it seemed they were all good friends, talking and laughing as another bottle of wine was opened.

Then he glimpsed a reflection in a gold-framed wall mirror and felt himself flinch as he faced his Soviet officer's uniform. He reached for Luba's hand under the table and brought himself back to the reality of the moment: they were safe, full of American food and wine, and with a completely different life than the one they had awoken to that morning.

"I forgot to tell you that as long as you are on West German soil, I will be your advisor and protector," Schubert told them. "Once you have decided where you want to live—for instance, in Great Britain or in the USA—my duty will end. Tonight, or perhaps for several days and nights, you will stay in the guest rooms here in our headquarters. Our military campus cannot grant you political asylum. But do not worry for a second! Here with us you are safer than in any embassy anywhere in the world. Our military security is legendary. So, until tomorrow, *Gute Nacht!*."

"*Gute Nacht,* Lieutenant Colonel! And thank you for everything!"

Chapter 44

Heidi was determined to spend her day off by doing next to nothing. Together with Fred, she had many times explored the entire Washington, DC, area. She was proud of living "just across the river" from the nation's capital. From Alexandria, where they had rented a comfortable apartment one block from the Potomac, Fred could report to work at the National Airport or at Andrews Air Base in less than half an hour. Heidi's ride to work was a bit more complicated since she needed to cross either the Arlington Memorial Bridge or the wider, but always crowded, Theodore Roosevelt Memorial Bridge, to get to Macy's in downtown DC.

Today she had driven her car to the Capitol Building and parked there. Then she walked to the National Mall—first to the Washington Memorial, and then to the Lincoln Memorial. That walk had been further than she had expected.

Now she was sitting on the steps of the Lincoln Memorial, stretching her legs and taking in the warm sunshine. Since she had forgotten to take along some drinking water, she felt a bit tired and dozed off into a half-sleep. Being totally relaxed, her mind took her on a reminiscent tour.

She saw herself standing next to Fred at the small church in Sumner, Iowa. A voice behind her at that church whispered,

"This is your wedding day." As she looked down, she saw that she was wearing a white wedding dress. A sudden fog seemed to diffuse her vision and even her hearing. When this fog just as suddenly lifted, she saw the pastor turn to Fred, saying, "You may kiss the bride!" That old-fashioned phrase made her laugh out loud, because they had kissed many times before without a clergyman's permission. Still, the laughter woke her up.

Now fully conscious again, Heidi looked out across the beautiful green lawn but let her mind drift back to Sumner, starting with attending Sunday church service the day after the wedding. She had been hopelessly distracted by her recent wedding memories and her first night as a newlywed. As a hymn came to an end and the pastor started to speak, she tried to concentrate on his words. All of a sudden she saw him push aside his sermon notes, and she heard him announce:

"Heidi's testimony about how God led her to become a follower of Jesus Christ was so powerful that I felt our entire congregation would greatly benefit from hearing it.

"Heidi, or, rather, Mrs. Fred Harrington, would you please come to the front and tell us about your fascinating pilgrimage from being an atheist to becoming a believer!"

Just recalling the memory of that moment of shock, Heidi felt her throat tighten, but it wasn't as bad as that day in the packed Baptist church in Sumner.

"The pulpit is yours this morning, Heidi," the pastor said encouragingly. "Take all the time you need...you have an hour if you want!"

She could not remember one thing she had said…just that she made it through alive! Never would she forget how warmly the people had hugged her afterwards—especially her new husband!

Then she and Fred had flown to Sarasota, Florida, where they stayed at an exceptionally nice bed-and-breakfast on Siesta Key. The pure white, crystal-sand beach was amazing. Spending nearly all her life in Germany, Heidi had never heard of a beach where the sand consisted of 99 percent crystal. The sunsets over the Gulf of Mexico painted her honeymoon memories with pink-golden warmth.

One evening, dining at one of Sarasota's fine restaurants, they happened to get in a conversation with a local celebrity. He was the co-owner and top performer of the *Ringling Brothers' Barnum and Bailey Circus*. As a wedding and honeymoon gift, he handed them two tickets for the next day's show, and they could not have enjoyed themselves more.

Heidi remembered Fred's remark on the way back from the circus. "Well, that was a super-circus performance! Is there anything you Germans cannot do?"

"But Fred, the *Ringling Circus* is an American company," she had protested.

"Just look at your program, Heidi. Fifty percent of the performers have German names, and when they had a speaking role, they sounded German."

"Just like me, when I speak, right?"

"No, my love! You have the voice of an angel, with or without a German accent."

445

Heidi, lost in her daydream, was startled by a man's gruff voice.

"Excuse me, lady! Smoking is not permitted here," he said.

Heidi looked around, somewhat annoyed.

"But I am not smoking."

"Oh, I made a mistake," the man said. "Sorry! Would you perhaps have a dollar or more for a hungry guy like me?"

Heidi had encountered many beggars in her life and had learned to tell the difference between a truly hungry man and a swindler. She was about to decline his request, when he suddenly took several steps toward her. "You could invite me to a cozy restaurant," he said in a loud whisper, "and afterwards we could have some fun—" Just then a policeman walked up from behind the beggar and addressed Heidi.

"Is everything okay, young lady?"

"It was until this man showed up, pretending to be a hungry beggar."

"Okay, buddy," the policeman said to the man, "You better move on."

Heidi thought that the policeman's remark was too kind and diplomatic. Why did he not raise his club and chase him away, as German police would have done in an instant? But then, in America, everything was done in a kinder way—even in regard to pesky vagabonds.

"Your time is up here!" the policeman warned the man. The grubby man spit, turned, and ambled off.

"Thank you, officer!" said Heidi, quite relieved.

"No trouble at all!"

"There was no trouble because of your help."

"That's my job. As I said, just checking everything is okay."

Then Heidi was alone again, but the disturbing encounter had chased away her mood for romantic daydreams. She gathered her sandals and jacket and walked back to her parked car at the Capitol. She wanted to get back to the apartment in plenty of time in case Fred called at four o'clock, her time, as they had tentatively agreed.

Fred had flown President Eisenhower to All-Africa Summit meetings in Kenya, which was scheduled to last one week. Having been married to Fred for almost two years, Heidi had learned to be flexible, at least as it concerned her husband's work schedule. She had seen important meetings suddenly canceled, or Presidential visits of three or four days extended to one week or longer. Working for the US Commander-in-Chief was an unbelievable honor and responsibility, but also an unpredictable task.

Sometimes everything worked out just as planned. The phone rang at four o'clock and Heidi ran to answer it. "How was your day, darling?" Fred asked.

"It was my day off. I spent some hours in the sun on the steps of the Lincoln Memorial."

"I envy good old Abe! Did you have a good time?"

"I'll tell you all about it when I see you—which is when?"

"We should be back home on schedule. No side tours this time. Are you going to pick me up from the airport?"

"I wish I could pick you up *today*, Fred," said Heidi with a sigh. "I really miss and need you very much."

"Stay strong, girl! This time I was only gone for a week."

"For lovers like us, that is a long time."

"I love the way you put it, Heidi. Since I cannot say that *I'll come running*, I will say *I'll come flying,* though not soon enough."

Chapter 45

Nothing could stop the desperate freedom-seekers. No efforts by the East German government and the occupying Soviets prevented the exodus to the West, and even harsh punishment was no deterrent. The talk of Berlin was the trials of those who were accused of helping DDR citizens flee to West Germany. Shortly before Easter of 1956, two men and one woman were sentenced to life imprisonment for this "crime."

A few months into 1957, the DDR regime issued a new "passport law," announcing that anyone making an unauthorized trip outside the borders of East Germany would be sentenced to a minimum of three years in prison.

In 1958, Major General Molotov employed the law against "Slandering the DDR" to arrest 19 visiting students from East Germany's *Jena* University. They were sentenced to three years in prison. Furthermore, Molotov strongly suggested to the DDR rulers to pressure all East German educators to introduce "Compulsory Polytechnic Education," which was Molotov's high-sounding term for forcing all schoolchildren to work for stated periods in industry and agriculture.

East German border police were told to shoot without warning anybody crossing the "Security Zone," the narrow strip between the West and East border created by the DDR.

The Soviet Union, led by the feisty Soviet Premier Nikita Khrushchev and emboldened by their 1957 accomplishments in space with *Sputnik I and Sputnik II*, openly resolved to dislodge what Khrushchev called "Berlin, the bone in Russia's throat" once and for all. In his Moscow speech in November, 1958, he charged:

The West German militarists are thinking of swallowing up the German Democratic Republic, annexing Poland's western lands, and staking claims on the territory of Czechoslovakia and other socialist countries.

The Premier's bold, though irrational speech unfortunately was supported on Christmas Day, 1958, when Soviet Foreign Minister Andrei Gromyko warned the West: *Any provocation in West Berlin could start a big war, in the crucible of which millions upon millions of people would perish, and which would bring devastation incomparably more serious than the last war.*

Had the world learned to live with the never-ending tensions created by the Soviet Union, especially in Germany? Many Berliners felt that politicians in the West thought that by ignoring the problems, they would eventually disappear.

When the youthful John F. Kennedy became the 35th US President in January, 1961, Soviet Premier Khrushchev thought that it was time to "get rid of West Berlin." Even the First Secretary of the Communist *Social Democratic Party*, Walter Ulbricht, admitted publicly that he was embarrassed that the world was watching East Germany deflate like a balloon, as year after year, refugees spilled into West Berlin and West Germany. By the end of July, 1961, about three million people—one in every six—had fled the "workers' paradise."

On August 13, 1961, the time for action had come. Shortly after midnight, East German soldiers and the *Folk Police,* riding atop Russian Army trucks, streamed down *Unter den Linden,* Berlin's majestic 8-lane boulevard. At various points, armed troops and workers were dropped off to erect barbed-wire barricades along the entire 103 miles of the West Sector boundaries.

Norbert Anleger stood among the bewildered West Berliners watching the feverish activity of their East Berliner "colleagues" who were sweating under the glare of floodlights, and from fear that West Berliners might stop them. But neither the West Berliners nor the Western Allies did anything as the *VOPOs* (People's Police) and *GREPOS* (Border Police) dug up big cobblestones to put up fence posts, between which they strung barbed wire. These barbed wire fences ran down the middle of streets, through neighborhoods, across schoolyards, and along canals, following the border between the Soviet and the Western Sectors of the city.

Many West Berliners hoped for Allied intervention. However, none of the Western leaders were willing to risk a military confrontation by knocking down these new barricades.

Norbert had not slept one wink during the night from Saturday to the *Stacheldraht-Sonntag* (Barbed-Wire Sunday). By mid-morning, Norbert was among 2,000 outraged West Berliners who had gathered on the west side of the *Brandenburger Tor,* yelling to the armed soldiers and police.

"Put down your guns!" "Act like Germans!" "Hang Walter Ulbricht, not wires!"

Norbert and the rest of the crowd watched the workers on the Eastern side who continued their work in grim silence—as always, following orders.

While the fence construction with wires and cement blocks was going on, some East Berliners clambered over the barricades, and others swam across either the *Spree Kanal* or the *Teltow Kanal.*

After a few months, when many wire barricades had been replaced by solid concrete, the rage and protests of the West Berliners calmed down. They realized that the US troops in Berlin could not shoot at East German *Vopos* or Russian soldiers. Even tearing down the newly-erected fences, which more and more were transforming into solid walls, might have triggered World War III. Even family members who had been cut off from each other and had been the loudest of the outraged protesters, became resigned.

A ray of hope sprung up in the heart of the West Berliners when President Kennedy sent 1,500 troops to add to the US contingent in Berlin. He also assigned General Lucius Clay, who was admired and loved by West Berliners as the hero of the 1948-1949 airlift, to serve as his personal representative in Berlin.

In October, 1961, Clay had the chance to demonstrate his staying power. After American soldiers had been prevented from driving into East Berlin, General Clay stationed ten Patton tanks and three personnel carriers at Checkpoint Charlie, the US border crossing at the wall. Each time the police stopped an American military vehicle, US Jeeps equipped with machine guns were sent to escort the challenged vehicles across the border, forcing the East German and Russian police to step aside.

Two days later, the Soviets decided to meet intimidation with intimidation by posting ten Russian tanks on their side of Checkpoint Charlie. With Soviet and US tanks face-to-face, only 100 meters apart, all Germans and millions of Americans wondered if the long-feared US/USSR clash over Berlin was finally at hand. Norbert and hundreds of his friends and clients actually wished for such a confrontation, knowing that the USA would come out the winner. Still, even Norbert and other Berliners did not believe it was worth the risk of another major war.

After about two years, it appeared that life, work and leisure were nearly the same as found in other nations' capitals. Perhaps with one exception: in Berlin, more than anywhere in the world, people knew that all their reconstruction efforts, all their sacrifices during the blockade, and all their honest attempts to normalize their relations with Eastern Bloc nations, including East Germany, would be swept away overnight, should a war break out.

In May of 1963, Norbert received a letter from his brother-in-law, Fred, saying that President Kennedy planned a 10-day tour of Europe, starting out in Germany. He also wrote that fortunately, Heidi would be able to accompany him. In a casual conversation, Fred, the President's Chief Pilot, had mentioned that Heidi was born and raised in Berlin, and Kennedy was the one who suggested Heidi come along. Fred also wrote that he and Heidi might have a few free hours to visit with Norbert in Berlin.

Had it not been for Fred's letter, Norbert would not have known of President Kennedy's coming to Berlin. Quickly Norbert told his staff that he would be gone for half a day. Then he jumped into his car and drove to the US Military Headquarters in *Berlin-Zehlendorf,* right at the edge of the Grunewald Forest.

A friendly, middle-aged receptionist recognized Norbert and took him to General Clay's personal secretary. "Hello, Mr. Anleger! Good to see you again. What can I do for you?"

"I need urgently to speak to General Clay. Would you please put me in touch with him?"

"Oh yes, young man, General Clay will be very, very happy to *be in touch with you*—as you put it. As a matter of fact, he has tried for several weeks to be in touch with you. He had me and the other staff searching everywhere for your address or telephone number."

Norbert was surprised that the famous US Military Headquarters had not been able to round up at least his phone number. "Well, here is my business card," said Norbert, a little irritated. "That will make your future searches easier."

"You don't understand, Mr. Anleger. The General needs to talk to you right now. Your coming here today was a godsend," she said, already reaching for the red phone to instantly connect to the General.

Within a minute, the door opened and out came General Lucius Clay, looking very glad to see Norbert. "Mr. Anleger!" he said, shaking Norbert's hand. "We have not seen one another since the Freedom Bell dedication."

"Good to see you again, sir."

"My colleagues remember you as the genius interpreter. My memory of you is different. Sure, you translated Mayor Reuter's speech, and did a superb job with my own speech, as expected. But then you got that damned bell to finally ring, which was unexpected."

"How could I forget the moment when you, sir, pushed the button and nothing happened. I left you and the mayor in shock and bolted to the top of the belfry in the *Rathaus* Tower to ring my friend, the Freedom Bell."

"And how did you do that?" Clay asked.

"Sorry, General, that will always remain my secret," Norbert answered, "or let's just call it a miracle." The General nodded, then led Norbert into his private office.

"General Clay, I don't know why you have been looking for me," Norbert began. "I have come here today to ask you a favor. President Kennedy will visit Europe in June. Would there be a chance for me to accompany him as his interpreter—"

"Don't say another word," the General interrupted. "President Kennedy's trip is the reason why we needed to talk to you. To make it short, Mr. Anleger, could we have you as his special Berlin guide and his general interpreter from the middle of June to middle of July? Sorry for the short notice!"

Norbert looked straight at General Clay as he answered. "It would be the greatest honor for me and my company to be of service to the President, and to you, sir."

"I knew we could count on you! You are still the same dynamic guy as when we met you the first time in

1950—always on top of the job, and committed to building bridges of understanding between the nations."

"Yes, sir. I am glad you recognize me as your partner in building bridges. Please let me know soon when exactly you want me to report for duty."

On the way back to his office, Norbert decided to drive to the *Schöneberg Rathaus*, still West Berlin's City Hall. He parked his car in a visitor's spot and took the *U-Bahn* and then the *S-Bahn* to *Jannowitz Brücke*. After walking some left-and-right streets in the Soviet Sector, he came to an old but noble-looking four-story apartment house in the *Lichtenberger Strasse,* where a noble-looking young woman lived whom he had come to know and admire during the last year. She was an opera singer at the *Berliner Staatsoper* in East Berlin. Since she had no telephone, Norbert had frequently been frustrated when trying to reach her. He thought that she would be at home today and he needed to tell her why he would not be free to see her for several weeks during the summer.

Norbert rang the doorbell. "Just a moment, please!" he heard Amanda's beautiful voice from behind the closed door.

Oh, good, she was at home! Now he could explain to her why his upcoming assignment with the US President would take priority over all previous plans.

When Amanda's door cautiously opened, he had the same breathtaking feeling as always when he saw her. She was stunningly beautiful, even without the usual makeup he was used to seeing at her opera performances.

Soon they were sitting at a small table in the living room, holding hands, looking admiringly at each other, and sharing their plans for the coming weeks away from each other.

Amanda's name was actually Gertrud Steinmetz. As a singing artist rising in national and international prominence, she had changed her name to "Amanda" as she thought it sounded more theatrical. Each time when somebody asked Norbert how he had met her and when they had started dating, he felt like sighing, "Here it goes again!" The fact was that people really were interested in how these two unlikely persons had gotten to know each other. She was already quite well-known.

It all had started with Norbert hearing her sing at a rare East/West event, when the *Berliner Kultur Palast* was dedicated. Never before had he heard such a brilliant and beautiful voice. What a depth of interpretation! Amanda made the opera come alive, and watching her made Norbert feel more alive than ever before.

A month later, Norbert attended the opera again and saw Amanda at the after-party.

This was the first time in his busy life that he had felt a fire burning in the area where his heart was beating. He had rarely given romance a thought, disciplining himself to focus on mastering his interpretation skills, and then on building his entire translation organization.

Now, all he could think of was Amanda, and he wasted no time introducing himself to her at the party.

At this unexpected moment in his life, when the sun was shining and Berlin's intoxicating air could almost be tasted, she had accepted his invitation to dinner at the Kempinski Hotel on the *Kurfürsten Damm*.

"May I pick you up in my car?" he asked.

"I think it would be better if I take my car."

"What do you mean?" Norbert had asked, naively. "You want to pick *me* up?"

"You know what I mean, Norbert. Your car has a West Berlin license plate, yes? My car is registered in East Berlin. We can avoid lots of stupid questions at the border if we travel in separate cars. Agreed?"

Since Norbert was a good friend of the manager of the Kempinski restaurant, he was able to reserve a table away from the crowded dining areas. It had rained all afternoon, and the pedestrians were avoiding the large water puddles. Norbert's eyes were searching for Amanda in the eastern direction. Suddenly it dawned on him that he had failed to ask her what kind of car she drove. No wonder he could not see her!

"Hello, Norbert!" a lovely voice startled him. "I finally made it. Sorry for being late!"

When Norbert looked around, he saw Amanda standing under the streetlight with hundreds of illuminated raindrops running off her hair and down her raincoat.

"Is that really you, my friend?" he asked, sounding concerned. "What happened to you? Where is your car? Why did you get so wet?"

"Because it is raining, you sweet dummy!"

Norbert put his arm around her, as if protecting her from further rain. Then he led her into the hotel lobby, where three employees (recognizing the beautiful opera star) rushed to help her remove the raincoat and gave her a small linen towel for her face and hair.

Shaking the rain from her skirt, Amanda groaned at her soaking-wet shoes.

"Have you ever seen me in such a crumpled condition?" she asked Norbert.

An answer came from the foyer manager: "Miss Steinmetz, even if rain should turn into a flood, nothing will ever dampen your beauty!"

She gave the uniformed manager a surprised look, but he had more to say.

"Miss Steinmetz, I have heard you singing, and seen you on stage many times. Permit me to say, you are my absolute favorite opera singer."

The time had come for Norbert to gently push aside the admiring hotel employee, even though Norbert agreed with the man's high opinion.

"I believe our table is waiting for us. Please take us to the dining room."

As soon as they were seated, the chef came out to their table.

"It truly is an honor for us to have you dine with us this evening. *Mi casa es su casa!* Please accept our complementary aperitif to show you our readiness to serve you most excellently!"

Such a royal and magnificent welcome Norbert had never experienced before. Amanda was much better known and more popular than he had realized. Tonight *he* wanted to get to know her much better, too. All he had to do was force himself to speak as little as possible and let Amanda do the talking.

Before a waiter came to ask for their order, Norbert had to get an answer as to why Amanda had been so deplorably wet. Either she must have parked several blocks away from the hotel, or perhaps she had not been able to drive her car at all.

"Norbi," Amanda responded sweetly to his concern. "I am alright. Sitting here with you is so wonderful, I don't even notice—I just hope I don't look frightful!" Then after a brief giggle she continued, "I parked my car way down the road at the *Kaiser Wilhelm Gedächtnis Kirche,* because I wanted neither the STASI nor the paparazzi to find out where and with whom I am dining. I know you understand."

For a moment Norbert wondered why the STASI (*Staats Sicherheits Dienst*, i.e., East Germany's Secret Service) would be concerned with Amanda, but then he remembered they would of course be monitoring anyone with such a high public profile.

"You know, Amanda, when I was waiting for you in front of the hotel, I was embarrassed that I had never asked you what kind of car you are driving."

"That is true. We never talked about cars. When I bought my first car, a *P50 Trabant,* it was more of a headache than a reliable vehicle. But very recently, our GDR government, which is not known for its generosity, surprised me by giving me a brand-new *Trabant P601,* one of the first cars of the 1963 model."

"You got a car for free, even though you are not a Communist SED Party member?"

"Yes! Some East German leaders attended the opera and apparently liked my singing. They gave me the car three weeks ago, even before it was available in dealerships. They asked me to be the poster girl for the new *Trabant,* but I declined. You don't know my history yet, Norbert, but my thinking is that the East German communists and the Russian occupiers owe my family much more than a free car."

Just when Norbert wanted to caution Amanda not to be too free (and too loud) with her critical remarks about the DDR, a waiter appeared, ready to take their order.

The meal was absolutely delicious, and the service was delightful, as was the trio of classical musicians in the background. Since the rain had gained in strength, it was only natural that they would linger even longer at their table, relaxing with the help of a bottle of fine wine and superb pastry.

As their table was being cleared, Norbert reached for Amanda's hand, and looked straight into her eyes. "Forgive me this once for being impolite, but how old are you?"

"My! I would call that a blunt question coming from a sophisticated man like you! But I like your straightforward approach. I was born in 1940, which makes me 23 years old."

"That makes me eight years older than you," Norbert said. "You see, I was born in 1932 here in Berlin. In which part of the world did your cradle stand?"

"My mother gave birth to me when my parents lived in Vyborg, north of Leningrad.

"Both my parents were of German descent. As a medical doctor, father was drafted into the Russian Army. When the German troops reached Vyborg in 1942, my father packed up his practice and moved his family to Germany. For a few years, we lived in Breslau and then moved to Berlin, where my grandfather once had received his medical training."

"Wait, my dear Amanda! I need to get that straight. You come from a German family, where both your father and grandfather were medical doctors. You were born in Vyborg, Russia. I know from one of my clients that many people there still speak Finnish, Swedish, and German, along with Russian."

"Yes, but in our house our family spoke mainly German and Russian. Only the original Finns ever master the Finnish language."

"Does that mean that none of your family is from Finland?"

"At the risk of boring you, Norbert, let me give you a brief version of our family history. The city of Vyborg had been Swedish until Peter the Great captured it in 1710. For about 200 years it remained Russian. After the Russian Revolution in 1917, it became Finnish. By then the Vyborg population was a mix of Swedes, Fins, Russians, Germans, Gypsies, Jews and Tartars. Are you still following me, you sweet Berliner?"

"Yes, my sweet—are you Russian or German?" Norbert asked.

"One more development to note, then I am done explaining my history," Amanda said. "In 1944, when the German troops were pushed from Moscow's suburbs all the way back to German territory, Vyborg fell to the Red Army and has remained Russian ever since."

"So you are Russian, Amanda?"

"Yes and no! When the Soviet Union stole or annexed Vyborg from Finland, my family had already lived in Germany since 1942. We had officially become full-fledged Germans. So *yes* because I was born there, and *no* because when I was two years old my nationality changed to German."

"Amanda," said Norbert, "I don't mean to sound like a KGB interrogator."

"But I don't mind telling you about my Russian-Finnish-German family," answered Amanda with the most charming smile. "I know, Norbert-Darling, you only wanted to treat me to an exquisite dinner at West Berlin's finest restaurant."

It was not lost on Norbert that she had called him "darling" for the first time.

"Yes, Amanda-Darling!"

They laughed over the new names they had given each other. Both felt as if walking on clouds as Norbert walked Amanda to her car. The rain had stopped, but it was now so foggy it took a while to find her car, yet neither was anxious for the evening to end.

That first date now seemed so long ago to Norbert as he sat across from Amanda at the small table in the living room of her apartment. He smiled as she told him she was glad to see him, yet wondered why he had come so unexpectedly. "There is an important matter I need to discuss with you," Norbert said as he reached across the table to hold both of her hands as he spoke.

Amanda, not knowing what to expect, looked at Norbert with intense curiosity.

"Since the time we started seeing each other, our duties have taken you and me to a number of cities in Europe. Our feelings for each other have not suffered from these periods of separation. Am I right?"

Without waiting for Amanda's answer, Norbert continued. "Another separation is coming up. Even though it should be three weeks at the most, I want you to be prepared for possible surprises.

"I have been approached by the US government to be President John F. Kennedy's interpreter during his 10-day tour of Europe in June. On June 26, Kennedy will be speaking to the people in Berlin on the *Schöneberg Rathaus* Square."

"Isn't that where you interpreted for Mayor Reuter and General Clay during the Freedom Bell Dedication?" asked Amanda, full of excitement.

"Yes, Amanda-Darling. He will give a speech right there. The City Manager anticipates that at least 150,000 Berliners from both sides will gather at the square on that day. There is something else that makes me very happy. As I have told you, my brother-in-law, Fred Harrington, is the Chief Pilot on

Air Force One. When he told the President that his wife—my sister, Heidi—is from Berlin, Kennedy immediately invited her to come along on the trip."

"What a wonderful opportunity for Heidi and Fred! Some people have all the luck in the world!" Amanda said with words that were loaded with special meaning—at least that is how Norbert interpreted her remark.

"It will be wonderful to meet your sister and Fred," said Amanda.

"And perhaps even the President of the United States of America," Norbert added, proudly.

"You know, Norbi, presidents come and go—but meeting Heidi, your flesh-and-blood sister, will have a special meaning for me."

After Norbert left so Amanda could get ready for a rehearsal, he climbed into his car with his heart racing with excitement. He knew how strong his feelings were for her, and he was starting to believe she felt the same for him. Could this woman with such outstanding talents and deep feelings really be the person who would be willing to spend the rest of her life with him as his wife?

That night, the hours crawled by as his mind raced, without giving him much sleep. In the morning, as he took an early cold shower, it came to him what to do: he would ask his sister for her opinion of Amanda. Should Heidi have the same impression that this lovely opera singer from East Berlin was the right match for him, he would be confident enough to ask his Amanda-Darling to be his wife.

Chapter 46

Today, June 23, 1963, was Norbert's great chance to meet President John F. Kennedy at Berlin's *Tegel* Airport. Since the American President and his entourage would come to Berlin in the large Air Force One, *Tegel* was better for landing and handling security than the aging *Tempelhof* Airport.

The moment the American and German governments had agreed to make Norbert Anleger not only Kennedy's interpreter but also his guide during his tour, he had started scribbling down ideas he wanted to share with President Kennedy.

Now Norbert stood with Berlin's government dignitaries and high-ranking guests from West Germany close to the spot where Air Force One would land. When the plane arrived and the engines were shut down, it took less than a minute for the door of the aircraft to be pulled open.

Looking as young and vigorous as Norbert had imagined him to be, the thirty-fifth president of the United States emerged and suddenly Norbert's heart was racing. Since most of the German officials spoke or understood English, Norbert did not have to translate at the moment, but he remained at hand and ready.

West Germany's Military Honor Guard showed off its new glory. A military band played both the US and the German national anthems. Because a large, official reception had been planned for that evening, President Kennedy's core group was put into limousines and whisked away to the US Military Headquarters in Berlin-*Zehlendorf.*

Fred Harrington and his flying crew had to stay put until the President's entourage had left for the headquarters. Then there was the small window of opportunity for Fred and Heidi to greet Norbert, whom they had not seen for years. The brief reunion was a joyous moment. After greeting the Harringtons, Norbert looked around and then asked, "And where is your little Prince Calvin?"

"You mean our seven-year-old boy? He attends school and could not come with us.

Besides, President Kennedy unofficially calls this Europe trip the *Harrington Tenth Anniversary Celebration.* It would be in poor taste for us "young" lovers to have our child along. Don't you agree?"

"I am not a specialist in marriage or family etiquette," laughed Norbert, "as you can see from my empty ring finger and—" Norbert stopped abruptly, looking at his sister.

"It would seem to me that you have brought along another prince, or princess?" he said to Heidi in German.

"Only you would come up with such a welcoming remark," she answered in German, as her faced flushed. "On the other hand, I must compliment you for being so observant. Yes, Norbi, you are right. God is giving us another precious gift—I have a feeling it's a girl."

"Are you two siblings fighting already?" asked Fred, who had not been able to follow his wife's German conversation with Norbert.

"On the contrary! Norbert has detected our family secret."

"Which is not an easy task, considering how slim and trim you look."

"Thanks, dear Hubby! Just don't let your lie show too much!"

The happy reunion and wonderful surprise was interrupted when a young officer asked Fred and Heidi to follow him to a limo, which was to take them to the Kempinski Hotel.

"Oh, you are not staying with the President at the US Headquarters?" asked Norbert.

"No, only President Kennedy and his closest staff will be there," said Fred, "and perhaps you, as his chief interpreter. The flight crew and the press are lodging at Kempinski's, which is not a shabby place! But don't worry, Norbert, our paths will cross many times every day, the way the President's schedule had been set up—for instance tonight." Fred checked his wristwatch. "As a matter of fact, in less than four hours we will all meet in Kempinski's Grand Ballroom for the gala reception."

"Yes," said Norbert. "I saw that on my itinerary."

"I almost forgot!" Fred said. "President Kennedy and his Chief-of Staff want to meet with me in one hour for a briefing."

"Doesn't your President ever sleep?" asked Norbert.

"He slept on and off on the plane," answered Heidi, "even though his staff would not call those catnaps real sleep."

"And when do the staff sleep?"

"Never," said Fred, "at least not for four or eight years, depending on how many terms he is the Commander-in-Chief."

President Kennedy had arrived in Berlin on June 23, which was a Sunday. To respectfully acknowledge the international leaders who had come to meet him in Germany, Kennedy's Chief-of-Staff had set aside the first workday on German soil for a number of receptions and interviews.

On Monday, the President wanted to spend two hours with his speech writer, Ted Sorensen, and with Norbert Anleger, who would be his interpreter. In Kennedy's typical perfectionistic manner, he went over every sentence and paragraph of the speech he would deliver on June 26. Norbert was a little surprised that Kennedy worked so diligently, with Norbert's help, practicing one line which he wanted to say in German without translation. They spent fifteen minutes on the proper pronunciation of *Ich bin ein Berliner,* which Kennedy planned to embed in his speech.

When Norbert finally had a little time to himself, he received a phone call from Fred Harrington. "Heidi just told me that you have a pretty steady girlfriend in Berlin. Is that true?"

"Well, Fred, I would say that *pretty* is right, and so is *steady*. As to the title 'girlfriend,'

I am not so sure. We do like each other a lot. Unfortunately, our jobs often take us to different places and in opposite directions. Why do you ask?"

"We just thought you might want to bring her along to tonight's dinner and gala. Most of the people will be couples except for the President and his staff. What do you say, Norbi?"

"Amanda—that's her name—lives in East Berlin. She has more freedom to move between East and West Berlin than most of the East Germans. Still, very often she has to overcome many obstacles. For instance, she has no telephone. But, yes, I think that would be terrific to bring her to the gala. I'll try to reach her through her next-door neighbors who have a phone connection."

"No phone? Does she live in the back-district of Siberia?" Fred asked.

"No, she lives and works in East Berlin and in several other East Bloc nations. She is an opera singer with engagements all over Eastern Europe and occasionally in the West."

"Sounds fascinating! Invite her, please! Tell her that she will meet the President of the United States! Tell her that Heidi would like to meet her! Tell her anything that will make her come!"

"I'll try my best," said Norbert. As he walked away he changed his mind about heading for a phone and instead ran to his car. He reached Amanda's apartment in record time and bolted up the stairs to the front entrance.

When Amanda opened the door, Norbert saw that she was beautifully dressed as if going to the theater. In his breathless stupor, he asked the silly question, "Are you going somewhere, Amanda? You are dressed to kill!"

Flattered by Norbert's compliment but still a bit embarrassed, Amanda answered, "Call it a premonition or what, I had the strange feeling that you and I might be going out tonight."

"We are, Amanda-Darling! That is why I am here. In a few hours we will be part of the Presidential Reception and Gala at the Kempinski Hotel. Since you are already dressed for a special occasion, we should leave right away. You know how the communist goons at the checkpoint react when they see a West Berliner with an East Berliner in a West-registered car."

"Maybe we should take my car, then."

"No way! That might complicate the border crossing even more," warned Norbert.

Amanda took only a minute to grab her purse and cape and they left, with her locking the apartment door behind them. They hurried down the stairs, rushing more out of excitement than anything. A few minutes later they had to stop at the *Invaliden* checkpoint, the crossing for West Berliners. About ten cars were lined up ahead of them.

"Look at the long line," said Amanda. "This could mean a border crossing disaster."

"Which I have experienced more often than I care to remember," added Norbert.

Eventually, a uniformed *Vopo* asked for their identification documents. Noting that Norbert was from West Berlin, he said in a rather polite tone, "From you, sir, I want to see the

471

receipt for the 25 West Marks you paid when you drove into East Berlin."

Irritated over the crossing delay as well as the unjustified East German rule that forced each Western visitor to pay 25 West Marks per day regardless of whether he planned on staying there for 24 hours or only half an hour, Norbert's reply was harsh.

"I wish you would give me back my 25 marks which I just gave to your colleague," he said as he handed over the receipt which showed he had paid the crossing toll less than thirty minutes before. The border guard was shocked at the impertinent tone. He looked up and took a deep breath, ready to exhale a tirade of admonishments. Suddenly he recognized Amanda.

"*Hallo, Fräulein* Steinmetz! What an honor to help you cross the border! Your papers are all *in Ordnung*. The gentleman's are okay as well."

Amanda managed a polite smile and nodded. "Incidentally, I saw your performance two weeks ago," the crossing guard said. "You were magnificent! Please—go ahead!"

Soon they were in West Berlin and on their way again. "What a ridiculous idiocy, having all these border checkpoints in one city! Germans controlling and hating other Germans!"

"I am glad you did not say that to the *Vopo*. He might have kept us back just to prove how powerful East German police are these days," Amanda said.

"What you call powerful, I call insane," replied Norbert.

"And I agree with you," Amanda said, feeling like she had just taken a big risk just by that admission.

A few hours later, inspired by the music of a string quartet and enjoying an upbeat, friendly atmosphere with excellent food, President Kennedy, along with Allied military brass and German government officials, relished every minute of the reception dinner. When Kennedy found out from Norbert that there was a professional opera singer among the guests, he seemed especially delighted. He asked an aide to bring the woman to speak to him at the head table, then he asked Norbert to interpret for him as he planned to ask her if she would sing a song during this interlude between dinner and the gala. "I happen to know she speaks English, so you can make your request of her yourself, if you like," Norbert said, barely able to control his excitement. He turned to look at the musicians as Amanda spoke with the President, but after only a moment he heard her unmistakable voice call to the orchestra leader.

"Play *Of Thee I Sing* by George Gershwin!" she said, referring to the sharp and witty musical comedy and satire on presidential politics which had won the Pulitzer Prize for drama in 1932. The guests were spellbound when Amanda sang. With cheers and lots of laughter all around, Kennedy asked her to sing two more selections. Fred Harrington felt especially glad that he had convinced his brother-in-law to invite his "girlfriend" to the reception.

The reception ended with President Kennedy thanking all who had a hand in planning and making the evening a great success. In good German tradition, he shook everybody's hand. Only the women got hugs. When he approached Amanda, he gave her an especially warm hug.

473

"Your songs were the best welcoming treat Berlin could have given us. And thank you for choosing Gershwin's spoof on presidents."

"You are most welcome, Mister President!"

For Tuesday, June 25, Kennedy's Chief-of-Staff had planned an all-day city tour under the guidance of Norbert Anleger, a son of the city. Norbert had expected one big limousine to pull up with the President and a free seat reserved for his tour guide. He had not counted on a whole convoy of limos showing up, occupied by US Secret Service personnel, German *Sicherheitsdienst* officers, and the press. When the Chief-of-Staff saw Norbert's surprise, he leaned close to him.

"You are here for the President, period," he said in a low voice. "That means for him alone. Ignore all the others, or better yet, pretend they do not exist. Got it?"

That was valuable advice, which Norbert used as guiding rule throughout the entire day. The night before, Norbert had again reviewed his plan. He had given careful consideration to what the President might like to see, and what he should see as a first-time visitor to Berlin. Norbert had been given total freedom except for the iron-clad order: *Whatever you do, wherever you go, do NOT cross into the Soviet Sector of Berlin—that might cause an international calamity!*

President Kennedy insisted that Norbert sit next to him. "I am all yours, Mr. Anleger, at least for today," laughed the President. "Let's roll!"

Norbert had chosen the Free University of Berlin, located next to the US Military Headquarters, as the first drive-through site. As the convoy was traveling across the campus, Norbert provided the commentary.

"The *Freie Universität Berlin* was formerly opened in December 1948 in Berlin-*Dahlem.*

The need for an alternative to the once world-famous Humboldt University, located in the Soviet Sector of Berlin, became evident when the communists began ousting professors and students who did not conform to the ideology of Communism. By the way, the US Ford Foundation contributed major funds for classrooms, an auditorium, and a library." Norbert's narration stopped abruptly.

"Mister President! I know my city well, perhaps too well. I was about to tell you that West Berlin is 185 square miles. You probably do not want to be bombarded with too many details such as this. Forgive me, and stop me anytime if am I am boring you. My problem is that I love this city so much that I forget that people from other places might not have the same interest."

"Mister Anleger," the President said, "don't think for a moment that Berlin and its fate are not of the greatest interest to me! I watched on television when Russian soldiers and East German police blocked the streets from East to West Berlin in August of 1961. I saw them first build barbed wire fences, then they used hollow cement blocks. A few weeks later, they erected high walls made out of poured concrete.

"And of course I remember August 13. My family and I were taking a few vacation days, relaxing aboard my sailboat off Hyannis Port, Massachusetts. An emergency phone call from Secretary of State Dean Rusk informed me about the tragic events in Berlin. Watching later on TV made it clear to me that our troops in Berlin could neither fire on the East German police, nor tear down the barriers—without risking war with Russia."

After this rather touchy conversation, Norbert asked the chauffeur to drive to Checkpoint Charlie, the hot spot of East/West military confrontation. Standing on the West Berlin side, Norbert pointed out to Kennedy the structure of concrete blocks and wire fence barricades on the Soviet side, designed to prevent high-speed breakthrough escapes.

"And what are those crossed beams behind the high screen fence in the back?" asked the President.

"They are vehicle traps to catch motorized fleeing East Berliners still on the Russian Sector side."

From there, the caravan drove to the Soviet War Memorial in the British Sector near the Brandenburg Gate. Two Soviet soldiers stood ceremonial guard, rifles strapped across their chests. Since the stop was not an official government visit, President Kennedy did not get out of the limo to lay a wreath at the memorial or exchange any words with the Soviet guards.

Norbert directed the limo to stop by the flower-decorated, unofficial memorial site of 18-year old Peter Fechter, who had been killed there by East German bullets on August 17, 1962. Norbert urged the President to exit the car and walk with him up to the site as he told Kennedy the background.

Fechter had used his lunch break time to attempt an escape to the West. In bright daylight, he had managed to climb to the four-meter-high top of the wall, when a woman shouted to the police guards: *"Schießt doch mal!"* ("Go ahead! Shoot!")

Several shots were fired, and Fechter was hit. He cried out for help, clinging to the crown of the wall for 55 minutes, while bleeding to death. His mother, who had been informed of his fate, had rushed to the wall, where she had to endure his death cries just a few meters away. Once Fechter died, DDR border police and GDR soldiers pulled his body back into the East.

President Kennedy was deeply moved by the story and asked, "The East German police and soldiers just watched the boy die without rendering help?"

"Yes, Mister President. He was the thirtieth fatality since the building of the *Berlin Wall.*

"The anti-West propaganda has brainwashed the DDR police and military guards to shoot at the escapees, calling them *subversive elements not worth living.*

"Please look across the wall. From where we are standing, you can see the so-called 'No Man's Land.' What an irony! Putting up a barbed-wire and a concrete wall smack through Berlin, surrounded by rifles, hand grenades, guns, land mines and search lights—that's what I would call a death strip of the worst kind, not a no-man's-land."

"Norbert, do you have some literature explaining the structure and length of the wall?"

"Not with me, sir, but I can get it for you. In the meantime, you have to trust my memory. As you see, it is between three and four meters high. The total length is 107 kilometers. It has 295 observation towers and more than 40 bunkers."

"How do you know these statistics so well?" Kennedy wanted to know.

"When you live in West Berlin, you keep an eye on what is happening in East Berlin. Sometimes you really wonder which side feels more like living in a heavily-guarded camp."

The President headed back to the limo, with Norbert and two secret service agents close behind. As they were waiting for a break in traffic to leave, the President turned to Norbert.

"Doesn't it drive you crazy to live in this enclave in the middle of communist East Germany, which one day could get devoured by the Soviets?"

"No, sir, never! First of all, we West Berliners do not think that the USA will ever sell us out to the Russians. Second, human beings get used to many things, good and bad. I know it may sound strange, but we in West Berlin have learned not to constantly have angst over the infamous wall, which the communists call the *antifascist wall of protection.*"

The President reached over to grab Norbert's hand. "Norbert, you really represent the best in this *island of freedom.*" Norbert quietly registered the compliment from the American President. Then he told the chauffeur to drive to the Airlift Memorial at the Tempelhof Airport. There, Kennedy and his entire entourage got out of their cars. They walked up to the middle of the street where they looked at the high memorial, honoring the 79 American, English, French and German men, who had lost their lives during Berlin Airlift from 1948 to 1949.

As they walked back to their cars, Kennedy said he was very thirsty. Actually, his thirst had started when he had seen an English graffiti on the western side of the wall, announcing, "Last Coke for 10,000 miles!" Norbert noticed how Kennedy was searching for something.

"May I help you with something, Mister President?" asked Norbert.

"I doubt that you can. A Coca-Cola would be what I need right now."

"How about a typical Berliner bratwurst with a Coke?" Norbert asked.

Moments later, Berliners had the first-time-ever experience of seeing four black limousines stopping simultaneously right in front of "a hot-dog stand," as the President called it. The President had the privilege to be the first to order. "Bratwurst with lots of sauerkraut, and a Coke," he said to the vendor.

"Not a beer?" the vendor asked in English.

"You heard me right, I want my sausage with a coke."

The middle-aged vendor operated his business in partnership with his wife. As fast as possible, both tried to satisfy the sudden large group of customers, who all ordered bratwurst. Never before in their lives had such a rush of customers overwhelmed their stand, not even after victorious soccer matches. When Norbert told him who his famous customer was, he refused to accept payment. The President asked Norbert to please translate into German that he insisted the man accept the money, and that the quick service for his crowd was appreciated.

While the rest of the group chewed their fried sausages, Norbert showed the President a map of Berlin printed in *East*

Germany, which had become a novelty souvenir for Western visitors. This version of a Berlin map depicted West Berlin as a white desert, totally blank, except for the inscription "West Berlin." No streets, landmarks, or districts were identified.

As Norbert was explaining the city layout, he looked up to see none other than his sister, Heidi. On a walk, she and Fred had seen the unmistakable entourage of men in suits and black limos and were crossing the street to see if they could find Norbert. As they approached, Norbert let the President know they had company.

"And how is my faithful Chief Pilot, and his lovely wife today?" asked Kennedy, cheerfully.

"Couldn't be better, Boss!" Fred dared to answer in a style far from the official protocol.

"Would you like a good German bratwurst, Heidi?" Kennedy asked. "Or maybe you don't eat anything fried like that…"

"Anything cooked, fried or grilled in Berlin is good for me, Mister President. If I come across something that really is not my taste, I only have to think of the hunger-years after the war, to make ALL food just fine with me."

"Hey, Colonel," Kennedy said to Fred, "Where did you find your wonderful and smart wife?"

"In Berlin, Mister President."

"I think when my son has reached the age to begin meeting lovely girls, I will send him to Berlin."

"Thank you, Mister President!" said Fred and Heidi at the same time. The four shared a laugh, but then it was time for the President's tour to continue. An aide escorted Fred and Heidi to the bratwurst vendor and paid for their lunch as Norbert and the President climbed into their limo.

The next stop was the *Reichstag,* the still badly war-damaged former seat of the German Parliament. This was also the place where, in May of 1945, the Soviet troops had hoisted the Red Flag as a sign that Germany had been defeated and that World War II was over in Europe.

When Norbert noticed that Kennedy was not impressed with the badly bombed-out skeleton of the formerly magnificent structure, he felt like apologizing to the President.

"Mister President," he began, hesitantly. "I have been given strict orders not to guide you to East Berlin, which I know well, too. The trouble is that, unfortunately, Berlin's most celebrated landmarks are in East Berlin, like the Pergamum Museum, the former City Hall, the German State Opera, the Humboldt University, the State Library, and even Hitler's Bunker."

"Don't worry, Norbert. Considering that this once world-famous city was almost totally destroyed by 1945, you have managed to show me so much more than I had expected to see.

"Besides, with your running commentary, you have succeeded in revealing to me the inner heart of the city, something that only a person born and raised in Berlin could do. So go ahead, and don't hold back!"

Norbert needed to hear such encouraging words. As a result, he took President Kennedy to Spandau Prison, where the Nazi leaders who had not been hanged were imprisoned.

After a brief stop there, the motorcade proceeded to take its distinguished sightseers to the Olympic Stadium where the 1936 Olympic Games were held. Kennedy confirmed with Norbert that this was where Hitler had refused to shake the hand of the US winner of four Gold Medals, Jesse Owens, just because he was of the black race.

In the tour, Norbert also included the restored *Charlottenburg Palace*, which now was the home of several government agencies. After a full day of interacting so closely with President Kennedy, Norbert could read him well enough to know he had experienced enough of Berlin for one day. The last thing Norbert wanted was for the President to start getting bored, or irritated with one too many pot holes. The day had gone well and both men felt a deeper bond had developed between them than could have been anticipated. This was to have a lasting effect on both.

When Kennedy's limo arrived back at the U. S. Military Headquarters, the President stretched and shook his limbs.

"Thank you again, Mister Anleger! By the way, seeing how complicated life in Berlin can be, I might change my mind about sending my son John here when he is grown up."

"Yes, my sister and her husband, Fred, your Chief Pilot, were more than a little fortunate that they met here."

"Yes," said President Kennedy, "they seem to be a lucky couple whose match was made in heaven. Hopefully heaven will be just as generous with you. Your friend Amanda strikes me as just as beautiful and intelligent as your sister, Heidi. Have you ever talked to Amanda about getting married?"

"No, Mister President. Not yet."

Chapter 47

Berlin had its share of fog, rain, and in winter, even snow. But one thing Berliners knew: June always brought at least a few days of perfectly sunny weather. School vacations always started in June and lasted until end of August. Today was just that kind of blue-sky June day, and Norbert was thinking that the timing of President Kennedy's visit was good as he was experiencing the beauty of Germany in June.

Norbert asked President Kennedy for permission to leave and have breakfast with Heidi and Fred Harrington. "Go ahead!" Kennedy said. "I'm having breakfast with my staff this morning, anyway." Then he laughed as he said, "And I'm pretty sure they all speak English!"

Norbert was glad to finally have the chance to ask Heidi for her impression of Amanda.

"Norbi," said Heidi, while they were sitting down in one of Kempinski's breakfast rooms, "I absolutely adore your Amanda Steinhof."

"Steinmetz," corrected Norbert.

"Sorry, Mister Interpreter! I meant to say Amanda Steinmetz," laughed Heidi, unconcerned. "The point is, she seems to be a real darling."

"That's what I call her—either Darling-Amanda or Amanda-Darling," said Norbert. "And she does the same with my name."

"Well, that sounds pretty serious! Has she always lived here in Berlin?"

"Most of her life. She lives in East Berlin in the *Lichtenberger Strasse.*"

"I know where Berlin-*Lichtenberg* is, but I have not heard of *Lichtenberger Strasse.*"

"It is a short street that runs from the *Strausberger Platz* to the *Friedrichshainer Platz.*"

Just at that moment the restaurant door opened and in walked Amanda. Norbert jumped up to greet her. "Amanda-Darling," he said, "what a wonderful surprise!"

"Didn't you tell me you might try to have breakfast with the Harringtons during these days?" said Amanda. "My neighbor wasn't there for me to borrow the use of their telephone, so I took a chance, hoping to find you three here this morning."

"We have to get you a phone!" Heidi said quickly.

"This is not the USA, Heidi. I have been on the waiting list for a phone for three years."

"But you are a famous opera singer, a professional artist. Should you not have your own telephone?"

"Each time I ask the bureaucrats to move up my phone installation date, they tell me they have to follow their pecking order. First: party leaders; second: medical doctors; third: pub and restaurant owners; fourth: nationally recognized athletes; fifth: lawyers; then, perhaps, artists."

After they had placed their order, Norbert continued his story of how he had met Amanda, even though Amanda could listen in now.

"When Heidi left Berlin in 1960, it was a huge loss for me. My three brothers and parents were already dead. Then my Aunt Hanna died, and her husband, Uncle Theo, moved into a senior citizens' home. Even Uncle Fritz Brenner, my mother's brother, who had returned from many years of deportation in the Soviet Union, died of uranium poisoning at a fairly young age.

"In order to get over the feeling of emptiness, I buried myself in work, work, work. That did pay off, I must admit. After my early success, I opened the second and then the third Center for Interpretation and Translation. But it was not easy, by any means. I came across hundreds of stories of torn-apart families, destroyed businesses, stolen properties, and expatriated, uprooted individuals. My heart ached for them. I did help them with foreign language paperwork and document translations, but I could not take away their pain and feelings of despair and helplessness.

"Then one day, at the dedication of the East Berliner *Kultur Palast,* I heard a voice that melted my heart. It was the voice of Amanda Steinmetz."

Amanda, looking embarrassed, softly put her hand on Norbert's arm. "Norbi-Darling, let Heidi and Fred enjoy their breakfast." Norbert looked down, ready to stop talking.

"No! Let him talk!" urged Heidi. "We had the same parents and belong to the same family. Norbert speaks for me, too."

The breakfast get-together which had started out as an innocent gossip hour was reaching an ever-deepening layer. The four people from such diverse backgrounds, including the fact they were originally from three different countries, found more and more commonalty as their discussion continued. They listened to each other, and opened their hearts to one another. Each remark, each story, each confession, and each occasional silence brought them closer together, as the minutes ticked away.

Fred was the first to remember his present duties and excuse himself from the group. "I have to see JFK within the hour. He wants to discuss tomorrow's flight to Bonn."

"And I need to change and get ready for the luncheon the Lord Mayor is giving for the American guests," said Heidi.

"May I stay close to you for the rest of the day?" Amanda asked Norbert.

"Amanda-Darling! Nothing would please me more."

Norbert insisted on paying for everyone's breakfasts, and with hugs and kisses he and Amanda said goodbye to Fred and Heidi.

The huge area in front of the *Schöneberg Rathaus* was overflowing with people long before President Kennedy's open limousine reached Berlin's famous square. In the limo stood President Kennedy, West Berlin's Mayor Willi Brandt, and West Germany's Chancellor Konrad Adenauer. Originally, they had been sitting until Kennedy suddenly said to Adenauer, "I think the people can see us better if we stand up."

A uniformed chauffeur drove the limo with the three dignitaries, plus Norbert, up to the front of the *Rathaus*. Close to 1:00 p.m., other city officials joined them on the platform. Everyone seemed to be very excited. Only the President and Norbert felt the weight of the important task ahead, delivering and translating a speech which was certain to be heard not only in Berlin, but around the world.

After greetings and introductions, President Kennedy was ready for his 20-minute speech.

"I am proud to come to this city as the guest of your distinguished Mayor, who has symbolized throughout the world the fighting spirit of West Berlin. And I am proud to visit the Federal Republic with your distinguished Chancellor, who for so many years has committed Germany to democracy and freedom and progress, and to come here in the company of my fellow American, General Clay, who has been in this city during its great moments of crisis and will come again if ever needed.

"Two thousand years ago the proudest boast was '*civis Romanus sum.*' Today, in the world of freedom, the proudest boast is '*Ich bin ein Berliner.*'

"I appreciate my interpreter translating my German!

"There are many people in the world who really don't understand, or say they don't, what is the great issue between the Free World and the Communist world. Let them come to Berlin. There are some who say that communism is the wave of the future. Let them come to Berlin. And there are some

487

who say in Europe and elsewhere, we can work with the Communists. Let them come to Berlin. And there are even a few who say that it's true that communism is an evil system, but it permits us to make economic progress. 'Lass sie nach Berlin kommen.' Let them come to Berlin!

"Freedom has many difficulties and democracy is not perfect, but we have never had to put a wall up to keep our people in, to prevent them from leaving us. I want to say, on behalf of my countrymen, who live many miles away on the other side of the Atlantic, who are far distant from you, that they take the greatest pride that they have been able to share with you, even from a distance, the story of the last eighteen years. I know of no town, no city, that has been besieged for eighteen years that still lives with the vitality and the force and the hope and the determination of the city of West Berlin.

"While the wall is the most obvious and vivid demonstration of the failures of the Communist system, for all the world to see, we take no satisfaction in it. For it is, as your Mayor has said, an offense not only against history but an offense against humanity; separating families, dividing husbands and wives and brothers and sisters, and dividing a people who wish to be joined together.

"What is true of this city is true of Germany—real, lasting peace in Europe can never be assured as long as one German out of four is denied the elementary right of free men, and that is to make a free choice. In eighteen years of peace and good faith, this generation of Germans has earned the right to be free, including the right to unite their families and their nation in lasting peace, with goodwill to all people. You live in a defended island of freedom, but your life is part of the

488

main. So let me ask you, as I close, to lift your eyes beyond the dangers of today to the hopes of tomorrow, beyond the freedom merely of this city of Berlin, or your country of Germany, to the advance of freedom everywhere, beyond the wall to the day of peace with justice, beyond yourselves and ourselves to all mankind.

"Freedom is indivisible, and when one man is enslaved, all are not free. When all are free, then we can look forward to that day when this city will be joined as one, and this country, and this great Continent of Europe, in a peaceful and hopeful globe. When that day finally comes, as it will, the people of West Berlin can take sober satisfaction in the fact that they were in the front lines for almost two decades.

"All free men, wherever they may live, are citizens of Berlin, and, therefore, as a free man, I take pride in the words

'Ich bin ein Berliner.'"

The roaring applause of the crowd seemed to have no end. Again and again, thousands from West and East Berlin shouted encouraging slogans. The fearless Amanda Steinmetz was one of them. She was proud to have personally met and talked with the President, and was certain of his sincerity.

Overwhelmed by the thundering response, President Kennedy later said to his speech writer, Sorenson: "Today is the 26th of June, 1963. We will never have another day like this as long as we live."

The truth of Kennedy's statement was a tragic premonition, because only a few months later, on November 22, while the President was riding in an open limousine in Dallas, Texas, he would be shot and killed.

As America and the rest of the world would deal with the shock, just how much the Berliners loved Kennedy would be demonstrated when they followed Mayor Willi Brandt's radio appeal to place burning candles in their windows as symbol of their sympathy and solidarity. One could see candlelight in just about every window of West Berlin's apartments and houses.

Certainly Kennedy's speech that day in Berlin where he pointed to the wall as an example of the failure of communism had endeared him to the Berliners, and to freedom-lovers worldwide, forever.

Amanda listened intently, and felt her heart would burst with gratitude for Kennedy's uplifting words and truly inspirational speech which was having a profound affect even as each word was spoken. After the end of the speech, "*Ich bin ein Berliner*," the crowd erupted and made it nearly impossible for her to push through to the front and side of the platform. Secret servicemen prevented her stepping up until Norbert saw her and came to take her hand, helping her up to stand beside him as more and more people came to shake the President's hand.

"You did a wonderful job, Norbert!" shouted Amanda, but her words were drowned out by the jubilant Berliners. Not understanding what Amanda said, Norbert put his arms around her neck and yelled, "I love you, too."

Fred and Heidi Harrington were among those who had clearance to be allowed up to shake the President's hand. They thanked him for his inspiring speech.

"Mister President! Your speech was the nicest anniversary gift any *half-Berliner* couple could wish for," said Heidi.

Kennedy just smiled. He had told Fred many times how fond he was of Heidi, and what a nice couple they made.

Norbert made an effort to take in the scene and etch it in his memory. It was breathtaking, really, to stand with his dear Amanda, his beloved sister and her husband, and the President of the United States, looking out at the mass of people who were cheering—not just for the speakers, but for freedom and liberty for all.

One day after the Berlin speech, Fred was flying President Kennedy to Bonn, West Germany's provisional capital. Flying with him were Heidi, Norbert and Amanda. Fred thought this was his most precious cargo transport to date.

For Heidi, being in Berlin again and breathing the legendary *Berliner Luft* (air) had invigorated her. If Kennedy, after being in Berlin only a few days could say, *"Ich bin ein Berliner,"* she realized she could, and should, more fully embrace her heritage as a Berliner, the bad along with the good. Returning to Berlin on this special trip was made even more interesting by the fact that Heidi had met Amanda Steinmetz. Since neither Heidi nor Amanda had been in the picturesque city of Bonn before, both women made up for it by using every moment for sightseeing and shopping.

When it was time to leave Bonn, Amanda traveled by train back to East Berlin, while Fred flew President Kennedy and his staff, plus Heidi, Norbert, and a few selected reporters to Rome, where Kennedy was involved in several government meetings until Saturday night.

"Remember, Fred, tomorrow is Sunday," Kennedy said. "After breakfast, you, Heidi, Norbert and I will get an extensive tour of the city, and Norbert will not have to say a word."

"Why is that?" asked Norbert.

"Because the Italian government is giving us their best interpreter. He knows Rome better than the President of Italy."

"That will be fine with me," Norbert said. "I just wish Amanda was still with us."

"Well, young man, I guess you'll have to marry that wonderful young lady to have her at your side all the time. She might even widen your knowledge of the Russian language, an effort which would be tax-deductible."

"I don't think Germany grants such tax breaks, sir."

"Then you'll just have to collect her and all your things and move to the US. We would be happy to have you both on our staff."

"That is a most generous remark, sir. But please, don't forget: *Ich bin ein Berliner.* Somebody has to stay in Berlin until freedom truly rings."

On the long flight from Rome back to Washington, DC, President Kennedy visited Fred Harrington in the cockpit. Fred turned around to greet Kennedy.

"Keep your eyes on the controls! I just wanted to tell you that your brother-in-law, Norbert, is not only an excellent interpreter, but he also is one of the finest young Germans I have ever met."

"As is his sister," added Fred, with a wink.

"We both agree," the President said, and both men laughed.

"By the way, Colonel, there will be no flying for us on the Fourth of July."

"Which is in two days."

"I realize that. Just get us safely to the US. I need to spend the long holiday weekend with my wife and my two children, who I miss dearly."

"I understand, sir."

"Good! At ease, Chief Pilot! And smooth flying."

"Thank you, Commander-in-Chief!"

Instead of walking back to his comfortable easy chair, the President steered toward his secretary. "Please connect me with Norbert Anleger in Germany! I forgot to ask him an important question." In less than a minute, Norbert was on the line.

"Mister Anleger, thank you again for all the details you were able to provide me—very useful as I am working on what to include in my briefing. I meant to ask you to tell me more about East Germany's obscene, new *fundraising* strategy. You mentioned that the GDR has begun to ask the West German government to pay ransom for people they are willing to release from their prisons, if the price is right. Is that correct? I want to include this outrageous development in my report, and I want it to be accurate."

"What I told you is the full truth, Mister President. The GDR, or DDR, economy is close to bankruptcy. This prisoner trade-for-money scheme is despicable, but it gives back freedom to many innocent prisoners, and is seeming to help the GDR economy to recover.

"In the beginning, the Eastern authorities emptied many high-security prisons and sent dangerous criminals to the West—for cash! The West had offered to pay 5,000 German Marks per head. When the West discovered how twisted this deal was, they decided to pay only for verifiable persons who had fled, or had unsuccessfully tried to flee, East Germany. In return, the DDR regime raised the ransom price, in some cases to 40,000 marks. The West paid! Money spoke louder than reason and decency."

"Thank you, Norbert, for clarifying what I could remember only vaguely," the President said. "Frankly, I find East Germany's trading arrangement appalling. Reminds me too much of the times of the slave traders who sold human beings to the highest bidder. Surviving Berlin after the war has been one trial after another, hasn't it, Norbert?"

"Yes, sir. But please don't hesitate to call me with any question, as you have today. I miss being in your presence, and the hope you give to so many."

"Well, that's all, my friend. Thanks again for all your work on my behalf. Stay well!"

"You too, Mister President."

Norbert replayed his air-to-land phone conversation with President Kennedy over and over in his mind, and each time he marveled at Kennedy's interest in Germany's wellbeing. Feeling a stronger connection with the US now, more than ever, Norbert began to follow every news story out of Washington, especially any about President Kennedy.

Then came the disastrous Friday, the 22nd of November, when the horrific news raced around the world: **"US President John F. Kennedy has been assassinated!"** Norbert dropped all his plans and arranged for a flight to Washington, DC, where Kennedy's funeral was to be held on November 25. Amanda tried to quickly get a US visa and an overseas flight ticket. At the East Berlin Visa Office, a communist official said to her: "When a damned American president dies, that is no reason for upright citizens of the German Democratic Republic to rush to his funeral. Visa denied!"

Norbert flew to the States in the company of the official German government delegation. He stayed with Heidi and Fred in Arlington. As millions of people around the world mourned the death of Kennedy, the people living in Virginia and Maryland just outside Washington were especially grief-stricken because many of them knew or had met the President personally. Without a doubt, Fred, Heidi, and Norbert were among those at the funeral who were most deeply affected.

All too soon, Norbert had to say goodbye. On the day he had to fly back to Germany, he saw Fred only for a few minutes. Fred was busy in briefings with his new boss, President Lyndon Baines Johnson. Heidi took Norbert to the airport, making him promise to come back and visit under better circumstances.

When Amanda greeted Norbert at the Tempelhof Airport in Berlin, he seemed to have aged. At first they both were silent during the taxi ride. Then Amanda snuggled closely to him; she could feel that he needed her comfort.

"Norbi-Darling," Amanda said softly, using the term he liked hearing from her lips.

"Christmas is just around the corner. Why don't we take a two or three week holiday? I would give anything if I could take you to my family's ski lodge in Krynica, near Zakopane in Poland. We could spend a wonderful time there, skiing, sunning and relaxing in Poland's High Tatra Mountains. Unfortunately, the Steinmetz Lodge was confiscated and badly ruined by Soviet soldiers after the war. When my father visited there last year, he found it in an abominable condition. We'll have to think of somewhere else for a vacation spot."

"How about in the *Riesengebirge* right here in Germany—I mean in the DDR," said Norbert, correcting himself in a mocking tone.

"That sounds good to me. We would not have to travel as far, and you would certainly be able to secure an East German visa, I mean a DDR visa," Amanda mocked, too.

The taxi took them to Amanda's apartment, where they continued discussing their possible vacation plans. Both believed that here they were safe to openly discuss Amanda's ultimate destination: West Germany or West Berlin.

"Norbi-Darling! While you were in Washington, I had lots of time to think. You know our government doesn't recognize Christmas or Jesus' birth in any way, but they do plan all kinds of festivities dedicated to *Father Frost* during the Yule season. We have no opera performances before and after Christmas, which means I will not be working."

Suddenly Amanda stopped talking, got up and looked around in her living room.

"What's wrong, Amanda-Darling? Did you lose something?"

"No, Norbi, I just wanted to make sure that my apartment didn't have any uninvited guests while I spent so little time here during President Kennedy's visit."

"You think somebody might have taken a closer look around, or installed listening devices in your apartment?"

"I am afraid so! The lower window curtains are drawn shut, which I have never done as long as I have lived here."

"In your rush to meet me, Heidi, Fred, and the President you might have pulled the curtains without thinking about it."

"You could be right! Besides, what would the police or KGB suspect here?"

Encouraging each other not to be over-suspicious, Amanda and Norbert continued making their tentative vacation plans.

"Perhaps looking up your Steinmetz Lodge in Krynica is not such a bad idea after all," said Norbert. "If we discover that the condition is really terrible, we could put in a full day of skiing and then look for a more comfortable hotel on the Czech side, right across the border. I doubt that anybody in the High Tatra would bother asking for our ID."

"I still think we should have visas for every country we might visit," said Heidi.

"As you please, my Lady!"

Lieutenant Vassily Zhukovski, the new Soviet deputy of Major General Andrey Molotov and successor to the defector, Sergey Svertlov, adjusted his ultra-sensitive earphones. It seemed that his careful effort to tap the conversations in Amanda Steinmetz's apartment was paying off. For days now, he and soldiers under his command had tried to spy on Amanda's Western visitors and friends with the help of electronic bugs they had installed. Since Miss Steinmetz had no telephone, they had not been able to listen to phone conversations. Having direct access to live conversations in her apartment, however, was even better.

Zhukovski was eager and ready to make notes on what the two people in Amanda's apartment were planning to do.

"You know, Norbert, if we drive from Poland to Czechoslovakia, we could either travel the long route to Prague, or the shorter route to Budapest, or to Vienna. I always wanted to visit these beautiful old cities."

"Darling, have you ever been in Salzburg? That is the most charming city in Austria. I have a number of clients whom I helped travel from Salzburg to Munich."

The Soviet officer's hair stood on end. The more he listened the more obvious it became that an escape plan was in the making. He was convinced that he was listening to a man and Amanda preparing to flee East Germany. The hateful remark about the Russians having ruined the family lodge in Krynica fit with the information he had received concerning Amanda and her friends being anti-communists. "Putting in a full day of skiing" most likely was code for staying near Krynica for one day only. The idea of crossing from Poland to Czechoslovakia without visas was a criminal breach of border laws, yet they discussed it so casually.

The fact that they might then travel to Hungary or Austria made everything even more suspicious, as was the very likely possibility of them escaping from Salzburg in Austria, to Munich in Germany.

What was developing here in Fräulein Steinmetz's apartment looked like another opportunity for Zhukovski to demonstrate his skill of ferreting out disloyal East Germans.

He just had to be extremely careful and patient. And he was glad that many years ago, his grandmother had taught him the German language so well.

Zhukovski closed his eyes a moment to better focus on what Amanda was saying.

"This will be an important trip for us, Norbi-Darling. We've had incredibly hectic schedules. We both really need to get away."

Zhukovski smiled.

"Instead of making more detailed plans for our Christmas vacation, let's have a glass of wine with the delicious cookies you brought from America," Amanda said. "And then you have to tell me all about President Kennedy's funeral."

As interesting as Norbert's account of Kennedy's funeral was to Amanda, for Lieutenant Zhukovski it was a waste of time. Kennedy was dead and buried. Vassily Zhukovski and his Soviet comrades were more interested in who this new President Lyndon Johnson was. Would he hold the same strict line against the Soviet Union as his youthful predecessor?

Even after several glasses of wine had loosened the tongues of Amanda and Norbert, they said nothing more of importance for a report Zhukovski had to give to General Molotov. He would use his notes about their so-called vacation to back up his assertion of their intention to flee East Germany. He felt very pleased with himself, and, in his elevated mood, almost decided to include in his report the passionate love scene dialogue from the end of the evening, but thought better of it.

During the following days, Norbert and Amanda met only at places outside her apartment, as they had thought more about the clues that someone had been there, which meant it was highly probable the place was bugged. They met either in West Berlin or in small *Berliner Kindl Kneipen* (saloons), where Norbert hated the bitter taste of the DDR beer. In spite of the shabby beer, the food usually was good. Amanda and Norbert just wanted to be somewhere where no one was listening.

It did not take them long to agree on a departure date: December 14, 1963. They knew that on Saturdays and Sundays, traffic would be light. They would travel in Heidi's Trabant, creating the least suspicion in Eastern European countries. For Amanda it was easy to secure visas for these countries. Norbert was not a typical West Berliner since he had extensive experience traveling across the borders of many countries on business. He was able to avoid application obstacles and delays to get the desired visas in record time.

By now, both knew that Amanda would not return to East Berlin or the DDR; instead she would stay in West Germany or West Berlin. This secret end-goal made their planning extremely difficult. On the one hand, Amanda wanted to take along as many of her belongings, trophies and international souvenirs as possible. On the other hand, luggage filled with sentimental valuables would make the East German *Vopos* suspect that she was attempting to escape to the West.

Sure, Amanda Steinmetz was an opera singer, an artist, or as the DDR called her, a *Kulturschaffende* (creator of culture). However, since when did singers drag along trophies won as cultural prizes and at singing contests? And did skiers really need several suitcases of clothes and household items when going on a holiday trip? Wasn't the requested visa of three to four weeks unusually long?

With a heavy heart Amanda left behind many treasured belongings in her apartment.

The packing for the trip became an intriguing task. It also was a rather silent job, since neither Amanda nor Norbert talked to each other so that no carelessly spoken word would give away their real intention.

Two pairs of skis and ski poles were attached to the roof of Amanda's car. What they did not want to be so conspicuous was all of Amanda's luggage, which proved difficult to conceal in the little Trabant. Luckily, Norbert's baggage consisted of only one duffel bag, which he pressed under his seat.

"Amanda-Darling!" Norbert said, loud enough to be heard by the curious neighbors. "Our Trabi will have to work extra hard when we get into the mountains of the High Tatra."

"Have a good trip!" one of the neighbors called out. "*Hals und Beinbruch!*" Norbert waved and smiled. He also automatically thought of the English version of that bidding, "break a leg," and shook his head to dismiss that image.

"Thanks! See you soon!" Amanda shouted to her neighbor.

Then the heavily loaded Trabant was on its way to the south. Norbert drove straight to Dresden, where they took a lunch break. Both needed to catch their breath before crossing the border to Czechoslovakia. As far as they could tell, they were not being followed. The traffic toward Dresden had been very light. In spite of displaying their skis on top of the car, they had no intention of driving to Krynica. Prague, the capital of the CSSR, was their next destination. Both had visited Prague before, but this was not a sightseeing trip. In the DDR, as well as in Czechoslovakia, danger could pop up at anytime.

The border crossing from the DDR into Czechoslovakia posed their first problem. The military Czech border guards were a mix of Czech and Russian soldiers. One of the officers spoke German and asked: "Did you get lost?"

"No! Why?"

"You have visas for skiing in Poland's Carpathian Mountains; but you have traveled in the wrong direction."

"Officer! As you can see from our baggage load, we want to do a lot of sightseeing in the east, south, and west. We will fit in our skiing as well."

"Ah, but why do you drag so many suitcases with you?"

"Are you married, sir?" Norbert asked.

"No! Why do you ask?"

Norbert smiled slyly. "Then you have never traveled in a small Trabi with a beautiful wife. *My* only cargo is this duffel bag here under my seat."

The guard and two others nearby joined Norbert in a laugh. The IDs and stamped passports were returned and the Trabant was waved on. Amanda waved a "thank you" to the inspector, who shouted after them: "Don't break your neck! Mountains can be dangerous."

"We know! Thanks, anyway."

In the evening they reached the Golden City of Prague. They stayed overnight at the first hotel they saw, not minding how run down and dusty it was. The hotel manager hardly looked at their passports. In broken German he explained his guests that they could eat supper right at the hotel.

"My wife is good cook, and price is good," he said with an inviting smile. "Honeymooners, yes?"

"You said it!" Amanda answered.

The next morning, Norbert and Amanda debated whether they should allow themselves a vacation day in this beautiful city.

"What if somebody keeps track of our travel?"

"So what! We have not done anything wrong, yet," replied Norbert.

"Right—not yet!"

"Do you think it would be smarter to keep on traveling to Vienna?" Norbert asked.

"Smarter yes, but staying here for one more day will be more fun."

"You are right, Darling-Amanda, like always. Let's explore the ancient beauty of Prague today! Tomorrow we will continue to Budapest."

"Shall we stay a few extra days in Budapest, too?" Amanda asked.

"This time I have to disappoint you with a *no*. With our skis on top of your car, we better head for an area where we can use them. That would be the Alps in Austria, agreed?"

"Oh yes, Norbi-Darling. To use the skis finally is just what we need."

Norbert and Amanda enjoyed every step of their sightseeing in Prague. When total strangers smiled or nodded at them, Amanda said, "We really must look like a honeymoon couple, Norbi."

"Yes, and we also act like honeymooners."

At first, Amanda constantly took notes of what they had seen. Finally, she tired of all the writing and decided to just look and enjoy the sights. "Maybe it's just a tourist attraction," she said to Norbert as they walked through the Old Town Square, "but I've always wanted to see the medieval astronomical clock here."

"I'm not sure I've ever heard of that, but I'm sure we can find it if you want to see it. Who knows if we'll ever return to Prague?" The clock adorns the southern wall of the Old Town City Hall in the Old Town Square. It announces every hour with 12 apostles passing by the window above the astronomical dial, and with symbolic sculptures moving aside. When Amanda looked up and saw it, she smiled so beautifully, Norbert could hardly take his eyes off of her to view the amazing clock himself.

The following day tested the durability of the Trabant as they drove nearly 600 kilometers to get to their next stop, Budapest. The guard at the Czech/Hungarian border was kind and efficient. When they finally arrived in Budapest, they were struck by the friendliness of its citizens. It seemed to Amanda and Norbert that the further away they got from East Germany, the better. Their first glimpse of the spectacular Danube River, which separates the Buda Town from the Pest Town, helped them to decide on a hotel which faced the river, and a room with a view of the Danube.

They noticed right away that most people had no anti-Western attitude, but there were overtones of anti-Russian sentiment. During dinner at a nice restaurant with an outstanding international reputation, the couple shared fond memories of President Kennedy's visit to Berlin, and lamented his tragic death a few months later. Suddenly, one of the four young men dining at a table next to them leaned toward Norbert.

"Excuse me," he said in German. "I heard you say something about the American President Kennedy. Did you know him?"

"Yes, we did. You see, as his interpreter, I was with him during the ten days he spent in Europe—especially in Berlin."

Now all four got up from their table, and they surrounded Amanda and Norbert.

"You really knew this wonderful man?" they wanted to know.

"Yes, we did," answered Amanda. "As a matter of fact, I had the privilege of singing three songs for him at the reception gala in Berlin."

That did it! The four men bombarded them with one question after another, some asked in German, some in English, others in Russian. Amanda asked one of them, "Why did you ask me your question in the Russian language?"

"Because I am Russian. I moved to Budapest to study medicine. Here I can get a much better education than in Soviet universities. But I asked you in Russian, because there is something beautifully Russian about you I really cannot describe in words. Do you speak Russian?"

"Yes, I do; and I sing in Russian, too."

The waiter assisted as they moved their tables together to make one large enough to all sit around. The evening continued with pleasant chatter and with many toasts to friendship with Germany, America, Hungary, and Russia (and notably not with the Soviet Union).

At last Norbert stood, thanked the friendly intruders for a splendid time, and pulled out Amanda's chair for her to stand as well.

"Sorry, guys! We had a long trip today coming from Prague. Tomorrow we want to spend the whole day exploring your beautiful city. We have to get some sleep now. Good night!"

"You'll need more than one day to see this wonderful city," said one of the men. "Or at least an excellent tour guide, which I happen to be able to put you in contact with."

Norbert hesitated, and the man continued, though he was now addressing Amanda.

"There is so much you need to see and know about Budapest and Hungary. Just don't take one of the official government guides! They will tell you lots of BS about the heroic Soviets coming to Hungary to save the people from the Nazis and from Western influence."

Amanda nodded, knowingly.   "Well, luck is on your side," the man said. "You have just run into Hungary's best tour guide—my friend, here, Janos." He tapped his friend on the shoulder, while telling Amanda that Janos knew everything there was to know, and could lead their tour in Hungarian, German, English, French, or Austrian, whichever she prefers.

"Wait a minute!" interrupted ~~Heidi~~ Amanda. "The Austrians speak German."

"*Ja*, but not the way Janos speaks it!"

They all had a good laugh. Then Norbert spoke up again.

"Where I come from, we speak the REAL German. *Ich bin ein Berliner!*"

"I know," said the Hungarian one who had been quiet until now. In English, he told Norbert that he was pretty sure he remembered him from Berlin-*Schöneberg* at the dedication of the Freedom Bell in 1950. "Berlin's Mayor and the American General Clay spoke, interpreted by a rather young man. If your name is 'Anleger,' then it was you who translated."

"Yes," answered Norbert. "How is it that you remember my name?"

"I was only a young school boy. When somebody announced your name, I thought that was a strange name to have. My father, a former embassy employee in Berlin who is German but was born in Hungary, thought so too. He speaks fluent German—'Anlegen' means a ship is anchoring, or a boat is mooring."

"That is what *anlegen* means, indeed. And I am impressed that you remember the Bell Dedication in Berlin."

"As a matter of fact, I was so impressed with how you could make us understand what General Clay had said in English, that I decided right there and then to become an interpreter."

He spread out both of his arms and said, "Voila! You are looking at this former school boy whose dream came true. Today I am a full-time professional interpreter and tour guide. And it would please me if you would choose me as your guide tomorrow. By the way, the tour is free for you and your lovely wife. No charge, okay?"

As promised, Janos was at the couple's hotel the next morning at nine sharp. He had brought along his German-speaking friend, two large baskets with sandwiches, juice, apples, a coffee thermos, and four mugs.

"I brought some picnic foods from home," he explained. "Eating on the run will save us valuable time—although we will have to stop for some Hungarian cake! Let's go! There is so much to see!"

The day was packed with sightseeing, adventure, historic information, and an endless number of stories and anecdotes from Janos which kept everyone mesmerized. They spent the bulk of the day on the Buda Castle Hill where they could walk in the courtyards, visit the museum and gallery inside, take a look at the Matthias Church, taste a Hungarian cake in Cafe *Ruszwurm*, and marvel at the Buda Castle and the Presidential Palace. The group had their picnic on the grass of the Castle Hill.

When Amanda and Norbert finally said goodbye to their new Hungarian friends, there was much hugging and even tears.

"Come and see us in Berlin!" said Norbert to them—and he meant it.

"How about you coming back to us soon, with more time for longer sightseeing tours?" Janos countered Norbert's offer.

After a romantic night overlooking the river reflecting a full moon, Amanda and Norbert had some trouble changing gears the next morning when they had to pack the Trabant and head toward the Austrian border. Their concern about the car's East German license plate causing trouble was lessoned when Janos suggested they use a border crossing known to seasoned travelers for accepting bribes in American dollars. Thanks to the helpful hint and Norbert's foresight to carry these, the crossing into Austria was a breeze.

Before sunset, Norbert and Amanda saw the beautiful silhouette of the City of Vienna. Amanda turned to Norbert.

"Being in Austria feels almost like being safely at home. For the first time in my life I can smell freedom from Soviet oppression in the air. Oh, Norbi, now we can start our skiing vacation!"

509

"Skiing in the city of Strauss and Mozart?" Norbert teased,

"No Norbi-Darling! After seeing the sites in Vienna, we will drive further west into Austria's gorgeous mountains."

"Yes, my Love, and together we will conquer one of Europe's highest mountains, the *Großglockner,* in the *Hohe Tauern."*

"Not so fast!" said Amanda. "It's been so long since I skied, I'm not about to tackle that 3,800-meter-high monster!"

"We will see when we get there!" said Norbert.

Vienna, "the dream city where nothing happens when nothing happens," as a 20th century writer put it, was a dream city also for Amanda and Norbert. Away from the hectic life of Berlin with its post-war hustle and bustle, Vienna felt like an over-grown, sleepy town—just what they had been looking for and what they needed.

"Have you ever been here before?" asked Norbert.

"Yes, I have. I was only twenty years old, so I guess it was 1960. Out of the blue, my singing instructor showed up at my door and said: *'Young Lady. You better start packing, because next week I will drive you to Vienna!'* I was so surprised that all I could say was, *'Vienna? What is in Vienna?'"*

"Well, of course you knew Vienna has a rich history in the music world," said Norbert.

"That's what Professor Streber said—rather harshly, I might add. He was never one to joke around, but his reputation in the opera singing world is still renown. I was very fortunate to have him as an instructor."

"Why did he insist you go to Vienna?"

"That is the amazing thing, Norbi. He actually thought well enough of me to give me the opportunity to perform at the *Staatsoper*. Vienna's famous Selma Rupert had taken ill and asked my teacher to find a replacement for the performance at the *Staatsoper*. I had sung in the Strauss operetta, *Die Fledermaus*, locally, so Professor Streber chose me to fill in."

Amanda looked at Norbert, hoping she was not boring him. "Well, to make a long story short, Professor Streber helped me get my travel documents, put me into his *Volga*, and off we went to Austria. The whole experience was just amazing. And, the next year, the Director of the Vienna Opera called me back to perform in Johann Strauss' *Der Zigeuner Baron*. So you see, Vienna is very, very special to me. It's where my international career started, really."

"You never told me about your Vienna connection," said Norbert, still surprised.

"That is the problem with us, darling. We never seem to have enough time for ourselves."

"Let's change that, from now on! For me, there is nothing more important and wonderful than being with you. You know what? I think we should spend the rest of our vacation days right here, simply enjoying being together."

"Norbi, that is the most wonderful suggestion you could have surprised me with. To be in Vienna, the capital of classical music, and to walk the streets of Mozart, Beethoven, Schubert and Strauss—" She pulled Norbert into her arms and began to sing and waltz to *The Blue Danube*.

Their days in Austria were filled with laughter, joy and love. Instead of traveling in Amanda's Trabant, they rented a bigger car which had no difficulty climbing steep mountain roads and high passes. They visited the town of Linz and skied in the *Salzkammergut.* From Innsbruck they could see the *Zugspitze*, the highest mountain in Germany. They stayed for two days in the famous health resort *Bad Aussee.* The fresh air in the mountains, the daily sun, and the vigorous ski excursions left them with the wonderful feeling of contented exhaustion.

They preferred to keep to themselves, but did meet another young couple on the ski lift who lived in Vienna and offered to show them around. Norbert politely declined, but did ask for their recommendation of the very best and most romantic restaurant in the area. That evening he took Amanda to the famous restaurant, known for its thick straw-thatched roof and fabulous food. "This is the perfect end of a perfect day," Amanda said.

"The evening is not quite over, my darling," Norbert said as he pushed back his chair and stood up. He knelt on the floor beside her and reached into his pocket. Guests at nearby tables stopped talking and stared at Amanda and her gallant, kneeling knight.

"Amanda Steinmetz, you are the love of my life! Will you marry me?" Norbert asked, extending his hand which held a ring that sparkled brilliantly in the romantic dining room candlelight. Amanda's expression revealed that she had not expected such a formal, wonderful, or any other form of proposal.

"Yes! Yes!" replied Amanda, her eyes filling with tears of joy. The guests broke into applause and called out congratulations. Even Herr Augsburger, the owner and chef of the restaurant, came over to congratulate them and told Norbert that there would be no charge for their meal. He also announced to all the guests that for this very special occasion, he would be bringing out his finest wine to serve, complements of the house.

"Speech! Speech!" shouted a few patrons, and Norbert stood to address the room.

"My name is Norbert Anleger. I am from Berlin, where I work as an interpreter. I could start bragging about some of my extraordinary clients, including the late President John Kennedy—however, my greatest achievement was convincing this lovely young lady, Amanda Steinmetz, to marry me."

The audience applauded, and some raised their glasses while others whispered, "Steinmetz? The opera singer?"

Then it was Amanda's turn to speak.

"I am Amanda. I am an opera singer, or as they call me in East Germany, a *Kultur-Schaffende*. I am from Berlin, too. When other girls of my age had boyfriends, I only paid attention to classical composers and their music. Now the time has come to give myself to this wonderful man, Norbert Anleger, to have and to hold, forever."

"Champagne for everyone!" Herr Augsburger shouted, as everyone applauded for Amanda and Norbert.

The following day was Norbert and Amanda's last day in Austria. They returned the rental car and drove the Trabant to the city office of motor vehicles, where they were able to change the registration to show Norbert as the owner, and to obtain an Austrian license plate to replace the East German one.

Originally they had intended for Amanda to fly from Munich to West Berlin. When they were told that no German citizens were allowed to fly commercially from West Germany to West Berlin, they booked Amanda's flight from Vienna to Berlin-Tempelhof. Once Amanda was in the air, Norbert would drive the Trabant via Munich and Hannover to Helmstedt, the crossing point to East Germany. Helmstedt was only 200 miles east of Berlin.

The next day began with an early departure time for Amanda. Norbert gave her sufficient West German Marks and told her to take a taxi from the Tempelhof Airport to the *Hermann Strasse* in *Neukölln*, where he lived.

"I might see you there late tonight, or more likely, tomorrow morning. And, Amanda-Darling, don't worry about a thing! I love you!"

"I love you, too, my darling husband-to-be," replied Amanda, fighting back tears as she boarded the plane.

A few hours later, an undercover KGB agent phoned Lieutenant Vassily Zhukovski, reporting that the *Republik-Flüchtige* (fugitive) Amanda Steinmetz had arrived at the Berlin-Tempelhof Airport and had taken a taxi.

"I have been successful in following the taxi to Neukölln, where she got out at Hermann Strasse 245. That is the five-story building where the West Berliner, Norbert Anleger, lives," the agent was pleased to report.

"Nice job, officer!" said Zhukovski. "I know all about Anleger, including his latest crime of helping Amanda Steinmetz flee to West Berlin. Thank you for your help. The case is closed for you. *Spasibo!*"

Chapter 48

Although he lived and worked in West Berlin, Norbert Anleger knew his way around most all of West Germany. His business had taken him to every corner of the newly formed Federal Republic of Germany, as well as to neighboring countries.

Once Amanda had left for Berlin, Norbert was anxious to catch up with her—an impossible goal, regardless of how fast he could drive. His first task was to drive from Vienna to Munich in the American Zone of West Germany.

As he was driving, Norbert questioned himself as to why he had changed the East German license plate into an Austrian plate. He should have waited until he was back in West Germany. Now he was driving a car built in East Germany, with an Austrian license, on the West German autobahn, intending to drive through the German Democratic Republic to eventually get to West Berlin! How much more complicated could he have made it for himself and for the dim-witted *Vopos* in the DDR?

He was making good time and was close to where he would have to face DDR border police and People's Police. When he reached the Helmstedt/Marienborn border crossing to East Germany, Norbert cleared the West German control very quickly. Then he approached the control point on the East German side, where many cars were lined up in front of him.

As Norbert was waiting to get closer to the customs shed, he noticed that the DDR Police used plenty of lights in the section where they checked out cars with non-East German license plates. After a ten-minute standstill, he became too impatient to just sit behind the wheel and got out of the Trabi.

Norbert stood, staring at the concrete wall. *This is what the damned communists have done to my country*, Norbert thought. *All around West Berlin they built this Death Strip with electric fences, patrols, floodlights and vehicle traps between the inner and outer walls, and they call this monstrous wall the 'Antifascist Protective Barrier'. Ha! It's a monstrosity in the formerly innocent landscape of rural Saxony-Anhalt. Now, barbed-wire, armed guards in towers, vicious dogs… families, friends and neighbors no longer dare to even wave to each other across the strip.*

"Hey, you there!" a border policeman barked at Norbert. "Get back into your car, you idiot! Now—or I will shoot!"

Norbert could not see the person yelling at him, but he was smart enough to obey the angered officer. The last thing he wanted was more delay getting through the checkpoint and home to Amanda. It took a good—or rather *bad*—full hour until his car reached the inspection shed.

"Are you German or Austrian?"

"I am German on the way back from a skiing vacation in Austria."

"Did you steal the Austrian license plate from somebody?"

"No, my friend gave me her car when we were in Vienna. To make the gift legal, the Austrian authorities issued me an owner's registration and gave me an Austrian license plate."

"Such a generous girlfriend," the guard sneered. "And where is your friend now?"

"She was so exhausted from skiing, we decided she should fly home. She lives in West Berlin, just like I do. Actually, she is my fiancée."

"Perhaps you exhausted her too much!" the guard said with a gruff laugh.

Norbert said nothing in reply.

"Open the trunk and all four doors!"

Norbert stepped out of the car, opened the doors and the trunk and started to climb back into his car—at least that was his intention. Two rough hands on each shoulder stopped him cold.

"Step back! Turn your face toward the wall!"

Norbert's fear of possible trouble at the East German border was proven justified sooner than he had expected. He turned toward the guard as he wanted to explain his unusual situation.

"I told you, stay where you are!"

In the meantime two Soviet soldiers joined the DDR policeman, asking the agitated East German questions about the traveler he was having a problem with.

"Do you speak Russian?" a soldier asked Norbert.

"Just so-so," he replied in Russian.

Hoping that Norbert would understand more than he admitted, they asked him a barrage of questions about the car's registration, the license plate, the skis on top of the car, the luggage inside the car, and about his missing fiancée. Norbert noticed that it was easier to deal with the Russian soldiers than with the angry East German customs official. Suddenly the East German excused himself, saying he had to make a phone call in his office. Norbert quickly handed each Russian ten American dollars. They nodded silently and pocketed the money.

When the East German came back, he began to report to the soldiers.

"I have just spoken to my Lieutenant. He said—"

"Stop! Stop, Tovarish," one Russian interrupted. "Everything is okay with this man and his car. Let him go through."

The guard became even more red in the face but said nothing, knowing he was outranked.

Norbert cautiously got back into the car and rolled slowly out of the danger zone. He had bribed Eastern European officials before, but this was one of the most drastic mood changes he had ever bought with twenty dollars.

After crossing the Elbe River near Magdeburg, Norbert hit another control point. This time the two officials were interested in Norbert's passport only. They also asked why he had two pairs of skis on top of his car, since he was the only traveler.

"Two are better than one," Norbert answered, "especially when you are not good at skiing. You never know—just in case!"

One of the East Germans was especially keen to see the skis. In a hushed voice, he asked Norbert, "Now that you are on the way home without broken skis, would you sell me one pair?"

"Yes, I would," Norbert quickly replied. "How much would you give me?"

"One hundred marks."

"What? These skis cost me more than 400 West Marks."

"I have only East Marks," the customs agent answered.

"Okay! It is a special price for you. Give me 300 East Marks and unlock the ski pair on the left. But do it quickly! I am in a hurry."

In few minutes Norbert was on his way again, now with only one pair of skis on the car roof. Shortly before the town of Brandenburg, Norbert pulled his car to the side of the autobahn. In the dark of night, he could see a farm house not too far off the road which was dimly lit. Carefully, he drove off the autobahn and up the short muddy road to the house. In front of the house he noticed the German sign, *Post.* He was in luck. Post offices, even in East Germany, had telephone connections. A man with gray hair quickly answered the door after Norbert knocked.

"Was ist los?"

"I am sorry for disturbing you so late. I need to make a few urgent phone calls."

The man invited him in after Norbert showed him his ID card.

"I don't have a calling card," said Norbert. "I will pay with cash, in West Marks."

"*Das ist gut, sehr gut!*" the man said, nodding and smiling.

At first Norbert called his own number at the apartment in Neukölln. No ring! Then he remembered that he had put his phone on "Vacation Hold," which meant no phone calls would come through. Then he dialed his company. Thanks to the helpful postmaster, Norbert could make a quick connection. At two Centers, he reached only the answering machine. At the third Center, a human voice answered: "Who is calling so late?"

"You really could answer a bit more politely!' admonished Norbert. "It is me, your boss, Norbert Anleger. I am calling you from a post office in Brandenburg."

"What are you doing in—?"

"Listen to me, Franz. No time for questions. Please do me a big favor and drive to my apartment, where Amanda Steinmetz has arrived today. You know the address. Incidentally, she is my fiancée since a few days ago."

"Oh! But what are—?"

"Tell her that I phoned from Brandenburg," Norbert interrupted. "And that I will see her tomorrow morning if everything goes well. Explain I cannot call her because when

I left, I put the phone on Vacation Hold. You will have to give her the message in person. Talk to you later! Bye!"

Then Norbert paid the postmaster in West Marks and pulled out an extra American twenty-dollar bill, as a gift. The man could barely speak as he called out his thanks to Norbert, who was already out the door and climbing into the Trabant.

Now Norbert had only one more East German control point to clear before reaching West Berlin. He could almost smell the famous *Berliner Luft* (air). With some luck, he could make it to his apartment in less than two hours. Hopefully Amanda would be waiting there for him.

Life as fiancés—and soon husband and wife—could begin.

The only thing bothering Norbert were the headlights behind his car. They had followed him the moment he had left the post office in Brandenburg and reentered the autobahn. Then he could make out two more lights. Two cars were now behind him, keeping the same speed with his car!

Norbert gently pushed the Trabi a little faster, seeing in his rear-view mirror that the cars behind him did the same. Then he drove still faster. He tried to dismiss the thought that the cars behind him might be police cars. Perhaps the drivers behind him were happy they had found a car to follow that dared to ignore the silly speed limit of 100 km/h.

All that changed when Norbert's car reached the intersection where the road proceeded either north to the West Berliner *Glienecke* Bridge (leading to Wannsee), or south to Potsdam in East Germany. Suddenly there was a burst of lights in red and blue and piercing white searchlights from all directions. For a second Norbert thought of out-racing his pursuers. Then he saw that there were just as many bright lights beside the autobahn as ahead of him. He managed to come to a quick stop, and two Russian soldiers quickly posted themselves close to his bumper, leveling their automatic weapons at him.

So close to West Berlin, and now this?

The two Russian soldiers made him get out of the car. While one pushed the barrel of his gun into Norbert's chest, the other quickly rummaged through the luggage items in the car. Even though Amanda had taken two large suitcases on the plane, that still left many smaller suitcases, bags, and boxes in the car.

The soldiers demanded he give them his papers, then called for their commanding officer to come. When he showed up, he was accompanied by an East German border police sergeant. The latter took over the interrogation.

"Let me see! What have we here?" he asked with a voice of mockery and self-importance.

"You live in West Berlin. You have three business centers in three districts of Berlin. The public thinks of you as an interpreter, because you have translated speeches for many important foreigners who are enemies of both the Soviet Union and our German Democratic Republic."

Norbert said nothing, but looked directly at the officer's face which was both squinting and smiling at the same time.

"Are you not surprised how much we know about you? Let me continue the list of your crimes! You have forged hundreds of documents to help Eastern Block and Warsaw Pact members get to the West—and I don't mean for vacation!

"Your so-called skiing vacation started out in the company of one of our famous opera singers, Amanda Steinmetz, who is missing since this morning. Where might she be? Did you help her flee, or did you kill her when she refused your insistence that she defect?

"And then there is what just came today over the teletype! You manipulated the ownership of Miss Steinmetz's car by forging her registration documents. Just a few hours ago, you bribed two Soviet soldiers with American dollars. In Brandenburg, you left the autobahn illegally to make phone calls to West Berlin."

The sergeant looked up in disgust.

"Look here! The list goes on and on, even mentioning that a few years ago you were arrested twice for anti-Soviet and anti-DDR activities."

"But your authorities always cleared me of any wrongdoings," Norbert said. "Even the high-ranking Commander of Soviet Troops in East Berlin, Major General Andrey Molotov, declared me innocent."

"I don't care who you have deceived! You are a miserable, capitalistic *Unterhändler* of the lowest kind. You think of yourself as an innocent man? Less than half an hour ago you broke the law by driving 165 in our 100 km/h zone. If it were up to me, I would put you away for life."

By now Norbert knew that this fanatic DDR Officer was out to nail him for good. He decided right then to keep his mouth shut, and also to keep his eyes open for a possible chance to escape. For the next few minutes, the DDR Officer consulted in Russian with the Soviet Officer.

"*Charasho*," the Russian said, "let's move this criminal to the police station at the *Schönefeld* Airport. There we have a legal court and a prison, if we need one or both."

Norbert understood enough Russian to be prompted into action. In his mind, he imagined the route they would take to get to the *Schönefeld* airport, which was located very close to the Berlin Wall, south of Berlin. He realized that traveling from Potsdam via *Teltow* and *Mahlow* to get to the Airport would give him no chance to escape. The autobahn stretch they would drive was too far from the West Berlin border. Besides, trying to flee on foot and unarmed would be suicide.

While Norbert was going through the agony of being insulted, arrested, and hand-cuffed on an autobahn in East Germany, his new fiancée woke up in freedom, yet feeling sad and a little worried that Norbert had not yet made it home. On the other hand, Amanda knew about the probability of checkpoint delays, and the often-heavy traffic in West Germany, especially on the autobahn leading to Berlin.

Then her doorbell rang. It was Franz, who apologized for not showing up sooner.

"Somehow I messed up your address. I am here to tell you that Norbert phoned last night from a post office in Brandenburg. He said he hoped to be here soon. Is he?"

"Is he what?" asked Amanda.

"Has Mr. Anleger come home?"

"Not yet! I wish he had. Perhaps my car broke down, or he might have pulled off the road somewhere for a nap."

"I am sure that he is okay. He always knows what to do. He wanted you to know that you cannot receive any phone calls here because the number is temporarily on vacation hold. By the way, congratulations on your engagement! Looking at you, I can only repeat that he always knows what to do."

"Thank you for the nice compliment, I think! And for your congratulations!"

Then Amanda was alone again. She had breakfast—and waited. She started reading a book from Norbert's shelf, played her favorite classical music—and waited. She studied the score of a new opera—and she waited.

Amanda told herself to remain calm. When the grandfather clock chimed four times, she noticed that she had forgotten to eat a noon meal. Well, she could make up for it now. But she discovered that the breadbox was empty and the pantry was rather barren since the apartment had stood empty for weeks. If she left to walk to a store and buy food, she might miss Norbert's return. *Why is he not here yet? Has he been in an accident?*

The clock moved up to six and then seven. It was dark outside and Amanda was having a hard time trying not to panic. She rested on the couch, closing her eyes and hoping she could nap to pass the time, but she was too worried and too cold. She found some firewood and used it in the wood stove to heat the apartment. Norbert would appreciate stepping into a warm home on this cold winter night in January. Amanda tried her best to think of the happy reunion they would soon have, and of other happy times from their vacation. Had they stayed in Austria longer, they now would have been drinking hot cider, hot chocolate, or some stronger drink to keep warm.

Walking around in the apartment, she found a brochure advertising the 1964 Winter Olympics to be held in Innsbruck, Austria, January 24 to February 9. Norbert must have been thinking of attending the Olympics before they decided on having their skiing vacation, which eventually had brought her here to his apartment in West Berlin. She would not have been free to travel with Norbert to the Olympics in late January anyway, because of her opera commitments.

Opera commitments? Suddenly it struck her that her employment with the Opera in Berlin was over—forever over! Even the communist Eastern part of the world would be taboo for her for many years to come. She would have to look around for a singing or acting position in West Berlin, West Germany, or in other Western countries. *In the FREE world*, she reminded herself.

Norbert's handcuffs cut into his wrists like cold, sharp steel. With his sleeve, he wiped clear a spot on the military car window where he sat in the back seat, his breath in the freezing car fogging the glass. He looked out, wondering what might have happened to his Trabant he had to abandon back on the autobahn. The tightly-packed suitcases and packages were full of Amanda's belongings. Would the Soviet and East German thugs be willing to give back the *Trabi* and its contents?

The car door opened.

"Dawai, dawai! Get out of the car!"

Hindered by his cuffed hands, Norbert eventually managed to obey the command.

"Stand here and wait!" a Russian soldier ordered.

Standing outside in the cold wind, Norbert asked, "What are we waiting for?" The only answer he got was a heavy-handed push into an electric cart. He was driven to a massive building with a huge Russian sign above the entrance door: "Court House." Inside, it was unbearably hot, but it was just the right temperature for the freezing man from West Berlin. Then even Norbert's feet were cuffed, which made him walk like a drunk.

Norbert was led into a large courtroom, where a uniformed judge waited for him. In the most casual manner, the judge asked both the Soviet and the German officers who had accompanied Norbert into the courtroom to present their case. Norbert looked around but saw no lawyer nor any other legal personnel, except for an elderly stenographer.

The entire process of having Norbert's case introduced, the charges examined, and the judgment pronounced took less than fifteen minutes. Norbert was required to speak Russian during his allotted two minutes to defend himself, and he stumbled through his proclaim of innocence as best he could. Norbert's sentence was four years of imprisonment at the *Uranium Ore Prison in Aue*, near Zwickau in DDR's *Erzgebirge*.

When Norbert heard his sentence, he did not blink one eye. He had promised himself to show no reaction. He had succeeded, to the amazement of the few people in the courtroom. Some thought that perhaps he had not understood the sentence. Norbert had understood the judge's pronouncement, even though his mind was far from accepting it. To Norbert, this rush-through kangaroo court was a big farce, and had the mark of dishonesty and incompetence just like everything else in the DDR.

Before Norbert was led out of the courtroom, one of the guards removed the shackles from his legs, but not his handcuffs. Only one soldier remained with Norbert as they walked over to the airport terminal which was part of the same building. He signaled for Norbert to sit down and wait. Norbert, however, pretended not to understand any Russian.

"Sit, sit, Tovarish!" the guard ordered. When Norbert did not move, ignoring him completely, he snorted loudly, "Okay, then keep standing, you idiot!"

Both men did not speak for about twenty minutes. Just when the Russian was rolling a cigarette made from fag-ends, a loudspeaker announced that the flight from Schönefeld to Karl-Marx-Stadt would be delayed by three hours.

"Is that where we are going?" Norbert asked the soldier in German. No answer!

"Hey, Ivan!" Norbert tried again. "Can I make a phone call to my fiancée?"

"Njet! Nein!"

Norbert finally sat down, and not a word was spoken for another hour.

"I have to go to the toilette!" Norbert said in German. Again, no response! Norbert stood up and stamped his feet.

"Hey, Ruskie! Ich muß scheissen! Understood? I have to shit!" said Norbert, using a vulgar Russian expression.

The Russian's answer was one English word he must have picked up somewhere:

"*Shit-bag!*"

Norbert nodded, stomping with his feet even harder and louder.

"*Gde?*" ("Where?") asked Norbert in Russian.

"*Na levo!*" ("To the left.") came the laconic answer.

Norbert showed the soldier his handcuffs, hoping he would remove them.

"Njet!"

Okay, thought Norbert. *the cuffs stay, but I go!* Norbert, who knew many airports like the back of his hand, unfortunately had never been at this East German *Schönefeld* airport. He saw no toilette signs. Several doors he tried to open were either locked or led to other rooms with locked doors.

The window of time for escape was very small. He knew he had to get away now during this one moment he was not being guarded. Suddenly he felt a blast of freezing cold air on his face as one door he pushed on opened up to the outside. He instantly changed his grimace to a smile of relief and hope. *This is the air of freedom!* he thought.

Norbert faced a large courtyard with trucks, carts, and other airport paraphernalia. He ran to the edge of the open yard. When he still saw nobody, he kept on running to a group of pine trees that formed a thick curtain. He would hide there!

But why stay here and wait until the airport police and their dogs come? So he kept on running. Even though Norbert had not been here before, he knew the small town of Schönefeld, and east from here Berlin's even smaller suburb *Bohnsdorf*. Would the people in those East German towns help him? And how would he cross the wide death strip?

I wish I could get rid of these handcuffs, he thought as he noticed his wrists were bleeding. As he was struggling to get further north, he encouraged himself with the German saying he often used to encourage his own employees: *Where there is a will, there is a way.*

He saw no way around the runway ahead. He would have to race across it as fast as he could, though without the use of his arms he found it hard to keep his balance. After only a few strides, an ear-blasting siren stopped him in his tracks. They had detected him! Within seconds there were Jeeps and fast-moving vehicles all over the airfield.

Norbert threw himself to the ground. He was convinced that if the sloppy Russians did not shoot him, the over-anxious German police and their dogs would chase him down. In no time Norbert was surrounded by yelling policemen, barking dogs, and scowling Russian soldiers.

His flight to freedom was over, but the airplane flight to *Karl-Marx-Stadt* was still on. First, however, with no civilians around, four men took the opportunity to kick Norbert with their boots as he lay on the ground. When one jerked him up to stand, the others pummeled his mid-section as he tried to shield himself with his cuffed hands. If anyone did happen to witness this, they would know to never accuse the police or Russian soldiers of brutality.

With a bruised and bloody passenger on board, the small plane destined for Schönefeld left three hours later than scheduled and landed in *Karl-Marx-Stadt*, formerly *Chemnitz*. When the plane landed, two camouflaged Jeeps left immediately for the infamous labor camp in *Aue*, which was reserved for serious criminals or dangerous enemies of the DDR. Norbert Anleger was about to begin his four-year sentence.

Chapter 49

Early reports, out all over the German Democratic Republic press, broadcast the breaking news that the famous opera singer, Amanda Steinmetz, had been kidnapped by ruthless West Berliner thugs who had dragged her through several Eastern European countries before making her disappear in the West. People in West Berlin and West Germany knew, or suspected, the truth: Amanda had fled to the West with the help of her fiancé, a citizen of West Berlin. But later the same day, the news broke that Miss Steinmetz's fiancé, Norbert Anleger, was actually the one who had been kidnapped, arrested, and taken to an unknown location in the DDR.

More than one week had passed since Amanda opened the door to Norbert's apartment in Berlin-Neukölln, where she had expected to be joined by him within hours. Instead, she had one visitor the next morning delivering the one and only message she had received from Norbert. Franz, an employee of Norbert's, had told her two pieces of disturbing news: the apartment telephone was not in service, and Norbert had been on track to arrive the night before. Why was there this frightening silence now?

Amanda contacted Franz to ask if he'd had any word. Then she contacted the West Berlin police. She had even contacted several East German police agencies. The result from Western sources always was the same: Norbert Anleger, driving an East German Trabant with an Austrian license plate, was last seen by a postmaster at a post office in Brandenburg, in the DDR. No further information was available.

Amanda knew she would go crazy if she continued to stay in the lonesome apartment and let her mind worry the same dreadful thoughts all day, every day. She knew almost nothing about the area, but felt drawn to take a taxi to Wertheim's Department Store, where Norbert's sister once had been a manager. Even though Heidi was not there, talking with the clerk who knew her was of some comfort to Amanda who felt desperately disconnected from everything and everyone she knew. With the help of Norbert's neighbors, she found a grocery store which was well-stocked with Western food items, though she (as a former East Berliner) was not familiar with many of them.

One sleepless night, she decided that the next day she would go to the nearest office of Norbert's company. She wanted to introduce herself as both Norbert's fiancée and as a new West Berlin citizen. Franz offered to give her a tour of the Center. She caught herself staring at a telephone which sat on a secretary's desk, willing it to ring and to be a call from the secretary's boss, her darling Norbert. At the end of the tour, Franz sensed that Amanda was more than a little distressed about Norbert's disappearance. He assured her that, at least, the company was so well organized and well-staffed, it was operating well enough in spite of Norbert's absence, though of course they were all terribly anxious for his return. Then, an idea occurred to him which would be helpful to everyone involved.

"I'm sure you are terribly busy, Miss Steinmetz," Franz said. "but could you possibly find any time to come and assist here at the Center? With Mr. Anleger away, we are swamped with work to be done."

It took Amanda only a few days to understand the nature of Norbert's business and to take on jobs which normally Norbert would have tackled.

As the days turned into weeks and the weeks into months, there was still no word from Norbert. Amanda took the initiative to visit the other two Centers, and even managed to give them a little pep talk to keep their spirits up in the absence of their leader, who had always provided the recognition and motivation the workers needed.

Even though Amanda still felt horribly alone, she got some satisfaction from her work as she seemed to have a knack for business and making things work smoothly. One day, the managers of Norbert's three Centers got together and voted to officially employ Amanda and make her the interim Director of the Interpretation and Translation Centers, with salary! Until then, Amanda had worked as a volunteer, without pay or title.

Even though Amanda had received job offers from operas and theaters in West Germany and beyond, she declined them all. She had come to West Berlin to be with Norbert and to live in freedom. The least she could do now, without him, was to continue his work, which he had loved so much.

At an office party, one manager casually mentioned that he had read somewhere that Amanda had studied acting under the world-famous Max Reinhardt, and singing under equally preeminent teachers.

"So why are you now spending your days with us *regular Joes* translating other people's speeches and legal documents?"

"I can see your point, and I could give you a long and complex answer. But, it really boils down to the fact that I am doing what I can for my beloved fiancé, which right now is to maintain and grow his business. When he returns, we will get married and then I will do what I can for him as his wife."

A secretary who had heard the conversation remarked to her colleague: "Miss Steinmetz shoots straight from the hip, just as Mr. Anleger used to do. I really like her as my new boss!"

For Norbert, the relentless and grueling labor in the uranium mine was easier to take than the lack of freedom. All his fellow prisoners were Germans, some from the West and some from the East. Except for the *Gefängnis* warden, who was Russian, all other prison personnel were German. That made life even less tolerable for Norbert. If foreigners such as the Soviets from Central Asia were pushing him around, inflicting punishments and depriving him of sleep and food for several days, he would have to bear it. But to be degraded, shamed, and mistreated on a daily basis by other Germans was harder for him to swallow.

To the prison guards, he was "A-1478-64." The "64" indicated the year he had been admitted; "A" was the designation for "Political Prisoner." The guards usually did not know or care about the names of the convicts, addressing them only with a sharp "Hey!" or by their number. Most prisoners were too exhausted at the end of long work days to carry on conversations with each other. To add to the isolation, they had no access to newspapers or radios. The guards even punished anyone who scribbled calendar markings on their cell wall. They literally were cut off from civilization, lost in space and time.

Rumor had it that during the Nazi regime, the *Aue* prison had been operated as a concentration camp with about 110,000 inmates, of whom about 20,000 had died and were buried in unmarked mass graves. When Germany capitulated in 1945, the Soviet conquerors quickly moved in and converted the concentration camp into a prison hell for former Nazi members and enemies of the new communist government.

Norbert had never been a Nazi, and his hatred for communist rule had grown each time he had lost family members or friends to senseless deaths. Even now, when it would have been wise to work willingly and keep his mouth shut, Norbert became known as an agitator who liked to criticize and defame the glorious DDR. Prison officials, for example, knew that Norbert mockingly called the town of *Wandlitz* where the DDR party bosses enjoyed a luxurious life, *Bonzograd* (Big-Wig-Grad). But Norbert used his anger and small retaliations to fuel his will to survive. He never let himself think he would actually have to stay in this hell for four years.

Norbert was not permitted to receive any mail. Once, during the evening meal, Norbert asked a guard whether he could write to somebody. A nasty laugh was the response, and he was kicked out of the dining hall.

With Franz' help, Amanda finally got the telephone service restored, even though it was still in Norbert's name and not hers. This gave her a sense of freedom she hadn't even realized had been sorely missing. Today she was off work and in the mood to write a letter and/or call someone, just to reach out, not to share any news since there was none of importance. Whom should she call? Whom should she write? Her parents, who still lived in East Germany, must have read in their newspapers that their daughter had been kidnapped by West German thugs and was now missing. Amanda had already written them a letter, but assumed it was almost certainly intercepted and confiscated, preventing them from knowing the truth.

I will write to Heidi and Fred in the US, she thought. *They need to know that Norbert is still missing, but that I am holding down the fort as best as I can.*

In previous letters, Amanda had written to Heidi about her engagement to Norbert, and about their wonderful skiing vacation in Austria. She hated to again have to write that there was absolutely no news of Norbert, or clues from any agency. She hoped Heidi would write a letter in reply soon, just because it felt so good to hear from someone who loved Norbert, too. Heidi and Fred both had told Amanda that they were praying for Norbert, and that they had faith he would return alive, one day soon.

On a windy, cool September morning, there was a rap at the door of the downtown Center for Interpretation. Amanda, who shared her office hours between Norbert's three Centers, looked out to the street entrance and saw a man with a faded red blanket wrapped over his shoulders. Thinking it was a beggar, she handed one of the young office workers two German Marks, which he was to give to the man.

From the office window Amanda saw how the man refused the gift. She could not hear what he was saying, but it seemed he was pleading to be let inside. To clear up the situation, she hastened to the door. There she heard the stranger protest:

"No, I will not accept your money! Tell the manager that I have news about the boss of the Center!"

Amanda rushed over to the shivering man and pulled him inside. Once they were in her office, the scrawny, emaciated-looking man looked at Amanda and asked meekly, "Are you Miss Steinmetz?"

"Yes, my name is Amanda Steinmetz. I am the acting Director of this Center."

"Fräulein," the stranger said, as tears ran down his cheeks. "I have good news for you. Norbert Anleger is alive!" Then his voice broke. Amanda stared at the blanket-wrapped man.

"Please sit down and tell me more!" Amanda said as she motioned for her assistant to bring some hot coffee.

Emil Schiller began to tell Amanda about the *Aue* Prison Camp, and that he had befriended Norbert there. Schiller had endured eight years of hard labor, and said that both he and Norbert had helped each other cling to the hope of a miracle to be set free.

"My day of freedom came one week ago, when *Vopos* brought me from *Aue* to the border of West Berlin, gave me ten East German Marks and said, 'Take the *S-Bahn* to the Mariendorfer Station. Ask the people how to get to the

Marienfelder Refugee Center. Everybody there knows where it is.' I did take the *S-Bahn*, but not to the Mariendorfer Station. I came here."

"Norbert surely would tell you to come here," said Amanda. "Oh, Emil, we are glad you made it, but please tell me when in the world Norbert can come, too! Is he only a few days behind you?"

Then Emil Schiller proceeded to tell Amanda about Norbert, how he had been arrested near Brandenburg, how the police had taken everything from him including Amanda's car, and that he had been sentenced to four years in the Uranium hell of *Aue.*

"But what had Norbert done to get such a severe sentence?" Amanda cried out.

"Miss Steinmetz! Your fiancé is innocent except for driving too fast on the autobahn in East Germany. Please believe me! I was innocent, too. They used my frequent negative remarks at work about the DDR regime to arrest me and slowly kill me in that Uranium hell. But as you see, I am still alive!"

Now it was Amanda who could not hold back her tears. She slumped to the floor and sat beside Emil's chair, sobbing. "My poor Darling-Norbert!"

Chapter 50

When Amanda walked into the Center, she noticed her coworkers acting rather strangely and whispering behind her back. "Amanda, you better go directly to your desk. You have mail waiting for you," said the manager.

When Amanda looked at mail on her desk, she noticed a letter with East German stamps first. Reading the incomplete address of the sender, *Aue Prison Camp,* she quickly closed her office door. Then she tore open the envelope.

Dearest Amanda! I have been allowed to send you this short note from the prison camp in Aue, even though I do not know where you might be. Rumors put you in different places. Hoping this letter will reach you, I am sending it to my office—or what used to be my office.

All I am permitted to write is that I am "alive and well." I hope to be released in ####

The rest of the letter was blackened out by dark ink, until the signature: *Always, your Norbi.*

Amanda had to put down the letter, which by now showed many tear stains. *Norbi is alive!*

He was incarcerated in *Aue,* geographically not too far from her, yet an impossible distance of injustice…she knew he would be allowed no visitors. Until Emil Schiller had reported to her where Norbert had been imprisoned, she had struggled to hold out hope that he was alive. She knew in her bones that he would have contacted her if at all possible, that he must be in jail or dead. Now she had the most reliable proof that he was alive in *Aue*, East Germany, somewhere close to the Czech border.

The next piece of mail which caught her eye was from London and was addressed:

Herrn Norbert Anleger, Esquire
Interpretation & Translation Centre
West Berlin – Mitte
FRG – Germany

Dear Sir:

It gives me great pleasure, Sir, to inquire on behalf of Her Majesty the Queen Elizabeth II, whether your translation and interpreting services would be available on May 27, 1965, when Queen Elizabeth and her husband, Prince Philip, will be visiting Berlin.

You come highly recommended as a most proficient interpreter and, if need be, a very knowledgeable Berlin guide.

His Worship, the Mayor of West Berlin, Willi Brandt, will also be in the visiting and touring party.

Her Majesty's visit to Berlin will end with a Grand Ball Reception at the Charlottenburg Schloss the same evening.

The Royal House is looking forward to a positive reply at your earliest convenience.

Thank you for giving your speedy attention to this matter.

Amanda sat down in her desk chair, still holding the heavy-paper letter in her trembling hand. All at once she felt relieved and yet heartsick over Norbert's letter, and then excited and and yet angry about the extraordinary letter from England. She was thrilled that Queen Elizabeth must have heard of Norbert's exemplary service to international dignitaries in the past, but what was to be done now? It was horribly unfair he wasn't there, right then, to read and reply to this amazing opportunity.

She quickly called for a meeting of her three Center Managers. They all agreed that this was a difficult situation. There was no way that they would decline an invitation coming from such an esteemed person of worldwide fame.

"One of you will have to be the Queen's interpreter," said Amanda. "Since you three are all experienced and excellent interpreters, we probably should cast a lot to determine who will serve."

For a brief moment the managers looked at each other. Then the senior manager spoke.

"Thank you, Miss Steinmetz, for your confidence! I think I am speaking for the three of us, when I suggest that you should take Mister Anleger's place."

"Me? But I am not a professional interpreter," protested Amanda with genuine humility.

"Don't even say so!" another manager said. "You would be Mister Anleger's choice, we believe. You run the company with so much competence and poise, attributes essential to this opportunity. We all have heard you translate skillfully in English, Russian and —"

"Enough," interrupted Amanda. "If you really think that I am up to it, I will write to the Queen and ask for her permission to take Norbert's place."

A few hours later Amanda's letter was ready to be mailed to Queen Elizabeth II, informing her about Norbert's political imprisonment in East Germany, and her willingness to fill in for her fiancé.

Amanda returned to her duties, more often recalling to mind the handwritten note from Norbert than the letter on royal stationary. In less than one week, she received a telegraphed message that simply told her the time and place she would be picked up to be taken to meet the Queen's delegation in Berlin. After putting it on her calendar, Amanda stayed so busy with work at the Centers that she found no time to properly prepare herself for the illustrious visitor from England, or even to shop for a new outfit.

May 27, 1965, was to become "another unforgettable day for all West Berliners," as a Western newspaper called it. A black Mercedes government limo picked up Amanda in the late morning and took her to the Kempinski Hotel, Berlin's flagship hotel. She was escorted to a private meeting room where Mayor Willi Brandt greeted her.

"Come, Miss Steinmetz, let me introduce you to Queen Elizabeth II and Prince Philip," said Brandt, as if this was the most normal thing to do. Walking up to the royal couple, Amanda regretted that she had not dressed a bit more sophisticated for the occasion. But when the British Monarch greeted her semi-formally and Prince Philip even reached for her hand with a big smile, Amanda decided to be herself instead of being star-struck.

Brandt, to Amanda's relief, briefed her on the Queen's requests and itinerary and told her he would be available to her during the entire visit should she have any questions. The Queen had indicated that among the noteworthy sites she wanted to be taken to, the *Schöneberg Rathaus,* definitely should be included. This was where, two years earlier, President Kennedy had proclaimed, *"Ich bin ein Berliner."*

A large crowd gathered in front of the *Rathaus.* The excited Berliners cheered the Queen with shouts in English and German. Queen Elizabeth won the hearts of the Berliners with her short speech, which ended with the following words:

"Much of what I see in Berlin is of very personal interest for me, remembrances of earlier generations of my family. My soldiers live in Berlin today as your friends and protectors. God bless you all!" Translating Amanda's voice matched that of the Queen, both in tone and strength.

During the following sightseeing tour of Berlin, Mayor Brandt graciously stepped back and let Amanda give most of the explanations of Berlin's most interesting places.

The Grand Ball Reception in the evening at the *Charlottenburg Schloss* was an outstanding success. The City of Berlin had decorated the Queen's table with 800 roses and 700 carnations. The menu was the Queen's favorite: Helgoland Lobster Cocktail with Asparagus Tips, among other special dishes. The dessert was the typical Berliner "Lemon Parfait Berolina."

To Amanda's surprise, as the evening meal came to an end, Prince Philip lightly tapped her shoulder. "I just found out that you have not always been an interpreter, but rather an opera singer," he said very softly. Amanda could guess what was coming!

"The Queen and I love the music of operas and operettas. If it is not asking too much, would you mind honoring the Queen and the reception guests with a song?"

And so, at the Queen's Grand Ball Reception, Amanda delighted the entire international audience with her brilliant voice. Even Her Majesty the Queen told Amanda so, as they said goodbye to each other.

Riding in the elegant limousine back to Norbert's apartment where she was still living, she was suddenly overcome with grief. *No doubt, today has been an unforgettable day for me. Still, I feel guilty about it, because it was not intended for me but rather for you, Norbert. You should have been here. You would have done a better job. While I was in the illustrious company of Queen Elizabeth and Prince Philip with the best food I have eaten in years, you, my darling, had to slave in a Uranium mine, feeling forgotten, starving and exhausted. I cannot bear this any longer. You would not even be in trouble if you had not been trying to help an East-Berliner—me!*

Chapter 51

Though physically spent at day's end, Norbert almost never slept well at night. In the stillness, his mind had free rein to race with self-reflection and analysis. Occasionally he just lay awake, while his entire life seemed to roll by like a film. but without an ending.

For more than 30 years Norbert's life had been filled with many surprises—good and bad. When he was seven years old, World War II had started, which was a thrill to most young German boys. By the time the cruel war had ended in Europe in May of 1945, it had robbed him of his three brothers and his mother. Then he learned that his father had died in a German concentration camp. Only his sister Heidi had made it through the war alive, having somehow survived traumatic experiences.

For several years after the war, both Soviet military and East German police had hunted him for reasons that were never clear to him. Somehow, he always escaped their snares. When Norbert was sixteen, the Soviet Blockade had greatly affected him and all people living in West Berlin where he resided. Suddenly West Berlin was without food, water, and electricity. The store shelves were empty. Young children went to school hungry, and went to bed at night very cold and still hungry—if they had the luxury of sleeping in a bed.

Thank God for the Western Allied troops who, under American leadership, supplied the more than two million West Berliners with food, coal, and other necessities for life! Their planes, boats and trucks transported the precious cargo to distribution centers and stores, where Berliners, always forming long lines, could buy what they needed to survive if they had sufficient ration cards. During the Berlin Airlift, which lasted from June, 1948 to September, 1949, Norbert, along with thousands of other Germans was fortunate to work for the Americans, whom they called "Amis".

To discover that his sister Heidi, the last member of his immediate family, had survived the war, was one of the most beautiful surprises for Norbert. Then, he was surprisingly fortunate enough to be able to make his part-time interpreter job for the US Air Force and the West Berlin government into the full-time profession of his life.

The last life-changing surprise he could remember as he lay in his dark prison cell was falling in love with the gorgeous half-Russian, half-German Amanda Steinmetz, a famous opera singer who had become his fiancée. He had helped her escape from East Berlin.

Then luck had turned against him and he landed in this miserable Uranium hell in East Germany, where the world seemed to have forgotten him. Once he had been thrown into *Aue* Prison in 1964, there had been no more pleasant surprises, just daily bone-crushing work. The shocking thing was that he was never fed properly and no prisoner had medical care even when their situation was dire. Given the abysmal conditions, it was not surprising that absolutely no communication with the world outside was permitted.

When Norbert was finally allowed one time to write to anybody in East or West Germany, it came as a real surprise. Even though he knew that he was not permitted to get a reply, he could always hope that his letter to Amanda had reached her at the Interpretation Center. Norbert's other hope was that his buddy Emil Schiller had been able to find Amanda in Berlin and tell her where he was. Amanda needed to know! Everyone needed to know what was going on in *Aue*, but he knew that would come later, much later.

Another grueling year went by and Norbert again was allowed to write one letter. Again, he sent it to Amanda in care of the main office of his company, but it had been returned, unopened, stamped "Addressee Unknown."

In 1967, the *Aue* Prison published a four-page News Bulletin, "*Current Events You Need to Know About.*" Any unbiased reader would have called it "trashy, useless, communist propaganda." But to Norbert it was at least something in print, regardless whether worthy or unworthy to be read.

He read that a total of 17,000 "invading" American soldiers had been killed in Vietnam since 1961 by the victorious Vietnam defenders, with the help of their brave Chinese allies.

Norbert also read the surprising news that Stalin's forty-three year old daughter, Svetlana Aliluyeva, had defected to the monopoly capitalism of the United States, stabbing her motherland Russia in the back.

"My, my! What a distortion of facts and history!" Norbert said, ready to throw the bulletin into a waste basket, when he heard a sharp knock at the door. One of the prison guards entered and, without looking at Norbert, shouted:

"Prisoner A147864! Follow me!"

What was going on? Norbert was not aware of any wrongdoing or rebellious behavior on his part. Silently, he followed the guard to the office of the warden.

"Sit down! If you don't sit, you will when you hear the good news, Norbert Anleger."

Norbert could not believe that the warden, for the first time, had addressed him by his name. After shuffling some papers, the warden finally looked up.

"You checked into our house of correction in January of 1964. You were condemned to four years hard labor. The Prison Board has looked at your record and decided to shorten your sentence. You have performed your duties, even though often you could have shown better acceptance of your situation. It is hoped that you have learned your lesson and will return to be a loyal German citizen. Even though you will be returned to the decadent West Berlin, you must not cause trouble for the noble German Democratic Republic. You will leave here in four days."

The warden searched for something on his desk.

"Here are two vouchers for your train ride to Berlin, *Friedrichstrasse Station,* from where you will have to walk the short distance to the official crossing into West Berlin."

"And for whom is the second voucher?" Norbert asked.

"It is a souvenir for your girlfriend."

"I have no girlfriend, just a fiancée."

"That's even better. Fiancées are easily more jealous."

Norbert did not quite understand the warden's joke or what the second voucher was really for, but it did not matter. He did not want to delay leaving the Uranium hell another moment. Still, he appreciated the Warden's sudden humane attitude. "One more question, Warden. Am I permitted to phone my fiancée or to write her about my upcoming discharge?"

"No, you are not! Things might change." He paused and curled his mouth into an insincere smile before speaking in a softer tone. "Then she would be disappointed if you did not show up," the warden said.

Then the guard took Norbert back to his cell.

A few days later, Norbert stepped out into a blindingly bright, sunny day and made his way to the train. He could hardly believe he was traveling through the beautiful *Erzgebirge* landscape. The blue sky made the colors of the wild flowers shine a deeper purple, and the tall spruce trees look greener.

He arrived in Berlin early in the afternoon. The moment he crossed over from East to West Berlin, he stepped into a phone booth to call the Center, hoping beyond hope Amanda would answer the phone.

"This is the downtown Interpretation and Translation Center. May I help you?" he heard an unfamiliar voice say. Norbert struggled to keep his composure.

"I would like to speak to Amanda Steinmetz, please."

"May I ask who is calling, please?"

"It is Norbert Anleger, your boss – if you are working at my Center."

"Yes, sir, I am. Mr. Anleger, I am not positive that Miss Steinmetz is in her office. I am very, very sorry to ask, but would you mind holding a moment?"

Norbert waited, his heart racing. When Amanda picked up the receiver, there was silence on both ends of the line. Norbert choked back tears and cleared his throat until he thought he could perhaps utter a word.

"Amanda?"

"Norbert-Darling! Is that really you? Are you free? Where are you?"

"I walked from the *Friedrichstrasse* to the official Sector Crossing into West Berlin."

"I know where that is, Norbi. Don't walk any further. I will pick you up in ten minutes."

Norbert's tears made it impossible for him to speak. Stepping out of the phone booth, he felt weak and had to sit down with his worn cap in his hand. He had to close his eyes. She is coming! Amanda is coming to get me! Suddenly he heard a voice. "God bless you, poor man!" Opening his eyes, he saw an old woman dropping a coin into his cap. When she saw that the cap was empty, she quickly gave him another coin. He imagined how he must look, and would appear to Amanda. He hoped she wasn't too frightened by his gaunt and tattered looks.

What a reunion it was between Norbert and Amanda! They held each other, determined never to let go again.

Then Amanda suggested that they drive straight home. With considerate affection, Amanda offered to let Norbert drive.

"But I have not driven a car for almost four years!" Norbert said.

"Darling! This has always been your car. You know Berlin well. And when you are driving, you can tell me what happened to my venerable Trabant and if I ever will see it again."

"I think, you never will. Let me first put my luggage into the car!" Norbert laughed.

"Yes, where is your luggage, my love?"

Norbert pointed at his chest. "You are looking at it! It is what you see on my body plus an extra train voucher for a ride from *Aue* to Berlin. Believe me, never before have I traveled this lightly."

"And you never will again!" Amanda said emphatically. "For sure not when I travel with you."

Norbert felt almost in a daze as he drove the familiar, yet strange, streets leading to his apartment where Amanda had lived for over three years without him. He asked her to wait, to not begin all the stories she would need to tell him about his business and the Centers to fill him in. It was enough for now that he knew they were still in existence. He just wanted to bathe, rest, and be where he could see, smell and touch Amanda.

"I must tell you something, darling," Amanda said.

"Yes, you must tell me something. You must tell me everything. I miss hearing your voice so much!"

"I miss hearing your voice, too. And thank goodness we are here, together, safe. But, I do not feel right staying here as my residence now that you are back living here. We are not married."

"But we are engaged!" replied Norbert.

"That is not the same. Being engaged, as we are, is a stage of *hoping* for a future together.

"But being married means being *committed to each other* for the rest of our lives."

Norbert was reminded of just who this smart, good woman was that he had the incredibly good fortune to be engaged to.

"Then let's get married!" he said.

"Yes, Norbert-Darling, let's get married!"

Two weeks later, Norbert had fully recovered his strength and was in the best of spirits as he held Amanda's hand during a small civil ceremony. They did not need a honeymoon; they were together forever! Now the Centers for Interpretation and Translation were operated by Mr. and Mrs. Anleger. It was amazing how fast Norbert managed to reconnect with the business he had been deprived of for several years. Amanda was just as proud of Norbert's fast reintegration as he was of Amanda's successful operation of the Centers in his absence.

Things went rather smoothly during the rest of the year, 1967, when Norbert could have still been serving out his prison sentence. He threw himself into his work, doing his best to distance himself from the hellish memories. He found that with Amanda as his full-time business and life partner, he was accomplishing more than he had ever dreamed possible.

The year 1968 proved to be more challenging. On April 4, the world reeled from the tragic news that the freedom activist and Civil Rights leader, Reverend Martin Luther King, Jr., had been assassinated. He was only 39. On June 5, Senator Robert F. Kennedy, the brother of the late President J.F. Kennedy, was shot while campaigning for president. He died 24 hours later, at 42 years of age.

In both cases Norbert Anleger felt deeply saddened, since he had known both leaders through his work as an interpreter. However, as tragic as these assassinations were for America, they did not affect the ever-increasing number of international clients who seemed to be constantly traveling the world and requiring more and more translation and interpreter services. Norbert spent more time than ever interviewing and hiring more personnel for his Centers, while maintaining extremely high standards.

In March of 1968, hundreds of Czechoslovakians secretly, or sometimes openly, came to Norbert's Centers, seeking a way to leave their communist nation for the West. Many of them had fled Czechoslovakia via Austria, to Germany, to vote with their feet—they no longer wanted to live under Moscow-directed rule.

In Europe, people already talked of a "Spring of Prague," thinking that with new Communist Party Chief, Alexander Dubcek, a new season of hope—a new spring—had started. That hope was crushed when, on August 21, Soviet tanks rolled into Prague and other big cities in Czechoslovakia, taking over the government rule after Dubcek had been arrested. That ruthless attack prompted an even larger flow of refugees escaping across the border to Austria and spreading into West Germany and even West Berlin.

The Centers received daily requests for help. In one case, they were asked for money to buy weapons and ammunition "to fight the Soviet and Warsaw Pact occupiers." Even after the Spring of Prague had faded, the stream of refugees and asylum-seekers did not stop. There were limits to how and how much the Anlegers could help, but they used every resource possible to act as a bridge to freedom.

When the German Democratic Republic passed a law that East and West German citizens now needed passports with visas to travel between the two Germanys, the Centers had to extend their office hours to handle the influx of requests for help.

In the midst of the Czechoslovakia and East German exodus, Norbert Anleger received a letter from the White House, announcing President-elect Richard Nixon's intention to visit Europe for eight days in February, 1969. Nixon's Chief-of-Staff had recommended Norbert Anleger as the first choice to serve as Nixon's tour guide and interpreter when in Berlin.

Already overloaded with client work, Norbert's first thought was to delegate the assignment to one of his senior interpreters. Amanda was out of the picture because she was to give birth to twins around Christmas, 1968. When Norbert made a quick study of the future president who would be inaugurated in January, 1969, he discovered that Richard Milhous Nixon (then a US Senator) had seen very little of the world outside of the USA. Norbert decided to accept and fill the role himself. He wanted not only to be Nixon's interpreter and tour guide, but also his historical and geographical consultant.

Norbert knew more than anyone in his company, and perhaps as much as anyone in the world, about Berlin's recent and significant history. He felt it was both an opportunity and a responsibility to give the next President of the United States a truthful and complete picture.

Frankly, without discussing it with his coworkers, he was proud that several international dignitaries had chosen his Interpretation and Translation Centers to receive competent language and guiding help, notably President John F. Kennedy in 1963, Queen Elizabeth of England in 1965, and hopefully President Richard M. Nixon in February 1969.

Norbert set the letter from Washington down on his desk, leaned back in his chair and closed his eyes. *I am alive. I love my work, and my wife. I am about to become a father. Life is good...all because I am free.*

Chapter 52

The birth of healthy twin babies to Amanda and Norbert on Christmas Day of 1968 was a memorable event for all relatives and friends of the Anleger and Steinmetz families. In addition to the usual happy fuss over a couple's first child, the fact there were *two* new bundles of joy seemed to more than double the excitement and congratulations coming from near and far.

The baby boy received the name Leo, and the girl was named Venus. When Norbert's Center employees heard the names, they could not help but tease their bosses. "Have you joined a group of astronomers to call your babies Leo and Venus?" And friends asked, "Have you become star-gazers?"

Naturally, such questions were asked in a light-hearted way. In mid-January, Amanda and Norbert thought it would be a great way to warm up the bleak and freezing days by hosting a "welcome home" party for the twins. They invited all of the local Center employees, and also Wolfram and Dora Siemens to their apartment in Berlin-Neukölln. Plenty of good food, wine and beer put everybody into the best of moods. Before the party ended, Norbert got everyone's attention.

"Thanks, dear coworkers and friends, for helping us celebrate this very special event in our family. You are all like family to us, and it means a lot to Amanda and me to share this with you. We want to thank you also for your nice and meaningful gifts—especially for the 20-kilogram box of diapers! I believe that Mary and Joseph in Bethlehem would have appreciated these more than the gold, myrrh and frankincense!" Everyone laughed, and toasted Norbert and Amanda.

"And now," continued Norbert, "now I will answer the question on everyone's mind—why we gave our babies such lofty names. Were we so star-struck when they were born that we stared into the heavens and saw the constellation, Leo, and the planet, Venus? I want to explain that these names represent Amanda's and my conviction for our *Firma*—our company—that THE SKY IS THE LIMIT!"

"Hear, hear!" the guests shouted. The ever-faithful Franz who had helped Amanda from day one raised his glass and called out, "Here's to the Gemini twins…and their stellar mom and dad!" More "cosmic" joking followed, including predictions the children would grow up to be astronauts. Amanda reminded everyone that she and Norbert really did believe that, with everyone working together, they could achieve the greatest success, especially since each one on the company's team was such a "super star."

Fred and Heidi in the USA liked the names of their nephew and niece even more. First of all, the names were the same in German and English. The second reason Fred wrote in his congratulatory note:

"Venus and Leo—great names! I have spent many years of my life flying VIPs all over the world. I am just waiting for the day a President asks me to take him to the moon! We can't let the Ruskies own the universe, can we? In this time of early space exploration, I think the sky names are perfect. Maybe the children will be inspired to become aerospace engineers or astronauts. As soon as they are old enough, I look forward to giving them their first plane ride, anyway!"

February 27, 1969, was an extremely busy day for Norbert. President Nixon had arrived the night before, and Norbert was required in all the greeting ceremonies and introductions. The day of the President's introduction to Berlin started early and was a full schedule for Norbert. Norbert was truly in his element as interpreter and city guide in Berlin, his energy far surpassing that of President Nixon, who was suffering jet lag.

Late at night, when Norbert came home, he found Amanda still awake.

"Why are you still awake, darling? I hope you did not wait up for me," Norbert greeted his wife.

"No, Norbi, I did not, but our babies did! How was your day?"

"Frustrating, and a little disappointing. Nixon is quite different than Kennedy. He's equally intelligent, but he is a very high-strung, nervous person. He listened to my narrations and explanations about Berlin but asked very few questions. I got the impression that he was already thinking of the next stopover in Europe."

"That's alright, my perfectionist darling! I am sure you gave him the best possible tour of our interesting city," said Amanda, as she stroked Norbert's face.

"You know, Presidents should never spend just one day in any capital city of the world."

"I agree with you, Norbert-Darling. Still, now President Nixon knows a lot more about Berlin than he did before... and he knows exactly where it is, which so many people do not. Did you tell the President that last year the DDR declared itself a Socialist State with Berlin as its capital?"

"Yes, but only briefly. If he had shown even the slightest interest I would have liked to have talked about the difference between socialism and social democracy, for instance. Nixon thinks in extremes: *Communism* is red and bad. *Socialism* is not quite red, but still bad. *Social democracy* is no real democracy. *Capitalism* is the ideal political form for all progressive nations in the world. For this man there seems to be no room to define any form of government which could be in-between."

"Next time," Amanda said, giving Norbert a comforting smile, "perhaps you should invite him to our Centers of Interpretation and Translation and have him read some of the many articles you and our coworkers have written for German newspapers and international magazines."

"Keep on dreaming, Amanda! Presidents are absurdly busy people. What keeps US Presidents from making a real difference in the world is that after about two or three years on the job, they start spending all their time plotting to get reelected for their next four-year term."

The sudden crying of their two-month old babies kept them from digging deeper into the bottomless pit of politics.

"I'll be back, darling. Our little boy and girl are hungry, as you can hear," Amanda said, as she hurried away. Norbert's eyes followed lovingly the quick steps of his wife, now also the mother of his wonderful twins.

561

Enjoy these days, my sweet children, he said to himself. *When you need something, you cry and people come running to help.* With a big yawn he went to bed and fell asleep instantly, with a smile still on his face.

Covering a big yawn with his hand, Fred Harrington sat up in bed and looked over at his wife, still asleep, her blonde hair curling softly around her face. He slowly and carefully climbed out of bed so as not to disturb her. He liked the rare mornings when he was back in Virginia, at home, and could rise early to make breakfast for Heidi. It was a labor of love to make all her favorite things to create a perfect German-style breakfast including bread rolls, jam, ham, sausages, soft-boiled eggs and coffee. It warmed his heart when he saw her surprised smile.

"I have been thinking, darling," Fred began, as he poured more coffee for them both.

"Good for you! I like thinking men," Heidi said.

"Seriously, my love! My thinking includes you. I figured out that this year is my 22nd year with the Air Force. That is about two more years than the average professional airman puts into service. I started out in 1948, when I was only 19! And as you know, five years later I was promoted to Air Force Captain. Then, on January 1, 1953, I flew my first flight as Chief Pilot of Air Force One."

"I will never forget how proud you were when President-elect Eisenhower made you his co-pilot on his secret trip to Korea," said Heidi.

"He had planned on navigating the small plane in Korea by himself. The Secret Service and his whole staff had a fit. Finally he had to agree to have a co-pilot fly with him as a back-up. That was incredibly lucky for me."

"On that trip you told President Eisenhower about me being in Germany, and that you had not seen me for two years," remembered Heidi.

"Yes. That was when he asked me to become Air Force One's Chief Pilot. Right after that, I left Korea and was stationed in Washington, DC."

"And I was able to follow you to America a few months later," Heidi remembered. "I still can feel your strong arms hugging me when we greeted each other at the National Airport. But tell me, why are we talking about old times today?"

"I was thinking perhaps the time has come to retire from active service in the Air Force."

"Didn't we talk once about you retiring in 1973, after 25 years of military service?"

"Yes, darling, we did. I would be forty-four years old."

"You meant to say, forty-four years *young*," Heidi corrected. "You would still be in your prime." All of a sudden Heidi jumped up, ran to their study and returned immediately, waving a big brown envelope in her hand.

"I am so sorry! This letter from Germany arrived yesterday for you. I totally forgot to give it to you."

"That's okay. Wow! That is a heavy envelope! The sender forgot to put their name and address on it. Let me see!" Fred used his butter knife to slice the envelope open.

"It is from Wolfram and Dora Siemens, our friends in Berlin. I wonder what made them write to us."

When several colorful travel brochures slipped out of the envelope, they were even more curious. Written in English, it was a fairly lengthy letter, typical for German writers. But since Wolfram Siemens was a businessman, he came right to the point after a few polite greetings.

...Frankly, the day you walked into my office in Neukölln, I liked you both very much. When you, Fred, introduced yourself to me with 'Ich bin ein Berliner,' you instantly won my heart. I did not tell Heidi, but I would have given you a more substantial discount, had you asked for it. After all, you were my first tenants.

Dora and I were delighted to find we would all become such good friends, as well. It was especially thoughtful of you to make me the first person to know that you were going to get married. That was even a surprise to Heidi, I think.

Well, this time it is my turn to surprise you. We are retired now, and free to go wherever we like, whenever we want. For many years we have worked on a project—our dream to fly around the world. In spite of World War II, we have seen much of Europe and have visited North, Central, and South America.

Our plan now is to circle the world, visiting not only nations that are well-known, but also exploring those countries that usually are not on the agenda of travel agencies. Here is our plan: Starting out in Germany, we will fly to Greece, Turkey,

Syria, Iraq, Iran, Pakistan, India, Nepal, China, Thailand, Borneo, New Zealand, and Australia.

You may be interested to know that while in Australia, we will have the opportunity to attend an opera at the Sydney Opera House, thanks to your dear sister-in-law. When we went to the Anleger's for a celebration party to welcome the new babies (they are so, so precious!) we told them of our world-travel plans. Amanda still has some very important connections in the opera world, apparently, and got us tickets to an opera which normally are sold out as much as a year before the performance. From Sydney we fly to the USA, where we will primarily visit California and Wisconsin.

Why do we write you in such detail? Because once we have visited my Siemens relatives, we will look up also Dora's relatives. And then—we want to spend a few days or perhaps even a week with you in Washington, DC, or more accurately, in Virginia, where you live.

Then, we will continue north to Baffin Island in north-eastern Canada. Baffin Island is the fifth largest island in the world, yet has a population of only 11,000 people. When I was a young boy, we German kids read Karl May's books about the native Indians in North America, and my favorites were the stories about Canada's Northern Territories, especially Baffin Island.

From there we will fly to Greenland, Iceland, Norway, Sweden and back to Germany.

As you might guess, the tickets are a special promotion called "Around the World in 100 Days," with unlimited stopovers. We are not as confident as we would like to be about our financial picture as retirees, or I would have also purchased tickets for you as well. Maybe we will have enough at the end of our lives to leave you both the means to enjoy such an adventure.

For us, the fulfillment of such a dream is coming up in a very short time, and we hope to get together with you soon. By the time you are reading this, we may already be on our way to the Mediterranean and beyond. You don't even have to write us whether we are welcome or not —we will be coming anyway!

Your friends forever, Dora and Wolfram

Fred and Heidi's excitement about seeing the Siemens was short-lived. Starting out in the spring of 1970, the Siemens enjoyed the tourist sights of Greece and Turkey, survived sand storms in Syria and Iraq, and were thrilled to see the ancient ruins of Iran, where Dora mailed a post card to Heidi. In Pakistan they ran smack into the worst hurricane storms the country had ever experienced.

It took the Air India pilot two attempts to land at the Jinnah International Airport in Karachi, where all passengers were quickly ushered into flimsy storm shelters. Instead of being taken to Islamabad, Pakistan's capital, they had to seek shelter in trench-like ditches, where a number of the passengers quickly perished in the turbulent, hot sand drifts and falling debris.

It took the government several weeks of search and rescue work to announce that nearly 250,000 people had been killed in the deadly storms and following floods. Tragically, Wolfram and Dora were among the victims. Fred was able to confirm the news through contacts at the Karachi Airport and the Red Crescent Organization.

Fred and Heidi took the shocking news very personally, especially since the Siemens letter and post card were sitting right on their kitchen shelf, reminders now of a sad loss instead of the wonderful reunion they had been looking forward to. Dora and Wolfram never fulfilled their dream to circle the world, but the dream didn't die with them. Fred and Heidi vowed to one day follow the Siemens mapped route and complete the *Around the World in 100 Days* adventure, in their honor.

Chapter 53

The year was 1971. The USA had been involved in the Vietnam War since 1961. In those ten years of battle, over 56,000 American soldiers lost their lives. Now the war was spilling over into Cambodia. The American troop strength in South Vietnam still was 185,000. Opposition to continued US involvement made itself known in Washington, and on university campuses across the nation.

In Germany, ten years after the building of the Berlin Wall and the long wall between East and West Germany, both Germanys seemed to have settled for a *status quo.* In East Berlin, however, the Communist *Polithauptverwaltung* (Political Main Administrative Department) had made elaborate plans to celebrate the tenth anniversary of the building of the Wall.

One of the most absurd ideas was the creation of a *Geländespiel* (Cross Country Game) for the *Free German Youth (FDJ)* on August 13. The "Young Pioneers" from all over East Berlin were to reenact the erecting of the Wall. They were to act in silence, having some youngsters act as patrol lookouts. Other youth were to quickly build barricades, or search in the imaginary hinterland for hidden political enemies, instigators, weapons or anti-DDR propaganda material. They even were to look and pretend to discover spy tunnels used by fleeing East Germans. Adult leaders of the Communist *SED* (*Sozialistische Einheitspartei Deutschlands*) concluded the event by informing the youngsters of the happenings ten years ago, when the DDR finally "protected" itself against capitalistic Western infiltrators by building the *Antifascist Protective Wall* which would guarantee the DDR peace and glorious socialism.

One of the speakers was Gerhard Jahn, the FDJ top leader, who called the thirteenth of August "a festive day for the DDR and a day of calamity for the decaying West."

In preparation for this questionable anniversary, teachers were pressured to use many school hours to get their students excited. One teacher in the Soviet Sector of Berlin played following word game with her pupils.

"What do you call the people living in Poland?"

"Polish."

"What do you call people living in England?"

"English."

"And what do you call people living in the German Democratic Republic, the DDR?"

"German."

"No, no! You are wrong! They are citizens of the DDR."

Students and parents alike were not only confused but fearful that they were not going to always know what was, or was not, permitted. Nothing was as it once was. Even the term "East Germany" was never to be used by teachers of any age group: only the term DDR was allowed.

The year 1972 brought two exceptionally interesting events for Fred Harrington.

In February, his assignment was to fly US President Richard Nixon to the People's Republic of China. This was an unprecedented and history-making trip. It was the first time China had allowed a foreign diplomat to enter the country since the Cultural Revolution, and, it was the first time in American history that a President visited China. Despite the impossibility of adequately preparing the staff, the Secret Service, and the President for such unknown territory, the weeklong visit became a political success, especially when the two involved nations agreed toward lessening the risk of war, to normalize relations, and to increase scientific and cultural ties.

The other event, memorable not only for Fred but for the world, was President Nixon's visit to Moscow in May. Several important agreements for both nations were signed, including the one for a joint space flight in 1975.

In China as well as in the USSR, Fred, as the Chief Pilot of Air Force One, had to make the arrangements for landing permits, refueling, maintenance and security of the President's plane. The visits were ice-breakers, but the deep degree of mistrust between both China and the Soviet Union toward the USA prompted Fred to use the sleeping accommodations aboard Air Force One, instead of sleeping in the closely-watched downtown hotels.

Since the President's February visit to China had prevented Fred from making plans to attend the Winter Olympic Games at Sapporo, in Japan, Fred investigated a possible trip to attend the Summer Olympics in Munich, West Germany. Heidi was much more enthusiastic to go to Olympics held in *München*, and Fred happened to know the Olympic swimmer, Mark Spitz, who would be competing for America.

As luck would have it, last-minute rearranging of the President's schedule forced Fred and Heidi to cancel their anticipated private trip to Germany. They were especially disappointed because they were going to get to meet Norbert and Amanda at the Games, and then spend one beautiful extra week together in Germany's Alps.

Even though they were heartbroken that their American relatives had to cancel, Norbert and Amanda left their twins (now nearly four years old) in the care of their trusted nanny, and drove from Berlin to *München*.

The Games were scheduled for August 26 to September 11, 1972. Mark Spitz did extremely well. Before the games were over, he had set an Olympic record by winning seven gold medals. Spitz was so busy with practicing, swimming, giving interviews, and more swimming, that Norbert never had a chance of introducing himself as the brother-in-law of Fred Harrington, who Spitz knew well.

Fred had recommended that Norbert and Amanda catch the basketball competitions. Neither Norbert nor Amanda could believe that the acclaimed US Basketball Team failed to win the Gold Medal for the first time since 1936, Since the Anlegers knew very little about basketball, they got over the loss fairly easily.

One morning, Heidi asked Fred if they could spend some time sightseeing in Munich. She knew that every day at 11 a.m. and noon, a crowd of people gathers in front of Munich's Town Hall on Mariensquare to hear the traditional Glockenspiel chime. They decided to enjoy themselves in Old Town, and head over to the Olympic Stadium later in the afternoon, or perhaps not until the next morning.

The earth shattering news that reached them that night, September 5, left them sad, outraged, and terribly relieved that they had not attended the Games that day. Arab terrorists of the "Black September Group" had entered the Olympic village, killed two Israeli coaches, and taken nine Israeli athletes hostage. All nine were killed along with five terrorists and a German policeman in a shoot-out at the nearby *Fürstenfeld* Airport.

Even though the Olympics resumed after a suspension of games and memorial observance for the victims, the Anglegers drove back to Berlin. Norbert had experienced enough killings during World War II, and he did not want to expose Amanda to any more potential violence—not to mention the entire event had lost all trace of joy or fun.

While driving home from Munich, both talked very little. Norbert had not the slightest fear driving through the DDR to get to Berlin. This time nothing would stop him from reaching West Berlin! But he feared that human brutality, race hatred, political enmity and international hostilities would not only be a curse of the past, but would most likely be a rising danger and self-destructive trend in the future.

Chapter 54

Because of the continuous attempts by East Germans to flee from the East to the West, Berlin remained a rebellious problem child for the Soviets. The economic blockade had not brought the city to its knees as they had anticipated, since the Allied airlift from 1948 to 1949 helped Berliners to survive. Even the Berlin Wall, built in 1961, had not destroyed West Berlin, the tiny island of freedom surrounded by the red communist sea. Numerous international leaders and high-ranking politicians visited West Berlin over the years, expressed their disdain for the Wall of Shame, and had gone home without being able to change anything. The West was in a deadlock with the East.

Even the US President, Ronald Reagan, had stood at the Berlin Wall in June of 1987 and given the challenge, "Mister Gorbachev, tear down this wall!" But the new leader of the Soviet Union resided in Moscow, thousands of kilometers from Berlin, and did not hear or heed the President's plea.

In October, 1989, Soviet President Mikhail Gorbachev was invited to come to East Berlin to speak at the Fortieth Anniversary of the German Democratic Republic. The communist leaders of East Germany had hoped that Gorbachev would instruct the 325,000 Soviet troops stationed in East Germany to suppress the rising flood of discontent with the government and stabilize their communist regime. But when Gorbachev gave his speech, he warned the East German Moscow-pundits that "He who acts too late, will be punished by history." The majority of East Germans understood his words to be a signal to act then, and bring about a major political reform.

Less than two weeks later, thousands of demonstrators gathered in the cities of Leipzig and Dresden to demand democracy and free elections. The demonstration wave quickly spilled over to other large cities in the DDR and found its most powerful expression in East Berlin, where more than 500,000 citizens took to the streets. Nervous police arrested hundreds and filled all available prisons.

Actually, the severe unrest among the East German population had begun back on July 17, 1989, when the politically more liberal Hungarian nation had lifted its border controls with Austria. Immediately, East Germans made their way to Hungary, and from there they continued their move to freedom by crossing into Austria in cars, on bicycles and on foot.

A truly historical event was the *Peace Picnic* on August 19, which Otto von Habsburg, the Crown Prince of Austria, Hungary and Bohemia, had organized in Sopron, a small town at the Hungary-Austria border. When the Hungarian officials in charge of the picnic opened the wooden border gate just a crack to let a few individuals pass through, the East German picnic attendees pushed the flimsy gate wide open. About 600 German men, women and children escaped to Austria. The bewildered Hungarian border policemen just stepped aside and let things happen.

Norbert Anleger and his Center coworkers had heard of the picnic organized by the Crown Prince von Habsburg in Sopron. Norbert also knew about the forced breakthrough of the gate leading into Austria. Quickly, Norbert issued hundreds of official-looking passes with big Red Cross markings, which he named *"Permit de Voyage."* The Anlegers sent these documents by couriers to the German embassies in Budapest, Prague and Warsaw. Hundreds of East German asylum-seekers used the passes to board special trains which had been sent by the West German government, and were soon on their way to Bavaria in West Germany.

Norbert and Amanda heard of the escapes and decided to print (forge) more Red Cross Passage Way Bills (*Permits de Passage*) even though they knew they had no government authorization and it was a high-risk endeavor. But breaking news stopped them in their tracks.

The Hungarian government announced on September 10 that ALL East German citizens would be allowed to cross the border. On that very day, 8,100 crossed the Hungarian-Austrian border into West Germany, followed three days later by 18,000 freedom-seeking German refugees, who had come from the embassies in Poland, Hungary and Czechoslovakia.

The total count of relocated East Germans was 31,000 before the Berlin visit on October 7 of Soviet leader Mikhail Gorbachev and his wife, Raissa Gorbachova. The DDR anniversary that should have been a glorious time of parades, band music, and marches, led to even larger demonstrations all over East Germany.

The 1,378 kilometer long Wall from the Baltic Sea in the north to the Czech border in the south that had been erected to separate 17 million East Germans from the West, now revealed irreversible cracks.

The beginning of the end of the East German government came on October 18, when the DDR top leader, Erich Honecker, was stripped of his position, which he had held for 18 years.

The East German Government ship was sinking!

Then, on November 9, 1989, with more than one million East Germans gathered on Berlin's *Alexander Platz,* the pressure on the government had become so great that it exploded.

Very few people in the world, and not many people in West Berlin, suspected that the twilight of the ninth of November would usher in the night that would change Germany forever.

Amanda and Norbert Anleger had been invited to the home of Berlin's former actor and movie director, Ulrich Schamoni, to help him celebrate his fiftieth birthday. He was one of Norbert's favorite clients and they had met several times both in the Center and out, over lunch. Amanda heard that East Germany's most popular folk singer, Helga Hahnemann, would be among the invited guests. She, the former opera singer, and Helga, the *chanson* singer, knew each other well. One night they had become friends when an Eastern journalist had interviewed them both. Amanda had beautifully explained her somewhat complicated background with regard to her Russian birthplace, her German nationality, and her love for Berlin. Then the reporter had turned to Helga.

"I know that you were born in Berlin. May I ask you what you like best about Berlin?"

"Naturally, the people of Berlin," Helga Hahnemann answered.

Such a plain answer given by a singing idol from East Berlin had impressed Amanda. Now they all were together to celebrate with Ulrich Schamoni, a man who was loved by West and East Berliners alike. When he unexpectedly was called to another room, his guests suspected he had a birthday congratulations phone call.

Suddenly Schamoni, his face shockingly pale, rushed back into the room, shouting:

"The Wall is open!"

Helga Hahnemann was the first to respond. "Oh, really, now. You've already had *that* much champagne? Very funny, Ulrich darling."

"No, really! The DDR will open up the Wall tonight!"

Another guest hung up a telephone call and rushed into the room. "Schamoni's announcement is the truth!"

Everyone began to talk at once, daring to believe the impossible might be happening. After toasting, hugging and kissing one another, they stormed into the streets of West Berlin, where the good news was already known to hundreds of jubilant Berliners. Some of the birthday party guests jumped into their cars and headed either to the *Potsdamer Platz* to Checkpoint Charlie, or to the new wall opening at the Bernauer Strasse. Here they found East German Police and soldiers were removing the first concrete slab, in order to make a better passage for the thousands of East Berliners waiting to get through.

Norbert and Amanda raced to their apartment in Neukölln to pick up Venus and Leo.

"Put on something warm and come with us to the *Mauer*!"

"What is going on at the Wall?" Leo wanted to know.

Venus, who was half- asleep, complained, "I was almost sleeping. Now you want me to go out into the cold November night?"

"Oh yes, my lovely Venus!" said Amanda, who had come in from the cold. "You will get your coat and you will come out—NOW!"

Wow! Was that my lovely mother who said that? Is the building on fire? "Please tell us what is happening, Mother!" said Venus.

"East Berlin's government is opening up the Wall for all East Berliners and DDR citizens," said Norbert, trying to contain his surging emotions. He desperately wanted to believe the news, but he needed to see it for himself. "Let's go!"

That was all the Anleger twins, now twenty-one years old, needed to hear. They all raced to the car and Norbert headed for the *Brandenburger Tor*, where they were met by thousands of predominantly young men and women dressed in pullovers and windbreakers who, approaching from the west, filled every inch of space at the foot of the Wall, many climbing up to the top of it. The tall, bright lights, originally intended to keep East Berliners from crossing the death strip and into West Berlin, now illuminated the climbers and the cheering crowd.

To all who had come here from West Berlin, the sudden opening of the Wall and the rapid influx of East Berliners was an unexpected *Wahnsinn* (frenzy). Soon one could hear West and East Berliners yelling out, using the German term *Wahnsinn* or the English, "madness," over and over again.

Almost within touching distance of the Brandenburg Gate, the celebrants on top of the Wall danced, sang, drank and hugged each other. West Berliners helped East Berliner brothers climb up the cursed Wall. Germany embraced Germany! For 300 to 350 meters, the people-covered structure was now a bridge between East and West, no longer an impenetrable wall dividing the free from the oppressed. Twenty-eight years of separation between the two Berlins seemed to have come to an end!

Before midnight of the historic ninth of November, the first East German cars made their way through the wall openings to West Berlin. Throngs of people cheered as East German-built Wartburgs, Czech Skodas, and Russian Ladas drove through the now scarcely-guarded control points by the Brandenburg Gate. West Berliners greeted them with flowers and champaign. When the small but very popular Trabants drove through, "Wessies" (West Berliners) wanted to touch the funny looking "Trabis." They used their fingers to drumbeat the metal car hoods. One intimidated driver begged the excited Wessies: "Be careful with my Trabi- she is delicate! Don't ruin my car! I had to wait for 14 years to get it!"

Checkpoint Charlie was still closed to those "Ossies" (East Berliners) who had no travel permit. At 10 p.m. about 600 East Berliners jammed the crossing point. Shortly before midnight, the pushing crowd had grown to more than 3,000.

After a few East Berliners with crossing permits cleared the control checkpoint, the nervous *VOPOS* could no longer hold back the masses. They stepped back and yielded to the pressure to keep the gates open without further checking.

No West Berliners remained asleep in their warm beds; like a suddenly opened valve, people poured out of their homes to join the madness. East German cars, decorated with red roses, paraded through the streets, the crowds bringing beer and champagne to the drivers. "*Wahnsinn!* Beautiful Madness!" was the shout of the Berliners from both sides.

For a few hours before sunrise on Friday, November 10, 1989, Berlin took a short nap.

Even the most excited celebrants needed a bit of sleep. When the employees of the Anlegers' Interpretation Centers came to work early the next morning, they found the doors locked. Hand-printed notes attached to the doors at all three Centers announced:

> *We are closed until Monday morning.*
> *Enjoy and celebrate a new wind of*
> *Freedom with our Eastern visitors!*
> *Let freedom ring over all Germany!*
> *—Norbert & Amanda Anleger*

East Berliners, who on that morning reached for their usually dull *NEUE ZEIT* communist newspaper, laughed their heads off when they read a so-called obituary on page one, written by one of their East Berliner journalists, Bernd Schmidt:

Suddenly and totally unexpected,
For all of us incomprehensible,
The Mauer has died.
August 13, 1961 – November 9, 1989
We do not mourn its death with a single tear.

All East Berliners and DDR citizens received a welcoming gift of 100 West Marks the moment they drove or walked into West Berlin. Many could not believe their fortune and quickly ran into stores to find out whether the money they had just received was real money, or a Western trick. Some bought bananas, oranges, kiwi and other foods they had sorely missed by being cut off from the West. Just as many rushed into bookstores to pick up maps of Berlin, which featured *both* Berlins, and some loaded up with educational and geography books. A few took the opportunity to buy their first Playboy magazine.

However, the majority of those who had come across from the East just stood and stared at the Wall from the western side. Some tried to decipher the graffiti.

"I always wanted to see what the Wall looked like in West Berlin," said a man with tears streaming down his face. He held his six-year old son high up above his head. "Look, Andreas, look! This is the ugly wall that your uncle climbed, when trying to escape. East German policemen shot him to death."

"They did, Daddy? Why?"

"They thought they did it for their country…they were ordered to do it."

The real surprise for many shoppers came when store loudspeakers welcomed the Eastern visitors to West Berlin and encouraged them to select what they needed and take it to the cashier. "And don't worry about not having enough money for all items! Just have the items properly checked out at the cash register, and we will take care of any price difference!"

One older woman looked up to the store loudspeaker, squinted with her eyes and blurted out: "What? They want to give me things for free, if I have not enough money to pay? I am 72 years old, and I have never before heard of such a generous offer."

"Believe it!" said a middle-aged couple standing in the same line. "Here is something else for you, your children and grandchildren." With that, the generous West Berliner couple emptied their entire shopping bag into the woman's half-empty paper bag.

One man from East Berlin with a remarkable conscience, whose name will always remain unknown, drove his car to the "American Memorial Library" in Berlin-*Kreuzberg*. He returned two books, which he had borrowed on August 9, 1961!

"The Wall made it impossible for me to return the books sooner. I am sorry that the books had to sit on my bookshelf for 28 years! I thought of throwing them across the Wall…but you know, my intention to one day return these books helped me hang on to hope that someday we could again pass freely through all of my city, my Berlin."

The stunned librarian just stared, feeling both the urge to laugh and to cry. Then she quickly figured out how high the overdue fine would be: 2,573 West Marks. She waved the fee with a blown kiss.

Naturally, the Anleger family was in the midst of it all! They had quickly eaten breakfast and hurried out the door, Venus and Leo heading in a different direction than their parents. When Amanda started to ask their kids to stay with them, Norbert said, "Let them go! Today everybody in Berlin deserves full-blown freedom. And our children need to mingle with those who have had no freedom for many decades."

Around noon, Norbert and Amanda, by chance, ran into the twins. They had been watching young people giving away pounds of candies and cookies. When they looked closer, they recognized that Leo and Venus were among them.

"Hey, kids! What are you doing here?"

"Making life sweeter for the Ossies!"

"Good for you!" said Norbert. "Wait! Let me give you some more money. You are almost out of the treats. Better yet, let's all take a break first and have some coffee across the street."

All four were so excited about what was going on around them that they could barely force themselves to sit down, even for a short while. As they were drinking their coffee, Leo, who was born in 1968 and therefore had never seen Berlin as a united city, had many questions for his parents, who also were still trying to digest the events of the last days.

"Dad! You are from West Berlin, and Mother came from East Berlin. You were too much in love and smart enough not to be held back by the Wall, to finally get married and have us cute twins."

Venus gave him a sharp kick under the table. "Speak for yourself!" Venus said. "I'm just as smart as I am cute."

"Okay then! I will direct my question to my intelligent and cute sister. How long has this terrible Wall existed?"

Norbert was quick in helping out his daughter, who most likely did not know the answer.

"Believe it or not, kids, 10,315 days. When I expanded our Centers a few years ago and put you two in charge of the new Travel Agency branch, it was my hope that within a few years you would arrange not only tour groups to Africa, Australia, and the US, but also to Eastern Europe."

Just as Norbert wanted to continue with his family talk, a woman ran up to their table and stood, breathless, in front of Amanda. "Miss Steinmetz!" the woman exclaimed. "I never thought I would see you again! Are you performing here in West Berlin? My mother used to take me to see you at the opera in East Berlin all the time!" As Amanda started to chat with, and update her fan, Leo and Venus lost interest in the history lesson and hurried off to join a group of their peers still handing out candy. Norbert and Amanda left shortly after and went back to their apartment.

As they were walking in the door, the telephone rang. Amanda answered the phone. Surprised as she was, she could not help but ask, "Listen, Heidi, your voice sounds so clear today. Are you phoning from your house in Reston?" After Fred had retired from 26 years of active Air Force service shortly after his boss, President Nixon, had been forced to resign the presidency, Fred and his family had moved from Arlington to Reston, Virginia, a brand new suburb of Washington, DC.

"Reston? No. I am calling from the Berlin-*Tegel* Airport. Should we take a taxi, or do you want to pick us up?"

"What are you telling me? You are in Tegel? And who is with you?" Norbert motioned for Amanda to hand the receiver to him.

"Hello! Where are you, really?"

"Well, we wanted to see with our own eyes this amazing news for Berlin—for Germany—for everyone! You must be terribly busy, but if you have room and a bit of time for us, we will come to you. Otherwise the Kempinski Hotel will be our home."

Several hours later, after unpacking at the Anlegers and having a short nap, the American guests were anxious to be taken to where the revolutionary action was taking place. Norbert and Amanda were the ideal tour guides, as always, but especially now in the midst of the political changes.

For the next three days, Heidi and Fred could not hide their amazement and astonishment at how much Berlin had changed. Wherever they drove, there were people on the sidewalks and in the streets debating, waving, praying and smiling. Never tiring, Norbert and Amanda told them all they knew about the old and new Berlin, even at the risk of sounding like broken records.

Heidi, in German, and Fred, in English, talked to at least one hundred Ossies, trying to get their life stories. They interviewed East Berliner policemen and members of the military. They shed tears with those who were crying, and they laughed with those who were jubilant. Heidi even reverted to her original Berlin slang which she had spoken as a young girl. When the East Berliners heard Heidi speak "Berlinish" flawlessly, their hearts overflowed with love and trust toward this former Berlin woman and her American husband.

Some of the men reached into their pockets and shoulder bags and pulled out splinters of the Wall that they had chopped off as souvenirs.

"How did you get those nice pieces?" Heidi asked one of the bearded men.

"Young lady! There is nothing nice about this terrible Wall. Can you hear the continuous sound of picks and rock hammers breaking into the Wall? Men and women have brought chisels and any tool they can find to get a few chips off. We call them our *Spechte* (woodpeckers). Those splinters will make good souvenirs one day, because I guarantee you, in less than 12 months there will be nothing left of the *Wall of Shame*. Here, have a few pieces! And tell your friends in America that we thank them for helping us, when the rest of the world seemed to have forgotten us."

"Are you thinking of the airlift during the Blockade? My husband, here, was one of the pilots who supplied you with food, coal, and even candies."

"Ah, how can we Berliners ever forget the *Rosinen* Bombers with the little handkerchief parachutes? I was only a young kid then, but the parachute attached to the candies which I found, I have saved to this day. I even missed some days of school when I was on the lookout for dropped candies." The man reached out to shake Fred's hand. "A belated thank-you, sir. Here, have some more of the Wall chips to give to your grandchildren some day. We all must remember—" He stopped speaking as his voice cracked with emotion.

The people in Berlin had their "Wall woodpeckers," but all of Germany along the East-West Border buzzed like a beehive in anticipation of even greater things to come—perhaps even a reunion of the two Germanys?

The City of Berlin had transformed into a place of unending celebration and jubilation, drawing visitors from all over the world. For instance, the Russian cellist, Mstislav Rostropovitch, who lived in Paris and had watched on TV the world-shaking events, flew in a private jet to Berlin. On Saturday, November 11, he placed his priceless cello on the dusty pavement at Checkpoint Charlie and played pieces by his favorite composer, Johann Sebastian Bach. After several hours playing in the cold weather, he put his instrument into its protective case and spoke briefly with one of the Western reporters who had been listening, along with the crowd which had gathered.

"Walls are never built for eternity," Rostropovitch said. "Here in Berlin, I am playing from my heart. *Lebe wohl*, Berlin!" (Take care of yourself, Berlin.)

Another person to be moved by the events was the US Ambassador, Vernon Walters. He had criss-crossed Berlin from west to east and north to south for two days. Then he stood at the *Glienicker Brücke* (bridge) in West Berlin's extreme southwestern corner, from where he could see the wide East German landscape. "Never before in my life have I seen so many men crying tears of joy," he said.

The former Mayor of West Berlin, Eberhard Diepgen, who had accompanied the Ambassador, put his arm around his American friend and said in English:

"The power of freedom is stronger than concrete and steel."

Chapter 55

Heidi and Fred had enjoyed their short visit to Berlin tremendously. Their family ties with Norbert, Amanda and the grown-up twins had been strengthened. Unfortunately Heidi's foremost wish of walking through the *Brandenburger Tor* had to be postponed to a future visit. The long, dividing East/West Wall from north to south of the two Germanys now had many cracks and openings, as had the Berlin Wall. But as long as the *Brandenburg Gate* remained a locked gate, it was no gate at all. The locked and guarded Brandenburg Gate was the most visible and shameful indication that the relations between East and West still resembled a solid wall, a useless gate to nowhere.

Yet rumors in and around Berlin were spreading that East Berlin intended to open the *Brandenburger Tor* on Christmas Eve. Could it be that the narrow openings in the Wall on November 9 had led not only to many more and wider openings in a few weeks, but now were to climax in the opening of the world famous symbol of Berlin, the Brandenburg Gate? Paris had its Eiffel Tower. London had its Trafalgar Square. Berlin needed its 20-meter high, 65-meter wide *Brandenburger Tor,* which had been built and opened to public traffic in 1791.

One hundred seventy years later, in 1961, communists had built the Berlin Wall and had made even this historic symbol of free passage the victim of political insanity. East Berliner workers, assisted by Soviet military troops, had sealed shut the Gate with concrete blocks and barbed wire.

Now, 28 years later, the telephones at Norbert's Centers had been constantly ringing for days with inquiries. "Can you tell me … " "I'm with the press. Is it true that … " "I just heard that the East Germans will open up the *Brandenburger Tor.* Is that true?"

Norbert, Amanda and their coworkers were hesitant to make firm predictions. The West German Chancellor Helmut Kohl seemed to be confident that it would happen. However, he had been wrong before when it came to news items about East German events.

On December 21, as Norbert watched heavy earth-moving equipment being taken to the Gate inside of the Wall, his hope won out over pessimism. Something revolutionary was in the making! He was not the only one who thought so. In spite of heavy rain, thousands of East Berliners gathered at the Brandenburg Gate on the afternoon of December 22 to witness the moment of the possible opening. Nothing happened during the rest of the day, but hundreds stayed and waited through the entire rainy night, many with only small umbrellas or no covering.

By noon on December 23, about 40,000 Berliners had gathered in the *Unter den Linden* Street and at the *Pariser Platz* in excited anticipation. The rain did not dampen their enthusiasm of hoping to see the Gate open after 28 years. Some were holding posters or banners:

"KOMMT ZUSAMMEN!" ("Come Together!") and, *"WIR SIND EINE FAMILIE"* (*"We are ONE Family"*). Many bottles of champagne were shared with total strangers. While the rain kept coming down, there was a sudden loudspeaker announcement:

"Today the Romanian people have overthrown their dictator, Ceausescu!"

At first there was a silence of disbelief. Then a thousand-fold scream of joy and applause filled Berlin. The last communist dictator in Europe had fallen! Now the real celebrations in Berlin could begin.

The two government Celebration Delegations approached the *Brandenburger Tor* from opposite sides. The police on both sides had put up steel fences to protect the dignitaries as they walked through the anxious crowd of people shoving forward to move nearer the Gate. On the West Berliner side, about 30,000 spectators had gathered. A striking sight near the Wall was a huge banner with the fitting quote from a well-known German Christmas carol:

Macht hoch die Tür, das Tor macht weit! (Raise up the door, make wide the gate.)

On the eastern side, the delegation with Prime Minister Hans Modrov and East Berlin's Mayor Erhard Krack reached the Gate exactly at 3 p.m. The crowd quieted as the loudspeaker came on.

"Please welcome Bundeskanzler Kohl and West Berlin's Mayor Walter Momper!"

As the West Berliners waited for their delegates to deliver their speeches, the unexpected happened. Thousands of jubilant East Berliners squeezed through the single three-meter wide opening in the Brandenburg Gate, toppling the steel fences and concrete barriers. Many youngsters climbed on top of the Wall again, where they waved black-red-gold West German flags.

The government representatives gave their short speeches. The crowds on both sides were too excited to listen. Everyone was absolutely frantic to get themselves through the Gate's opening—before it was possibly closed again, cutting them off from the freedom they so desperately longed for. They wanted to walk through the *Brandenburger Tor* and touch the ground on the other side. The cold rain continued coming down, but the Germans would not be dissuaded from reuniting with their German brethren.

Walking through the deep mud in *Tiergarten Park* next to the Brandenburg Gate, Norbert looked at Amanda and his children, who were trying to protect themselves from the steady rain by huddling under a shared raincoat.

"Don't you think it is time to go home, family?" asked Norbert.

"Not yet!" they all indicated.

"This is too amazing! Such thrilling days will never happen again in my lifetime!" shouted Leo, purposely splashing a water puddle in the direction of Venus.

"Here is another memorable thrill for you!" laughed Venus, as she pushed him so that he stepped into a huge puddle.

Once they were back in the dry safety of their car, Norbert looked lovingly at his family.

"What a crazy bunch you are! By Christmas Eve, you all will be coughing and have runny noses."

"But it was worth it all! Don't you agree, kids?" asked Amanda as she pushed her wet hair out of her eyes.

"You said it!" both answered simultaneously, as twins do.

"The first order for tonight is to have hot tea and more hot tea," said Norbert.

"Sure, Dad. That will cure our colds and our crazies!" said Leo.

Everyone laughed through their shivers, glad to be heading home after such a fantastic and world-changing day.

Norbert had added eight people to the staff at his three Centers in 1989 to handle the large number of asylum-seekers and hundreds of other clients with equally urgent needs. Everybody noticed that his employees did their overtime duties with happy rather than heavy hearts. The Anlegers and their team did whatever it took to hold up their part in building a bridge to freedom for anyone who came to them for help.

By the end of December, 1989, the long Wall had 60 official border crossings between East and West Germany. Amanda and Norbert Anleger were among the many German citizens who were working and hoping for a full reunification of the two Germanys in the near future.

They continued supporting the East German demonstrations for free elections and freedom. These demonstrations were now called *Peaceful Revolutions* and, since many demonstrators carried candles, the *Revolution of Candles*. Candles in Germany had become the symbol of life, hope and peace.

Eventually, the many discussions and negotiations led to the first free election in the German Democratic Republic on March 18, 1990. Then came a negotiating session, which resulted in a "Unification Treaty." In cooperation with the Soviets and the Western Allies, the "Two-Plus-Four Treaty" negotiators promised full sovereignty to the two Germanys, whenever they would become ONE united German State.

It was so complicated that Norbert struggled to clearly explain the situation in a letter he was writing to Fred and Heidi, full of family news and current events. It wasn't long before the Anleger's heard back.

"Can't you Germans get your act together?" Fred had written in his response. "Just shake hands, swallow your political pride, and unite to one Germany!" Norbert had to shake his head when he read Fred's letter.

"The Americans don't understand the complexity of our political misery in Germany," Norbert said to Amanda. "The USA has never been occupied by Soviet or French or British forces who want to have their continued say in political matters. Just last week, Mrs. Thatcher stated before British parliament that she was in favor of a German reunification—but under no circumstances, sooner than five years from now. And we all can guess what the Soviets have in mind: the total collapse of West Berlin and West Germany."

On October 3, 1990, the miracle occurred! The German Democratic Republic and the Federal Republic of Germany agreed to form the reunited nation of Germany. Berlin became a "single" city and Germany's capital again. The *Wiedervereinigung* (reunification) had happened! Germany's unity had been successfully forged and the black-red-gold German flag, now the symbol not only of West Germany, but of all Germany, was hoisted on top of the *Brandenburger Tor.* The next day, the press called the third of October, the *"Tag der deutschen Einheit"* (Day of German Unity). A German postal stamp was issued in commemoration: "German Unity Day – October 3, 1990."

Finally the last celebratory beer was finished and all the guests and employees left the main Center where Amanda and Norbert had hosted a spontaneous party celebrating the *Wiedervereinigung.* Exhausted, the Anlegers hurried home and fell into bed.

Tired as they were, their minds were racing with the day's excitement and their many conversations with clients, friends and staff.

"Are you asleep?"

"Not any more, darling," Amanda replied. "I was thinking…"

"Oh no, not again!" Norbert joked.

"I was thinking—how the terrible war and the post-war years have kept us from getting a solid academic education. But Norbi, look how far you have come in your effort to make the world a better place! You have traveled to so many countries. Through the Centers, you have not only translated documents and speeches, you also have helped many uprooted and defeated people get a grip on their life…on hope. You have interpreted the happenings in the world and converted tragedies into victories."

For a while Norbert said nothing. He just gently reached for Amanda's face in the dark, kissed her forehead, and then spoke to her softly.

"You, my Amanda-Darling, better look at yourself! Starting out as a little baby called Gertrud in Russia, your parents moved with you to Breslau in Germany, and after the War, to Berlin. There, the charming, little Russian-German girl became the beautiful, internationally known opera singer, Amanda Steinmetz. Look how far *you* have come!"

Amanda snuggled closer to Norbert. "And then I fell in love," she said.

"Yes, then we met and fell in love," Norbert said. "And you made your desire to live in Berlin come true, not knowing that your life would undergo drastic changes. When I was imprisoned in East Germany, you took the reigns of my business into your hands and operated the Centers with amazing skill and strength. Never, never will I be able to thank you sufficiently!

"In spite of international acclaim as a singer, you never looked back when you became my full-fledged business partner. Instead of singing for opera-goers all over Europe, you worked with penniless, downtrodden refugees and desperate people in need. God has given you not only an absolutely beautiful voice, but also a loving, golden heart."

They held each other, quietly, in an embrace which had become familiar to them over the decades, entwined as one.

Amanda sighed a small sigh and then whispered in Norbert's ear.

"If it was not so dark, cold and late, I would make you get out of bed, walk with me to the piano and sing, *Grosser Gott, wir loben dich. Herr, wir preisen deine Stärke!*"

"Holy God! We praise thy name. Lord of old, we bow before thee," said Norbert. "Did I get the translation right?"

"Of course, darling, you are the best interpreter in all the world!" Amanda said as she and Norbert both sat up. They climbed out of bed and walked to the living room where Norbert turned on the lamp before they sat down on the piano bench together. Amanda shivered when she touched the cold ivory keys.

"Amanda-Darling, if you sing the beautiful old German hymn, *Grosser Gott, wir loben Dich,* then we both will sing—if you care to make it a duet—another very meaningful song, *Nun danket alle Gott mit Herzen Mund und Häenden.*"

Surprised neighbors could not believe their ears when, in the middle of the night on this historic day for Germany's Reunification, they heard the wonderfully strong piano chords, blended with Amanda and Norbert's voices, giving thanks and honor to God, who had made this day possible against all odds.

1. Nun danket alle Gott, Mit Herzen, Mund and Händen, Der grosse Dinge tut An uns und allen Enden Der uns von Mutterleib Und Kindesbeinen an Unzählig viel zu gut bis hierher hat getan.

2. Der ewig reiche Gott Woll' uns in unserm Leben Ein immer fröhlich Herz, Und edlen Frieden geben Und uns in seiner Gnad' Erhalten fort und fort Und uns aus aller Not Erlösen hier und dort.

1. Now thank we all our God with heart and hands and voices Who wondrous things has done, in whom the world rejoices; Who from our mother's arms has blessed us on our way With countless gifts of love and still is ours today.

2. Oh may this bounteous God through all our life be near us With ever joyful hearts and blessed peace to cheer us, To keep us in his grace and guide us when perplexed And free us from all ills of this world and the next.

Post Scriptum

The final and necessary steps to restore Germany's independent status happened when the last Western Allied Forces left Germany in early 1994. The Soviet Union withdrew its last soldier on August 31, 1994.

About the Author

Dr. Reinhold Kerstan was born in 1931 in Germany. His experiences growing up as the son of a Baptist pastor in East Prussia (now Poland), in Berlin, and in Czechoslovakia during World War II are published in his autobiography, *Blood and Honor* (David C. Cook Publishing, 1980).

After completing high school in Berlin, he attended college to study pharmacy and graduated from the University of Frankfurt in 1957. As a pharmacist, he settled with his new Swedish wife, Inger, in Wolfsburg, Germany's city famous for producing Volkswagen cars. After working there for only one year, his career took a completely different turn as he felt God's calling lead him to Switzerland.

Kerstan and his wife studied at the theological seminary in Switzerland and then immigrated to America where Reinhold spent another year of study in Sioux Falls, South Dakota. God led the Kerstans into pastoral church service in Winnipeg, Canada, and in 1965, to Wisconsin in the USA. The young Kerstan had already traveled the world extensively to countries such as Morocco, Spain, France, Holland, Italy, Greece, and Egypt.

In 1968, he became the editor and communications director of the North American Baptist Conference in the Chicago area. Traveling, visiting and reporting on mission stations in Cameroon, Nigeria, Brazil, and Argentina became part of his many duties. Kerstan also was able to study and earn his Ph.D. at Northwestern University.

In 1980, his mission field expanded to include the whole world when he became the Director of Communications and Director of Study and Research for the Baptist World Alliance, an international organization headquartered in Washington, DC.

Over the years, Kerstan met with world-renown evangelist, Billy Graham, at conferences and international events. In 1982, Graham appointed Kerstan as his interpreter for the crusade in communist East Germany. One year later, Graham republished Kerstan's book, *Blood and Honor*, with a new foreword written by Dr. Graham. His organization distributed 380,000 copies; within two years other publishers picked up the book, which was eventually translated into six languages besides English—German, Swedish, French, Spanish, Portuguese, and Russian—selling a total of 1.2 million copies.

In 1992, McMaster University in Hamilton, Ontario, called him to teach as a full-time "Professor of Preaching and Communication." Kerstan found this especially fulfilling and remained there until his retirement in 1999. After that he began to write down his ideas for a new book, this time an historical fiction drawing from his own experiences and extensive research on Berlin from 1930 to 1990. *The Bridge of Love to Freedom: Surviving Berlin after World War II* was published in 2015 by Suncoast Digital Press, Inc.

The Kerstans have three children, and each of their family of five was born in a different country. Today his children are married with own families and are living in Utah, Illinois and Florida. Reinhold and Inger Kerstan reside in Sarasota, Florida, and spend summers in Georgia's Blue Ridge Mountains.

What Readers are Saying...

"*The Bridge of Love to Freedom* is an excellent story of post-war Germany. Dr. Kerstan skillfully narrates the difficult times people in Germany, and especially in Berlin, had to endure for many years after the war had come to an end. Germany was divided in four occupation zones, and Berlin, the former capital, was a disastrous puzzle of four administrative sectors. The territory occupied by the Soviets was under communist leadership. But even the Germans living under Western Allied rule had a hard time to survive physically. I was born 1924 in Berlin. After doing my duty in the German military and avoiding imprisonment, I was fortunate to obtain the permission to immigrate to the USA in 1952. Kerstan brings back to my memory hundreds of critical and often dangerous situations in Germany before, during, and after World War II. These sometimes haunting memories will always be with me. I thank Dr. Reinhold Kerstan for writing this truly fascinating book. It is important that the twelve years under Nazi rule, and then the period under the Four Power occupation will not be forgotten."

Helmut Maass, CHA
Retired Regional Director of Franchise Operations
Howard Johnson Hotel Company

603

The Bridge of Love to Freedom

"As both a professional educator and daughter of the author, I was mesmerized by the gripping action and historical significance of this novel as it portrays life after World War II. The aftermath experienced by the war's victims, both US and European, is portrayed by way of a fictitious German family. Together, the characters and reader live through both trials and victories. Reading about the Airlift in Berlin took me back to my high school social studies class when I learned about modern European history, but did not completely understand the lessons to be learned from the past. As I read *The Bridge of Love to Freedom*, I thought about how much more meaningful my classes would have been if I had been given the opportunity to read personal stories like this to bring history to life. Dr. Kerstan, who is both my professional mentor and my father, inspired me to enter the amazing field of education many years ago, in an effort to make a difference in the lives of children. After reading this book, I feel confident that it will be the source of inspiration to both the adults and young people who choose to tap into its brilliance."

Annette Codelia
Executive Director of Elementary Schools
School District of Manatee County, Florida

"When reading *The Bridge of Love to Freedom*, I was immediately whisked back in time to the end of World War II. Kerstan's knowledge of the German culture, folkways, and mores is obvious from the beginning of the work and is only emphasized as the reader is caught up in the intrigue, hopelessness, tragedy and the desperate struggle for survival. The author's use of history demonstrates a scholar's approach to explain the importance of the nations of the world rising to meet the needs of a people needing help. To explain the depth of the tragedy befalling the German people after the war's end, there are the attractions that grow into love stories, and the trials and travails they endure before culminating in marriage are truly strokes of genius. I am confident that scholars as well as students, and those who read for pleasure will all enjoy this novel and gain a new perspective on what war really and truly means to those who survive. As well, to the contemporary reader, there is a parallel to the world events of today and the desperate plight of those who sacrifice all to survive the ravages of war. My respect for this author's knowledge and love for the German and American people, which comes through as a loving desire for freedom for all, grew with each page. Kudos for such a moving and authentic narrative."

Patricia S. Burgess, Ph.D.
Executive Director
PATH Homework Help, Inc.
www.pathwhelp.org

Made in the USA
San Bernardino, CA
30 December 2016